I0831474

Under the Sun of Satan

UNDER THE SUN OF SATAN

A Novel

Georges Bernanos

Translated from the French SOUS LE SOLEIL DE SATAN
by Harry Lorin Binnse

CLUNY
Providence, Rhode Island

CLUNY MEDIA EDITION, 2022

For more information regarding this title
or any other Cluny Media publication,
please write to info@clunymedia.com, or to
Cluny Media, P.O. Box 1664, Providence, RI 02901

VISIT US ONLINE AT WWW.CLUNYMEDIA.COM

ISBN: 978-1944418939

Cover design by Clarke & Clarke
Cover image: Vincent van Gogh, *Olive Trees with Yellow Sky and Sun*, 1889, oil on canvas
Courtesy of Wikimedia Commons

CONTENTS

Prologue

THE STORY OF MOUCHETTE

1.

HERE IS THE evening hour the poet Toulet loved. Here is the horizon losing its sharpness—a great ivory cloud in the west and, from the earth to the top of the heavens, a twilight sky, a vast loneliness, already chilling—full of a liquid silence.... Here is the poet's hour, as he distilled life within his heart, in order to extract from it its essence, hidden, embalmed, baneful.

Now the human swarm stirs in the shadows, with its myriad arms, its myriad mouths; now the boulevard unfurls and glows.... And he, elbows resting on the marble slab of the table, watched the night arise, like a lily.

Here is the hour when begins the story of Germaine Malorthy, of the township of Terninques, in Artois. Her father was one of those Malorthys from the Boulonnais, who are a dynasty of millers and bolters, all men of the same flour, keen to get their full measure from a bag of wheat, but easy to deal with and good trenchermen. Malorthy the father was the first of his clan to settle in Campagne, where he married and, quitting wheat for barley, went in for politics and brewing, at neither of which was he particularly apt. The flour-merchants of Desvres and Marquise thereafter regarded him as a dangerous dolt, sure to end in the gutter, having meanwhile brought dishonor on businessmen who had never asked anyone for anything more than an honest profit. "We are liberals, as were our fathers before us and as our sons will be after us," they said, meaning to indicate thereby that they were solid tradesmen, beyond reproach.... For the rebellious doctrinaire, of whom time makes deeply ironical sport, is ever the founder of a line of peaceable progeny. The intellectual offspring of Blanqui, apostle of blood-letting, has peopled the civil service, and the sacristies are cluttered with that of Lamennais.

The village of Campagne possessed two lords and masters. Gallet, a public-health officer suckled on the bacteriological and radical scientism of Raspail and deputy for the district, was one. From the heights whereon his destiny had placed him, he still stood melancholy watch over the paradise lost of bourgeois life, his remote small town, and the ancestral parlor done in green rep, where his nonentity had swollen with air. He honestly believed himself a threat to the social order and to property; this he regretted, and, by invariably remaining silent or aloof, he hoped to prolong their dear death throes.

"No one does me justice," this wraith one day cried out, and with touching sincerity. "After all, I have a conscience!"

During those same years and in the same place, the Marquis de Cadignan lived the life of a king without a kingdom. Keeping posted on the world's great happenings through the "Social Notes" in the monarchist *Le Gaulois* and the conservatively republican political reporting of the *Revue des Deux Mondes*, he continued to cherish the ambition of restoring to France the forgotten sport of hawking. Unhappily, the dubious Norway falcons with distinguished pedigrees, which he had bought at great expense, betrayed his hopes and ransacked his meat-lockers; so he had wrung the necks of all these Teutonic Knights and, more modestly, trained sparrow hawks to pursue larks and magpies. Betweenwhiles he gave hunt to the girls; at least so it was said, for the public spite had to rest content with scandal and idle talk, since the sly fellow poached for his own account exclusively, silent in chase as a wolf.

2.

FATHER MALORTHY HAD by his wife one daughter, whom he at first wished to call Lucrèce through devotion to the republican cause. The schoolmaster, honestly believing this virtuous matron to have been the mother of the Gracchi, made a brief speech on the subject and recalled that, before him, Victor Hugo had paid tribute to the great maternal memory. The records of the civil registry office were thus for once adorned with the confused glory of this name. Unfortunately, the village priest, stricken with scruples, talked of awaiting the archbishop's counsel, and, like it or not, the fiery brewer had to suffer his daughter to be baptized under the name of Germaine.

"Had it been a boy, I would not have put up with it," said he, "but for a young lady..."

The young lady reached the age of sixteen.

One evening at supper time Germaine walked into the main room of the house, carrying a pail full of fresh milk.... Two steps from the threshold she stopped short, her knees buckled, and she blenched.

"For heaven's sake," exclaimed Malorthy, "the girl's having a spell."

The poor little thing pressed her hands to her belly and burst into tears. Mother Malorthy's glance caught her sharp in the eye.

"Leave us alone a moment, Father," she said.

As not infrequently happens, after a thousand vague and barely admitted suspicions, of a sudden the obvious blazed forth, exploded. Neither pleas, threats, nor even blows were able to drag anything out of the stubborn girl except childish tears. In such crises the most shallow-witted damsel will display a clear-headed composure which is, in all likelihood, merely the loftiest achievement of the instinct; where a man will mumble and falter, she keeps her mouth closed. By overexciting curiosity well does she know that she disarms wrath.

A week later, however, between two draughts on his comfortable pipe, Malorthy said to his wife, "Tomorrow I'm going to see the Marquis. I have ideas of my own. I see through the whole business."

"The Marquis!" said she. "Antoine, pride will be your downfall; you know nothing for sure; you'll be laughed at for your pains."

"We shall see," her goodman replied. "It's ten o'clock. Go to bed."

But next day, as he sat deep in a large leather armchair in his formidable opponent's parlor, he at once felt oppressed by his own foolhardiness. His anger had cooled; "I'll go too far," he told himself.

For he had thought himself capable of handling this business, like many another, as a sly peasant, without self-conceit. For the first time passion's voice was the louder, and it spoke in a tongue to him unknown.

Jacques de Cadignan had then reached his forty-fifth year. Of middling height and already grown stout with age, he at all seasons wore a brown moleskin suit, which made him seem heavier still. Regardless of this, he was nonetheless charming, by virtue of a species of cordiality and rustic courtesy which he applied with a sure touch. Like many of those who live in the spell of pleasure and in the presence—whether real or imaginary—of a feminine consort, no matter what care he might take to seem gruff, willful, and even a trifle coarse, he betrayed himself by his speech; his voice was of the richest and most varied, with the outbursts of a spoiled child, urgent and tender, secret. From an Irish mother he had likewise pale blue eyes, limpid and shallow, full of an icy light.

"Good evening, Malorthy," said he. "Do sit down."

Malorthy had actually stood up. He had worked out his little speech, and now was astounded not to remember a word of it. At first he spoke as in a trance, waiting for wrath to unloose his tongue. "Monsieur le Marquis," he said, "it's about our daughter."

"Oh!..." said Cadignan.

"I have come to talk to you man to man. Ever since we became aware of it, five days ago, I've been thinking it over, weighing the pros and cons; we can only understand each other by speaking frankly, and I'd rather see you before going any further. After all, we're civilized people!"

"Going where?..." asked the Marquis. Then he added quietly, in the same tone of voice, "I'm not making fun of you, Malorthy, but damn it, you're talking to me in riddles! You and I are both of us too well along in years to deal in such dodges and beat about the bush. Shall I tell you what you're trying to say? Well then, the girl is pregnant, and you're trying to find a dad for your grandson.... Is that it?"

"The child is your doing!" cried the brewer without further delay.

The stout man's calm sent shivers down his back. Of all the arguments he had rehearsed, one by one, irrefutable arguments, he found none he dared even suggest; in his brain the evidence was fading away like smoke.

"Let's stop joking," replied the Marquis. "I do not intend to be rude before hearing your reasons. We know each other, Malorthy. You know that I have a soft spot for the girls; I've had my good times like everyone else. But upon my word! There isn't a child procreated over the whole countryside but what your damned gossips try to pin it on me, with their *ifs* and *ans*, their *maybe this*'s and *maybe thats*.... The days of the feudal lords are over: whatever I take, I have been freely given. The Republic includes everyone, by God!"

"The Republic!" thought the brewer, astounded. He took this profession of faith for mere bluff, although the Marquis spoke frankly and, a peasant at heart, felt drawn toward a government which promotes agricultural meetings and awards medals to well-fattened animals—the Campagne lord of the manor's ideas on politics and history being, after all, with minor differences, those of the lowliest of his tenant farmers.

"Well?..." said Malorthy, still waiting for a yes or no answer.

"Well, I forgive you for having allowed yourself—as the saying goes—to get your dander up. You and your devilish deputy and indeed all the ill-willed fellows hereabouts have built me up as a Bluebeard. The Marquis here and the Marquis there, serfdom, feudal rights—all that nonsense. Even though I am a Marquis, I have a right to justice, haven't I? Do you want to be fair, Malorthy, and straightforward? Tell me frankly what idiot advised you to come here, to my home, to tell me a nasty story, and to accuse me in the bargain?... There's a woman behind it, eh? Oh, the hussies!"

He was laughing now, good, jolly laughter, music-hall laughter. A little more, and the brewer would have laughed in his turn, as though after a hard-struck bargain, and would have said, "Shake on it, Monsieur le Marquis! Let's have a drink together!..." For by birth a Frenchman is hearty.

"Come, Monsieur de Cadignan," he sighed, "If I had no other proof, the whole countryside knows that you were paying court to the girl, and have been for a long time. Why look—barely a month ago, as I was going down the Wail road, I saw you both, in the corner of the Leclercq pasture, sitting side by side on the edge of the drainage ditch. I said to myself, it's just a flirtation—it won't last. Then, too, she had given her promise to the Ravault lad; she has so much self-respect! But now the damage has been done. A wealthy man like yourself, an aristocrat, is not one to trifle with questions of honor.... Of course I'm not asking you to marry her; I'm no such fool. But neither must we be treated like nobodies, you having your fun and leaving us high and dry, for all the world to laugh at."

As he said these last words, he had unwittingly resumed the tone of a peasant who is getting down to cases, and spoke with an insinuating, slightly whining good nature. "He doesn't dare deny it," thought he; "he has an offer to make...he will make it." But his worthy foeman let him talk into the void.

The silence stretched out for a minute or two, during which all you could make out were faraway strokes on an anvil.... It was a lovely August afternoon, filled with hummings and dronings.

"Well, then?" the Marquis finally asked.

During this brief respite, the brewer had mustered his forces. He replied, "It's up to you to make a proposal, sir."

But Cadignan pursued his own line of thought. "Is it long since she last saw this Ravault?"

"How should I know?"

"You might find a clue there," the Marquis quietly answered. "It would be an interesting bit of information.... But fathers are so stupid! In two hours I should have handed you the guilty man, bound hand and foot!"

"You don't say so!" exclaimed Malorthy, as though thunderstruck. He knew very little about that superior form of cheek which the clever call cynicism.

"My dear Malorthy," continued the other in the same tone of voice, "I have nothing to advise you; what's more, when he's hard hit, a man like you won't take advice. I simply tell you this: Come back in a week; between now and then, calm down, think it over, divulge nothing, accuse no one; you might run into some people less patient than I. What the devil! You're no longer a child! You have no witnesses, no letters, nothing, A week is enough to hear people talk and from some small matter to draw a large conclusion; you can see how things are shaping up.... Do you understand what I'm driving at, Malorthy?" he concluded in jovial tones.

"Maybe," answered the brewer. At this moment the tempter hesitated; for a second his voice had faltered. "He wants me to say my say," thought Malorthy; "I'd better watch out!" This sign of weakness restored his courage. Moreover, he became more excited as he felt his anger rise.

"Make inquiries," Cadignan resumed, "and leave the young girl alone. After all, it won't get you anywhere. That young game bird is like a corn crake in alfalfa, she'll walk about right under your keenest dog's nose, she'd drive an old spaniel crazy...."

"That's exactly what I meant," Malorthy asserted, emphasizing each word with a nod of his head. "I've done what I could; I'll gladly wait for a week, or two weeks, as long as is wanted.... Malorthy owes nothing to anybody, and if his daughter turns out badly, she will bear the brunt of it. She is old enough to let herself be seduced; by the same token she knows how to fight back."

"Come! Come! No idle talk!" cried the Marquis.

But the brewer had got going; he thought he was frightening his adversary.

"You cannot shake off a pretty young girl as readily as you can an old gaffer, Monsieur de Cadignan—everybody realizes that.... You are well known, you know, and she herself will tell you her story, by God! Face to face, in public, for she can get her dander up, that little girl!... If the worst comes to the worst, at least the laughter will be on our side...."

"By heaven, that's something I'd love to see!" said the Marquis.

"You shall see it," Malorthy promised.

"Go ask her," exclaimed Cadignan, "go ask her yourself, my friend!"

Fleetingly the brewer glimpsed that pale small face, resolute, undecipherable, and that prideful mouth, which for a week had refused to tell.... Then he cried out: "Devil take it!... She's told her old father the whole business!"

And he stepped back a pace or two.

The Marquis looked aside for a moment, then scanned him from head to foot; his eyes grew steely. The pale blue of his eyes turned greenish. At that moment Germaine could there have read her fate.

He moved over to the window, closed it, and came back to the table, saying nothing. Then he shook his sturdy shoulders, moved close enough to his visitor to be able to touch him, and said only, "Swear it, Malorthy!"

"I swear!" replied the brewer.

This lie at once seemed to him an honest dodge. Then, too, a retraction would have been terribly embarrassing. Nevertheless one idea alone kept going through his mind, an idea he could not quite grasp, and all he felt was its anguish. Between two roads open to him, he had a certain vague impression of having chosen the wrong one, and that he had committed himself to it for good, irreparably.

He expected an explosion; he would have preferred it. Meanwhile the Marquis calmly continued: "Go about your business, Malorthy. It is better to leave things as they are for today. You in one way, I in another, are both the dupes of a little baggage who told lies before she knew how to talk. Listen to me!... The people who furnish you with their advice are perhaps shrewd enough to spare you a couple of blunders, of which the silliest would be that of trying to intimidate me. I don't give a damn for what people may think of me. In short, the law courts were not made for the use of dogs, if you have a mind to turn to them.... So, good day!"

"Time will tell!" the brewer haughtily replied. And as he tried to think of a further rejoinder, he found, himself outside the door, alone and nonplussed.

"What a fellow," he said later on; "were he to fob off grains for barley, you would still tell him thank you."

As he walked along, he rehearsed every detail of the interview, gradually—as usually happens—working out a flattering role for himself. But try as he might, his common sense had to grant one fact overwhelming to his self-esteem: this encounter between the powers, from which he had expected so much, had settled nothing. Cadignan's last words, so full of mysterious meaning, likewise kept worrying him about the future. "You in one way, I in another, have been prettily duped...." It seemed as though that little girl had sent them both equally packing.

Glancing up, he saw through the trees his fine red brick house, the begonias set in its lawn, the brewery smoke drifting straight up in the evening air, and he no longer felt unhappy. "I'll get even," he murmured, "this is going to be a good year." He had for twenty years been dreaming this dream of one day being the peer of the lord of the manor; now he had achieved it. Incompetent to frame a general idea, but endowed with a keen sense of real values, he no longer had the least doubt of being his little town's first citizen, of belonging to the race of masters, whose laws and customs in every age reflect their own image and likeness—half merchant, half man of independent means, owner of a water-gas motor, symbol of science and modern progress—equally superior to the titled peasant and the political doctor, the latter merely a bourgeois who had lost caste. He made up his mind to ship his daughter off to Amiens for her confinement. There was one consolation: he was at least sure of the Marquis's discretion. And what was more, the Wadicourt and Salins notaries made no secret of the chateau's imminent sale. The ambitious brewer anticipated this squaring of accounts. He could dream of no happier event, not having enough imagination to wish a rival dead. He was one of those stalwarts able to carry hatred in their hearts, but whom hatred never carries away.

It was a morning in the month of June; in the month of June a morning so bright and resonant, a bright morning.

"Go see how our animals have spent the night!" Mama Malorthy had told her (for the six fine cows had been in the meadow since the evening before).... Always would Germaine see once again that tip of the Sauves forest, the blue hill, and the great plain stretching toward the sea, with the sun on the dunes.

The horizon which already was warming and growing hazy, the hollow road full of shadow, and the pastures all about, with their hunchback apple trees. The light as fresh as the dew. Always would she hear the six fine cows, sneezing and coughing in the bright morning. Always would she breathe the mist, with its smell of cinnamon and smoke, which pricks the throat and makes you sing. Always would she see once again the hollow road, with the water in its ruts afire from the rising sun.... And, more marvelous still, at the edge of the woods, flanked by his two dogs, Roll-to-Death and Killjoy, her hero, smoking his briar pipe, wearing his moleskin suit and his big boots, like a king.

They had met three months earlier, on the Desvres road, of a Sunday. They had walked side by side, as far as the first house.... One by one, words of her father's came back to her, and so many a blasting article in the *Reveil de l'Artois*, pounded out with thumps on the table—serfdom, oubliettes—and then again that illustrated history of France, Louis XI in a pointed cap (in the background a corpse swung from a gallows, and you could see the big tower of Plessis).... She answered without prudery, her head held high, with a pretty courage. But at her recollection of the republican brewer, she shivered all the same, a shiver only skin-deep—already a secret, her secret!...

At sixteen, Germaine knew how to love (not, indeed, to dream of love, which is merely a society game).... Germaine knew how to love, which means that she fed within her, like a fine ripening fruit, a curiosity after pleasure and hazard, the bold confidence of those who risk their whole fate on one throw, brave an unknown world, begin afresh with each generation the history of the ancient universe. This young girl of the middle class, with her fresh-milk complexion, her unaroused eyes, her so gentle hands, plied her needle in silence, awaited the moment to dare and to live. As bold as could be in imagining and desiring, but doing everything with order, her choice settled, with heroic good sense. A fine battlement, which ignorance, in the case of one naturally impetuous, inspires at each heartbeat to sacrifice everything to something it does not know! The elder Malorthy woman, born ugly and rich, had herself never hoped for any other adventure than a suitable marriage, a business requiring only a family lawyer, virtuous by reason of its estate, yet she nonetheless retained a very keen awareness of the unstable equilibrium in all feminine life, like that of a complicated structure which the least shift can rend asunder.

"Papa," said she to the brewer, "our daughter needs some religion...."

She would have been much abashed to say anything more, except that she thought it a good idea. But Malorthy would not let himself be persuaded. "What's she need a priest for? To learn in the confessional all the things she should not know? Priests warp children's consciences, as all the world will tell you."

For this reason he had forbidden her taking the catechism course, and even that "she associated with any of those pious simperers who," as he put it, "sow dissension in the best households." He spoke also, in mysterious and prophetic terms, of secret vices which ruin young ladies' health, and of which they learn the theory and practice in convents. "The nuns twist girls to the priest's advantage" was one of his favorite saws. "Before the event, they wreck a husband's authority," was his final judgment, as he slammed his fist on the table. For he would put up with no joking on the matter of conjugal rights, the only rights which certain liberators of mankind want to keep absolute.

Then, when Madame Malorthy complained that their daughter had no friends and scarcely ever went outside their small garden of trimmed and funereal yews, he replied, "Let her be. The girls of this damned country are full of mischief. With his Young People's Society, his Children of Mary, and all the rest of it, the parish priest holds on to them for an hour every Sunday. Look out for such things! If you wanted her to learn about life, you should have obeyed me and sent her to the high school at Montreuil; by now she'd have her diploma! But at her age, schoolgirl friendships aren't worth a thing.... I know what I'm talking about...."

Thus spoke Malorthy, pinning his faith on the Deputy Gallet, whom these delicate problems of feminine education did not leave indifferent. The poor little chap had once, indeed, been appointed doctor for the Montreuil high school, had extensive knowledge of the young ladies, and did not hide it.

"From the scientific point of view...." he would occasionally say, with the smile of a man who had got over many illusions, was full of forbearance for the pleasure of others, but no longer sought his own.

In the garden of trimmed yews, under the veranda, the wholly naked veranda, which smelled of scorched putty, there it was that she grew weary of waiting for no one knows what, and for what never comes, the eager little girl grew weary.... There it was that she started her journey, and she traveled further than the Indies.... Luckily for Christopher Columbus, the earth is round; hardly had the storied caravel set her course than already she was on her way home.... But another way can be tried, straight, unbending, which ever leads astray and from which none returns. Were Germaine, or others who tomorrow will follow her, able to speak, they would say, "What purpose is served by setting out for once on your right road, which leads nowhere? What would you have me do with a universe round as a ball?"

This man, whom a tragic fate awaits, seemed born for a quiet life. A surprising fact, you say, quite unforeseeable.... But facts are nothing: the tragedy lay in his heart.

If his self-esteem had been less deeply wounded, Malorthy would of course have made up his mind to give his wife an honest account of his visit to the château. He thought he would do better to hide for a time his anxiety and his embarrassment beneath a haughty silence, pregnant with threats. Then, too, he wanted to even the score, and thought he could readily do so by staging a dramatic scene at home, with his daughter as its victim. For many a conceited simpleton whom life disappoints, the family serves an essential purpose, since it places at his disposal, and, as it were, within his grasp, a handful of weak creatures whom the veriest coward can terrify. Impotence loves to reflect its own emptiness in the sufferings of others.

This was why, the moment supper had been cleared away, Malorthy suddenly said in the voice he used for giving orders, "Little girl, I have something I want to talk to you about...."

Germaine raised her head, slowly laid her knitting on the table, and waited.

"You have failed me," he continued in the same tone of voice, "gravely failed me. A girl who goes wrong in a family is like a member of that family who goes bankrupt.... Everyone can point his finger at us tomorrow—at us, people beyond reproach, who honor all their commitments and do not owe anyone a penny. Well, then! Instead of begging our forgiveness and dealing frankly with us, as would be fitting, what have you done? You weep as though you were going to die of it, you moan and groan and ceaselessly lament. But as for informing your mother and your father, not a bit of it! Hush and keep mum—that's all you're good for! It's going to stop right now," he finished, striking his fist against the table, "or I'll know the reason why! Enough tears! Will you speak, yes or no?"

"I ask nothing better," replied the poor young thing, in order to gain time.

The moment she had been awaiting and dreading had arrived, of that she had no doubt; and at once, with the crisis, the ideas she had been silently maturing for a week all surged into her mind together, in a terrible jumble.

"I've just seen your lover," he continued, "seen him face to face.... So Miss had her eye on a Marquis; her father's beer was too low for her?... Poor ninny, she thought she was already the lady of the manor, with counts and barons and a page boy to carry the train of her dress!... Anyway, he and I had a little talk together. Let's see if we truly understood each other: you are going to promise me to mind your *p's* and *q's*, and to obey without question."

She was crying noiselessly, spasmodically, her eyes clear through her tears. The humiliation which had so frightened her beforehand terrified her no longer. "I'll surely die of shame at it," she had kept saying to herself, only the previous evening, as hour by hour she waited for the explosion. *And now she sought for that shame, and found it no more.*

"Will you obey me?" Malorthy reiterated.

"What else can I do?" said she.

He reflected a moment: "Monsieur Gallet will be here tomorrow.

"Not tomorrow," she interjected, "on the free market day. Saturday."

Malorthy looked at her an instant, jaw dropping with amazement. "That's so. I'd forgotten," said he. "You are quite right. Saturday."

She had made this remark in a clear and composed voice her father had never before heard her use. In her chair by the fireside the old mother felt its impact and groaned.

'Well, then...Saturday! I say Saturday," continued the brewer, who was losing the thread of his discourse. "Gallet is a chap who knows life. He has discretion and feeling.... Keep your tears for him, daughter! We'll go call on him together."

"Oh, no!" she said.

Because the die had been cast, in the very thick of the battle, she felt herself so free, so alive! That *no* seemed to her as bittersweet on her lips as a first kiss. It was her first defiance.

"I'll be damned!" the old fellow thundered.

"Come, now, Antoine!" said Mother Malorthy, "give her time to catch her breath! What do you want the poor young thing to tell that deputy of yours?"

"The truth, by God!" shouted Malorthy. "In the first place, my deputy is a doctor—point one! If the child is born out of wedlock, he will at least say a word for us some place in Amiens—point two! What's more, a doctor means education, means science...he's not just a man. He is the republican's parish priest. And then you make me laugh with your secrets! Do you think the Marquis will speak up before we do? The girl was not of age, at the time, perhaps it was an abduction; that could get him somewhere! And we'll drag him there, in the criminal courts, by thunder! He with his high and mightiness, he with his taking you for an idiot, he with his denial of the obvious, he with his lies at every breath—a Marquis in clogs!... Ungrateful brat!" he cried, turning his back toward his daughter, "he struck your own father!"

He had not planned this last falsehood, which was merely a rhetorical outburst. The outburst, moreover, failed in its purpose. The heart of the young rebel beat faster, less at the thought of any outrage done her lord and roaster than at the glimpse of the hero in his magnificent wrath.... His hand! That terrible hand!... And with a traitorous glance, she tried to discover what mark it had left upon her father's face.

"Give me a chance," then said Madame Malorthy; "let me say something."

She took her daughter's head between both her hands. "Poor silly girl," said she, "to whom will you confess the truth if not to your father and to your mother? When I began to suspect things, it was already too late… but ever since! Now you know what men's promises are worth! They're all of them liars, Germaine! Young Miss Malorthy?… What the devil! I don't know her! And you would not have enough pride to make him swallow his own lie? You would let people believe you gave yourself to a nobody, a farm-hand, a tramp? Come, admit it! He made you promise not to say anything?… He won't marry you, daughter! Do you want me to tell you the truth? His Montreuil notary already has orders to sell the Charmettes farm, mill and all. The château will go the way everything else has gone. One of these fine mornings, and there you'll be! He'll be gone too! And what will be left for you but sly smiles from everybody?… But answer me, you blockhead!" she cried.

"He'll be gone, too…" Of all the words she had heard, she retained only these. Alone… Abandoned, stripped of her crown, relapsed… Alone in the common herd…repentant! What was there to fear in the world except loneliness and boredom? What was there to fear except this house bereft of joy? And then, crossing her hands above her heart, she artlessly sought her young breasts, that small deep bosom, wounded already. She pressed her fingers upon it, under the light material, until a new certainty burst forth from her pain, with a cry prompted by instinct: "Mother! Mother! I'd rather be dead!"

"Enough," said Malorthy; "you shall choose between him and us. As sure as my name is Antoine, I give you one more day to make up your mind…. Listen to me, you wicked girl! Not an hour more!"

Between herself and her lover, she saw looming this rabid, thick-set man, the scandal beyond repair, her adventure at an end, the only door to the future and to joy tight shut.... Assuredly she had promised silence, but that also was her shield.... This stocky man, now, whom she detested.

"No! No!" she said again.

"Lord God! she's lost her mind!" groaned Madame Malorthy, raising her arms toward heaven, "gone stark mad!"

"I'll certainly go crazy," replied Germaine, weeping the harder. "Why are you tormenting me, after all! Do what you please, beat me, throw me out, I'll kill myself.... But even then, when I'm dead, I won't tell you anything. And as for Monsieur le Marquis, it's a pack of lies; he has never even touched me."

"Slut!" the brewer muttered between his teeth.

"Why ask me questions if you won't believe me?" she asked in a childlike voice.

She was braving her father, defying him through her tears; she felt stronger with all her youth, with all her cruel youth.

"Believe you?" said he. "Believe you? It would take a sharper one than you to pull the wool over your papa's eyes.... Do you want me to tell you? He finally admitted it, that fine sweetheart of yours! I gave him a kick in the teeth after my own fashion; 'Deny it if you will,' said I, 'the little girl has told us everything.'"

"Oh! Mo...ther! Mother!" she stammered, "he...dared...he dared!"

Her fine blue eyes, suddenly dry and burning, turned violet; her forehead paled, and she vainly twisted the words in her parched mouth.

"Keep quiet, you'll be the death of her," Mother Malorthy kept saying. "Bane of our lives!"

Yet even though she said nothing, her blue eyes had already said too much. The brewer caught her glance, laden with scorn, stealthy. One who defends her young is less awesome, less swift, than she who sees torn from her flesh that flesh, her love, that other fruit.

"Go away, get out!" stuttered the outraged father.

She waited a moment, her eyes lowered, her lips trembling, holding back the avowal which stood ready to burst forth as ultimate insult. Then she picked up her knitting, her needle, and her ball of wool, and proudly strode across the doorsill, glowing more deeply than a woman who binds sheaves in harvest time.

But once free, she cleared the stairway in two hindlike bounds and closed her door behind her like a gust of wind. Through the half-open window she could see, at the end of the garden path, between two begonias, the white-painted, cast-iron gate, which closed in her little universe, at the edge of a leek-field. Beyond that, other small brick houses, in a row, to the turn in the road, where steamed a shabby thatch roof, supported by four cracked mud walls, the habitation of old man Lugas, the village's last beggar.... And that crumbling thatch, in the midst of handsome glazed tile, was still another beggar, another free man.

She stretched out on her bed, her cheek buried in her pillow. She tried to gather her wits, to tidy them, and in her mind heard only the buzz of anger.... Oh, poor little one! whose fate is settled on a child's bed, shining indeed, and smelling of furniture wax and clean linen!

For two hours Germaine concocted enough schemes in her head to conquer the world, had the world not already its master, over whom young girls are not in the least concerned.... She groaned, cried out, wept, without being able to budge the pitilessly obvious. Now her escapade was known, her guilt confessed, what chance would there be soon again to see her lover, ever again to see him? Would even he countenance such a meeting? He believes I have betrayed his secret, she told herself; he'll have no more use for me. "One of these fine mornings, and there you'll be!" Mother Malorthy had exclaimed only a little while ago.... How strange! For the first time she had felt a certain anguish, not at the thought of being deserted, but at her loneliness to be. Betrayal did not frighten her; she had never dreamt of it. This cozy, middle-class, respectable life, the house of honest brick, the prosperous brewery with its water-gas motor—the good behavior which is its own reward—the consideration owed to herself by a young person who is the daughter of a well-known businessman—yes, the loss of all these goods together did not give her a moment's worry. For seeing her in her Sunday best, hair discreetly combed, for hearing her fresh and lively laughter, Malorthy had not the least doubt of his young lady's accomplishments. "Brought up like a queen," as he would say from time to time, not without pride. He likewise said, "I have my conscience; that's enough." But the only thing with which he ever confronted his conscience was his ledger.

The wind freshened; far away small-paned windows one by one flared up and went dark; the sanded path outside was only a vague whiteness, and the silly little garden broadened and abruptly grew immeasurably deep, with the dimensions of the night.... Germaine awoke from her rage as though from a dream. She jumped out of bed, went to listen at the door, heard nothing more than the brewer's accustomed snoring and the solemn ticking of the clock, came back toward the open window, prowled a dozen times round her narrow cage, noiseless, lithe and stealthy, like a young wolf.... What now? Midnight already?

Deep silence—already here is peril and adventure, a fine gamble; great souls spread out therein like wings. Everything sleeps; no trap is set.... "Free!" she said, of a sudden, in that low, hoarse voice not unknown to her lover, and with a sigh of pleasure.... And indeed she was free.

Free! Free, she repeated, with growing certainty. And assuredly she would have been unable to say who made her free, or what chains had fallen from her. She merely expanded in the abetting silence.... Once again a young female animal, at the threshold of a lovely night, tries timidly, and then with frenzy, her adult muscles, her teeth and her claws.

She left all the past behind her as though it had been a day's lodging.

Gropingly she opened her door, went down the stairs tread by tread, made the key grind in the lock, and felt full in her face the outdoor air, which never had seemed to her so soft. The garden slipped by like a shadow...the iron gate was passed...the road, and the first bend in the road...she did not breathe till she had gone beyond it, leaving the village behind her, in the trees, compact, hidden.... Then she sat down upon the bank at the road's edge, still quivering with the pleasure of discovery.... The distance she had covered seemed vast to her. The night before her opened up like a refuge and like a prey.... She made no plan; in her head she felt a delicious void.... "Away from here! Get out!" Father Malorthy had said, not long ago. What was simpler? She had gone.

3.

"Here I am," she said.

He jumped up, dumfounded. A cry of tenderness, a word of reproach, would surely have made him explode with wrath. But he saw her standing straight and unaffected in the doorway, seeming barely touched by any emotion. Behind her, her soft shadow stirred upon the gravel. And at once he recognized that serious, impassive look he dearly loved, and that other little gleam as well, just beyond reach, in the depths of her sparkling pupils. They recognized each other, both.

"After Papa's visit, with thunderbolts hanging over my head—in my own house at one in the morning—you deserve a spanking!"

"Lord, I'm tired!" said she. "There's a rut in your driveway; I fell into it twice. I'm soaked to the knees.... Give me a drink, won't you?"

Up to that moment, a perfect understanding, and even something more, had changed nothing in their accustomed way of speech. She still called him "sir," and occasionally "Monsieur le Marquis." But that night she used the intimate second person singular for the first time.

"No one can deny it," he joyfully cried out, "you have a will of your own."

She gravely took the proffered glass and raised it to her mouth without trembling, but her little teeth chattered against it, and her eyelids fluttered without being able to hold back a tear which slipped down to her chin.

"Phew! You see," she explained, "my throat is all choked up from crying. I cried on my bed for two hours. I was nearly crazy. They'd have ended up by killing me, you know.... Oh! A fine pair of parents I have! They'll never lay eyes on me again."

"Never?" he exclaimed; "don't talk nonsense, Mouchette"—that was her pet name—"young girls are not allowed to run about the fields like a midsummer partridge. The first policeman who sees you will take you back home in his gamebag."

"Is that so?" said she. "I have money. What prevents my taking the Paris train tomorrow evening, for instance? My Aunt Egle lives in Montrouge—a fine house with a grocery store. I shall work. I shall be very happy."

"You little idiot, are you of age? Yes or no?"

"I shall be, in time," she replied, undismayed. "I have only to wait."

She looked away for a moment, then, quietly fixing her eyes on the Marquis, she asked, "Will you take me in?"

"Take you in—for heaven's sake!" cried he, pacing up and down the better to conceal his embarrassment. "Take you in? Nothing stands in your way, does it? Where would I put you? Do you think I have at my disposal a secret dungeon for the safekeeping of young girls? You'll only find such things in novels, sly-boots! Before nightfall tomorrow, they'd all be on our backs, your father with the police, half the village with pitchforks and all.... Even the Deputy Gallet, that rascally doctor, the great lumbering dolt."

She burst into laughter, clapping her hands, then abruptly stopped, turned suddenly serious, and remarked in a quiet voice, "Oh, yes! Monsieur Gallet? I was to go to see him tomorrow with Dad. One of his notions."

"One of his notions! One of his notions! The way she says it! I've told you a hundred times, Mouchette, I'm not a bad man, I know I've done wrong. But in the name of all that's holy! I haven't a cent left to my name. By selling every last thing I own, I shall still have enough not to starve to death—a mere pittance! Yes, I have rich relatives, my Aunt Arnoult first and foremost, but at sixty as solid as oak, rich as flint, a woman fit to bury me.... I've sown too many wild oats. I must play a cautious game this time, Mouchette; and above all I must gain time."

"Oh!" she said, "how pretty that is!... Lord, it's pretty!" She was turning her back to him, with both hands stroking a small Louis XV chest of drawers in pagoda lacquer, with bronze-gilt decorations. With her fingertips she traced mysterious signs in the dust on the violet breccia marble.

"Don't fuss with that chest of drawers," said he. "I have an attic full of such old trash. Perhaps you would be good enough to give me an answer?"

"What answer can I give?"

And she looked him in the face, with the same placid eyes.

"What answer!..." he began. But he could not help avoiding her gaze. "Let's not trifle, girl, and let's put the dots on our *i's*. Moreover, I don't want to lose my temper. You must understand that it is to the advantage of both of us to let the storm blow over. Tell me—can I marry you tomorrow? Well, then, I don't suppose you claim you can stay here and your father be damned? We'd see some fine goings-on! It is half past one," he concluded, pulling out his watch. "I'm going to harness Bob and drive you fast to the road. You'll be home before daylight without anyone's being the wiser. And tomorrow you'll put up a bold front to Malorthy. When the time comes, we'll get in touch with each other. That's a promise. Come on! Away with you!"

"Oh, no!" she said. "I'll not go back to Campagne tonight!"

"Where will you sleep, stubborn?"

"Here. Along the road. No matter where. What do I care?"

This time he lost patience and began to swear up and down, but in vain. He put you in mind of that effigy of their legendary monster which the people of Tarascon parade through their town, snarling and gnashing its teeth at the end of each abusive couplet sung in its honor:

Em un prim seden de moupo
L'embourgino, L'adus que broupo...

"How innocent I am to hope to persuade an obstinate girl. Go ahead, if you want to—sleep with the larks. After all, is it my fault? I could have done better, but I needed time; another month and the old shack would have been sold; I would have been free. Today your father falls on top of me like a bombshell and threatens me with the police; in other words, a hell of a scandal. Tomorrow I'll have the whole neighborhood on my hands. That old hoot-owl will be enough to attract a hundred crows. And why? Who's to blame? Because a little girl, who now has decided to be stubborn, got frightened and turned us in bound hand and foot, to the devil with the consequences! Father's been told all, as though at confession...and after that, you, my boy, shift for yourself! I don't blame you, my dear, but after all!... There! There! Don't cry any more, don't cry."

She leaned her forehead against the windowpane, weeping silently. And, thinking he had convinced her, it already seemed less difficult to him to relent and to feel sorry for her. For by nature a man hates his own suffering in the suffering of another.

He tried to turn the obstinate little head toward him; with both hands he pressed the fair hair on the nape of her neck.

"Why do you cry? I didn't mean a word I said. After all, I can see the whole thing in my mind's eye: old man Malorthy, with the bullying airs of a small-time politician addressing a meeting... 'Answer me, you miserable wretch!... Tell your father the truth....' He would have ended by giving you a whipping.... At least he didn't whip you?"

"Oh, no!" she said, sobbing.

"Heads up! Mouchette, that much is over and done with."

"He doesn't know a thing," she cried, clenching her fists. "I didn't say a thing!"

"I'll be damned," said he.

True enough, he little understood this outburst of wounded pride. But he saw with even greater astonishment an unknown Germaine standing erect before rum, her eyes wicked, her forehead creased with a frown of masculine wrath, and her upper lip a trifle drawn back, showing the full whiteness of her teeth.

"Come," he finally said, "you should have told me sooner."

"You would not have believed me," she replied after a brief silence, her voice still trembling, but her glance already clear and cold.

He looked at her, not without some wariness. This whimsicality, this bold and fiery mood, these remarks as short as a hare's tooth had become commonplace to him. But in the heat of the chase he had, until now, seen in all this simply the trifling defenses of an artful, pretty girl in whom an ultimate qualm maintains, the illusion of remaining free at the moment when she no longer refuses herself. Sturdy maturity readily inspires a blind self-assurance, and in love, the most cynical experience is much closer than you might think to a very nearly unadulterated credulity. "The mouse scampers around in front of the cat," he would sometimes remark, "but it is soon recaptured." In short, he had not the least doubt of having recaptured her. How many lovers thus welcome into their arms a stranger, the perfect and the agile enemy!

Fleetingly the countryman, in all his plainness and simplicity, for the first time had a foreboding of some close and unaccountable danger. His cluttered living room, full of piled-up furniture recently brought down from the loft, where it had been rotting away, suddenly seemed to him enormous and empty. And he opened wide his eyes in order to make out, beyond the circle of lamplight, the thin, motionless silhouette, the sole and silent presence.... Then he burst into happy laughter.

"So then? Papa Malorthy's word of honor was just so much talk?"

"What word of honor?" she asked.

"Nothing. A little private joke of my own.... Do turn around and close the window."

Behind her, indeed, the door had opened abruptly but without a sound. A brief, salty-tasting gust of cold wind, come from the open ocean but laden in its passage with all the stale mist of the tidal pools, caused the leaves of paper scattered over a table to flutter up to the ceiling, and sucked out of the lamp chimney a long red flame which fell back in a flurry of soot. The wind was still freshening. From one end of the grounds to the other, the fir trees came awake and roared in unison.

She turned the key in the lock and sulkily walked back.

"Come on over a bit closer," said Cadignan.

She moved a couple of paces further away, however, and by a dexterous maneuver put the table between herself and her lover; then she perched herself on the edge of a chair, little-girl fashion.

"Are we going to spend the night like this, Mouchette? Shame on you and your sulking!" he cried out with a forced laugh.

He was, of course, readily making the best of a stubbornness which he well knew he would not master; yet more than the desire for a caress which bored him, the thought of a risk to be run swelled his heart. "Tomorrow will certainly come soon enough," thought he with a kind of joy. For rest is good, but even more delectable is a short breathing space.

What was more, he had reached the age when feminine intimacies soon become unbearable.

"Would you mind waiting a moment?" Mouchette coldly asked, without raising her eyes.

All he saw of her was her shining forehead, obstinately lowered. But the sharp small voice echoed queerly in the silence.

"Take five minutes!" he exclaimed cheerfully, to hide his perplexity, for this cold pertness had abashed his gay temper. (In such fashion a friendly, gangling dog has his nose scratched by a watchful claw.)

"You do not believe me?" she resumed, after long pondering, as though she were thus concluding a monologue within herself.

"I do not believe you?"

"Don't try to fool me—nothing doing! I've done a lot of thinking during the last week, but in the last quarter of an hour it seems to me that I understand everything—yes, all life! You can laugh at me! At first I did not know myself at all—I—Germaine. You are joyful, unwittingly, at a mere nothing, at a fine day of sunshine...at foolishness.... But at last so joyful, with a joy fit to choke you, that you are well aware you desire something else in secret. Yet what? And something you already have to have, too. Oh! Without that, all the rest is nothing! I was no such fool as to believe you faithful. Don't think that! We boys and girls don't keep our eyes in our pockets; you learn more along the hedgerows than in the parish priest's catechism class! We talked about you: 'My dear, he gets the prettiest ones!...' Thought I, 'Why not me!' Every dog has his day.... And to realize now that Father's big eyes scared you.... Oh! I hate you!"

"I swear she's stark, staring mad," Cadignan cried out. "Mouchette, you haven't a grain of sense; you talk like a cheap novel."

He slowly filled his pipe, lit it, and said: "Let's be sensible."

What sort of sense? How many others before him had cherished the illusion that they were pulling the wool over the eyes of a pretty sixteen-year-old, at full alert? A score of times you would have thought her beguiled by the crudest lie, which she did not even hear you utter, her attention fastened upon a thousand nothings we disdain, upon eyes refusing to meet hers, upon an unfinished word, upon your tone of voice—that voice better and better known, possessed—patient in finding her way, falsely tractable, little by little sucking into herself the experience of which you are so proud, and that less by slow toil than by a sovereign instinct, of lightning flashes and sudden illuminations all compact, more skillful at guessing than at understanding, and never content until she has learned how to do injury in her own right.

"Let's be sensible: What do you hold against me? Have I ever pretended that in my old hovel—turrets and all—I was less of a pauper than any other bumpkin? Answer me frankly, can we take a chance at it? To close one's eyes on future troubles is all very well, and in love affairs the songster is not the last to be snared by his own song. But to promise what you very well know you cannot fulfill is really a stinking trick. Can you see the look on the faces of the parish priest and that strapping curate of his were we to appear hand in hand at Mass on Sunday? Once my Brimeux mill has been sold, and my debts paid, I'll have a good fifteen hundred louis to my name, by George! That's something to sink your teeth in. In short, fifteen hundred louis—two-thirds for me and the other third for you. I give you my word on it. Let's call it a bargain!"

"There! There!" said she laughing (but her eyes still full of tears), "what a lot of talk!"

He flushed with disappointment and, through the smoke of his pipe, studied the strange girl with a look in which anger was already beginning to break through. She met it without flinching. "You can keep your five hundred louis. You need them more than I do!"

Certainly she would have been very much put to it to justify her extraordinary pleasure and to give a name to all the complex feelings which crowded her dauntless heart. At that moment, however, she wanted nothing so much as to humiliate her lover in his poverty and to hold him at her mercy.

An hour earlier to have braved the night and darted after adventure, to have defied the good opinion of all the world, only in the end to find—O raging fury!—another country boor, another designing old codger! Her disillusionment was so strong, her scorn so sudden and so overwhelming, that in fact the events to follow were already, as it were, engraved upon her. Chance, you may say. Yet chance is stamped with our likeness.

Let the simpleton be amazed at the sudden outburst of a will long held in check, a will which a needful, barely conscious dissembling has already stamped with cruelty, that exquisite revenge of the weak, that everlasting surprise of the strong, that snare ever set! Such a fellow strives to pursue passion, step by step, in its whimsical wanderings—passion, more mighty and less graspable than the lightning's gleam—flatters himself as a keen observer, and knows about others only his own wry lonely grin as it comes reflected from his mirror! The simplest feelings come to life and stature in a darkness never fathomed; there they merge or spring asunder in a pattern of secret affinities, like the clouds of an electric storm; and from the gloom's surface, we capture only the brief glimmerings of the tempest's unattainable heart. Hence the best psychological hypotheses perhaps allow us to reconstitute the past, but not to foretell the future. And like many others, they offer our eyes alone a false semblance of a mystery the very notion of which overwhelms the mind.

After a final effort, the spent breeze had died away. The laurel bushes which afforded the old house a triple girdle had long since fallen back to sleep, while the powerful, black-foliaged trees, the sixty-foot pines in the center of the domain, still rustled at their tops, growling like bears. The lamplight shone with greater strength, warm and homelike at the end of the walnut table, sputtering monotonously. And, so close to the night seen in the opaque blackness of the windowpanes, the warm and slightly heavy air seemed sweet to breathe.

"Well, fume if you like, Mouchette," the Marquis quietly remarked; "you won't make me angry this evening. I swear it's a pleasure to see you here!"

He tapped down the ashes in his pipe with a careful finger and, half in earnest, half in jest, resumed, "It is all very well to refuse five hundred louis, sweetheart. But you don't spit in the hand of a poor devil who sincerely offers the last coins in his purse. But enough said between us. Utter poverty does not make me ashamed, darling...."

At these last words, Germaine blushed.

"I'm not ashamed of it, either," said she. "Have I ever asked you for anything, in the first place?"

"Not at all... Not at all...Mouchette. But your father, Malorthy..."

He stopped short, having spoken without meaning any harm, when he saw his mistress's mouth tremble and the beloved neck swell with a childlike sob.

"Well, what of it! Malorthy, Malorthy? What does all that mean to me! I'm sick and tired of it! It's a lie that I gave you away, a dirty lie! Oh, when last night...in my presence...he dared say...I was wild with rage! Look! I was ready to plunge my scissors into my throat. I was ready to kill myself in front of him, on purpose, right over the tablecloth! You don't know me, you two. To the devil with you! Your troubles are only just beginning!"

She was striving to fill out her frail voice, striking her fist on the table in a series of sharp little blows, somewhat laughable in her wrath, with that trifling emphasis whereby the most open-hearted of women distract themselves before making up their minds.

Cadignan, far from interrupting her, really admired her for the first time. A feeling other than desire, a kind of fatherly sympathy he had never before experienced, drew him toward this rebellious child, more eager and prouder than he, his feminine comrade...what!... Perhaps someday? He looked straight at her and smiled. But she thought he was defying her.

"It's wrong of me to get angry," she said coldly. "It was bound to happen. Yes, their brick house and their doll's garden would have ended by being the death of me.... But you, Cadignan"— hurling his name at him like a challenge—"I took you for a man of a different stripe."

She stiffened in order to finish the sentence without letting her voice break. However brash and sure she forced herself to seem, for the moment she saw no other outcome than the steel jaws of her father's dwelling, soon to snap closed upon her, the inescapable rat-trap she had fled two hours earlier, in such a frenzy of hope. "He has failed me," she thought. Yet, in conscience, she would have been unable to say why or how. And now the mistress and the lover, still face to face, no longer recognized one another. This credulous fellow past his prime believed he was doing enough by artlessly paying for his vulgar bliss with his last pennies, which the little savage would have loathed more than destitution and shame.... What had she journeyed to ask, through this first free night, of a gay dog already growing paunchy, whose peasant and soldierly blood had endowed him only with a purely physical energy and some sort of rough dignity? She had escaped, that was all; she quivered at the feeling of freedom. She had rushed to him as though to vice, to the long-indulged illusion of once and for all taking the decisive step, of ruining herself for good. Abruptly a certain book, a certain evil thought, a certain image half seen behind closed eyes, with the stove purring away and her hands idle over her forgotten sewing—all recurred to her memory with a frightful irony. The scandal of which she had dreamt, a scandal to turn people's heads, had very quietly taken on the proportions of a school-girl escapade. The return home, the discreet confinement, months of loneliness, honor regained at the hand of some stupid fool...and then years and still more years, all of them gray, in the midst of a whole population of little brats—all this she saw in a flash and groaned.

Alas! like a child, set forth one fine morning to discover a new world, who rounds the vegetable garden and finds himself back at the old well, having seen his first dream die, so had she done no more than take this one small idle step out of the cornmon rut. "Nothing has changed," she whispered, "nothing is new...." Yet against all this self-evident reality, an inner voice, a thousand times sharper and more positive, bore witness to the crumbling of the past, to a vast horizon laid bare, to something delightfully unexpected, to an hour struck beyond recall. Through the tumult of her despair she felt a great silent joy arise, like a foreboding. What matter whether she somewhere—here or there—found refuge! What mattered a refuge to one who had been able so easily to leave behind the accustomed threshold, and had found so light the door she closed behind her? This rake of a Marquis feared village opinion, which she took it upon herself to defy. So much the worse! She did not feel her own strength the less for having found its measure in the weakness of another. From that moment on, her immediate fate could be read in the depths of her arrogant eyes.

They had both grown silent. In the middle of the high, uncurtained window, the moon suddenly appeared through the glass, naked, motionless, all alive and so close that you would have liked to hear the murmur of its silver light.

Then, by a comical conjuncture, the same question put a few hours earlier by Malorthy took shape again on Cadignan's lips: "It's up to you to make a proposal, Mouchette."

But since she merely looked questioningly at him, fluttering her eyelids and saying nothing, he added, "Speak freely!"

"Take me away," she said.

And, after having appraised him with her eyes, weighed him, estimated him closely, exactly like a housewife sizing up a chicken, she added, "to Paris...anywhere!"

"Let's not talk about that yet—do you mind? I can't say definitely.... Once your confinement is over, and the little beggar born..."

At once she half raised herself from her chair, her mouth open, with a gesture of surprise which was utterly convincing and beyond argument. "Your confinement? The little one?"

Then she burst into peals of laughter, her two hands held against her bare throat, her head thrown back, more and more exhilarated at her resounding challenge, casting into the four corners of the aged room, like a war cry, that one tinkling sound.

Cadignan's face turned purple; still choking with laughter, she said, "My father was pulling your leg.... Did you believe him?"

The daring of her falsehood banished any suspicion. The unlikely does without proof. The Marquis did not doubt she had told the truth. For that matter, anger was choking him.

"Shut up," he cried out, pounding his fist on the table.

But she still was laughing, more restrainedly, with a certain prudence, her eyelids half shut, both her small feet tucked under her chair, prepared for instant flight.

"Damn it, God damn it!" the poor fellow kept repeating, wholly taken in and twisting the invisible dart buried in his flesh.

For an instant his glance met that of his mistress, and in this fashion he caught a whiff of the trap. "We'll find out who's telling the truth," he testily concluded. "If your simpleton of a father was pulling my leg, I'll fix him! And now, keep quiet!"

She wanted nothing better than to look him straight in the eye, to watch him from under her long lashes, to enjoy his confusion, her face pale at the thought of her being so dangerous and wily, as strong as a man.

He nervously fingered his mustache for a moment, thinking, "What an odd business...which of them is lying?" And yet never had a false word been so readily proffered, so freely, without reflection, like a gesture of defense, as spontaneous as a cry.

"Pregnant or not, I don't go back on my word, Mouchette," he said at last. "The moment the shack is sold, I'll surely dig up some quiet little nook for two, a game warden's cottage, halfway between the river and the woods, where one can live in peace. And, God help us, marriage will perhaps be the end of it...."

The poor chap was becoming mollified; she quietly replied, "Are we leaving tomorrow?"

"Oh, you fool!" he shouted, really aroused. "You talk about it, I swear, like a trip to town of a Sunday evening.... You are a minor, Mouchette, and the law is no trifling matter."

Three-quarters sincere, but sprung of too old a peasant stock to commit himself lightly, he was waiting for an outcry of joy, an embrace, tears, in short the emotional scene which would have rid him of his embarrassment. But the artful girl let him talk and kept derisively quiet.

"Oh!" said she, "I'll not wait very long for a game warden's cottage.... At my age! A fine figure I'd cut between your river and your woods!... If I'm not wanted any more, do you think I care?"

"It might end badly," the Marquis scornfully replied.

"I don't care how it ends," she exclaimed, beating her hands together, "and besides, I have an idea of my own.... I certainly have."

Cadignan having, however, merely shrugged his shoulders, she continued, goaded to the quick, "A lover, and I know just where to find him."

"You don't say?"

"Who'll refuse me nothing, and he's rich...."

"And young?"

"Younger than you.... Well, at least young enough to turn white as the tablecloth if I merely touch him with my foot under the table—So!"

"That's something...."

"An educated man, in fact a scientist...."

"I see—the deputy...."

"You're right," she exclaimed, blushing and watching him anxiously.

She expected an outburst, but he only replied, knocking out his pipe, "Much good he'll do you! A fine conquest, the father of two children and the husband of a lanky wife who keeps a sharp eye on him...." Nonetheless his voice was unsteady. His banter did not deceive the cautious young girl, who watched his every movement with keen attention—calculating the width of the table which separated her from her lover—her heart pounding, her palms moist and icy. But she felt as light as a hind.

Indeed, in days gone by, Cadignan had given short shrift to a mistress or two. Even the night before, he had felt more keenly the shame of being caught in an open lie by a ludicrous opponent than the fear of losing his fair Mouchette. Nor had he the least doubt that she had betrayed him, and, in his simple-minded selfishness, he held this weakness against her as a crime, and had not in the least forgiven her. But now the name of the man he hated the most, with a firm, rustic hatred, had stirred him to his depths.

"For a youngster," said he, "you don't let the grass grow under your feet.... After all, blood runs true. The father sells bad beer, and his daughter.... Well, we all sell what we have for sale."

She tried to shake her head in bravado; but not being as yet hardened to such things, the base insult, coming from so close, made her flinch for a moment: she began to sob.

"You'll hear worse than that, if you live long enough," quietly remarked the Marquis. "Gallet's mistress!... And under Papa's nose, I presume?"

"In Paris, whenever I want to," she stammered in the midst of her tears.... "Yes, in Paris."

Her ten little claws rasped on the table against which she pressed the palms of her hands. The buzzing ideas in her brain made her dizzy; a thousand lies, an infinity of lies murmured there as though it were a hive. The greatest variety of schemes—all of them outlandish, fading away as promptly as they took shape—there unwound their endless sequence, like the progress of a dream. From the activity of all her senses, there burst forth an unutterable confidence, similar to an outpouring of life. For an instant, the very boundaries of time and space seemed to bow before her, and the hands of the clock ran as fast as her young daring.... Having never known any restraint other than a childish system of habits and of prejudices, conceiving of no other sanction than the judgment of those around her, she saw no limit to the wonderful shore up which she now clambered from shipwreck. However long you may have savored its bittersweet delight, wicked thought is incapable of blunting beforehand the frightful joy of evil at last embraced, possessed—in a first rebellion like a second birth. For vice grows a slow, deep root in the heart, but the fine flower full of venom blooms in its full resplendence for one day alone.

"In Paris?" said Cadignan.

She saw plainly that he was burning to ask her more, without daring to do so.

"In Paris," she repeated, her cheeks still shining and her eyes dry. "Yes...in Paris, in my own place—a pretty room—and free.... All those deputy gentlemen have their girlfriends that way," she added with unshakable seriousness.... "Everyone knows that. Is it not they who make the law? Between the two of us it's an understood thing... and has been long since!"

It is true enough that the dour lawmaker of Campagne, whose marrow was harassed with fretfulness, and whom a strait-laced wife, herself gnawed by desire, exhausted but did not satisfy, had more than once displayed to the brewer's daughter those fatherly feelings regarding the true meaning of which a perceptive girl makes no mistake. That was all.... Yet on this trifling theme, faithless Mouchette felt strong enough to continue lying until daybreak. Each falsehood was a fresh delight, which tightened her throat like a caress; that night she would have lied despite insults, despite blows, to the very peril of her life; she would have lied for the sake of lying. Later she remembered this strange outburst as the most headlong expenditure of herself she had ever experienced, a sensual nightmare.

"Why not," thought Cadignan. "Look at the little fool, will you," he continued aloud. "Look at her! Believing the word of a dirty-bellied turncoat, a spellbinder, a clown of the worst sort! He'll treat you the way he does his constituents, my girl! A deputy's ladylove indeed!"

"Laugh away," said Mouchette, "there have been worse fates!"

The rustic's nose, usually pink and cheerful, was paler than his cheeks. For a moment, swallowing his anger, he walked up and down, both hands plunged under his generous moleskin jacket; then he moved a few steps toward his watchful mistress who, to keep out of his grasp, turned to the left and prudently left the table between her and her dangerous adversary. But he kept on with lowered eyes, went straight to the door, locked it, and slipped the key into his pocket.

Then he returned to his armchair and dryly remarked, "Stop pestering me, child. You asked for it; I'm keeping you here till tomorrow, free, for the fun of it.... I'm doing it at my own risk. And now be good and answer me, if you can find your tongue. This is all just talk?"

She was herself as pale as the collar of her dress. Between clenched teeth she gave him his reply: "No!"

"Go on!" he rejoined. "Do you truly expect me to believe that?"

"He's my lover, and I mean it."

She uttered this fresh lie the way you would spit out some burning, bitter liquid. And when she no longer heard the reverberations of her own voice, she felt her heart stop dead, as it does in a swing's descent. Her tone of voice came very near deceiving even herself and, while she hurled the word "lover" at the Marquis, she crossed her arms upon her breasts with a motion which was at once childlike and perverse, as though these two magic syllables had stripped her and shown her naked.

"For God's sake!" Cadignan cried out.

He had bounded up, so quickly that the poor young thing's first start, ill-directed, almost projected her into his arms. For a moment they stood face to face in one corner of the room, saying nothing.

Almost at once she dodged away, jumped on a chair which collapsed at the strain, thence to the top of the table; but her high heels slipped on the waxed walnut, and she threw out her hands in vain. The Marquis had grasped her by the waist and drew her briskly back. The violence of the impact dizzied her; the thickset, man carried her off like a prey. She felt herself roughly thrown on the leather sofa. Then for another moment she saw only two eyes, at first savage, little by little overcast by anguish, then by shame.

She was free once more; standing in the full light, her hair in disarray, a fold in her dress showing one black stocking, her eyes vainly seeking her detested lord. Yet all she could make out, and that only with difficulty, was a great pit of shadow and the lamp's reflection on the wall, so blinded was she by such rage as she had never known, suffering in her pride more than in a wounded limb, with a suffering physical, sharp, unbearable.... When at last she made him out, the blood welled back into her heart.

"Come! Mouchette, come!" said the uneasy countryman.

As he spoke, he gradually drew near, his arms outstretched, seeking to recapture her without violence, as he would have done with one of his skittish birds. But this time she eluded him.

"What's the matter with you, Mouchette?" Cadignan kept asking, his voice lacking all assurance.

She watched him at a distance, her pretty mouth twisted in a sly grin. "Is she dreaming?" he wondered.... For, having yielded to one of those outbursts of anger when suddenly desire is born, he felt less remorse than confusion, having never treated his mistresses much more gently than does a faithful friend playing his part in a brutal sport. He no longer recognized her.

"Will you answer me!" he cried out, incensed at her silence.

Yet she drew away from him, stepping slowly. Since she was making for the door, he tried to bar the way there by shoving his armchair across her narrow path, but she cleared the obstacle with an effortless leap and a cry of dread so ardent that he stood stock-still, catching his breath. A second later, when he veered to follow her, he saw her in a flash at the other end of the room, standing on the tips of her small feet, arms reaching up, stretching to grasp something on the wall.

"Hey there! Hands off! You crazy fool!"

Two strides would certainly have carried him to her and he could have disarmed her, but a false shame restrained him. He moved toward her without haste, and with the gait of a man not easily stopped. For he saw his own hammerless—a beautiful Anson—in his mistress's hands.

"Just try!" said he, continuing to move forward, and in the tone you would use with a snarling dog.

Mouchette, beside herself, replied merely with a kind of sigh of terror and of rage, raising the weapon arm's length the while.

"Idiot! It's loaded!" he wanted to tell her.... But the last word was as though crushed on his lips by the explosion. The charge hit him beneath the chin, shattering his jawbone into splinters. The shot had been fired at such close range that the tallowed felt wad went clear through his neck and was later discovered in his cravat.

Mouchette opened the window and was gone.

4.

DR. GALLET, HAVING finished his letter, was addressing the envelope in his tiny handwriting with its skillful downstrokes. Suddenly his gardener Timoleon appeared behind him: "Miss Germaine, sir..."

Miss Malorthy herself crossed the threshold, sheathed in her tight-fitting black coat, her umbrella in her hand. She had entered so quickly that the echo of her hasty steps on the flagstones had not yet died away behind her.

She burst out laughing in the gardener's face, and he laughed in return. The half-open window let in the ever compliant evening smell, and the tawny glow at the edge of the armchair at that same moment faded away.

"What can I do for you, Miss Germaine?" asked Dr. Gallet.

He hastened to seal the envelope.

"Dad was going to tell you himself that the next council meeting has been postponed until the ninth of this month, so... since I was going by..." She replied with her accustomed composure, so comically stressing the words "council" and "postponed until the ninth of this month" that Timoleon laughed again without knowing why.

"About your business," said Gallet brusquely, handing him the letter.

He followed his gardener with his eyes until the door closed behind him. Then: "What is the meaning of this?" he asked.

"You want to know right away?" she replied, laying her umbrella across the armchair. "Well then, I'm pregnant, that's all."

"Quiet, Mouchette," he murmured after a pause, in a voice already choking, "or else don't talk so loud."

"I forbid you to call me Mouchette," said Miss Malorthy dryly. "Mouchette—no!"

She tossed her coat over a chair and stood before him.

"Think it over," said she. "Nobody ever believes it when you first tell them."

"Since...since when?"

"About three months." She began quietly to unhook her skirt, holding a pin between her teeth.

"And you never hinted...now you admit it..."

"Oh! Oh! Admit!" she said, trying to laugh without dropping the pin. "What words you use!"

Her lips closed, her eyes laughed with the laughter of a child.

"You're not going to undress here, surely!" exclaimed the Campagne doctor, making a great effort to recapture his presence of mind. "At least you might go into my office."

"What difference does it make?" asked Germaine Malorthy. "Just turn the key in the lock. It's too chilly in your office."

He shrugged his shoulders indifferently, but at once glanced sidewise at her, his throat tightening. She, one of her legs hoisted onto an arm of the easy chair, the other bent beneath her, was quietly unlacing her boot.

"I'm taking advantage of the opportunity," she remarked. "See? They hurt me terribly. I've been tramping around in them all day. You'll give me the little doeskin shoes I left here Tuesday, won't you? They're on the shelf in the bathroom, behind the chest. And then, you know what? I won't leave tonight. I told Papa I should probably go to Caulaincourt, to see Aunt Malvina.... Your wife comes home tomorrow, I believe?"

Gaping, he listened to her without noticing that in the amazing mobility of her little face there was something motionless and clenched, a hint of weariness and obsession, which even distorted her smile.

"You'll end by wrecking everything with your rashness," he resumed plaintively. "At first I saw you only in Boulogne or Saint-Pol, and now all you are able to do is find excuses.... Did you notice Timoleon? As for me..."

"Nothing ventured, nothing gained," she said sagely. "Do go get my shoes, won't you? And take care to close the door behind you.

With her eyes she followed her strange lover as he shuffled along in his felt slippers, encased in his morning coat with its skimpy tails, its narrow collar, its shiny elbows.

About what was she thinking? Or was she thinking of nothing? All that was laughable and repulsive in this yellow-toothed disciple of cant had ceased even to astonish her. *Worse, she loved him.* As much as she could love, she loved him. Ever since the night when, by act beyond repair, she had killed at once the harmless Marquis and her own deceiving dream, the young Malorthy girl, Miss Malorthy, vainly struggled against her disappointed ambition. Flight, escape would have been too obvious an indictment; she had had to resume her place at home, brazenly beg her father's forgiveness, and, humbler and more silent than ever under the glances of unbearable pity, weave the lie around her, thread by thread. "Tomorrow," she told herself, eating her heart away, "tomorrow forgetfulness will come and I shall be free." But tomorrow never came. Slowly the bonds once severed tightened again their knots about her. By a bitter mockery, the cage had become a refuge, and she could no longer breathe except behind its formerly loathed bars. The character she pretended to be bit by bit destroyed the other, and the fancies which had sustained her one by one fell by the way, gnawed by the invisible worm of tedium. The commonplace small town she had defied had recaptured her, was closing in around her, digesting her.

Never was fall less swift, or more beyond recall. As she went over in memory each incident of the criminal night, Mouchette saw nothing there to justify the recollection she had harbored of it, as of a vast effort suddenly released, of a treasure swept into oblivion. What she had wanted, the prey at which she aimed, missed at her first try, gone forever—she no longer knew how to give it a name. Indeed, had she ever named it? On! it was not that heavy countryman stretched out at her feet.... But what was the prey?

Let other girls cringe and die under the linden trees, their lives having lasted but an hour or a hundred years! Life for a moment opened, spread out in all its breadth, the wind of space striking full... then folded back, plummeting like a stone.

Such as they, however, have not committed murder, or perhaps in a dream. They have no secret. They can say: "What a fool I was!" as they smooth the gray fillets under their frilled caps. Never will they be aware that, sketching their young claws one stormy night, they might have killed in sport.

After her crime, Gallet's love served Germaine as another secret, another silent challenge. She had at first thrown herself at the soulless and contemptible fellow's head, and had doggedly clung to this new bit of flotsam. But the mutinous child, with very sure cunning, had quickly enough lanced his heart, like an abscess. As much through delight in evil as through a dangerous game, she had made this ludicrous puppet into a venomous beast, known to her alone, hatched by her, like unto those monsters which haunt adolescent vice, and which in the end she dearly loved as the very image and the symbol of her own degradation. And yet of this sport she was already weary.

"There," said he, tossing her two shoes upon the rug.

Immediately he was amazed by the silence. At a glance, ever a sidewise glance, he espied in the shadow the little body stretched out on the armchair, knees bent back, head resting on her shoulder, one corner of her mouth very slightly drawn up, cheeks pale.

"Mouchette," he called out. "Mouchette!"

At the same time he moved forward quickly, caressing the closed eyelids with his fingers. They slowly came half open, revealing eyes still devoid of thought. Then she turned her head and sighed. "I don't know what came over me," she said; "I'm cold."

Then he saw that she was naked in her light wool coat.

"Well," he said. "Are you asleep? What's new?"

He remained standing, his head bent forward, ever laughing with his bitter laughter. "The crisis is over," he added, having taken her hand. "The pulse a little fast; that's usual. Nothing serious. You do not know how to take care of yourself.... You'll... You'll... Too bad! Do you cough?"

He sat down beside her, hastily pushing aside the half-closed collar. Her matchless shoulder, slipping away with animal grace, quivered for the moment it lay bare. But she pushed him away without any harshness.

"Whenever you like," said he. "You must grant, however, that I cannot give any opinion without a previous examination of the respiratory tract. That is your weak point. What's more, you take very bad care of yourself."

He continued for a time in the same vein. Then only did he notice that she was crying. Her eyes wide open and staring, her little face calm also, the arch of her lips ever drawn tight, she wept, without even a sigh.

For a moment he looked at her open-mouthed. A curiosity far above what was usual in him, the search for and fright at an unfathomable feeling in another person so close to himself for a moment ennobled him. But the expected utterance died on his lips; he blushed, turned away his eyes, and kept still.

"Do you love me?" she suddenly asked in a tone whose plaintiveness took on a strangely solemn and harsh note. At once she added: "I ask you because of an idea I have in my head."

"What idea?"

"Do you love me?" she abruptly repeated in the same tone of voice. As she said it, she arose, trembling in every fiber, laughably naked in her half-open coat, naked and thin, and in her eyes that same look from which pride had departed.

"Answer me!" she insisted. "Answer me quickly!"

"Now, now, Germaine…"

"None of that!" she cried. "Not that! Just tell me 'I love you!'… yes…like that!"

She threw back her head and closed her eyes. Between trembling lips he could see the hard white teeth, and her breath in its passage made a light whistling sound, just audible in the silence.

"Well…what?" said she. "Is that all? You don't dare say it?"

She let herself slip down at his feet and reflected a moment, with her chin cupped in her hands…. Then she turned up toward him again, eyes filled with cunning.

"I know…. I know…. I know very well," she said, nodding. "I know you hate me…. Less than I!" she continued solemnly. And at once added, "Only you…you don't even know what it is."

"What what is?"

"To hate and despise."

She then began to pour forth a torrent of speech, as she did every time a word uttered by chance awakened within her that elementary desire, not the joy or the torment of this hidden little soul, but the very soul itself. And in the pulsation of this body, frail and already withered under its bursting shroud of flesh, in the unknowing rhythm of the hands opening and closing, in the subdued spring of her shoulders and tireless thighs, there breathed something of the majesty of the animals.

"Do you want the truth? You have never felt…how can I explain it? It comes to you like an idea…like a dizziness…to let oneself fall, slide…to go to the bottom—all the way—to the very depths—where even the scorn of half-wits would not keep you company…. And then, old friend, even there, nothing satisfies you…you still lack something… Oh! in the old days…how I was afraid! of a word… of a glance…of nothing. For instance, that old lady Sangnier…(yes, indeed! You know her: Monsieur Rageot's neighbor)…did she play me a dirty trick one day! One day when I was crossing the Planques bridge—by hastily grabbing her little niece Laure away from my contaminating presence… 'A fine thing,' said I to myself, 'am I catching?' Oh, but now! Now…now…now, her scorn: I'd like to outdo it! What sort of blood flows in their veins, those women who are given pause by a glance—yes—whose pleasure would be poisoned by a glance, and who deceive themselves, they are honest, demure little things even in their lovers' arms…. We are ashamed? Well, of course, if you like, we are ashamed! But frankly, from the very first day do we seek anything else? What attracts you and repels you… What you dread and flee, but without haste—what each time you find afresh with the same shriveling in your heart—what becomes like the air you breathe—our very element—shame! It's true that pleasure must be sought for its own sake…its sake alone! What matter the lover! What matter the place and the hour! Sometimes… Sometimes…in the night… Two paces away from that big snoring hulk, alone…alone in my little room in the night…I whom all reproach! (reproach me for what, I ask you?) I get up…I listen…I feel myself so strong! With this mere trifle of a body, this poor little flat belly, these breasts which fit within the cups of the hands, I draw near the open window, as though I were being called from outside; I wait… I am ready… Not one voice alone calls me, you know! But hundreds! Thousands! Are these men? After all, you are merely boys—with plenty of vices, of course!—but boys! I swear to you! It seems to me that what calls me—here or there, no matter! In the murmurous ground swell…another…another takes pleasure and admires himself in me…man or beast…. So, I am crazy. Let me be crazy! Man or beast which holds me… Holds me fast… My loathsome lover!"

Her full-throated laughter suddenly broke off and, the glance which she held steady on her companion's eyes emptying of all light, she remained standing miraculously, like unto one who was dead. Then her knees gave way.

"Mouchette," gravely said the learned man, who had arisen from his chair, "for the last time, your hyperemotionalism frightens me. My advice is to calm down."

He might long have continued the same tune, for Mouchette no longer heard him. By an almost imperceptible motion, her chest had bent forward, her shoulders had come to rest on the divan, and, when he lifted the little head in his hands, he at first saw a face pale as stone.

"Dear God!" he exclaimed. Vainly he sought to pry her jaws apart, grinding an ivory spatula between her clenched teeth. The lip she had sucked in was bleeding.

He moved over to his medicine cabinet, opened the door, groped among the phials, chose one and sniffed it; his ears attentive the while, and his eyes worried, troubled by this quiet presence behind him, waiting, without admitting it to himself, for a cry, a sigh, a motion reflected in the panes of glass, for something or anything to break the spell…at last he turned around.

Her head now held up straight, quietly sitting on the carpet, smiling sadly, Mouchette watched him draw near. In this smile he read nothing save an inexplicable pity, bestowed from on high, from a superhuman sweetness. The lamplight falling full on the white forehead, the lower part of her face in the shadow, this smile, barely discernible, remained strangely motionless and secret. And at first he thought she slept. But abruptly she said, in her quiet voice: "What are you doing—tell me truly—with that bottle in your hand? Put it down! No, I beg you, put it down! Listen to me: I've been sick? I fainted? No! Truly? Suppose even I had died here, in your house!… Don't touch me! Above all don't touch me!"

He comically sat down on the edge of a chair, his phial still clutched in his strong hands. Meanwhile his face little by little resumed its accustomed expression of sly and sometimes fierce stubbornness. Finally he shrugged his shoulders.

"You can make fun of me," she resumed, her voice continuing calm; "that's the way it is. When I am carried away...carried away... carried away... I'm terribly afraid of anyone's touching me.... I feel that I am made of glass.... Yes, that's just it...a great empty goblet."

"Hyperesthesia...quite usual after nervous shock."

"Hyper-what? What a funny word! So you know about this? You have taken care of women like me?"

"Hundreds of them," he proudly replied, "hundreds of them. At the Montreuil *Lycée* I've seen far more serious cases. Such crises are not unusual among young girls who live together. Competent observers go as far as to maintain..."

"So," said she, "you think you have known women like me?" She became silent. Then suddenly: 'Well then, you lie! You've told a lie!"

She leaned toward him, took both his hands, gently lowered her cheek... and at the same instant he felt upon his wrist—even to the depths of his heart—the sharp bite of her teeth. Yet already the supple young animal was rolling about with him on the leather cushions, and all he saw above his head thrown back on the couch was that vast depth in the eyes where ripened its own joy.... She was standing before he could get to his feet.

"Go on, get up," she said laughing. "Go on, get up! If only you could see yourself! You're panting like an old hound. Your eyes are still askew. Women like me, old chap! There is not one—not another one—able to make you into a lover...."

She gloated over this depravity in full flower. For weeks, in fact, warming the Campagne legislator in her arms, she had afforded him a new life. "Our deputy is growing fat," said the good folk. For the poor devil, so spiritless in appearance, would at an earlier date have discouraged the shrewishness of any other woman than his wife, but now *he was putting on flesh.* Delight, rejoicing in pleasure, far from staying his hunger, was making him this new fat; and, through the necessity of keeping secret his miser's joy, he gorged himself on it, losing none of it in empty words, digesting it whole. His constant daily dissimulation surprised even his mistress. Without perhaps being fully aware of the extent of her power, she discovered its dimensions in the depth, obstinacy, and meticulousness of his lying. In this lying the unfortunate fellow took delight; it would have been cowardly sometimes to seek risk, to chance it; in the lie he tasted his bitter revenge. The long humiliation of his married life burst in it like a muddy bubble. The thought, once hated or dreaded, of his pitiless spouse had become one of the elements in his joy. That wretched woman came and went, slipped from cellar to attic, green with a chronic suspicion. She still seemed queen and mistress within these four detested walls. ("Perhaps I'm mistress in my own home" had been one of her challenges.) But what did it matter! She was so no longer.... The very air she breathed he had indeed stolen from her: it was *their* air she breathed.

"I love you," said the practitioner. "Before I loved you, I knew nothing."

"Speak for yourself," she rejoined. (And she was laughing anew, with that laugh, alas, daily more taut, more hard.) "As for me, you know I never had much appetite...a small appetite.... Oh! I know well enough—" (For he was listening to her with what he intended to be a light air of reproach and irony.) "—You are such a fool! You take me for a harlot! What rot!"

She laughed in vain: an animal pride breathed in her voice, which she had raised a trifle. Her eyes once again were focusing inward, losing themselves. And the only truly human thing they retained was an expression—barely perceptible—of vanity, of stubbornness, of a hint of candid besottedness which was a tribute to her sex.

"However," he tried to object.

She closed his mouth. Upon his lips he felt her five fingers: "Oh, how much fun it is to be beautiful. The man who seeks us is always beautiful. But a thousand times more beautiful he whose daily hunger and thirst we are. And you, my old friend, have the eyes of that man."

She pushed back his head in order to penetrate with her glance even beneath the soft eyelids. Never did that singular flame shine forth more visibly, dart higher, foolishly futile. For an instant the Campagne lawmaker truly thought himself another man. His mistress's tragic will was as though seeable and touchable, and toward her he stretched his arms, with a sort of groan.

"Mou…Mouchette," he pleaded, "my little Mouchette!"

She let him hold her tight. But from the very depths of her darted her look of the bad days.

"Good…good…you love me…."

"Look here," said he, "just now…"

"Just a moment; let me put on my clothes. I'm freezing."

When she next spoke, he saw her, already comfortably settled, her coat buttoned, her feet discreetly joined together, her hands crossed on her knees.

"And with it all, my friend, you haven't even examined me."

"Whenever you want."

"No! No!" she exclaimed. "What's the use? Another time will do. Besides, I know more about that subject than anyone else; in six months I shall be a mother, as the saying goes. A pretty mother!"

M. Gallet studied the design of the carpet. "That news surprises me," he finally said with comic seriousness. "I was about to explain myself a while ago. This pregnancy seems unlikely. Let me assure you, not without serious reasons…. But you'll fly off the handle again."

"No," said Germaine.

"We have not, you and I, either prejudices or scruples in matters of love. How are we to believe in a moral code which a science as exact as mathematics—hygiene—daily belies? Like everything else, the institution of marriage evolves, and the goal of this evolution we doctors call free mating. Hence I shall make no obtrusive allusion, respecting in you a woman free and mistress of her fate. I shall speak of the past with all possible reserve. But I have grave reasons to diagnose a more advanced pregnancy. I am persuaded that an examination—if you allow it—would confirm this *a priori* diagnosis. I ask you for only five minutes."

"No," she said. "I've changed my mind."

"Very well. So I'll leave it at that for the time being."

Vainly he awaited a cry of anger, a protest, or even a pout of vexation. Once again, however, a long silence put the finishing touch to his bafflement. Having heard him without emotion, his mistress was now pondering with all her heart, and at such moments Mouchette's countenance was frank and open.

"What a fine thing science is," she finally declared. "One can't hide a thing from you. Yet I have not lied.... Look yourself; it does not show.... So! In any case, you'll not leave me in the lurch, I am sure."

"What are you talking about?" he asked.

"I'll be delivered neither in three months nor in six. I'll never have a confinement."

Laughingly he said, "You astound me!"

But once again she bent her sharp glance upon him. "Go on, I'm not so stupid. I know how easy it is for you fellows. One, two, three and away! It's done with, flown off, gone...."

"What you're asking me to do, little girl, is a serious matter, forbidden by the law. As usual, I don't hide my personal views on the subject. But a man in my position has to take opinion into account—opinion, or, if you prefer, prejudices, perhaps respectable, certainly powerful.... The law is the law."

For from that moment he was convinced that Mouchette's imprudent request had given her away. Of how much less account is a mistress when she has divulged her secret.

"You can't teach me my trade, little one," he added complacently. "Love will never make me lose my head to the point of forgetting the elementary precautions involved.... What's more, perhaps you misinterpret symptoms which you little understand. But if you are pregnant, Mouchette, you are not pregnant by me."

"Let's change the subject," she exclaimed, laughing. "I'll travel as far as Boulogne—that'll settle it. Surely one might think I was asking you for the moon!"

"Simple honesty imposes another duty on me...."

"Which is?"

"I must warn you that surgical interference is always dangerous, sometimes fatal.... That's all."

"That's all!" she said.

Then, getting up, she reached the door, walking quietly, almost humbly. Vainly, however, did she turn the knob, with a motion at first hesitant, then more and more nervous, then bewildered. Of course absentmindedly, Gallet had bolted it. She stepped back several paces, as far as the desk, where she stopped short. The color drained from her face. She was talking to herself; several times she repeated in a blank voice: "*That reminds me of something, but of what?*"

Was it the sound of the rain against the windowpanes? Or the suddenly thick shadow? Or something more hidden? Gallet ran to the door, pulled on it, opened it wide. He opened it. And less for his mistress than for his fear, his own peril—he knew not what—which was in the air, within his reach—the word which was to be spoken and which must not be heard—for the mysterious avowal which the lips, already stirring, would no longer hold back. And his motion was so abrupt, so instinctive that, in the light, he was astonished at being there, face to face with his motionless mistress.

Fear of ridicule, however, gave him back his voice: "If you are in such a hurry to leave, my girl, I won't detain you. Only forgive me for having locked the door a while back," he added in an excess of politeness for which he was grateful. "I did it without thinking, absentmindedly."

She listened to him with her eyes cast down, unsmiling. Then she passed in front of him and moved away, at the same humble pace, head lowered.

Such unexpected docility completed the discomfiture of the Campagne doctor. Like many a fool who, when things get serious, always has something to say and thinks of it too late, a straightforward and silent ending to their quarrel was enough to nauseate him. During the very brief time Miss Malorthy took in reaching the street door, Gallet's little wit was unable to shape any final sentence, at once adroit and firm, which, without compromising his dignity, would have brought a softened Mouchette back to the green rep armchair. But when the beloved little hand touched the knob, when he saw the black silhouette already outlined in the door opening, his whole poor body could only utter the single cry: "Germaine!"

He seized her under the arms, held her bent form against his chest, and, violently kicking, shut the door, threw her into the empty armchair.

Then at once, as though this great effort had in a moment burnt up all his courage, he sat down on the nearest chair at hand, his features pallid. And on the instant she clambered toward him, her hair disheveled, her hands thrust forward, more beseeching even than her eyes, paled with anguish.

"Don't leave me," she kept repeating. "Don't leave me. Don't throw me out today.... I just had a dream.... Oh, what a dream...."

"Someone just closed the kitchen door. Timoleon is out.... Someone is in there...." muttered the conquered hero, as he gently pushed his mistress aside.

She, however, clasped her arms around his chest. "Look after me! I'm a crazy fool! I've never been afraid. This is the first time. Now it's all over."

Again he thrust her aside, stretching her out on the settee.

She immediately sat up. Already her cheeks were pink. Machine-like, she repeated, "It's over.... It's over," but in a different tone of voice.

Meanwhile Gallet had left the room. Almost at once he returned, uneasy. "I can't understand it at all," said he. "The laundry door is open, and so is the kitchen window. Yet Timoleon has not yet come home; I saw both his house shoes on the outside steps...." He raised his voice and said to his mistress with a horrible grimace, "What follies you force me to commit!"

She smiled. "This is the last one. I'm going to behave."

"Damn Timoleon! He leaves the house wide open, damn him!"

"What are you afraid of?"

"For a minute I thought it was my wife," innocently answered the great man of Campagne. Then he thought it more fitting to add: "She sometimes comes home that way, without warning."

"To the devil with your wife," replied Mouchette, now quite composed. "We'd have seen her. And what's more, I want to beg your pardon. I was so nasty, my dear! You would have done well to let me leave. I should have come back. I need you, kitten.... Oh! not for the reason you suspect," she exclaimed, taking his hand. "We won't quarrel over a poor brat who will never see the light of day, I give you my word! I don't want any scandal here. I don't care a damn about taking my chances. No, I need you because you are now the only man I can talk to without lying."

Then, as he shrugged his shoulders, she went on: "You think that's nothing." (She spoke quickly, quickly, with beguiling feverishness.) "Well, dearest, it's easy to see you're not much like me! When I was little, I lied often and without pleasure. Now, the habit's got the best of me. When I'm with you, I am what I want to be. How it hurts, not to act out your own part but the very part which disgusts you most! Why are we not like the beasts which come and go, eat and die, without ever bothering about what others think? At the very door of the public slaughterhouse, you will see cows eating hay two paces from the mallet, facing the butcher and his gory arms, who watches them and laughs. How I wish I were like them! I'll even tell you something else..."

"What are you chattering about?" interrupted Campagne's physician. "Tell me, rather, now and frankly, why, a little while ago?... Oh, well! You seem to reconcile yourself very meekly, very honestly, to my point of view; you seem resigned to ask others—I don't want to know who they are, I don't want to know their names—to perform the dangerous, dubious act for which I cannot accept responsibility; you go away without wrath, with the look of a whipped dog—whipped but submissive—and all of a sudden… Oh, I know! I must seem prying, but you can't understand: here is what we call a case, a very interesting case…all of a sudden, over a closed lock, a door which does not open to the first light push, you become hysterical, truly hysterical!… 'I just dreamt a dream. Oh! what a dream…' I dragged you back already in flight. You had so odd a look! Where were you off to?"

"You want to know? But you won't believe me."

"Tell me anyway."

"I was going to kill myself," Mouchette quietly replied.

He struck his knees violently with the flat of his hand.

"You're making fun of me!"

"Or, if you prefer," she continued calmly, "in my mind's eye, as clearly as I see you, I saw a corner of the Vauroux pond, near our farm, overhung by two willows, into which I was going to fling myself. Behind it among the trees, you can see the slate roof of the chateau. What do you want me to say? This is all nonsense, I know.… I was out of my wits."

"God Almighty!" cried out the doctor of Campagne, rushing toward the door, "this time, someone did stir up there! And it's *her* tread!"

And, since she was bursting with laughter, he threatened her so direly with his glance that she felt she had to smother the rest of her amusement in her tiny handkerchief.

She heard his ancient slippers sliding as far as the staircase; the bottom treads creaked, then all was silent. Once again he confronted her. "It's Zeleda," said he. "I saw her traveling case in the upstairs hall. She must have taken the two-thirty train to save the expense of a night at the hotel. How could I have failed to guess she would do it! She's been there for ten minutes—maybe for twenty-five, who knows? Away with you!"

He shuffled his feet with impatience, even though in the depth of his humiliation he tried to strike an attitude. Mouchette, however, coldly answered: "It's your turn to act the fool. What are you afraid of? Papa sent me with a message. I can't run away, as though I were a thief, it would be too stupid. What's more, the window of your room faces on Egraulettes Street, and she'll see me. After a three-day absence, to get up and go without a word would seem a little odd. Did she hear us? So much the better. You never hear anything accurately through a door. Don't argue. Laugh in her face! When she comes, we'll greet her politely...."

He listened to her, won over. In a moment Mouchette's agile hands put everything back in its proper place. The cushions resumed their elastic plumpness, armchairs primly turned their backs to the wall, the pharmacy withdrew behind closed doors, the lamp shone quietly under its dumpy green shade. When Miss Malorthy sat down again, the very walls were liars.

"Now let's wait," said she.

"Let's wait," Gallet echoed.

He gave a final glance around the room, his eyes fastening, reassured, upon his mistress. At a respectful distance from the man of science engaged in his priestly functions, the young and eager patient sat ready to receive the infallible oracle.

"How dare she cross her knees so high," was the only inner question to perplex him. Now that she had grown silent, he became well aware that he had just responded less to his mistress's arguments than to her voice and tone. "It's childish," he repeated to himself, "childish. There are a hundred reasons to justify her presence here!..." But at the thought of having shortly to follow this whimsical child's lead in lying, of having to stick to his role before his skeptical sly adversary, his tongue clove to the roof of his mouth.

Then, suddenly, when he once again sought to catch Mouchette's glance, he was no longer able to. Those treacherous eyes were fixed upon the wall above his head, already ripe with a new secret. He had a foreboding, a certainty, of a misfortune thenceforth beyond escape. His evildoing stood there, before him, in the full light of day, obvious, blazoning, and he had wanted to have this unimpeachable witness at his side! Had not fear held him clenched in its grasp, he would certainly at that instant have hurled Mouchette out through a window. He would have trodden upon her as a man tramples a lighted fuse near a powder magazine. But it was too late. The sluggard's dreadful resignation handed him over defenseless to the enemy of his bosom. And before she had uttered a word, he heard her (the voice, nonetheless, which broke the silence was clipped and smooth): "Do you believe in hell, my dear?"

"This is a fine time to talk nonsense," he replied in a conciliatory tone; "I beg you, at least keep your incomprehensible jokes for a more suitable occasion."

"Oh, come, come! No! The fit is over; don't worry. You'll drive me mad with your airs of a convict awaiting the hangman. What risk are you running now? None whatever."

"I'm only afraid of you," said Gallet. "Yes, you're none too reliable an accomplice...."

She did not deign to answer him and smiled. Then, after a lengthy silence, the same calm, bland voice once again asked: "Answer me right away, my dear; do you believe in hell?"

"Of course not!" he exclaimed, exasperated.

"Swear it."

He resigned himself. "Yes, I swear it."

"I knew it anyway," she said. "You do not fear hell, and you fear your wife. How stupid you are!"

"Mouchette, keep your mouth shut," he begged. "What is this leading to...?"

"What's it leading to, eh? You're mighty sorry you kept Mouchette here, a while back? If you hadn't, she'd now be in the frog pond, her dear little mouth full of mud and well stopped.... Don't cry, you big baby. You can surely see that I'm talking very quietly on purpose. You cowardly wretch! You are afraid of her, but you're not afraid of me!"

He pled with her: "What motive have you to harm me?"

"None, truth to tell, none. I wish you no harm whatever. Only why do you not fear me?"

"You're a good girl, Mouchette."

"Of course, a good girl. But a girl whose pleasures alone you will share. Didn't you just prove it—tell me, yes or no? Mouchette have a baby! Come, come!"

"It's not mine," he cried, beside himself.

"Suppose it isn't. I don't ask you to acknowledge fatherhood."

"No." (They were speaking very low.) "You merely demanded that I do something my conscience reprobates."

"We'll discuss your conscience shortly," answered Mouchette. "By refusing to do me a favor, you have finally opened my eyes. Don't think I'm picking a quarrel with you. I love you neither for your good looks—take a look at yourself—nor for your big-heartedness; in fact—no insult intended—you are on the stingy side! What is it I love in you? Don't look at me with those big, round eyes! Your vice.... You'll tell me that's cribbed out of some novel?... If you knew...what you soon *will* know...you would understand that I had just fallen to the depths, to your own level.... We are at the bottom of the same hole.... For you I don't need to lie.... No! You don't read my heart right, you think I'm getting back at you.... No, little one! What's more, today I can be wholly, utterly honest. So this, or never, is the time to speak. I have you cornered, my poor darling, you can't escape me. I defy you even to raise your voice.... So!"

She herself spoke in so low a tone that he automatically bent his head, artlessly. This intimate eloquence, this half-silence, Zeleda's quiet footsteps above them, Timoleon's humming the chorus of a silly song over his saucepans were enough to reassure him. Nevertheless he did not yet dare raise his eyes to meet the glance which he felt fixed upon him.... "How annoying!" thought he.

But the dire handwriting was already upon the wall.

Mouchette took a deep breath and resumed: "If I do speak now, what's more, it's for your sake, for your good.... Look: we have been lovers for weeks, and no one knows it, no one.... Miss Germaine to you... Mr. Deputy to me... isn't that it? Are we well hidden, thoroughly secret? Monsieur Gallet is making love to a girl of sixteen. Who suspects it? Even your wife herself? Admit it, you old wretch, you're unfaithful to her right here, under her nose, under her mustache (and she has one!), and that's half your fun. I know you. You don't like limpid water. Just so, in my favorite Vauroux pond, I see very old, very singular beasts; they are a little like centipedes, but longer.... For a moment you will see them floating on the water's clear surface. Then they suddenly dive and the place where they were becomes clouded with mud. And they're just like us! Between us and the fools around us there is a similar small cloud. A secret. A big secret... When you have learned it, how we shall love each other!"

Thereupon she tossed back her head, laughing silently.

"Strange girl!" said Gallet.

Childlike, she pursed her lips and stared at him a moment, worried. Then her features relaxed once more: "True enough, I talk too much," she admitted; "basically through fear. I talk so I'll not give myself away. Were Zeleda to enter the room this minute, would I really be pleased or put out? Now wait! wait! Above all listen to me carefully: you are not the father. No! Guess who? It was the Marquis.... Yes.... Yes.... The Marquis de Cadignan."

"Strange girl!" Gallet repeated.

Mouchette's lips were trembling.

"Kiss my hand," she suddenly said. "Yes, kiss my hand...I want you to kiss my hand!"

Her voice had faltered, just like the voice of an actor who has failed to make the effect he expected, who flounders about and grows stubborn. At the same time she pressed her palm upon her lover's mouth. Then she drew sharply away and said with extraordinary emphasis, "You have just kissed the hand that killed him."

"An altogether strange girl!" repeated Gallet for the third time.

Mouchette tried to laugh scornfully, but her laughter's pent-up explosiveness was so cruel and tearing that she became quiet.

"This is insanity," firmly announced the Campagne physician. "Even someone other than myself would recognize such symptoms as these. Moreover, you are a nervous girl, with alcoholism in your inheritance; you reached the age of puberty two or three years ago and are now precociously pregnant; in such cases, these accidents are not infrequent. Forgive me for talking this way: I am speaking to your reason, to your good sense, because I know that patients of your sort are never wholly taken in by their own delusions. Admit it: you're joking? A trifle more exaggerated than the sort of joke in which anyone might indulge? A bad joke."

"A joke," she finally stammered...

Mighty anger pounded in her breast, but she restrained it. The fire of disappointed pride wholly consumed what remained in her of foolish and cruel adolescence; she suddenly felt within her breast the indomitable heart, and within her head the cold and practical intelligence of a woman, that tragic sister to the child.

"Don't go fail me at such a moment," she cried out, "or it will be your turn to weep. Believe what you will; perhaps I am weary of keeping this secret, perhaps it is remorse? or sheer fright... Why shouldn't I be afraid, like anyone else? Believe what you will, *but don't wash your hands of it.* After all, I've talked too much already. Yes, it is I who killed him. On what day? The 27th... At what hour? A quarter to one in the morning. (I can still see the hand of the clock.) I took down his gun. It was hanging against the wall, under the mirror.... Perhaps I was not absolutely certain it was loaded. It was. I fired when the end of the barrel touched him. He almost fell on top of me. My shoes were full of blood; I washed them in the pond. I also washed my stockings, at home, in my own basin.... Now! Are you convinced?" she concluded with naive assurance. "Do you want *more* proof?" (So far she had not supplied any whatever.) "I'll give it. Just question me."

Unbelievable fact! Not for an instant did Gallet doubt that she had told the truth. From her first words he had believed her, so much more does the countenance tell than do the lips. But so great was the initial surprise that it paralyzed even those manifestations of terror which Mouchette already espied on her lover's countenance. The wretched fellow's distress, in its paroxysm, even though it did not explode outwardly, inwardly overexcited all the powers of the instinct and afforded the half-lucid brute an almost boundless capacity for dissimulation, for lying. It was not horror at the crime which held Gallet rigid; but in a flash he had seen himself forever linked to his appalling companion, accomplice not of the act but of the secret. How tell this secret without giving himself away? Since it was too late to stop its avowal, he would say, No! What else was he to do? No, and again No! to the very evidence itself. No! No! No! No! howled fear. Already he wished that he could make a blow out of that No, as though it were a closed fist striking the terrible, accusing mouth.... Only... Only.... The inquest was over, the verdict of no true bill rendered. Only: did he know all? Was Mouchette withholding some proof? Were she to betray herself, he would be able to ward off the blow: the obstinacy habitual among judges, the oddness of the crime, the oblivion which was already obliterating the memory of a man formerly feared or loathed, the Malorthy family's prestige —above all the testimony of the court physician—here was enough to overcome a magistrate's tender scruples. Mouchette's excitement and the probable vagaries of her wrath made plausible the hypothesis of an attack of insanity which, moreover, Gallet had no doubt would soon actually overcome her.... But then, sane or crazy, what would the treacherous girl say before the door of the padded cell could be closed upon her? However quickly these contradictory notions flashed through the unhappy man's mind, he recaptured his peasant shrewdness sufficiently to be able to say, without irony:

"I didn't mean to make you angry.... I do not judge your act, if ever you committed it. The trade of seducing fifteen-year-old children involves its own risks.... But I'll question you, since you beg me to. You are speaking to a friend...to a father-confessor." He lowered his voice despite himself, with a tone of anguish.

"...So you did not sleep at home during the night between the 26th and the 27th?"

"What a question!"

"How about your father?"

"He was asleep, of course," replied Mouchette. "To get out without being seen doesn't take much brains!"

"And to get back in the house?"

"That's not hard, either! At three in the morning, he would not hear God thundering."

"But next day, my dear, when they heard what had happened?"

"Like everyone else, they believed it was suicide. Papa gave me a kiss. He had seen the Marquis on the evening before. The Marquis had admitted nothing. 'He was scared, all the same,' said Papa.... He also said, 'As for the moppet, we'll manage; Gallet has a long arm.' For they wanted to ask your advice. But I didn't want them to."

"So you admitted nothing, either?"

"No!"

"And the moment the...the deed was done...you fled?"

"I only ran as far as the pond, to wash my shoes."

"You took nothing, carried nothing off with you?"

"What would I have taken?"

"And what have you done with your shoes?"

"I burned them, together with the stockings, in our oven."

"I saw the...I examined the body," Gallet continued. "Suicide seemed obvious. The shot had been fired at such short range!"

"Yes, right under his chin," said Mouchette. "I was so much shorter than he, and he was coming straight toward me.... He was not afraid."

"Did the...the deceased have in his possession any objects...any letters?..."

"Letters!" said Mouchette, scornfully shrugging her shoulders. "Why should he have any?"

"It all seems plausible," thought Gallet. And with surprise he heard his own voice repeating his thought aloud.

"You see," cried Mouchette in triumph. "It was really weighing too heavily on my mind! Let her come now, your Zeleda; you'll see. I'll be as well-behaved as a picture on the wall. 'How do you do, Germaine?'" (She arose, to make a curtsy toward the mirror.) "'How do you do, Madame?'…"

But the Campagne doctor was no longer able to dissemble. Shriveled with fear, he suddenly let himself go and let forth his ruse just as an animal, hard-pressed by dogs, will, when free of its pursuers, let flow its urine.

"My girl, you are crazy," said he in a long sigh.

"Eh? What?" cried Mouchette. "You…"

"I don't believe a word of the whole yarn."

"Don't say that again," said she between her teeth.

Smiling, he waved his hands, as though to pacify her.

"Listen, Philogone," she resumed in a pleading voice (and the expression of her face changed even more quickly than her voice). "I was lying a while back; I was putting on a bold front. Truly I can no longer live, nor breathe, nor even see the light of day through that terrible lie. But come! I've told everything now! Swear to me that I've told everything?"

"You've had a bad dream, Mouchette."

She pleaded with him anew: "You'll drive me crazy. If I have doubts of this, also, in what shall I believe? But what am I saying?" She caught herself, in a voice this time piercing. "Since when do people refuse to accept the word of an assassin who confesses and who is repentant? For I do repent. Yes… Yes… I'll play you the trick of repenting, I who say these words. And if you defy me, I'll go tell everyone my dream, my famous dream! Your dream!"

She burst into laughter. Gallet recognized that laughter and paled.

"I went too far," he stammered. "All right, Mouchette, all right; let's not discuss it any further."

She yielded to the extent of lowering her voice. "I frightened you," she said.

"A little," he rejoined. "You are at the moment so nervous, so impulsive.... Let's change the subject. I've now made up my mind."

She was trembling.

"In any case, you have nothing to fear. I have seen nothing, heard nothing. Moreover," he unwisely added, "neither I nor anyone else...."

"Which means?"

"That true or false, your story has all the earmarks of a dream."

"That is to say?"

"Who saw you go out? Who saw you come back? What proof has anyone? Not a witness, not a shred of evidence, not a word in writing, not even a spot of blood. Suppose I were to claim guilt myself. We would both be in the same position. No proof!"

Then... Then he saw Mouchette draw herself up before him, not at all pale, but, on the contrary, her forehead, her cheeks, even her throat so redly flushing that, under the temples' thin skin, the veins could be distinguished, quite blue. The small clenched fists still threatened him, though now the miserable child's eyes expressed only a terrible despair, like some ultimate summons to pity. Then this last glow died out, and delirium alone fluttered in her look. She opened her mouth and cried out.

In a single tone, now deep, now shrill, this superhuman wail resounded in the little house, already filled with vague bustle and hasty footsteps. With one initial movement, the Campagne physician had flung far from him the frail stiffened body; now he sought to close that mouth, to stifle that cry. He fought against that cry as a strangler fights the living heart beneath his fingers. If his long hands had by chance touched her vibrant neck, Germaine would have been dead, for each of the crazed wretch's motions seemed that of murder. But, with a sigh, all he could grasp was her lower jaw, and no human strength could have loosened its muscles.... Zeleda and Timoleon entered the room at the same moment.

"Help me!" he begged. "Miss Malorthy...an attack of violent insanity...at its most acute.... For God's sake, help me!"

Timoleon took Mouchette's arms and held them crossed on the carpet. After a moment's hesitation, Madame Gallet seized her legs. The Campagne doctor, his hands free at last, threw a handkerchief soaked in ether over the crazed girl's face. The frightful wailing, at first muffled, finally was wholly extinguished. The child, conquered, gave up.

"Run and fetch a sheet," Gallet told his wife.

They rolled Miss Malorthy up in it, and from then on she remained motionless. Timoleon hurried off to forewarn the brewer. That very evening she was taken off in an automobile to Dr. Duchemin's nursing home. She left it a month later, wholly cured, after having given birth to a stillborn child.

The First Part

THE TEMPTATION OF DESPAIR

1.

"MY DEAR CANON, my old friend," concluded Father Demange, "what more can I tell you? It is hard for me to consider your scruples legitimate, and nonetheless this disagreement troubles me.... I should gladly maintain that in this your refinement of thought is concerned over trifles, were I not sufficiently aware of your prudence and steadfastness.... But all this is to attribute much importance to a young priest scarcely weaned."

With a shiver Father Menou-Segrais pulled his coverlet back over his knees and stretched his hands from afar toward the hearth; he did not reply. Then, after a long silence, and not without a secret mischievousness which momentarily made his eyes sparkle, he said: "Of all the burdens of old age, experience is not the least, and I would that the prudence to which you refer had never increased at the expense of steadfastness. Of course there's no end to arguments and hypotheses, but to live means first of all to choose. Admit it, my friend: old people fear error less than risk."

"How like you!" tenderly observed Father Demange; "how little your heart has changed! I feel as though I were still listening to you in our courtyard at Saint-Sulpice, with you discussing the lives of the Benedictine mystics—Saint Gertrude, Saint Mechthilde, Saint Hildegarde—with poor Father de Lantivy. Do you remember? 'Why do you talk to me about the third mystical state?' he would say to you.... 'Of all these gentlemen, you are, to begin with, the greediest at table and the best dressed!'"

"I remember," said the pastor of Campagne...and suddenly his voice—so even—imperceptibly faltered. Turning his head with difficulty in the thickness of the pillows toward the large room already filled with shadow, and indicating with a glance his beloved furmture: "One had to escape," said he. "One always has to escape."

But at once his voice grew firm again and, in that same pert tone with which he liked to tease himself, to abash his great soul, he added: "Nothing better than an attack of rheumatism to give you a feeling and a taste for freedom."

"Let's return to our young friend," abruptly said Father Demange, with some gruffness, and without daring first to turn his glance upon his old friend. "I must leave you at five o'clock. I'll gladly see him again."

"What good will that do?" Father Menou-Segrais quietly replied. "We have surely seen enough for one day! He has dirtied my poor old Turkey carpet, and having with his accustomed tact chosen my most precious and fragile chair, he almost shattered its legs.... What more do you want? Would you weigh him and measure him again like some young conscript?... But of course, see him if you wish. God knows, however, what anxiety this great, clumsy puppy, all dolled up in black, affords me every day in the week amidst all my so foolishly cherished knickknacks."

Father Demange, however, too well knew the companion of his youth to be surprised at this mood. Years ago, when he had been Bishop de Targe's young private secretary, he had been fully aware of certain trials which Father Menou-Segrais's clear-seeing and sane genius had one by one overcome. A spirit of fierce independence, a common sense which might be called irresistible, but the application of which not infrequently involved an obvious cruelty all the more apparent to the sensitive because of his refined courtesy, his scorn for abstract solutions, his very lively taste for the highest spirituality—a taste hardly satisfied by speculation alone—had at first awakened the bishop's distrust. The youthful Demange's tactful influence, and above all the future dean of Campagne's irreproachable good breeding—he was at the time a cathedral curate—too late earned him the good will of the man who willingly allowed himself to be described as the last gentleman-prelate and who died a year later, leaving a tricky inheritance to Bishop Papouin, favorite candidate of the Minister of Cults. At first Father Menou-Segrais was politely kept in the background, then openly treated with disfavor after the first defeat, in the legislative elections, of the liberal deputy for whom that priest had certainly shown little enthusiasm. Radical Dr. Gallet's victory dealt the final blow to this sacerdotal career. Having been appointed pastor of Campagne—a curé, moreover, considered desirable—he thenceforward resigned himself quietly to serve the religious peace of the diocese, the two parties having become accustomed to agree at his expense, with the minister first lodging complaints against Aim and the bishop then disavowing responsibility. This game amused him, and no one better than he relished its pleasant oscillations.

Heir to a great fortune which he managed with wisdom—intending that the whole of it should go to his Segrais nieces—living on little, but not without distinction, a great lord in exile who brought into the very heart of the country something of the ways and customs of the court, curious about the lives of other men and yet the least of gossips, skilled at making people talk, groping for secrets with a glance, a haphazard word, a smile—then the first to request, to enforce silence—always admirable for tact and spiritual dignity, a delightful table companion and through politeness a good trencherman, on occasion talkative by reason of kindliness or charity, so perfectly polite that the simple pastors of his deanery, caught in the snare, always viewed him as the most indulgent of men, in intercourse agreeable and confident, perceptive without being sharp, tolerant by taste, even skeptical, and perhaps a bit suspect.

"My friend," Father Demange quietly replied, "I see what you are up to; you are deflecting upon your curate a blow intended for me. Covertly you are accusing me of lack of understanding, of prejudgment, of I don't know what else? Hidden thoughts that are charitable indeed at Christmastide, and stored up against a poor comrade on the retired list who will have to cover three leagues this evening before getting back to his own bed—all for love of you! Am I really capable of taking lightly a scruple which you have confided to me?... But as in the old days, your conviction seeks to carry all before it, to capture people by assault; only you do it more graciously.... You call upon me to come to a decision, and the elements at my disposal..."

"Who's said anything about elements!" interrupted the dean of Campagne. "Why not an investigation and full set of files? When the winning or losing of a battle is at stake, a man makes use of what he has at hand. All the while I was myself weighing the pros and cons, I did not call upon you, but the moment I reached certainty..."

"In a word, what you want is my approval?"

"Precisely," answered the old priest, unabashed. "A certain daring is part of my make-up, and my virtue is so small, my old age so slothful, I am so stupidly enamored of my habits, of my vagaries, even of my infirmities, that at the moment of decision I greatly need the sight and the voice of a friend. You have given me both the one and the other. All is well. The rest is my affair."

"You will be pig-headed!" exclaimed Father Demange. "You would like me to remain silent. When once again I am far away from you, this very night, I shall pray for your intentions—blindly—and never shall I have prayed more wholeheartedly. Meanwhile, even were you to use violence on me, to ease my conscience I shall sum up our conversation; I shall seek out what it leads to. Let me speak! Let me speak!" he exclaimed at the Campagne pastor's gesture of impatience,

"I shall not long detain you. I had reached the elements in the case record. I go back to them. Of course I don't attach much importance to his marks at the seminary...."

"What purpose is served by reverting to that?" asked Father Menou-Segrais. "They were poor, frankly poor, but God knows in what sense, and whether it is the poorness of the pupil that they prove, or that of the teacher!... Nonetheless, here is an excerpt from one of Bishop Papouin's letters which I have not read you.... Will you be kind enough to give me my portfolio—there, on the corner of my desk—and to bring the lamp a little nearer?"

First he glanced over the sheet with a smile, holding it very close to his nearsighted eyes. "*I dare not suggest to you,*" he began, "*I dare not suggest to you the only one remaining to me, recently ordained, with whom the dean—to whom I entrusted him—does not know what to do; he certainly has fine traits, but they are spoiled by a singular violence and obstinacy, without breeding or manners, a man of great piety more zealous than wise, in a word, still only very rough-hewn. I fear that a man like you*—here a little touch of fun, of episcopal irony—*fear that a man like you could not adapt himself to a little barbarian who, a score of times daily, would offend you despite himself?*"

"What did you reply?" inquired Father Demange.

"Approximately this: Adapting oneself is nothing, Your Excellency; it will be sufficient if I can put him to good use, or something to, that effect." He spoke in a tone of mischievous deference, and his handsome features laughed with assured boldness.

"In short," said the impatient old priest, "by your own avowal, the fellow corresponds to the description you had received of him?"

"He is worse," cried out the dean of Campagne, "a thousand times worse! After all, you have seen him. His presence in so comfortable a house offends all good sense, most assuredly. I ask you: the autumn rains, the equinoctial wind which stirs up my rheumatism, the overheated stove smelling of boiled suet, the muddy shoes of my visitors on my carpets, the salvos of late-season hunting parties—this is already quite enough for an old canon. At my age you await the good Lord in the hope that He will come without upsetting anything, on some ordinary weekday.... Alas! it was not the Lord Who arrived, but a gawky, broad-shouldered youth with a goodness of will so ingenuous it would set your teeth on edge, even more exasperating when he is tactful, when he hides his red hands, when he treads carefully with his iron-shod heels, when he lowers a voice created for horses and cows.... My little setter noses him with disgust, my housekeeper is weary of darning or removing the spots from the one of his two cassocks which still looks respectable.... Not a shadow of breeding. Of learning, scarcely more than is needed for passably reading the breviary. Granted that he says his Mass with praiseworthy piety, but so slowly and with so awkward a manner that it makes me break out into a sweat in my stall—even though that is, after all, a devilish cold spot! At the very thought of confronting from the pulpit so refined a public as ours, he seemed so unhappy that I did not dare put him under pressure, and I continue to torture my own poor throat. And what more can I add? You can see him all day long stalking the muddy roads, got up like a tramp, lending the carters a hand under the delusion of teaching these gentlemen a manner of speech less offensive to the Divine Majesty; and his smell, picked up in the stables, is offensive in the noses of pious ladies. To cap it all, I have not yet been able to teach him to lose a game of backgammon with good grace. Come nine o'clock and he is already drunk with sleep, and so I must forgo this diversion.... Do you need any more? Is that enough?"

"If your reports to the bishop are along such lines," Father Demange succinctly concluded, "I'm sorry for him."

The dean of Campagne's smile at once disappeared and his face—always extremely mobile—froze. "I'm the one to be sorry for, my friend," said he.

His voice had such a tone of bitterness, of unsatisfied hope, that it portrayed all old age at a single stroke, and the silent parlor was for a moment visited by the majesty of death.

Father Demange flushed. "Is it so serious, my friend?" he asked with touching confusion, a truly exquisite fervor of friendship. "I fear I have wounded you, and yet without knowing how."

But Father Menou-Segrais was already exclaiming: "Wound me, *me*? It is I who am stupidly causing you pain. Let us not mingle our petty affairs with those of God." Smiling the while, he reflected for a moment. "I'm too quick-witted; it leads me astray. There are better things for me to do than set you puzzles and find amusement in your distress. Oh! my friend, God also sets us puzzles.... I was living a quiet life, or rather I was very gently bringing it to a close. Ever since this clumsy fellow has appeared upon the scene, he draws everything to himself without being aware of it, and leaves me no rest. His mere presence forces me to choose. Ah, to be importuned by a wonderful adventure when one's blood runs so thin and so cold is a great and weighty ordeal!"

"If you present things in such fashion," said Father Demange, "I shall merely say to you: your old comrade demands his part in your choice."

"It is too late," resumed the pastor of Campagne, still smiling. "I shall bear it alone."

"...But to tell you the truth and in conscience," continued Father Demange, "I have seen nothing in this young priest which is worth affording a man like you trouble of spirit. What I have learned about him disturbs me without persuading me. It is a common species, these curates whose zeal is indiscreet, who are built for other, harder labors, and who, during the first years of their priesthood, spill over with an excess of physical energy which the restraints of the seminary..."

"Not another word!" exclaimed Father Menou-Segrais, laughing. "I feel I'm going to loathe you! Do you imagine that I have not already faced this objection? I have striven, willy-nilly, to pay myself off with such currency. One does not submit without a struggle to a superior force whereof one does not find the sign within oneself, which remains a stranger to you. Brutishness is abhorrent to me, and

I should be the last to let myself be caught with so vulgar a bait. Certainly I am no old woman! We have been rugged in our day, my friend, even though the fools knew nothing of it.... But here there is something other."

He hesitated and he also, this aged priest, blushed. "I shall not say the word; I should fear from you something, I know not what, which beforehand rends my heart. Oh! my friend, I was at rest; I was resigned, and resignation was sweet to me. I have never desired honors; my taste is not for administration but for command in the field. I should have wished that there might have been a desire to make use of me, but what of it? It was not to be; I was too weary. A certain intellectual baseness, that distrust or hatred of greatness which those wretches call prudence, had filled me with bitterness. I have seen the superior man hounded like a prey; I have seen the crumbling of great souls. All the same, I have a horror of confusion, of disorder, I have the sense of authority, of hierarchy. I was waiting until one of these misjudged ones should be dependent on me, until I should be accountable for him to God. That had been refused me; I no longer hoped. And of a sudden...when strength is going to fail me..."

"Your disappointment will be cruel," said Father Demange slowly. "Coming from another than you, this delusion would involve no danger; but I well know that you never do things by halves. You will turn topsy-turvy your life and, I fear, that of a poor, simple man who will follow you without understanding you.... And yet the peace of our Lord is in your eyes." He made a gesture of dismissal, indicating his desire to close a strange conversation.

Father Menou-Segrais understood him. "Time flies," said he, pulling out his watch. "I do regret that you cannot spend this Christmas Eve with me.... In your carriage you will find the demijohn of old brandy. I had it packed with much care, but the road is bad and it would be wise to watch out for it." He abruptly cut himself short. Silently the two aged priests looked at each other. Even and heavy footsteps were heard along the road.

"Forgive me," the pastor of Campagne finally said with visible embarrassment. "I must find out if my colleague d'Heudeline has finished confessions and if everything is ready for tonight's ceremony.... Will you lend me your arm? We shall cross the room and I shall go see you to your carriage."

He pressed on a bell and his housekeeper appeared. "Ask Father Donissan to come bid Father Demange good-bye," said he dryly.

"Father," she stammered, "I...I think that Father can scarcely do that...at least at the moment...."

"Can scarcely do it?"

"Well, you see...the roofers... Well, the roofers were talking about leaving the job unfinished...of coming back after the New Year's celebrations."

"Our belfry requires repairing, true enough," explained the dean of Campagne. "Its roof framework almost collapsed, under the autumn rains; I had to call in the contractor from Maurevert and hire here workers inexperienced at a task which is, to say the least, dangerous. Father Donissan..." He turned toward the housekeeper, and in the same tone of voice said, "Ask him to come down as he is. It makes no difference...."

"Father Donissan," he resumed as soon as the old woman had left, "asked me permission to lend a hand.... And he doesn't lend it half-heartedly! I saw him one morning last week, at the top of the ladders, his poor breeches stuck to his knees with the rain, guiding the joists into place, calling out orders through the gusts of wind, and obviously more at his ease on his perch than at his desk in the Major Seminary on a quarterly examination day.... Very likely he has gone back to the job today."

"Why call him?" said Father Demange. "Why embarrass him? What purpose will it serve?"

Father Menou-Segrais burst into laughter and, placing his hand upon his friend's arm, said, "I like to confront you two. I like to see you face to face. In this I am probably a little mischievous. But perhaps it is the last time, and, moreover, at the tip of this mischief is a very lively and very tender feeling, which I owe you by virtue of God's mercy, of His divine sweetness. How strong and subtle, indeed, is that grace, how straitly, indeed, does it encompass nature, that grace which by such different paths, without constraint, gently summons your two souls to unity, to the reality of a single love! How vain, in short, seems the guile of the devil, in its ponderous twistings and turnings!"

"I agree with you," said Father Demange. "Forgive me if I add this, which will seem to you very commonplace. I believe that the Christian of good will by himself maintains himself in the light above, like a man whose volume and weight are in so constant and so skillfully reckoned a proportion that he floats about in the water, if only he is willing to stay there, quiet. Thus—certain special destinies apart—I look upon our saints as being like powerful and good-natured giants, whose supernatural strength develops harmoniously, in a measure and after a rhythm which our ignorance cannot perceive, for it is aware only of the height of the obstacle and takes no account of the breadth and the range of the vital surge. The burden which we raise with difficulty, grinding our teeth and making wry faces, the athlete draws to himself like a feather, without a muscle in his countenance quivering, and he seems to all fresh and smiling.... I know that you will probably allege against me the example of your young friend...."

"Here I am, Canon," said a low and strong voice at their backs.

They both turned at the same moment. He who later would become the pastor of Lumbres was standing there in a solemn silence. At the threshold of the darkened hallway, his outline, lengthened by its shadow, at first seemed vast; then suddenly, the brightly lit door closing behind him, it seemed small, almost puny. His big iron-shod shoes, hastily wiped off, were still white with mortar; his stockings and his cassock were splotched with mud-stains, and his broad hands, half thrust through his girdle, were also the color of earth. His face, the paleness of which was at variance with the tanned redness of his neck, dripped perspiration and water mingled together, for at Father

Menou-Segrais's unexpected summons he had hastened to his room to wash. The disarray—or rather the almost squalid appearance—of his daily clothing was made all the more extraordinary by the odd contrast of a new padded winter coat, still stiff with sizing, which he had slipped on in such a flurry that one of its sleeves was laughably tucked up over a wrist as gnarled as a grapevine. Whether the prolonged silence of the canon and his guest put the finishing touch to his abashment, or whether he had heard—which later crossed the dean of Campagne's mind—the last words Father Demange had said, his expression, naturally distressed or even worried, suddenly took on such an accent of sadness, of a humility so heart-rending, that his homely countenance seemed at once resplendent with it.

"You shouldn't have troubled yourself," said Father Demange in his pity. "I see that you don't waste your time, that you aren't slack at your work.... All the same, I am happy to have been able to bid you good-bye."

Having given him a friendly nod, he immediately turned about, surely with affected indifference. The canon followed him toward the door. They heard upon the stairway the curate's heavy footsteps, perhaps a trifle earlier than usual.... Outside the coachman, chilled through, was snapping his whip.

"It distresses me to leave you so early," said Father Demange on the doorstep. "Yes, I should have liked, I should *particularly* have liked to spend this Christmas Eve with you. However, I leave you to One more powerful and more clear-seeing than I, my friend. Death has not much to teach old people, but a Child, in His crib! *And what a child!*... Shortly, the world begins."

Side by side they descended the brief stoop. The air was resonant up to the heavens. Ice crackled in the ruts.

"Everything is always at the beginning—until the very end," said Father Menou-Segrais, abruptly, sad beyond words.

The sharpness of the blast reddened his cheeks, circled his eyes with blue shadow, and his companion noticed that he was trembling with cold. "How is it possible!" he exclaimed. "You have come out bare-headed and without a coat, on such an evening!"

And indeed, more than any words, this imprudence on the part of Campagne's pastor indicated how infinite was his trouble of spirit. Now, to the even greater astonishment of Father Demange—or, more precisely, to his inexpressible amazement—he for the first time, for a first and a last time, saw a tear slipping down the delicate, familiar face.

"Good-bye, Jacques," said the dean of Campagne, forcing himself to smile. "If there be omens of death, so stupendous a breach in my accustomed habits, such a forgetfulness of elementary precautions, is a pretty sure indication…"

They were not to see each other again.

2.

FATHER DONISSAN DID not come in until very late that night. For a long time Father Menou-Segrais, holding a book which he did not read, heard his curate's regular footsteps pacing up and down his room. "It can't be long before we'll have it out together, and thoroughly," thought the old priest. He had no doubts that such a session was necessary, but he had up until then scorned to precipitate it, too wise not to leave to the young priest at once the advantage and the embarrassment of finally coming down to cases.

The last sounds had ceased save for that monotonous tread through the wall's sickness. "Why tonight rather than tomorrow or later?" reflected Father Menou-Segrais. "Father Demange's visit has perhaps set my nerves on edge." Nevertheless, stronger and more pressing than anything based on reason, the premonition of a unique, inevitable event made him wait, and each moment added to his anxiety. Then the hall door squeaked.

A hand rapped twice. Father Donissan appeared.

"I was awaiting you, my friend," was all that Father Menou-Segrais said.

"I knew you were," the other replied, his voice humble, But he at once drew himself up, faced the dean, and firmly said, all in one breath: "I must beg His Excellency to recall me to Tourcoing. I should like to implore you to second my request, without hiding anything of what you know about me, without sparing me in anything."

"Just a moment, just a moment," interrupted Father Menou-Segrais. "I *must* beg, you say? I must...why *must* you?"

"The parochial ministry," the priest resumed in the same tone of voice, "is a burden beyond my strength. Such was the view of my superior; I likewise feel that it is yours. Here, indeed, I am an impediment to goodness. The very least peasant of the neighborhood would blush at a pastor such as I, without experience, without enlightenment, without true dignity. Whatever effort I may make, how can I hope ever to supply that in which I am lacking?"

"Let it go," interrupted the Campagne dean, "let it go; I understand you. Your scruples are doubtless justified. I am willing to ask His Excellency for your recall, but that does not make the matter any less complicated. Here little was asked of you, after all. You say it is still too much?"

Father Donissan lowered his head.

"Don't be a child," cried the dean. "I shall probably seem harsh to you; I must be so. The diocese is too poor, my friend, to feed a useless mouth."

"Granted," stammered the poor priest with an effort. "Truly, I don't yet know.... Well, I had proposed...to find...to find a place in a convent, at least for the time being...."

"A convent!... The likes of you, sir, are always prattling of convents. The regular clergy, sir, is the honor of the Church, her reserve troops. A convent! A convent isn't a rest home, an asylum, a sick bay!"

"That is true..." was what Father Donissan wanted to say, but he succeeded only in sputtering. His scarlet cheeks, which his violent emotion could not succeed in blanching, trembled. Such was the only external sign of an infinite anxiety. And even his voice became firm enough to ask: "Then what would one have me do?"

"What would one?" replied the dean of Campagne. "Here is the first word of common sense you have uttered. Admitting yourself incapable of guiding and advising others, how would you be a good judge in your own cause? God and your bishop, my son, have given you a master; it is I."

"I recognize that," said the priest, after a fleeting hesitation. "However, I beg you..."

He did not finish. By an imperious gesture, the dean, of Campagne had silenced him. And with fearful curiosity he watched this aged priest, ordinarily so courteous, suddenly become harsh, imperturbable, his eyes so hard. "The matter is serious. Your superiors have allowed you to receive holy orders; I think that their decision was not lightly taken. Yet again, that inability which you have just admitted..."

"Allow me," the unhappy priest again interrupted, in the same expressionless voice. "Heaven help me!... I am not absolutely incapable of any apostolic work, one proportioned to my intelligence and my capacities. Happily, my physical health..." He became silent, ashamed in his sublime innocence of opposing to so many eloquent reasons an argument so wretched.

"Good health is a gift of God," gravely replied Father Menou-Segrais. "Alas, better than you do I know its value. The strength which has been granted to you, even your skill at certain manual tasks—here surely is the sign of a less exalted vocation to which Providence called you.... Is it ever too late, under the guidance of sure counsel, to acknowledge an unintentional mistake?... Should you try a new field of activity...indeed...indeed..."

"Indeed?..." Father Donissan had the courage to ask.

"Indeed, return to the plow?" the dean dryly concluded. "But what's more, please observe that I am asking the question today without giving it any answer. You are not, thank God, one of those impressionable young people whom a slightly abrupt word uselessly terrifies. You are not threatened by any dizziness. And, as for me, I have done my duty, even though with seeming cruelty."

"I thank you," the priest gently replied, in a tone grown strangely firm. "From the beginning of this conversation God has given me the strength to hear from your mouth some very harsh truths. Why will He not help me to the end? I beseech you to answer the question you have asked. Why have I any need to wait longer?"

"Good heavens..." murmured Father Menou-Segrais, taken aback. "I confess, a few weeks' reflection... I should have liked to give you leisure..."

"To what purpose, if I am not to be the judge in my own cause, and, truly enough, I cannot be the judge. It is your opinion I want to hear, and the sooner the better."

"Possibly you may be ready to hear it, my friend, but surely not to abide by it without reservation," replied the dean of Campagne with forced brutality. "Under such circumstances, to challenge that which one fears is less a sign of courage than of weakness."

"I know it, I grant it!" exclaimed Father Donissan. "You make no mistake. You see clearly within me. It is to your charity that I appeal—oh, sir, not even to your charity, to your pity—to deal me the last blow. That blow dealt, I feel, I am sure that I shall find the necessary strength.... There is no instance of God's not having given a helping hand to some wretch fallen on the ground...."

Father Menou-Segrais measured him with a sharp glance. "Are you so sure that my conclusion has been reached," said he, "and that no doubt remains in my mind?"

Father Donissan shook his head. "It does not take long to judge such a man as I," said he, "and you wish merely to spare my feelings. At least leave me the merit, before God, of total obedience, of absolute obedience: order me! command me! Do not leave me in suspense!"

"I approve you," said the dean of Campagne; "I can only approve you. Your intentions are good, even enlightened. I understand your impatience to conquer nature at a single stroke. But the word you expect from me may be a temptation beyond your strength. You want to know the decision; so be it. Will you carry it out?"

"I believe so," replied the priest in a muffled voice. "And, what is more, will I ever be better prepared than on this night to receive and carry a cross? It is time, believe me, Father, it is time. I am not merely an ignorant, uncouth priest, powerless to make himself loved. In the Minor Seminary I was only a second-rate pupil. At the Major Seminary I finally bored everyone. It took a miracle of charity on the part of Father Delange to convince the directors that they should admit me to the diaconate.... Intelligence, memory, even diligence are all lacking in me.... And yet..."

He hesitated, but at a gesture from Father Menou-Segrais, he continued with an effort: "and yet I still cannot wholly overcome one stubbornness...one pig-headedness.... The just scorn of others awakens in me...feelings so bleak...so violent... Truly I cannot struggle against them by ordinary means...."

He stopped short, as though frightened of having said too much. The dean's small eyes were focused upon him with extraordinary attention. In a voice of supplication he concluded, almost despairing, "So don't put it off.... It is time.... Tonight, I assure you.... You cannot know..."

Father Menou-Segrais arose so precipitately from his armchair that this time the poor priest blanched. The old dean, however, took a few steps toward the window, leaning on his cane and with an air of absorption. Then, hastily straightening himself, he said: "My son, your submission touches me.... I must have seemed brutal, and I shall be so again. It would be no great trouble for me to avoid this, in any number of ways; I still prefer to speak out. You have just confided yourself into my hands.... Into what hands? Do you know?"

"I beg you...." murmured the priest, his voice trembling.

"I shall inform you. You have just put yourself into the hands of *a man for whom you have no use*."

Father Donissan's face was ashy pale.

"*For whom you have no use*," repeated Father Menou-Segrais. "The life I live here is in appearance that of a well-heeled layman. Admit it! My semi-idleness makes you ashamed. The experience for which so many fools praise me is in your eyes profitless to souls, sterile. I could elaborate; that suffices. My son, in so serious a matter, the little civilities of worldly politeness are nothing; have I properly expressed your feelings?"

At the first words of this strange confession, Father Donissan had been emboldened to fix his eyes upon the terrible old priest, with a look of helpless amazement. He did not again lower his glance.

"I insist upon a reply," continued Father Menou-Segrais, "I expect it from your obedience, and before I give you my views on anything. You have the right to challenge me. I can be your judge in this matter; I shall not be your tempter. To the question I have asked, answer simply yes or no."

"I must answer yes," Father Donissan of a sudden replied, with seeming calm. "The trial to which you subject me is very hard; I beg you not to prolong it."

Tears, however, were flowing from his eyes, and it is doubtful whether Father Menou-Segrais heard these last words, low-spoken as they were. The unhappy priest earnestly reproached himself for his shy appeal to pity as having been a weakness. After a brief inner struggle, he nonetheless continued: "I answered through obedience, and now it should certainly be my part to wait and be silent...but... but I cannot.... God does not require me to let you believe.... In conscience, it was merely a thought...an involuntary feeling.... I am not saying this," he resumed in a firmer tone, "to justify myself; my disingenuousness is now known to you. Thus Providence strips me wholly naked before you.... And now... And now..."

For an instant his hands sought some support, his long arms flailed. Then his knees gave way under him, and he fell all in a piece, face forward.

"My little child!" Father Menou-Segrais cried out, in tones of true despair.

He awkwardly dragged the inert body to the foot of the sofa and with a great effort swung it onto that piece of furniture. In the midst of the russet leather cushions, the bony head was now of an ashen paleness.

"Come...come..." murmured the old dean, as he struggled to unbutton the cassock with his gout-stiffened fingers; but the worn fabric yielded first. Through the collar opening, the coarse cloth of the shirt appeared, spotted with blood.

Now the broad, deep chest was once more moving up and down. The dean bared it with an abrupt movement.

"So I suspected," said he with a sorry smile.

From the armpits to the base of the loins, the torso was wholly encased in a rigid sheath of the coarsest horsehair, loosely woven. The slender thong which held up the front of this frightful undergarment was so tightly drawn that Father Menou-Segrais undid it only with difficulty. The skin then appeared, burned by the unbearable rubbing of the haircloth as though by the application of a caustic; the epidermis, in places destroyed and in others swollen into blisters the size of one's hand, constituted one great wound from which oozed a watery liquid mingled with blood. The filthy gray and brown hairshirt seemed impregnated with it. And from a deeper wound in the fold of the flank, bright red blood dripped drop by drop. The unfortunate fellow had thought it proper to dress it as well as he could with a wad of hemp; this impediment removed, Father Menou-Segrais hastily withdrew his bloodied fingers.

The curate opened his eyes. His intent glance for a moment concentrated on each of the corners of the unrecognized room, then, fixing on the dean's familiar face, at first expressed growing surprise.

Suddenly his glance took in the broad opening of his cassock and his bloody linen. And then Father Donissan, throwing his head back vigorously, hid his face in his hands.

At once Father Menou-Segrais gently pulled them away, uncovering the rugged head with a gesture almost motherly. "My child, our Lord is not displeased with you," said he in a low voice, its accents defying description.

Then, at once resuming that customary tone of slightly distant benevolence behind which he liked to hide his tenderness: "Father, you will tomorrow throw that infernal business into the fire; something better must be found. God preserve me from speaking only the language of common sense; in good as in evil it is proper to play the fool a little. I merely reproach your mortifications for their indiscretion; a young priest beyond reproach should have his linen white.

"Get up," the strange old man went on, "and come a little nearer. Our talk is not over, but we have gone through the worst of it.... Come! Come! sit down here. I won't let you go."

He installed him in his own armchair and, as though inadvertently, chatting the while, he slipped a pillow under the aching head. Then, himself sitting on a low chair and drawing his woolen coverlet over him as though he were chilly, he reflected for a moment, he stared at the hearth, the flames of which could be seen dancing in his clear, dauntless eyes.

"My boy," said he at last, "the opinion you have of me is by and large quite just, but it errs on one point: I judge myself, alas! more harshly than you think. I am sailing into port with empty hands...." He calmly stirred up the flaming logs. "You are a man very different from me," he resumed. "You have turned me inside out like a glove. When I asked His Excellency for you, I had dreamed, a little naively, of introducing into my house...yes, I might as well say it...a young priest with a bad academic record and wholly lacking in those natural qualities for which I have so great a weakness, whom I should, as best I could, have shaped for the parochial ministry.... At my life's close, the Lord knows that this was a heavy burden to take on! Yet I was also altogether too happy in my solitude to die therein in peace. God's judgment, my child, must overtake us in the fullness of our labors.... God's judgment!...

"... But it is you who are shaping me," said the old priest after a long silence.

At these astounding words, Father Donissan did not even turn his head. His wide-open eyes expressed no surprise, and the dean of Campagne saw, by the movement of his lips alone, that he was praying.

"*They* had not the wit to recognize the most precious of the gifts of the Holy Spirit," he added. "*They* never recognize anything. It is God Who names us. The name we bear is only a borrowed name.... My boy, the spirit of strength is within you."

The three first strokes of the dawn angelus reverberated outside like a solemn warning, but they heard them not. The logs slowly crumbled into ashes.

"And now," continued Father Menou-Segrais, "and now I have need of you. No! Someone other than myself, supposing he had seen as clearly, would not have dared to speak to you as I have this night. It is, however, needful. We are at that one of life's hours (it strikes for every man) when truth imposes itself, by itself, with irresistible obviousness, when each of us has only to stretch forth his arms to reach at a single bound the surface of shadows, even the sunlight of God. Then is human prudence but a snare and a delusion. Sanctity!" cried out the old priest in a deep voice; "by saying this word in your presence and for you alone, I know the hurt I inflict upon you! You are not unaware of what sanctity is: a vocation, a calling. Up to the place where God awaits you you will have to climb—climb, or be lost. Expect no human help. In full awareness of the responsibility I am taking, having for a last time put your obedience and single-mindedness to the test, I felt that I did well in thus speaking to you. By questioning not your own powers alone but God's designs for you also, you were committing yourself to a blind alley; at my own risk and peril, I set you back upon your road; I give you to those who await you, to the souls whose prey you will be.... May the Lord bless you, my dear young boy!"

At these last words, like a soldier who feels that he has been hit and by instinct draws himself erect before falling, Father Donissan stood up. In his motionless face, with its closed mouth, its sturdy jaws, its obstinate forehead, the pale eyes betrayed a mortal hesitation. For a long moment his glance wandered without settling upon anything. Then this glance lit upon the cross hanging on the wall, at once shifted to Father Menou-Segrais, and, fixed there, seemed suddenly to flicker out. In it the dean no longer saw anything but a blind submission, which the tragic confusion of this soul, still agitated by terror, made sublime.

"I ask your permission to withdraw," was all the future pastor of Lumbres said, in a voice barely under control. "As I listened to you, I thought I had truly fallen into trouble of heart and despair, but now that is finished.... I...I believe...I am such...as you can desire... and...and God will not allow me to be tempted beyond my strength."

Having spoken, he disappeared, and behind him, the door was already noiselessly closing.

From then on, Father Donissan knew peace, a strange peace, and one which at first he dared not probe. The thousand bonds which held action back or slowed it down had all at once been broken; this extraordinary man, whom the mistrust or faint-heartedness of his superiors had for years confined within an invisible net, at last saw the field open before him and moved about it freely. Every hindrance withered under his frontal attack. Within a few weeks, the efforts of that will which nothing henceforward was to stop began even to liberate his intelligence. The young priest spent his nights devouring books formerly laid aside in despair, books he now understood, not without difficulty, but with a fixedness of attention which surprised Father Menou-Segrais as a miracle. It was then that he acquired that deep knowledge of the scriptures which at first was not apparent in his speech—he purposely kept that simple and commonplace—but which nourished his thought. Twenty years later he one day mischievously said to Bishop Leredu: "That year I slept seven hundred and thirty hours...."

"Seven hundred and thirty hours?"

"Yes, two hours each night.... And besides—between you and me—I cheated a little."

Father Menou-Segrais was able to follow upon his curate's countenance each vicissitude of this interior struggle, the outcome of which he dared not conjecture. Although the poor priest continued to take his meals with his pastor and strove to seem as calm as usual, the old dean could not observe without growing anxiety the physical signs, each day more obvious, of a will stretched to the breaking point which one further effort might shatter. However rich he may have been in experience and wisdom, or perhaps through an abuse of these very qualities, the pastor of Campagne only half disentangled the causes of a moral crisis to the limits of which he no longer hoped to set bounds. Too shrewd to wear his authority thin by vain words and useless counsels of moderation, which Father Donissan was surely in no condition to heed, he awaited an opportunity to intervene and did not find it. As happens all too often when a clever man no longer is master over the passions which he has aroused, he feared he might do the wrong thing and thereby aggravate the evil for which he had sought to supply a remedy. From anyone other than his strange disciple, he would more quietly have awaited the natural reaction of an organism exhausted by excessive labor, yet was not that very toil, under the circumstances, a remedy rather than an ill, and something like the grim relaxation of the wretched prisoner of a sole and persistent thought?

Moreover, Father Donissan had seemingly made no change in his daily activities, and carried on many undertakings at once. Every morning, at his rapid and slightly awkward pace, he was seen clambering up the steep path which leads from the presbytery to the Campagne church. Having said his Mass and after a prayer of thanksgiving whereof the extreme brevity long astonished Father Menou-Segrais, tireless, his long body leaning forward, his hands crossed behind his back, he made his way to the Brennes road and thoroughly scoured the great plain which, overrun with arduous roads, swept by bitter blasts, goes down from the crest of the valley of the Canche to the sea. Houses there are few, built in solitary places, surrounded by pasture lands with defenses of barbed wire. Through the frozen grass, which slides and yields under the shoe, you have often a long walk before you finally reach, in the midst of a little lake of mud dug out by animals' hooves, a sagging wooden gate which squeaks and opens stiffly between its rotten posts. The farmhouse lies somewhere, at the hollow of a fold in the land, and all there is to be seen in the gray air is a streak of blue smoke, or else the two shafts of a cart erect toward the sky with a hen perched thereon. The peasants of this neighborhood, a jeering race, covertly viewed with distrust the curate's tall silhouette as he stood erect in the mist, his cassock trussed up, and attempted a cough to indicate cordiality. At sight of him, the door opened hesitantly, and the attentive denizens of the house, pressing close to the stove, awaited his first word, which was slow in coming. At a glance, each recognized the peasant disloyal to the land and, as it were, a prodigal brother: to the appearance of respect and courtesy was added a touch of protective condescension, a trifle scornful, and his little speech was listened to throughout in horrible silence.... What return journeys, night having fallen, toward the lights of the village, with the bitterness of shame still in his mouth and his heart alone, forever!... "I do them more harm than good," sadly said Father Donissan, and he had won permission for a time to discontinue these visits, which his shyness made into a ridiculous martyrdom. Now, however, he lavished himself upon them anew, having even persuaded Father Menou-Segrais to allow him to take upon himself the most humiliating trial, the

Lenten collection, which the unhappy people, with distressing cynicism, called paying their round of drinks.... "He won't bring back a cent," skeptically thought the dean.... And yet each evening this stranger laid upon the table's edge the black woolen bag swollen to bursting. It was because he had little by little acquired over all the irresistible ascendancy of one who takes no account of risk and goes straight forward. For the crafty and the prudent at bottom humor only themselves. The laughter of the most uncouth stops short in his throat when he beholds his victim making a full offering of himself to the other's scorn.

"What a queer fish!" people said to each other, but with a shade of awkwardness. In days gone by, stationing himself in the darkest corner and fingering his ancient hat, the poor wretch long and in vain sought a skillful and happy opening, eager to give utterance to the words and sentences he had thought out while he was alone, and then he would leave without having said anything. Now he was too busy struggling against himself, overcoming himself. In overcoming himself, he did better than persuade or win: he conquered; he entered into souls as though through a breach. Just as before, he crossed the farmyard at the same rapid pace, amid the puddles of dung water and the flurried flight of hens. As it had been before, the same dirty-faced urchin, sucking his thumb, watched him out of the corner of an eye, while he noisily scraped off his muddy shoes. But now, when he appeared on the threshold, all arose in silence. No one knew the bottom of this heart at once greedy and fearful, which the slightest impediment would move to despair and which nothing was able to sate. Here was still that shamefaced priest whom a smile embarrassed to tears and who with great toil tore every word from his parched throat. But of this inward struggle, never again would any particle be outwardly visible. His face was expressionless, his tall frame no longer stooped, his long hands betrayed scarcely a tremor. At a glance, at that deep, anxious glance which did not waver, he had passed beyond petty politenesses, vague words. At once he was questioning, summoning.

The commonest words, those worn most threadbare by careless use, little by little regained their meaning, awakened a strange echo. "When he uttered the name of God, almost in a whisper, but with such an intonation," said an ancient tenant-farmer of Saint-Gilles twenty years later, "our stomachs went queasy, as though we had just heard a clap of thunder...."

No eloquence here, not even any of those amusingly innocent remarks which later would arouse the wonder of the sophisticates and almost all of which were of suspicious authenticity in the bargain. The speech of the future pastor of Lumbres was difficult; sometimes it even stumbled over every word, stammered. This was because it knew nothing of the handy play of synonyms and approximations, the twists of a thought which follows verbal rhythms, and takes its shape from them like soft wax. He had long suffered from the inability to express what he felt, from that clumsiness which provoked laughter. No longer did he shun this. He pushed straight on. He no longer evaded the humiliating silence when a sentence once begun comes to the end of its course and falls flat into nothingness. Indeed, he was to seek such silences. Each setback could only tighten the spring of a will thenceforth inflexible. He tackled his subject head on, in God's hands. He said what was to be said, and the most uncouth would soon be listening to him without resistance, would yield themselves ungrudgingly. This was because you could not for an instant believe yourself duped by such a man: where he led you, you knew that he would climb with you. The harsh truth, which suddenly, in a word long groped for, darted out to strike you full in the face, had wounded him before you. You knew well that it was as though he had torn it from his heart. No, no! there was nothing here for the learned, no rare spectacle. Here were very simple matters; you had to listen to the fellow, that was all.... The kettle quivered and sang on the stove, the limp dog slept, his nose between his paws, the great wind outdoors made the door groan on its hinges, and the black crow cawed as loud as it could in the airy wastes.... They watched him sideways, answered bashfully, excused themselves, pleaded ignorance or habit, and, when he became silent, became silent themselves.

"What on earth do you tell our good people?" asked Father Menou-Segrais. "Here they all are, back at their duties. When I speak of you, not one of them dares look me in the face."

For he avoided asking Father Donissan any of those direct questions which demand a yes or a no.... Why?... Through reasons of prudence, of course, but also because of a secret fear.... What fear? The work of grace in this already troubled heart bore marks of violence, of harshness which baffled him. Ever since that Christmas Eve when he had spoken so boldly, the pastor of Campagne had never been willing to resume a conversation of which he could no longer think without distress. Then, too, was not his curate ever straightforward, just as obedient and as perfectly respectful, beyond reproach?... None of his fellow clergy who came in contact with him had noticed any change in him. They treated him with the same slightly contemptuous forbearance; they praised his zeal and his piety. The pastor of Larieux, his spiritual director, a kindly old man, saturated in the Sulpician tradition, heard his confession every Thursday and gave no signs of surprise or anxiety. Yet this in itself, a thing which should have heartened him, disappointed Father Menou-Segrais and made him uneasy.

More than once, indeed, he thought he was reasserting his faltering authority in ingeniously roundabout fashion. Thus he would propose, suggest, give orders, in the desire—scarcely admitted to himself—of encountering some slight opposition. Even had he had to yield to more cogent reasons, at least that unbearable silence would have been broken! But Father Donissan's humble submissiveness nullified such subterfuges. He had only to suggest to be at once obeyed. Vainly did he put to the test by turns the poor priest's patience and his shyness, which he did with cruel shrewdness, as, for example, when, after having long dispensed him from Sunday preaching, he without warning required it of him. The unhappy fellow, on the appointed day and without a shadow of reproach, hastily assembled a few slips scrawled in his ungainly peasant hand, mounted the pulpit, and for twenty mortal minutes, pale and with, downcast eyes, glossed the gospel of the day, hesitated, stammered, gradually took courage, struggled to the bitter end, and finally achieved a sort of rudimentary, almost tragic, eloquence.... Now he was tackling it anew each Sunday, and, when he had ceased, a murmur, to which he alone was deaf, rustled from pew to pew, the deep sigh, like to nothing else in the world, of an audience for a moment held under a sovereign bondage that now was eased....

"It's going a bit better," said the dean after they had returned from Mass, "but it is still so vague...so confused..."

"Alas!" replied the priest, pouting like a child about to cry.

At lunch his hands still shook.

In the meantime, also, Father Menou-Segrais had come to a more serious decision: he had opened wide to his curate the doors of the confessional. That year the dean of Hauburdin went to the trouble of holding a retreat, preached by two Marists. One of these, succumbing to a bad case of grippe, had had to return to Valenciennes on the first day of Holy Week. It was at this juncture that the dean begged his Campagne colleague to lend him Father Donissan.

"He is young, he has no fear of spending himself, will do anything...." Up until that time, at the advice of Father Denisanne, who had given the dean a long account of his pupil, the pastor of Campagne had been rather parsimoniously careful of allowing his curate to exercise the ministry of penance. Ill-posted, and through a most excusable misunderstanding, the missionary father had assigned a part of his labors to the future pastor of Lumbres, who from Thursday to Saturday of Holy Week constantly heard confessions. The township of Hauburdin is large, on the borders of the mining country, but the success of the retreat was equally great. And surely none of the priests who on Easter Day took their places in the chancel, in their fine fresh surplices, and saw people without number kneeling at the

Communion table cast even a glance toward the silent young curate who, in darkness and in silence, had just for the first time immolated himself to man the sinner, his master, he who would not release him while he lived. Never did Father Donissan unburden himself to anyone of what he suffered during this peremptory glimpse into the future, or perhaps of its utter sweetness.... But when Father Menou-Segrais saw him again, on Easter evening, he was so struck by his distracted, absorbed appearance, that he at once questioned him with unusual abruptness, and the poor priest's simple answer fell far short of reassuring him.

One remark, nevertheless, which Father Donissan let slip very long afterward, casts a strange glow over this hidden period in his life. "When I was young," he avowed to M. Groselliers, "I did not know evil. I only learned to know it from the mouths of sinners."

Thus week after week slipped by; life resumed its peace and monotony with nothing to justify any strange anxiety. Ever since their last conversation on Christmas Eve, Father Donissan's silence had sadly disappointed his senior, and his obedience, the forced and passive meekness of the future pastor of Lumbres, had not cleared away the bitterness of a sort of misunderstanding the reasons for which the old man could not fathom. Was it merely a misunderstanding? Day by day, this experienced and knowing priest, so well fortified against the tyranny of appearances, felt an indefinable fear weighing upon his shoulders. The great child who every evening humbly knelt and received his blessing before returning to his room knew the dean's secret, and the dean did not know the child's. However tenaciously he watched him, he could not surprise in him a single one of those external signs which indicate the action of pride and ambition—anxious searching, alternate confidence and despair, a disquiet which does not deceive.... And yet... "Have I perchance perplexed this heart forever," he would say to himself, as he occasionally sought the glance that avoided his, "or is the fire that consumes him pure? His behavior is perfect, beyond reproach; his zeal is burning, effective, and even now his ministry bears fruit.... What can be said against him? How many another would be happy to grow old with such a man as helper! His outward bearing is that of a saint; nonetheless something in him repels, puts you on the defensive.... He lacks joy...."

Father Donissan, however, knew joy.

Not that which is furtive, unstable, now lavished, now refused—but another, more certain joy, equable, ceaseless, and, as it were, pitiless—like to another life within life, to the blooming of a new life. However far he pushed back into the past, he found there nothing which might resemble it; he could not even remember ever having had a presentiment of it, or having desired it. Even now he enjoyed it with a frightened eagerness, as though it were a parlous treasure which the unknown master would recapture, between one moment and another, and which already you cannot put aside without dying.

No outward sign had foretold this joy, and it seemed as though it subsisted as it had begun, borne up by nothing, a light whereof the source remains invisible, wherein every thought is swallowed, like some single cry across the vast horizon which does not pierce the first circle of silence.... It happened on the very night the dean of Campagne had chosen for the extraordinary ordeal, at the end of that night before Christmas Day, in that bedroom whither the poor priest had fled, his heart filled with perplexity, at the first glimmer of dawn. Something gray which you could hardly call morning crept up the windows, and the earth, gray with snow to infinity, crept up with it. But this Father Donissan did not see. Kneeling before his open bed, he reviewed each sentence of the strange conversation, striving to lay bare its meaning, then stopped short when one of the words spoken—too precise, too clear-cut, beyond warding off—suddenly rose in his memory. Then he struggled like a blind man against a new, more dangerous temptation. And his anguish lay in that he could not give it a name.

Sanctity! In his sublime artlessness, he assumed he would be borne at a stroke from the lowest to the highest rank, each in turn. He did not flinch.

"Whither God summons you, you must climb," the other man had said. He was summoned. "Climb or be lost!" He was lost.

Certainty of his powerlessness to live up to such a destiny even stopped short the prayer upon his lips. This will of God upon his poor soul overwhelmed him with a superhuman weariness. Something more intimate than life itself seemed to be suspended within him. The elderly artist found dead before a work newly begun, his eyes full of an unattainable masterpiece—the stuttering idiot who wrestles with images whereof he is no longer master, as though they were escaped animals—the jealous man, reduced to silence, who has only his eyes with which to hate, confronting the precious flesh, profaned, laid open—no one of these has felt to greater depths the sharp and treacherous prick, the stab of despair. Never had the wretched fellow seen himself (he believed) as clearly, as distinctly. Ignorant, fearful, a figure of fun forever enchained by the compulsion of a narrow, distrustful piety, shut in upon himself, lacking contact with souls, lonely, sterile in heart and mind, incapable of those excesses in goodness, of the glorious foolhardinesses which mark great souls, the least heroic of men. Alas! That which his master singled out in him—is it not the remnant of gifts received long since and frittered away! Choked seed will not sprout again. And yet it had been sown. There came back to him a thousand recollections of his childhood so strangely at one with God and those dreams, those very dreams themselves—maddening thought!—whose dangerous sweetness he had feared and which in his harsh zeal he had little by little buried.... So it was the unforgettable voice, which is heard only for a little while, before the silence should close in forever. Unaware, he had fled the divine hand outstretched—even the vision of the reproachful face—then the last cry beyond the hills, the ultimate distant cry, no louder than a drawn breath. Every step pushed him further into the land of exile; yet he was ever marked with the mark which only a little since the servant of God had recognized upon his forehead.

I could have... I should have... Words of dread! And were he for an instant to overcome them, he would once more be master; thus the defeated hero dictates his memoirs to his retainers, endlessly works out his plans anew and blows fresh life into the past that he may smother the future which still stirs within his heart. The strongest never yield themselves by halves. Steadfast good sense, the moment certain limits have been passed, will plunge to the depth of folly. This man who for forty years was to look upon the sinner with the eyes of Christ, whose hope the most rebellious would not weary, and who, like Saint Scholastica, obtained so much because he had loved more, had not at this tragic moment even the strength to lift his eyes toward the cross, through which all is possible. This simple thought, the first in any Christian soul, and which seems inseverable from the feeling of our powerlessness and from all true humility, did not come to him.

"We have squandered God's grace," repeated within him a voice strange, but with the timbre of his own, "we are judged, condemned.... Already I no longer am: I could have been!"

Twenty years afterward, the pastor of Lumbres, eyes filled with tears, said to Father de Charras, later Trappist abbot of Aiguebelle, who was bitterly bewailing the inner loneliness into which he had fallen, doubtful even of his salvation: "Stop, say no more.... You do not know how much certain words upset me, and indeed on my deathbed and in my Saviour's hands, I could not hear them unscathed."

Then, when the other priest would not be silent and begged that he be heard to the end, appealing to his confessor's love for souls, he saw him suddenly grow rigid, his eyes roving, his mouth tight, his hand convulsively clasped on the back of his rush chair.

"Not another word!" he cried out in a voice which stopped his amazed penitent short. "I command you!" Then, after a moment's silence, still pale and quivering, he drew Father de Charras's head to his bosom, pressing it tight with both his trembling hands, and said to him in touching confusion: "My son, sometimes I show myself as I am.... Poor souls who come to one poorer than they!... There are certain ordeals which I dare not reveal to anyone for fear that the incomprehensible kindness with which people treat me might transform my wretchedness into a further glory.... So greatly do I need prayers, and men bring me praises!... But they don't want to be undeceived."

It was now full daylight. The poor little room, in the sad December morning, disclosed all its humble disorder; the white wooden table under its scattered books, the folding bedstead pushed against the wall, one of its sheets dragging on the ground, and the dreadful faded wallpaper.... For a moment the wretched priest looked at these four walls so close upon him, and he thought he felt their weight upon his chest. The unbearable sensation of being caught in a trap, of finding in flight a corridor without egress, brought him to his feet with a start, his forehead icy, his arms limp in unutterable fright.

And all at once there was silence.

It was like that buzzing in the midst of a vast assembly which is the prelude to the total smothering of sound, in the suspense of waiting.... For another second the deep air wave slowly sways, withdraws. Then the enormous living mass, clamorous a moment since, in unison falls silent.

Thus the thousand contradictory voices which scolded, hissed, rasped in Father Donissan's heart, in a madness damned, grew quiet all together. Temptation was not allayed; it no longer existed. Father Donissan's will, at the end of its strength, felt the hindrance melt away, and the release was so abrupt that the poor priest thought he sensed it even in his muscles, as though the ground had given under him. This last ordeal, however, continued but for an instant, and the man who had, a few moments earlier, been hopelessly writhing, under a burden ceaselessly heavier, awakened lighter than a little child, indeed lost awareness of living in a void of delight.

It was not true peace, for true peace is only an equilibrium of forces, and inner certainty gushes from it like a flame. He who has found peace awaits nothing further, and he—this priest—was in expectation of heaven knows what new thing which would break the silence. It was not the weariness of an overwrought soul when it finds the depth of human sorrow and there takes its rest, for he desired something further, nor was it the self-abasement of a great love, since in the release of the whole being the heart is watchful and wants to give more than it may ever receive.... But he wanted nothing: he was waiting.

At first it was a stealthy, indiscernible joy, as though come from without, quick, unremitting, almost importunate. What was there to fear, for what to hope, in a thought unformulated, wavering, in a desire as little heavy as a spark?... And yet, as in the very midst of the orchestra's wild outburst the conductor catches the first and imperceptible vibration of a false note—too late, however, to stop its bursting forth—so the curate of Campagne had no doubt that that which he awaited and knew not had come.

Through the frosted windows, the horizon under the sky presented only a vague contour, almost invisible, and by contrast the full winter daylight lit the little room with a milky brilliance, motionless, full of silence, as though seen through water. And, with absolute certainty, Father Donissan knew that this indiscernible joy was a presence.

His torment vanished, there arose little by little in his memory the thoughts which earlier had aroused it, but those very same thoughts were now without power to harrow him. After a first start of fright, his memory, apprehensive, skimmed them over, one by one, cautiously—and then grasped them to itself. He grew enraptured the more he felt them mastered, harmless, turned into the humble servitors of his mysterious joy. In a flash all things seemed possible to him, the highest rung already scaled. From the depths of the abyss in which he had believed himself forever sealed, behold a hand had thrust him through such a space that here he would surely find his despair, even his faults, transfigured, glorified. Cleared were the boundaries of the world in which each forward step costs an aching effort, and the goal came to him with the speed of lightning. This inward vision was brief but dazzling. When it ceased, everything seemed clouded over once more, but he lived and breathed in the same gentle light, and the image, half seen, then lost, left behind it not a certainty, the pleasure of which he well knew would have shattered his heart, but an indescribable conviction of what was to come. The hand which had borne him had scarcely been withdrawn, stood ready, within his reach, would never quit him again.... And the feeling of this mysterious presence was so vivid that he abruptly turned his head, as though to meet the glance of a friend.

Nonetheless, in the very midst of joy, something yet continued to exist which the rapture did not consume. This bothered him, irritated him, as though it were a last link which he dared not sever. Were this link broken, where would the flood sweep him?... Occasionally this link was loosened and, like a ship dragging its anchors, his being was shaken to the keel.... Was this no more than a link, a hurdle to be cleared?... No: that which resisted was not a blind force. It felt, observed, schemed. It fought to have its way. *It*: was it not himself? Was it not the benumbed consciousness, slowly awakening?... The swelling of joy, according to the extraordinary words of the apostle, had been even unto the sundering of the soul and the spirit. It is impossible to go further without dying.

No! As Father Donissan turned his head, he met no friend's glance—but only, in the mirror, his pale and drawn countenance. In vain did he immediately lower his eyes: it was too late. He had caught himself in this instinctive movement; he sought to extract its meaning. What had he been seeking? This material sign of a worriment until then vague and indeterminate frightened him almost as much as a real, visible presence. Of this presence he had now more than a feeling—a clear-cut impression, beyond description. He was no longer alone. But with whom was he?

No sooner had the doubt taken shape in his mind than it became its master. His first impulse was to throw himself upon his knees, to pray. For a second time prayer stopped short upon his lips. The cry of humble distress would not be raised; the ultimate warning was to have been given in vain. The will already rearing back slipped from the hand enticing it; another was grasping it from which neither pity nor mercy must be expected.

Oh! how strong and cunning is that other, how patient when needful, and, when its hour has come, how swift, like a bolt of thunder! The saint of Lumbres would one day know his enemy's face. This time he had to suffer blindly his first attempt, receive his first assault. What would have been this strange man's life—a life which was no more than a frenzied struggle ending in a bitter death—had he at this moment, the stratagem thwarted, effortlessly surrendered himself to mercy—had he called for help? Would he have become one of those saints whose story is like a folk tale, one of the meek who possess the earth, with the smile of a child king?... But what does it serve to dream? At the crucial moment he accepted strife, not through pride, but swept on, irresistibly. As his adversary drew nigh, he was carried away not by fear but by hatred. He had been born for war; each turning in his road would be marked with a torrent of blood.

That mysterious joy, however, as though at the spirit's pinnacle, still kept its vigil, scarcely flickering, a tiny clear flame in the wind.... And it was against this—O folly!—that he now was about to turn. His barren soul, which had never known any gentleness other than a mute and resigned sadness, grew astounded, then took fright, became incensed at this sweetness beyond explanation. During the first stage of this mystical ascension, the wretched, giddied fellow's heart failed him, and with all his strength he was going to try to shatter this passive composure, the inner stillness whose seeming indolence abashed him.... How artfully that other one, who had slipped between this man and God, hid himself! How he drew forward and dodged back, came forward again, prudent, wily, intent.... How disciplined his every step!

The poor priest thought he had caught a whiff of the trap set to catch him, whereas both its jaws already held him in their grasp, and his every effort would tighten their clutch upon him. In the night which again was falling, the frail light set him at defiance.... He challenged, almost he cried out for the fullness of his anguish, which had miraculously melted away. Is not any certainty, even of the worst, better than the worrisome halt at a crossroads, in the treacherous night? This joy without cause can only be an illusion. A hope so secret, at the inmost, the deepest level, born in a flash—having no object—undefined, is too much like pride's presumption.... No! the action of grace has no such sensual attraction.... *He had to uproot that joy.*

The moment his mind was made up, he hesitated no longer. The idea of the sacrifice to be consummated here and now—within the instant—caused that other flame to flare up within him, the flame of bold despair, strength and weakness of this man without a peer, his own weapon which Satan would so often turn against his own breast. His face, now grown rigid, betrayed in the clouded eyes a determination to deliberate violence. He moved toward the window and opened it. For the handrail long since broken, the whim of one of Father Menou-Segrais's predecessors had substituted a brass chain, dug out of the depths of some sacristy closet. With his powerful hands, Father Donissan tore out the two nails by which it was affixed. An instant later this queer scourge whistled as it fell upon the naked back.

A word let fall by chance, the testimony of a few constant visitors, infrequent confidences couched in obscure terms alone allow us to imagine the pastor of Lumbres's rare and unique mortifications, for he strove to hide them from everyone, and with meticulous care. More than once his roguishness itself led curiosity astray, when some famous writer or other, a lover of souls (as the phrase runs), having come to see so fine a specimen, went home mystified. Yet if some of these mortifications—for instance, the fasts whose frightful rigor exceeded all reason—are fairly well known to us, he preserved within him the secret of other, harsher chastisements. His last request was to beg a friend that for pity's sake no doctor should attend him. The poor girl who was caring for him, since become Mother Mary of the Angels, then a servant in the town of Bresse, has recorded that the base of his neck and his shoulders were covered with scars, some forming calluses as thick as the little finger. Earlier, Dr. Leval, during a first serious illness, had remarked along his sides the deep marks of old burns, and, when he displayed a discreet surprise to his patient, the saint, reddening with shame, remained silent....

"In my time I have also committed certain follies," said he one evening to Father Dargent, who was reading him a chapter from the lives of the Desert Fathers.... And when the latter looked at him questioningly, he continued, smiling with deep embarrassment but also with innocent mischief: "You see, young people are very bold; they have to sow their wild oats."

Now, standing at the foot of the little bed, he struck and struck, without respite, in a cold rage. At the first blows, the welted flesh let only a few drops of blood seep through. But suddenly it spurted vermilion. Repeatedly the whistling chain, twisting for a moment above his head, darted to bite his flank and recoiled like a snake; he tore it back in a continuous motion and raised it again, systematically, carefully, like a thresher at work on the threshing floor. The sharp pain, to which he had first reacted by a muffled groan, then only by deep sighs, was, as it were, drowned in the flow of lukewarm blood which dripped along his loins, and of which he felt merely the dreadful caress. At his feet a ruddy brown stain spread without his seeing it. A pinkish mist lay between his seeing and the pale sky, at which he looked with dazed eyes. Then suddenly this mist disappeared, and with it the landscape of snow and mud, even the light of day. But he struck and struck again in this new dusk, and he would have struck until death. His thinking, as though benumbed by the excess of physical pain, was no longer directed at anything, and he felt no desire except to overtake and to destroy, within this unbearable flesh, the very principle of his evil. Each new violence summoned another and a stronger one, ever powerless to sate him. For he had reached that paroxysm where love betrayed has strength only to destroy. Perhaps he thought to clasp and abhor that part of himself, too heavy, the burden of his wretchedness, impossible of being dragged to the heights; perhaps he thought to chastise that body of death from which the apostle likewise wished to be set free, but temptation had thereby entered deeper into his heart, and he hated himself altogether. Like to the man who cannot outlive his dream, he hated himself.... Yet he held in his hand merely a harmless weapon, wherewith he tore himself in vain.

Meanwhile he struck without respite, soaked with sweat and with blood, his eyes closed, and surely the only thing which kept him erect was his mysterious wrath. A shrill humming now filled his ears, as though he had slipped steeply into deep water. Through his shut eyelids twice, thrice a flame spurted bright and high, then his temples beat with so fast a pulse that his aching head vibrated. Within his rigid fingers, at every blow the chain was more pliant and quicker, strangely nimble and traitorous, with a light rustling sound. Never afterward did he who was called the saint of Lumbres dare force the nature of so wildly daring a heart. Never did he offer it such a challenge. The flesh of his loins was all one burning wound, a hundred times torn and torn again, bathed in a frothy blood, yet all these rents were but a single pain—boundless, total, maddening—comparable to the dizziness produced by looking into too strong a light, when the eye no longer perceives anything except its own dazzling ache.... Abruptly the chain, too soon pulled out of its flourish and folding back upon itself, almost escaped from his hand and hit him hard on the chest. The last link nicked him so powerfully under his right breast that it gouged out a morsel of flesh like a chip pared off by a jointer-plane. Surprise, rather than the pain itself, drew from him a sharp cry, quickly stifled, as he again raised the brazen whip. The fire burning in his eyes was no longer of this world. The blind hatred which inspired him against himself was of the sort which nothing here below can appease and for which all the blood of the human race, could it be shed in a single flood, would be no more than a drop of water on iron heated red.... Nevertheless, as he lowered his arm, his fingers opened by themselves, and he felt his hand fall to his side. At the same time his loins gave way, and all his muscles went limp together. He slipped to his knees, made a tremendous effort to get up, tottered again, his arms held out, groping, shaken by a convulsive shudder. Vainly he tried to go back to the window, toward the pale brightness without, glimpsed without recognition through his half-closed eyes. The frightful, sustained struggle already had dwindled to a vague recollection, shapeless as a dream. Thus does uneasiness survive the nightmare, an invisible, inexplicable presence, in the dawn's peace and reverent silence.... He sat on the edge of the bed, let his head slip back, and fell asleep.

When he awoke, sunlight filled the room, he heard the bells ringing in the clear sky. His watch showed that it was nine o'clock. For a long moment the shadow on the wall was enough to engage his mind; then his eyes slowly circled the room, and he was astonished at the large shirring stain on the deal floor, at the chain cast down haphazard. Then he smiled with a child's smile. So the terrible task had been done; it was done, that was all. It was finished. The frenzy through which he had gone left him no bitterness whatever; as the details appeared in turn before his mind, he one by one cast them aside, without curiosity, without anger. Now his thought floated beyond, in a light so gentle! He felt his mind calmer, more lucid than at any other moment of his life, yet unutterably severed from the past. No longer was this the heaviness, the half-torpor of awakening. The last veils had been drawn asunder; he was himself finding himself, watching himself with a clear and active awareness, but with a superhuman disinterestedness.

The sun was already high. The Beaugrenant stage passed grinding along the road. Father Menou-Segrais's familiar voice arose from the little garden, and to it another, more strident voice replied, that of

Estelle the housekeeper.... Father Donissan listened and heard his name spoken twice. With an instinctive motion, he tried to get out of bed. But scarcely had his feet touched the floor when an excruciating pain wrapped itself around him, and he stopped short where he stood, in the middle of the room, his throat swelling with cries. The enchantment abruptly ceased. What had he done?...

For another minute, motionless, doubled over, he tried to recuperate for a fresh effort—a second step—all his harrowed flesh awaiting the wrench that would go with it. The mirror standing on his table returned to him a nightmare image of himself.... His sides, bare under the tattered shirt, were one great sore. Beneath his breast the wound still bled. But the deeper rents on his back and his loins girded him with an intolerable flame, and when he tried to raise his arm, it seemed to him that the tip of this flame reached as far as his heart.... "What have I done?" he repeated under his breath, "what have I done?..." The thought of appearing shortly, within a moment, before Father Menou-Segrais, the impending scandal, the treatments to which he would be subjected, a hundred other things envisioned put the final touches to his disheartenment. Not for an instant, moreover, did this incomparable man dare think, in his defense, of those servants of God whom a same sacred terror had on occasion armed against their own flesh. "One step further," was all that he said to himself, "and the wounds will open...surely I shall have to call for help." Glancing down, he saw his heavy shoes in a puddle of blood.

"Father?" said a quiet voice through the door. "Father?..."

"Yes, Dean?" he replied in the same tone.

"The last bell for Mass is about to ring, my son; it is late, very late.... I hope you're not unwell?"

"Just a minute, please," calmly answered Father Donissan.

He had made up his mind, the die was cast.

How did he manage, clamping his teeth, another step, a crucial step, as far as the hand basin, where he immediately wet the coarse, grayish-brown linen towel? By what further miracle did he suffer without a sigh the bite of the icy water on his back and on his sides? How did he succeed in wrapping around him, on the raw flesh, two of his miserable shirts? What was more, they had to be drawn tight for the slow bleeding to cease, and at every movement their folds cut deeper into him. He carefully washed the flooring, hid away his reddened linen, brushed his shoes, put everything in order, went down the stairs, and did not breathe easy till he reached the road—free—for he never would have been able to conceal from Father Menou-Segrais the chill of fever which made his jaws tremble.... But now the winter wind played full upon his cheeks, and he felt his eyes burning in their sockets like two live coals. Through the keen air, iridescent with the dusting snow, he kept his eyes sharply fixed upon the belfry overspread with sunlight. Couples in their Sunday best greeted him as they passed; he did not see them. In order to cover those three hundred yards, he had to catch himself a score of times, without allowing anything to reveal, in his ever even pace, the vicissitudes of his hidden struggle, on which he lavished, in which he spent recklessly those deep, irretrievable powers of which each living being has merely his reasonable portion. At the entrance to the little cemetery, the nails of his shoes slipped on the hard stone, and to recover his balance he had to make a superhuman effort. The door was now only twenty paces away. And now he reached it. And now that other low door to the sacristy, beyond the dizzying checkerboard of the black and white flagstones, where the reflections of the stained glass danced before his dazzled eyes.... And the sacristy itself, filled with the bitter odor of gum, of incense, and of spilled wine.... All around him the choirboys in red and white churned and buzzed like a swarm of bees. One by one he mechanically slipped the vestments over his head; his eyes were closed, and he chewed over the prescribed prayers in his mouth, his bitter mouth. As he knotted the tapes of the chasuble, he sighed, and to the very foot of the altar the same imperceptible sighing did not cease, rolled in his throat.... Behind him a thousand scattered sounds reverberated to the very vaulting, there to mingle into a single murmur—that resonant void which he would have to face at the moment of the Introit, arms outstretched.... He blindly walked up the three steps and came to a stop. Then he looked at the Crucifix.

O you who never knew anything of the world except colors and sounds without substance, soft hearts, lyric mouths in which harsh truths would melt away like a sugar candy—small hearts, small mouths—this is not for you. Your deviltries are proportionate to your weak nerves, to your mincing minds, and the Satan of your strange daily round is merely your own image distorted, for the devotee of the carnal universe is Satan unto himself. The monster watches you with laughter, but he has not laid his talons upon you. He is not in your driveling books, nor is he in your blasphemies or in your silly curses. He is not in your greedy eyes, in your treacherous hands, in your ears full of wind. Vainly do you seek him in the most secret flesh, over which your wretched longing roams without satisfying itself, and the mouth you bite yields only an insipid and faded blood.... Yet he is, nonetheless.... He is in the prayer of the Solitary One, in his fasting and in his penance, in the depths of his deepest ecstasy and in the heart's silence.... He poisons the water of purification, burns in the blessed wax, breathes in the breath of virgins, tears with the hair shirt and the scourge of mortification, corrupts every path. He has been seen uttering lies on lips parted to bestow the word of truth, pursuing the just man, in the midst of the thunder and lightning of the beatific rapture, up into the very arms of God.... Why should he vie over so many men with the earth, whereon they grovel like beasts, until that same earth covers them on the morrow? That unnoted flock by itself seeks out its fate.... His hatred has reserved the saints for his ministrations.

Then he looked at the Crucifix. Since the evening before he had not prayed, and perhaps he was not yet praying. In any case, it was no entreaty which rose to his lips. During the night's great strife, it had surely been enough to resist and give blow for blow; a man defending his life in a desperate struggle keeps his eyes fixed firmly ahead of him and does not search, the sky whence the immutable light falls upon the good and upon the wicked. In his exceeding weariness, his recollections pressed down upon him, but in array at one point in his memory, like the rays at the focal point of a lens. They made up one single pain. Everything had disappointed or cheated him. To him everything was a snare and a scandal. From the mediocrity where it was his despair to languish, the words of Father Menou-Segrais had borne him to a height where downfall was inevitable. Were not the former shortcomings indeed preferable to the joy which had led him astray! O joy, hated the more for having been, if briefly, so beloved! O frenzy of hope! O smile, O kiss of betrayal! In his eyes, which he kept ever fixed—without a word on his lips, without even a sigh—on the impassive Christ, there was expressed for once the violence of this frantic soul. Such was the face of the miscreant poor man, glimpsed at the splendid high window of the banqueting hall. All joy is bad, said those eyes. All joy comes from Satan. Since I shall never be worthy of that election which deludes my only friend, do not deceive me any longer, call me no more! Return me to my nothingness. Make me the passive matter of Thy labor. I do not want any glory! I do not want any joy! I no longer even want hope! What have I to give? What remains to me? That hope alone. Withdraw it from me. Take it! Were I able, without hating Thee, I would yield Thee my salvation, I would damn myself for those souls whom Thou hast entrusted to me in mockery—to me, wretch that I am!

And thus did he defy the abyss; he summoned it with a solemn suffrage, with a pure heart....

3.

THE CURATE OF Campagne took the Beaulaincourt road and went down toward Etaples across the plain. "It's just a good walk, at most eight miles," Father Menou-Segrais had smilingly remarked. "Go on foot, since you get so much fun out of it."

He was not unaware of the poor priest's boyish liking for railway trips. But this time Father Donissan did not blush as he ordinarily would have.... He even smiled, and not without mischievousness.

The dean of Campagne was sending him to his colleague at Etaples, who was quite worried about the closing exercises of a retreat. The two Redemptorists who thrice daily for over a week had sounded forth until they were hoarse were asking for a respite. It seemed out of the question to require of these weary men the ultimate ordeal of a day and a night in the confessional. "Your young assistant will surely be happy to lend us the aid of his zeal," the canon had written. And Father Donissan was hastening to comply with this simple request.

He was pacing along under a November rain, through the deserted meadows. On his left you could guess the presence of the ocean, invisible, at the boundary of a horizon weighted under a scudding, ash-colored sky. On his right, the last of the hillocks. Before him, the speechless flat expanse. The west wind wrapped his cassock around his knees and at intervals swept before it a fine spray of icy water with a briny taste. Still he marched on, straight ahead, his cotton umbrella rolled and tucked under his arm. What more would he have dared ask? Every step brought him nearer the old church, already discernible in the distance, so strangely helmeted in its lonely adversity. He pictured to himself within it the little crowd of women around the confessional, adroit at grabbing first place in line, quarrelsome, devout of mien, eyes holding and withholding, lips piously closed or drawn tight in an ugly crease—then, close beside this murmuring flock, standing so awkward and so stiff...the men. An odd thing and, as you might be forgiven for putting it in such a connection, exquisite! At this thought the violent young priest was moved by a troubled tenderness; unconsciously he hastened his pace, with a smile so gentle and so sad that a passing wagoner tipped his hat to him without knowing why.... They were awaiting him. Never did any mother on her way home, dreaming of the wondrous little body which would soon stand wholly within her embrace, have more impatience and purity on her countenance.... And now was hollowed out through the sand the bed of the brackish river, now the barren hill and the high silhouette of the white lighthouse amidst the black firs.

For weeks Father Menou-Segrais had no longer hoped to decipher anything in so secret a heart. The curate's dark silence of an earlier day had seemed less impenetrable than his present mood, always even-tempered, almost sprightly. A score of times had he questioned Father Chapdelaine, pastor of Larieux, who on every Thursday heard Father Donissan's confession. The old priest denied having found anything out of the ordinary in the utterances of his penitent and was honestly amused at his colleague's scruples. "A child," he kept repeating, "really a child, a very promising fellow." He laughed till the tears came. "But everywhere you find, dear friend, strange cases of conscience!... (Seriously) I wish you could hear his confessions. Come, come! We have all been through it, in the early days of our ministry: a bit of worriment, idle fancies, an exaggerated inclination toward prayer... (Wholly grave) Prayer is a very good, an excellent thing. Let's not abuse it. We are not Carthusians, my friend, we have to deal with good folk who are very simple-hearted and who for the most part have forgotten their catechism. We must not fly too high, lose touch." He laughed again. "Just imagine! He was scourging himself. I won't describe to you what he used for the purpose; you wouldn't believe me. I forbade him these absurd austerities. What's more, he at once gave in, without argument, I am certain he obeys me. Never have I met a more docile subject: a very promising fellow."

Father Menou-Segrais thought it inopportune to continue the discussion and, prudent as always, pretended to yield to so cogent a line of reasoning. Yet he asked himself with genuine curiosity: "Why on earth did the boy choose this idiot among so many available confessors?..." In the end, he lost the thread of his subtle deductions. The truth, nevertheless, was so simple! Out of all those at hand,

Father Donissan had quietly chosen the eldest. Not out of bravado or disdain, as might have been thought; but because this exaltation of old age seemed to him admirably wise and just. In the same spirit he listened every Thursday to Father Chapdelaine's little talk. No one else would have been capable of meditating such trifling words, and that with so much love that the poor old man, startled and flattered, finally himself discovered a meaning in his own confused sputterings.

Would this bold young priest, however, have dared admit to himself that he was seeking pious stupidity for its own sake? Perhaps he would have dared. Yet he knew so little about the great contest whereof he was the stakes! He was backing up an impossible wager and had no suspicion of it. Doubtless Father Menou-Segrais's solemn warning had disturbed him for a time, then another labor had so hardened his heart that it was as though he were physically insensible to the goad of despair. In the midst of the most daring combat a man has ever waged against himself, he had not the least hesitation in waging it alone; literally, he felt no need for any support. What could have been presumption was here no more than simplicity of heart: he was the dupe of his strength, as another might be of his weakness; he did not believe he was undertaking anything not commonplace, anything out of the ordinary. He had nothing to say about himself.

Before his eyes the little town grew dark, seemed to sink beneath the horizon. He quickened his pace. If only he could reach, unseen, the dark corner where, until supper time, and then into the evening, he would remain alone—alone behind the frail wooden screen, his ear bent toward invisible mouths! But he was disturbed about the unknown faces he would first have to confront. The old pastor, only glimpsed last Pentecost, the two missionaries—perhaps others?... For some months now the future pastor of Lumbres had been amazed at certain glances, at certain words, the meaning of which he did not yet understand, so odd that his simplicity had first mistaken them for distrust or scorn, but which little by little had created about him a strange atmosphere of which he was ashamed. In vain did he keep himself in the background, make himself more humble, flee all new friendships; his very solitude itself appeared to tempt the most indifferent, his slightly sullen timidity defied them, his sadness attracted them. Occasionally it was he himself who broke the silence, when a word let fall by chance suddenly besought his great soul. And up until the moment when the dumb surprise of all those around him had brought him back to himself and he had again ceased to speak, he talked, talked with that encumbered, stammering eloquence, the eloquence of a mind which seemed to drag the words after it, like a burden.... More often, however, he listened with extreme attention, his eyes eager and sad, while the secret prayers upon his lips caught by surprise the futile old priests in their innocent chit-chat. His strangeness was what first struck people. None, with a single exception, had any foreboding of this wondrous destiny. It was enough if he caused worry and set at variance.

Then again, what would you have recognized in this singular man? You would have observed him in vain. You could freely have spied upon him. At Father Chapdelaine's command, he had given up without discussion the mortifications whose frightful cruelty that credulous old priest scarcely suspected, even though Father Donissan had answered all questions with his habitual frankness. But that very frankness misled. To the curate of Campagne, here were facts of the past, episodes. He acknowledged them readily. He freely granted that a sharp flogging is only a trifling thing with which to subdue nature. Later the pastor of Lumbres would say: "Our poor flesh consumes suffering, as it does pleasure, with the same unfettered eagerness." I myself have seen, written in his own handwriting on the margin of a chapter of Saint Ignatius's *Exercises*, this strange behest: "If you believe you must chastise yourself, strike hard and briefly." He also used to say to his sisters at the Aire Carmel: "Let us remember that Satan knows how to take advantage of too long a prayer or too harsh a mortification."

"The fellow is now wholly reasonable," asserted the pastor of Larieux. It was true. His head remained cold and lucid. Never was he tricked by words. His imagination, rather, was on the short side. The heart consumed even its own ashes.

At twilight the wind died down; a light mist arose from the saturated earth. For the first time since his setting forth, the curate of Campagne felt tired. Still, he had passed Verlimont, and as far as the church, now close by, the road was easy and unmistakable. He stopped, nevertheless, and ultimately sat down on the ground, at the crossing of the Campreneux and Verton roads. A peasant woman saw him, bareheaded, his hands folded over the huge umbrella, his hat laid close at hand. "What an odd body," she said.

Thus it was that at times he bent under the burden, and conquered nature vainly bemoaned its distress. For he did not in the least struggle against her plaints: he no longer heard them. In all things he acted as though the sum of his energy were a constant—and perhaps indeed it was. At certain moments, and when all was about to fail him, the only rest he could conceive was to sink within himself and to examine himself with augmented sharpness. To this amazing man, weariness was no more than an evil thought.

And so he reviewed in his memory the events of these last months. It was true that he in no way yearned for the mortifications which for a time had spurred his courage. Even before Father Chapdelaine had asked him to sacrifice them, he had condemned them in his heart. Had they not afforded him consolation and ease? Had they not reopened within him that wellspring of joy which he had sought to dry up? Now he was more faithful than ever to the promise he had one day made before the cross, the promise suddenly revealed, instantly unforgettable. He would find no rivals for the part he had chosen. Never before him had any other bold spirit made this pact with darkness.

Had we not received from the very lips of the saint of Lumbres his confession—so simple and so heart-rending—of that which it pleased him to call the frightful epoch in his life, we certainly would refuse to believe that a man could deliberately, in totally good faith, as though it were a simple and ordinary thing, have committed a sort of moral suicide, the reasoned, refined, secret cruelty of which sends shivers down the spine. And yet it is beyond question. For days upon days, the man whose tender and knowing charity was to reawaken hope in the depths of so many hearts which seemed forever empty attempted to weed that same hope from his being. His elusive martyrdom, so perfectly woven into the web of his life, in the end became wholly blended with it.

At the outset it was as though he were possessed to gainsay and to deny himself. Reading, in which until then he had found not only his joy but his strength, he abandoned, then resumed, then again abandoned. Finding an excuse in an affectionate upbraiding delivered by Father Menou-Segrais, he began to annotate and write a commentary on the *Treatise of the Incarnation*. You should with your own eyes see this volume—in a rather rare eighteenth-century edition, one of the jewels of the pastor of Campagne's library—the margins of which, were crammed with Father Donissan's big handwriting! The awkwardness of these notes, the naïve pains the poor priest took to relate the author's words to the texts of the Gospel by means of references slightly comic in their preciseness—all this, even the blunders in his rudimentary Latin, gave proof of so great a labor that even the most cruel would not dare poke fun. Moreover we know that these memoranda were no more than the outline of a much more important work—surely just as ineffectual—now lost and probably moldering away at the bottom of some drawer, tragic and stumbling witness to the aberrations of a great soul. At first merely repulsive, this task quickly became insufferable drudgery. The pastor of Lumbres was ever a poor metaphysician, and experience alone can convey to you the meticulous torture which the obstinate struggling with an obscure text can inflict upon an intelligence lacking the requisite elements of understanding. This undertaking, rash enough in any case, was soon made more arduous by silly complications. Busy all day, Father Donissan could find leisure only after midnight, having by then lost the daily game of bezique with Father Menou-Segrais. It did not take the wily dean very long to lay bare this new secret. And it supplied him, after his fashion, with a number of discreet allusions which distressed his curate's simple-heartedness. So the poor fellow took on the additional burden of working by the dim glow of a night lamp and was soon suffering from neuralgia of the eyes which put the finishing touches to his exhaustion yet did not lay him low. For this last ordeal afforded him a pretext for new follies.

Up until this time the curate of Campagne had attained a certain rest and relaxation only in the prayer he loved, humble oral prayer. For a long time the saint of Lumbres's artlessness made him doubt whether he were capable of formal prayer, even though he practiced it daily and, it might even be said, at every hour of the day. He made up his mind to conquer himself yet once again.

I feel ashamed to report facts so bare, so lacking in interest, indeed so commonplace. After a night of toil, here was the poor priest pacing up and down his room, his hands behind his back, his head, lowered, holding his breath like a fighter husbanding his strength, trying his very best to think, to think according to the rules.... His subject, chosen beforehand, carefully located according to the best methods, properly Sulpician methods, he harried until he had extracted everything there was in it. Moreover, he sought the aid in this new enterprise of a sort of manual written by an anonymous priest in the year of grace 1849. "*Prayer Taught in Twenty Lessons, for the Use of Pious Souls*," announced the title page. Each of these lessons was divided into three sections: *Reflection*, *Elevation*, *Conclusion*, followed by a spiritual bouquet. A few bits of poetry (set to music by a monk, according to the preface) brought this miscellany to a close, and sang, in a tone dear to the sentimentally devout, the delights and fervors of divine love.

You can hold the dreadful little book in your hands, press it between your fingers. Its binding is protected by a black cloth envelope, solicitously sewn. Its much-fingered pages still retain a stale and rancid smell. A vile colored engraving bears on one left-hand corner, written in a fine, perfidious hand, its ink faded, this mysterious inscription: "To my dear Adoline, to console her for the thanklessness of certain persons...." Surely the ultimate testimony of some pious grudge.... Believe it or not, this was the book, the paltry little companion of him whose glance the proudest cannot say they bore without embarrassment as it read their thoughts—his companion—his intimate, the dear friend of the saint of Lumbres! What did he seek in these pages, like to each other as peas, where the vast boredom of an idle priest little by little found assuagement?

What did he seek and, above all else, what did he find? True enough, Father Donissan has left us no doctrinal or mystical work, but we do have a few of his sermons, and the recollection of his amazing private discourse is still all too vivid in certain hearts. None of those who ever went near him have cast any doubt on his acute feeling for the real, the sharpness of his judgment, the sovereign simplicity of his ways. No one showed more distrust of fine thinking, or even wholly ignored it when a firmer, harsher draught was in order. However forlorn we may imagine him to have been at this period in his life, can we believe these pious conceits actually nourished his prayer? Did he really recite these grandiloquent orisons without disgust, breathe the hateful chemistry of the spiritual bouquets, weep these theatrical tears? Did he pray, or, believing that he prayed, did he pray no longer?

You shudder as you close the little book; even the feel of its dirty cloth cover sets your teeth on edge. You would like to ascertain, to seek in human eyes, the secret of the derisive power which for a moment obscured the most luminous of souls. What then? Can even the grace of God thus be cheated? Will each of us always see, if he turns his head, his shadow behind him, his double, the beast which resembles him and was watching him in silence? How heavy is this little book!

Thus did the spite, which indeed pursued him until his last day, then succeed in the greater part of its attempts against the wretched priest. Having involved him in labors at once overwhelming and ridiculous—treacherously displayed to his conscience as an ingenious system of sacrifice and renunciation—having thus stripped him of all consolation from without, it now strove against the inward man.

Day by day the cruel work was easier and quicker. On fire to destroy himself, the stubborn peasant finally became his own maligner—and one sufficiently astute. There was no act of his humble life whereof he did not scrutinize the motive force, wherein he did not discover the intentions of a perverted will; there was no surcease which he did not scorn and thrust aside, no sadness which he did not at once interpret as remorse, for everything within him and without him bore the sign of wrath.

But the hour was surely come when this cruel labor would bear its fruit, would develop its full spitefulness. What fools we are to see in our own thoughts—thoughts which speech endlessly blends with the world of the senses—merely an abstract being from which we need fear no close and present danger! How blind he who does not recognize himself in the stranger encountered face to face, of a sudden, already an enemy by his look and by the hateful cast of his mouth, or in the eyes of the woman unknown!

Father Donissan got up and, momentarily scrutinizing the countryside which was three-quarters engulfed in shadow, felt disturbed by some vague worry, which he at first readily overcame. Ahead of him the road now dipped toward the valley, between two high banks covered with short, sparse grass. Whether it was because these wholly protected him from the wind (which, with sundown, had sprung up again), or whether for some other reason, the thick silence was no longer pierced by any sound. And although the town was close and the hour early, straining his ears he heard only the formless quivering of the earth, barely perceptible and so monotonous that the extraordinary silence was heightened by it. And then even this murmur ceased.

He started to walk—or rather; it later seemed to him that he had been walking very quickly, along a road smooth beyond criticism, very gently sloping, resilient to his step. His weariness had disappeared, and he discovered himself remarkably free and agile after his long tramp. Above all did the freedom of his thinking amaze him. Certain difficulties which had been weighing on him for weeks melted away as soon as he even tried to formulate them. Whole chapters in his books, so laboriously read and annotated, which he ordinarily wrested from his memory in shreds, suddenly were arrayed in their proper order, with their titles, their subtitles, the sequence of their paragraphs, and even their marginal notes. Continuing to walk, almost to run, he took a notion to leave the main highway and make a short cut over the paths of the Ravenelle, which, skirting the cemetery, leads straight to the front door of the church. He made his turn without even slowing his pace. Ordinarily furrowed even in midsummer by deep ruts at the bottom of which lies brackish water, this track is used almost entirely by fishermen and drovers. To Father Donissan's great surprise, the ground here seemed level and firm. He was delighted. Even though the unusual activity, the free bubbling over of his thought, had had a somewhat intoxicating effect, his eyes were on the lookout through the darkness for certain familiar landmarks as he moved along: the blot of a bush, a rapid turning, the slope of the bank in its reach toward the black sky, the road mender's cabin. Yet after having gone a fair distance, he was surprised to feel underfoot the opposite of what he expected, a slight slope upward, becoming much steeper, and then the thick grass of a meadow. Raising his eyes, he recognized the highway he had left a little earlier. Perhaps, without noticing, he had branched off on a cross-path, which had gradually led him back to his starting point, with his back toward the town? For he saw very clearly (why so clearly in the close night?) its first outlying houses.

"What rotten luck," he thought, but without disappointment or anger.

At once he started off again, determined to stick to the highway. This time he walked slowly, staring ahead of him, at every step feeling the rain-soaked sand grind beneath his heavy soles. The darkness was so thick that as far as his eyes could see, he could make out not only no glow of light, but not even a reflection, not even one of those visible rustlings which, in the deepest night, are like some radiation of the living earth, the slow rotting, until the day's return, of the day destroyed. Nonetheless he moved forward with increased assurance, wrapped, pressed down in this black night which opened up and closed behind him so straitly that it seemed to have physical weight. Yet this, all the same, occasioned him no distress. He walked at a relaxed, sure pace. Although he ordinarily approached the confessional laden with fears and scruples, he was not surprised this time to feel only a surge of almost joyous impatience. His train of thought was so supple that it made almost a physical impression upon him, that tingling of the skin, the need to spend in muscular activity an overflow of thought and images, that light fever well known to thinkers and to lovers. Again he hastened his steps, without the least fear. And the night ever opened before and closed behind. The road stretched out and slipped by beneath him; it seemed to be carrying him along-straight and easy, sloping ever so gently.... He was alert, keen, light-limbed, as though after good sleep in the morning's freshness. Here was the last turning. He hastily tried to descry the little house built of pink brick at the corner of the highway and of the road which he had surely just passed without seeing it. But he could make nothing out distinctly, neither the road nor the house—and in the town close at hand, not even a glimmer. He stood still, not worried but curious.... Then—and only then—in the silence he heard his heart beat, the pulse fast and hard. And he became aware that he was dripping with sweat.

At the same time the illusion which had borne him up until then suddenly melted away, and he felt himself jaded with weariness, his legs stiff and painful, his back breaking. His eyes, which he had kept wide open in the darkness, were now heavy with sleep.

"I'll clamber up the bank," he said to himself; "it's impossible that I shan't find what I'm looking for up there. The least landmark will certainly set me straight...."

He kept repeating the same words to himself with stupid persistence. And he suffered strangely throughout his body when, his mind at last made up, he hoisted himself on his hands and knees through the icy grass. Standing erect and sighing, he walked a few steps further, trying to guess at the line of the horizon, turning to and fro. And to his amazement he found himself once more on the edge of an unknown field in which the earth, lately worked, shone faintly. A tree that seemed huge stretched above him its invisible branches, and their light rustling was the only sound he heard. On the other side of a little ditch which he crossed, the firmer and more luminous earth, between two darker lines, revealed the roadway. Of the bank he had climbed, there was not a trace. On all sides, a vast plain, guessed at rather than glimpsed, indistinct, stretching to the borders of the night, empty.

He felt no fear; he was less worried than he was vexed. Meanwhile his fatigue was so great that cold had overcome him; he shivered in his cassock soaked with sweat. He lowered himself to the ground at random, unable any longer to remain standing. Then he closed his eyes. Without warning, into the very prostration of his sleep, there penetrated a certain anxiety which beckoned him. Before it could even be formulated, it took entire possession of him. It was like a nightmare that made sense, little by little gnawing his sleep away, awakening him bit by bit. However, although he was more than half conscious, he did not dare open his eyes. He was utterly convinced that the first glance cast about him would supply an object for his vague and uncertain terror. What would it be? Finally withdrawing his hands, the palms of which he had been holding against his tightly closed eyelids, he steeled himself for a moment to withstand the impact of an unforeseen and terrible vision. Abruptly opening his eyes, he became aware merely that he had for the second time returned to his point of departure, and to it exactly.

His surprise was so great, so swift the very disappointment of his fear, that he for a moment remained laughably cowering in the chill mud, incapable of any movement, of any thought. Then he took it into his head to examine the terrain about him. He walked to and fro, bent over double, occasionally feeling the ground with his hands, striving to find his own footprints and to follow them step by step to that mysterious point where he must have lost his way and unconsciously have reversed his direction. Even though he had his fear under control, it had sufficiently affected him so that he could not continue his journey until he had solved the puzzle—and he had to solve it. A score of times he tried to shatter the circle, in vain. At a certain distance, all tracks ceased and he was forced to realize that he had tramped through the grass of the field's edge—luxuriant enough so that his passage had left no trace. He likewise noticed that within a radius of several meters the earth was literally amass of footprints. An absurd discouragement, an almost childish despair made the tears spring to his eyes.

Less than anyone else the saint of Lumbres was what moderns in their gibberish call an emotive. Little by little the illusions and deceits of the night began to seem to his guilelessness obstacles he must overcome. Once more he set out along the road, at first slowly, then faster, then even faster, and finally at a dead run. He still believed that he was master of himself, and it was now no longer toward his destination that he hastened; it was on the night, on his dread that he turned his back: his last effort was an unconscious flight. Should he not long ago have reached the unreachable little town? Every minute of delay was hence a minute beyond explanation.

Again the two black banks surged up, flattened out, grew steep, and, when they wholly disappeared, it seemed dubious whether he even was dimly aware of the invisible plain, even though an icy cold wind, wholly soundless, struck him in the face.... He was certain he was already off the road without being able to understand at what moment he had left it. He ran faster, impelled forward, indeed, by the slope, his back bent, his cassock oddly tucked about his thin legs—a ridiculous phantom, so oddly active and gesturing, amidst moveless things. Head held low, he finally tumbled upon a yielding, frigid wall, against which he pressed his hands; he slid gently on his side, in the mud, and closed his eyes. And before he opened them, he already knew that he had *returned.*

He was not yet indignant. He got up with a deep sigh, and, hitching his shoulders as though to adjust a burden, set off once more, facing about unwaveringly. He progressed at an even, docile pace through earth which clung to the soles of his shoes, strode over low hedges and a barbed-wire fence, avoided other obstacles gropingly, without turning his head, tireless anew. His mind was not in the least unbalanced; he set himself no strange purpose; he accepted this so queerly interrupted journey as a run-of-the-mill adventure and quite simply bent all his thoughts to getting back as soon as possible, back to the Campagne rectory before daybreak. He had merely decided to repeat his long trip, but in the opposite direction. Were Father Menou-Segrais suddenly to have sprung up before him, no doubt, after a polite greeting, he would have briefly recounted the occurrence just as you might tell someone about a mishap no more than annoying.

Having crossed a final ditch, he now found himself on a dirt road, very narrow and barely discernible, in the midst of plowed land. He recalled having come along it, perhaps—an hour or two earlier. But *then he was alone*, it would seem....

For, ever since a moment ago (why not admit it?) *he was not alone*. Someone was walking at his side. He was certainly a small man, very lively, now on the right, now on the left, in front, behind, but whose outline it was hard to distinguish—one who at first scampered along without breathing a word. In so black a night, might they not help each other? Did they need to be acquainted in order to journey together, through this great silence, this dark night?

"A pretty dark night, eh?" the little man abruptly said.

"Yes, sir," replied Father Donissan. "Daylight is still a long ways off."

Here was certainly a jolly fellow, since his voice, without being in the least uproarious, had a tone of hidden gaiety which was truly irresistible. That voice fully reassured the poor priest. He even feared that his abrupt reply might have annoyed his jovial fellow traveler, himself so cheerful. How pleasant a human word can be when you hear it thus unexpectedly, and how soothing! Father Donissan remembered that he had no friend.

"In my opinion," then announced the dusky little pedestrian, "darkness brings people together. It's a good thing, a very good thing. When he can't see at all, the most standoffish chap has no pride. Suppose you had met me in the full light of midday: you would have passed by without even turning your head.... And so, you're on your way from Etaples?"

Without awaiting a reply, he moved quickly ahead of his companion, grasped the barbed wire of an invisible fence, and politely held it up at arm's length, making it easier to pass. Then he continued in his joyous, slightly muffled voice: "So you're on your way from Etaples, probably bound for Cumieres?...or Chalindry?...or Campagne?..."

"For Campagne," replied the curate, thus avoiding a lie.

"I'll not accompany you that far," he added, laughing briefly, a friendly laugh.... "We are short-cutting, across country toward Chalindry: I know the fences, I could go blindfold."

"I thank you," said Father Donissan, overflowing with gratitude. "I thank you for your kindness and your charity. So many strangers would have left me helpless; there are some good people fearful of my poor cassock."

The little man whistled in contempt: "Simpletons," said he, "ignorant fools, petty farmers who don't even know how to read. I run into such folk often enough, at fairs from Calais as far as le Havre. What silly nonsense you do hear! What wretched things! Why, one of my mother's brothers is a priest, yes indeed, one of my own uncles."

He bent over again, toward a short, thick hedge, bristling with thorns; having felt it and recognized it with his long and agile arms, he drew the curate to the right with a strange sprightliness and pointed to a wide opening. Stepping aside to let the other pass, he said, "You must yourself grant that it's nothing to me. Some other chap on such a night would go round in circles till morning. But I know this country."

"Do you live here?" almost timidly asked the curate of Campagne (for the further behind he left the town from which such a succession of inexplicable happenings had diverted him, a terror, seemingly quenched, muffled, mingled with shame—like the remembrance of an impure dream—deeply penetrated his heart and, its high point at last passed, left him weak, hesitant, and with a childish desire for the presence of someone reliable, able to help, for an arm he could grasp).

"I don't live anywhere, or the next thing to it," his companion admitted. "I travel in the interests of a Boulonnais horse dealer. Day before yesterday I was at Calais; Thursday I shall be in Avranches. Oh! life is hard, and I haven't time to take root anywhere."

"Are you married?" was Father Donissan's next question.

He burst out laughing. "Married to wretchedness. Where do you expect that I'd find time to think seriously of such things? You come and you go and you don't stay put. You take your pleasure on the go."

He became silent, and then went on, embarrassed: "I beg your pardon; one shouldn't say such things to a man like you. Bear hard to the right; there is a low spot near here full of water."

Such concern filled Father Donissan with fresh emotion. He was now walking at a very quick pace almost without fatigue. But to the extent that his weariness melted away, another weakness crept over him, took possession, permeated his will with a tenderness so cowardly, so poignant! Words came to his lips over which his consciousness had but a vague control.

"The good Lord will repay you for your trouble," said he. "He it was Who made our paths cross at a moment when my courage was leaving me. For this night has been to me a hard and a long night, harder and longer than you can imagine."

He was on the very verge of telling the candid, absurd story of his latest adventure. He wanted to talk, to confide in someone, to read in the eyes of another, even of a stranger, but of a friendly, compassionate stranger, his own worriment, the doubt which already assailed him, the dreadful dream. The glance he met when he raised his eyes, however, was more astounded than compassionate.

"Traveling by a moonless night is never very pleasant," was the unknown's evasive rejoinder. "Between Etaples and Campagne, I reckon there must be some nine miles of bad road. And had it not been for me, your walk would necessarily have been even longer. The short cut makes it at least a mile and a half less. But here we are at the Chalindry road." (The road, pallid in the night, thrust straight across the shapeless plain.)

"I shall soon let you go on alone," he added, as if regretfully. "After all, are you really in such a hurry to get back to Campagne?"

"I have already tarried too long," answered the future pastor of Lurnbres. "Much too long."

"I should have asked you...it might have been possible...even preferable...to await daylight along with me, in a little hut I know very well, on the edge of the la Saugerie woods—a sturdy charcoal burners' cabin with a good hearth and everything you need to make a fire."

Yet the invitation was obviously half-hearted, and the hesitancy in the voice which until then had been so open and sincere astonished Father Donissan. "He's afraid I may accept," thought he sadly. "Even he is in a hurry to part company with, me!"

This paltry testimony all at once poured a flood of bitterness into his heart. Once again his disappointment was so great, his despair so unexpected, so vehement that such a disproportion between cause and effect still worried what common sense and rationality he had left amidst his growing frenzy.

(Yet even if he could hold back some imprudent word, how could he dry up this flood of tears?)

"Let's stop for a moment," suggested the horse dealer, tactfully looking away from the poor priest shaken by his sobbing. "Don't be embarrassed: it's fatigue, you're worn out. How well I know; in one way or another, one has to give way." He at once added, however, half laughing, "I don't blame you, Father, you've come a long way! Your legs have covered a lot of ground!..."

He spread out his overcoat of coarse cloth on the crest of a bank. Almost by force he made his companion lie down on it.

How considerate, how tender, how brotherly is the gesture of this rude Samaritan! How not yield somewhat to this unknown gentleness? How refuse these friendly eyes the confidence they expect?

And nonetheless the wretched priest, so strangely humbled, still resisted, marshaled his utmost strength. However thick might be the night surrounding him, without and within, he judged himself harshly, thought himself childish and a coward, deplored this absurd exhibition of himself, the hatefulness of these silly tears. It was hard for him not to link this scarcely less mysterious adventure, willy-nilly, to the aberration which a few hours earlier had stopped him short upon his journey, had incomprehensibly kept him away from his goal.... And yet, on the other hand, why might not this most recent encounter be a relief, an abatement? Could he not humbly await advice from the man of good will who, by helping him, practiced—even though he knew not its right name—the charity of the Gospel?... Oh! It was too hard to keep silent, to rebuff a tendered hand!

He took that hand, pressing it, and at once his heart grew strangely warm in his bosom. That which a moment before still seemed to him silly or dangerous now seemed wise, needful, indispensable. Is humility scornful of any succor?

"I do not know," began the curate of Campagne, "I do not know how to make you understand...forgive.... But what's the use?... You will thus the better weigh my wretchedness.... Alas, sir, it is hard to think that a poor priest like me—so mean-spirited, so easily laid low—has no less as his mission the enlightenment of his neighbor, the kindling of his courage.... When God abandons me..."

He shook his head, made an effort to draw himself upright, and fell back heavily.

"You've taxed yourself to the limit of your strength," the stranger placidly replied. "Now all that's needed is patience. Patience is a good medicine, Father.... Less harsh than many another, yet how much more sure!"

"Patience..." began Father Donissan in a heart-rending voice. "Patience..."

Almost despite himself, he leaned his head upon his strange companion's shoulder. Nor had his hand withdrawn from the now familiar arm. Dizziness wreathed his head with a crown—a crown yielding, yet little by little drawn tighter, inflexible. Then he swooned, his eyes wide open, talking in a dream....

"No! It is not fatigue which has overcome me to such an extent: I am strong, sturdy, capable of a long fight—but not against certain—not, truly, in this fashion..."

It seemed to him that he was slipping down in the silence, a very easy, slanting fall. Then abruptly the very continuance of his slipping frightened him; he measured its depth. With an instinctive movement as swift as his fear, he drew himself up toward the shoulder which did not bend.

The voice, ever friendly, but reverberating terribly in his ears, was saying: "It's only a bit of giddiness...there...nothing more.... Lean against me: don't be afraid of anything! Ah! You've done a lot of walking! How weary you are! Long since have I been following you, watching you, my friend! I was on the road, behind you, when you were looking for it on all fours...your road.... Ho! Ho!"

"I didn't see you," murmured Father Donissan. "Is it possible? Were you really there? Do you mean to tell me...?"

He did not finish. The slipping began afresh, at a rate of fall endlessly accelerated, perpendicular. The shadows into which he sank whistled to his ears like deep water.

Spreading his hands apart, he clasped the solid shoulders with both his arms, and clung there with all his might. The torso which he thus pressed against him was hard and knotted like the trunk of an oak. It did not budge under the impact. And the poor priest's face felt the shape and the warmth of another, unknown face.

In an instant, for an almost imperceptible fraction of time, all thought abandoned him—aware only of the support he had found, of the density, the stability of the obstruction which thus held him back above an imaginary abyss. He leaned all his weight against it, with increasing, delirious security. His dizziness, as though dissolved by a mysterious fire in the hollow of his chest, slowly oozed from his veins.

Then it was, at that very moment, and suddenly, even though so fresh a certainty spread only gradually across the field of his consciousness—it was then, indeed, that the curate of Campagne became aware that that which he had fled the whole length of this cursed night, that he had at last met that thing face to face.

Was it fear? Was it the despairing conviction that what had to be at last was, that the inevitable was accomplished? Was it that bitter joy of one condemned who no longer has anything for which to hope or against which to struggle? Or was it not rather a foreboding of the pastor of Lumbres's destiny? However this may be, he was barely surprised to hear the voice saying: "Brace yourself well...don't fall until this little attack is over. I am truly your friend—my companion—I love you tenderly."

One arm circled his back in a slow, gentle, irresistible embrace. He let his head slump forward altogether, pressing it close into the hollow of shoulder and neck. So close that he felt upon his forehead and his cheeks the warmth of breath.

"Sleep upon me, nursling of my heart," continued the voice without change of tone. "Hold me hard, stupid fool, little priest, my comrade. Rest. I've sought you hard, hunted you hard. Here you are.

How you love me! But how you will love me better yet, for I am not ready to quit you, my cherubim, my tonsured beggar, my good old companion forever!"

It was the first time that the saint of Lumbres heard, saw, and touched him who was the most degrading associate of his sorrowful life, and if, in this connection, we are to believe certain persons who were the confidants of the witnesses of a certain secret ordeal, how many times was he again to hear him, until the ultimate release! It was the first time, and yet he had no trouble recognizing him. Even any doubt at this moment concerning the soundness of his senses or of his reason was denied him. For he was not one of those who innocently attribute to that Jack Ketch, our familiar—present at each of our thoughts, hatching us with his hatred, yet patiently and cunningly—any epic mien and style.... Anyone besides the curate of Campagne, even had he an equally clear mind, could not have repressed, under such circumstances, the first impulse of fear, or at least a convulsion of disgust. But he, shriveled with horror, his eyes shut as though to gather within him his essential strength, careful to spare himself any vain emotion, his whole will drawn out of him like a sword from the scabbard—he strove to consume his anguish.

Nevertheless when, in sacrilegious derision, the foul mouth pressed his own and robbed him of his breath, his terror was so complete that the very movement of his life was in suspense, and he thought he felt his heart pouring out into his entrails.

"You have received the kiss of a friend," quietly said the horse dealer, wiping his lips on the back of his hand. "I in my turn have filled you with myself, you tabernacle of Christ, dear simpleton! Don't be frightened at so small a thing: I have kissed others besides you, many others. Do you want me to tell you? I kiss you all, waking or sleeping, dead or alive. There's the truth. It's my delight to be with you, little men-gods, odd, odd, such odd creatures! Frankly, I don't often leave you alone. You bear me in your dark flesh, I, of whom light is the essence—in the triple fastness of your guts—I, Lucifer,

Light-Bearer.... I have you all numbered. Not one of you escapes me. By its smell I recognize every beast in my little flock."

He withdrew the arm with which he was still clasping Father Donissan's back, and withdrew himself a little, as though to afford the priest a place on which to fall. The saint of Lumbres's face had the pallor and stiffness of a corpse. Through his mouth, which was twisted up at the corners in a grimace of pain resembling a frightful smile, through his tightly closed eyes, through the contraction of all his features, he betrayed his suffering. But despite all this, he scarcely bent—and that the merest trifle—to one side. He continued to sit on the loose folds of the coat, ominously immobile.

Having scrutinized the priest with a sideward glance at once averted, the companion imperceptibly started with surprise. Then, sniffling noisily, he drew a large handkerchief from his pocket and, in the most commonplace fashion, wiped his neck and his cheeks. "Let's quit joking, Father," said he. "The night, toward its close, is mighty cold in this damned season!"

He gave him a friendly thump on the shoulder, just as you would playfully give a shove to some teetering object, or as children push at a snow man, which collapses on the spot, amidst their shouts of glee. The curate of Campagne, however, did not waver, though he did slowly open his eyes. And without the least relaxation of any of his features, a look black and fixed began to filter between his eyelids.

"Father! Reverend sir! Hey! Father!" called out the horse dealer in a loud voice. "You're dying, friend! You're cold.... Hey, there!"

He took both his hands in one of his own large palms, and with the other lightly slapped them.

"Get up, damn it! Get on your feet, confound it! I swear it's cold enough to freeze the blood!"

He slipped his hands under the cassock and felt the heart. Then, in a succession of quicker gestures—you might call them instantaneous—he touched his forehead, his eyes, his mouth. Again he took the hands within his own and breathed his breath upon them. Each of these actions suggested a slightly feverish haste, that of a workman who is finishing a delicate job and fears he may be overtaken by nightfall or by some intrusion. Finally, drawing his hands abruptly to his own chest, and shaken with a severe chill, as though he had slowly immersed himself in deep and icy water, he hastily clambered to his feet.

"I withstand cold," said he; "I *marvelously* withstand cold and heat. But I'm astounded at seeing you still there, on that icy mud, motionless, seated. You should be dead, I swear.... It is true that a while back, along the road, you bestirred yourself pretty thoroughly, my friend.... As for me, I'm cold and I admit it.... I am always cold.... Here are things you won't readily drag out of me.... They are true, nevertheless.... I am Cold itself. The essence of my light is an unbearable cold.... But enough.... You see before you a poor man, with the qualities and faults of his condition...a trader in nags from Normandy and Brittany...a horse dealer, as they say.... But enough of that, too! Think of me only as the friend, the companion of this moonless night, a good fellow.... Don't be obstinate! Don't think for a minute that you'll learn much more about this unexpected meeting. I want only to help you and then have you forget me immediately. I won't forget you. No, indeed. Your hands have greatly hurt me... and your forehead, too, your eyes and your mouth.... Never again will I warm them; they have literally chilled my marrow, frozen my bones; it's probably those anointings, your damned daubing with hallowed oils—pure witchcraft. Let's not speak of it any longer.... Let me go...I still have a long stretch of road. I'm not at my journey's end. Let's part company here. Let's each go our own way."

He was pacing up and down, distractedly, angrily, waving his hands about, but without moving more than a few steps away. And it was because Father Donissan was following him, here, there, with his dark, dark eyes. And now the lips no longer stirred in his motionless face.

What this face expressed from then on indeed was less fear than a boundless curiosity. You might have said anger, but anger stirs a flame in a man's eyes. Horror—but horror is passive, and no cry of anguish or disgust had loosened the jaws clamped in grim determination. Nor has an idle yearning after knowledge such sovereign dignity. Still humble in his triumph, each instant more complete and more sure, the curate of Campagne was well aware that victory over such an adversary is always precarious, fragile, short-lived. What matter if he saw the enemy momentarily at his feet, at his mercy? But here, here was the killer of souls, a few of whose secrets he must pry loose.

Suddenly the strange pedestrian stopped short, as though he had, in the course of his gesticulations, drawn tight invisible bonds, like a fettered bull. His voice, which a moment earlier had climbed to the highest pitch, resumed its usual tone, and with a certain simplicity he uttered the following words: "Leave me. Your trial is over. I did not know you were so strong. Probably we shall see each other again, later. Even, if you wish it, we shall never meet again. Since a moment ago, I no longer have any power over you."

He pulled the broad handkerchief out of his pocket and frantically wiped his face and hands. His breath made a painful whistling sound between his lips.

"Don't mutter your prayers. Shut up. Your exorcism isn't worth a damn. It's your will I was unable to break. Oh, what strange animals you are!"

He glanced right and left with increasing anxiety. He even hastily turned round and studied the shadows behind him.

"This bag of flesh and bones is beginning to weigh on me," he went on, shaking his shoulders violently. "I'm ill at ease in my skin sheath.... Command, and you won't find a particle of me left, not even a smell...."

He stayed still for a long moment, his face between his palms, as though to gather his strength. When he raised his head again, Father Donissan for the first time saw his eyes and groaned.

A man who, clinging with both hands to the ultimate tip of a mast and suddenly losing gravitational equilibrium, might see deepen and swell beneath him, no longer the sea but the whole starry abyss and, trillions of leagues away, the bubbling scum of the nebulae in gestation, across the void which nothing measures and through which he will plunge eternally—such a man would not feel in the pit of his stomach any more absolute vertigo. His heart beat twice as furiously against his ribs and stopped short. A nausea tore at his vitals. His fingers, clutched in despair, the only living part of a body petrified with horror, scratched the ground like claws. Sweat poured down between his shoulders. This fearless man, as though bent double and torn from the earth by the vast appeal of the void, now saw himself lost without return. Yet, at that very moment, his ultimate thought was still an obscure defiance.

Immediately, at a single bound, life in suspension again coursed through his veins, his temples pulsed afresh. Those eyes, still focused upon his own, resembled any other pair of eyes, and the same voice spoke to his ears, as though it had never become silent.

"I am going to leave you," it said. "Never again will you see me. A man sees me but once. Dwell in your stupid obstinacy. Oh! if only you knew the wages your master has set aside for you, you would not be so generous, for we alone—we, I tell you—we alone are not his dupes, and, as between his love and his hatred, we have chosen—through a sovereign sagacity, beyond the reach of your muddy brains—his hatred.... But why enlighten you on this topic, prostrate dog, enslaved brute, chattel who daily creates his master!"

Stooping over with peculiar agility, he picked up a random pebble from the roadway, between his fingers lifted it heavenward, and pronounced the words of consecration, which he ended with a gay chuckle.... Moreover, all this was done at lightning speed. The echo of his laughter seemed to reverberate to the utmost horizon. The stone reddened, whitened, abruptly burst, glowing wildly. And, still laughing, he tossed it back into the muck, where it quenched itself with a frightful hissing sound.

"That is just sport," said he, "childish sport. It isn't even worth seeing. But now we have reached the time when we must part forever."

"Go away," said the saint of Lumbres. "Who keeps you?"

His voice was low and quiet, with just the hint of a quiver of pity.

"A man greets us in terror," replied the other in a voice equally low, "but a man does not part from us without peril."

"Go away," softly answered the curate of Campagne.

The dreadful creature bounded up, turned completely around several times with incredible nimbleness, and then was violently hurled a few paces away, as though by an irresistible propulsion, his arms outstretched, like a man vainly trying to regain his balance. However grotesque this unexpected caper, the pattern of its movements, their calculated violence, even more their brusque interruption, had some singularity or other which made laughter out of place. The invisible obstacle against which the black adversary had flung himself was surely out of the ordinary, for although he had seemed to parry its impact with infinite litheness, imperceptibly but to its very depths, in the great silence, the earth trembled and sighed.

He drew back slowly, head lowered, and quietly, almost humbly, sat down.

"So, you are holding me back," said he, shrugging his shoulders. "Enjoy your powers for all the time that is given you."

"I have no power whatever," sadly replied Father Donissan; "why tempt me? No! That strength comes not from me, and you know it. Yet I have been watching you for the last few moments with some profit. Your hour is come."

"That does not make much sense," the other rejoined, speaking low. "What hour are you talking about? And indeed have I any hour?"

"It is given to me to see you," slowly stated the saint of Lumbres. "As much as this is possible to the eyes of man, I see you. I see you crushed by your sorrow, even to the bounds of annihilation—which will not be granted to you, O tormented creature!"

At this last word, the monster rolled from top to bottom of the bank and onto the road, where he squirmed in the mud, racked by horrible spasms. Then he grew still, his back tremendously arched, resting on his head and his heels, like one in the throes of tetanus. And at last his voice rose up, piercing, sharp, lamentable.

"Enough, enough, consecrated dog, torturer! You anointed animal, who taught you that of everything in the world, pity is what we fear the most! Do with me what you will.... But if you push me to the limit..."

What man would not have listened with horror to this lament expressed in words—and yet outside this world? What man would not at least have questioned his sanity? But the saint of Lumbres, staring at the ground, thought only of those souls which this other one had lost....

As long as his prayer lasted, the other continued to groan and gnash, but with diminishing force. When the curate of Campagne arose, he became wholly silent. He lay there like a corpse.

"What did you want of me, this night?" asked Father Donissan as calmly as though he were speaking to one he had long known.

From the motionless corpse a new voice arose: "It is permitted to us to test you, from this day forward and until the hour of your death. Then too, what have I done myself except to obey one more powerful? Don't blame me, O just man, threaten me no longer with your pity."

"What did you want of me?" repeated Father Donissan. "Don't try lying. I have means to make you speak."

"I'm not lying. I'll answer you. But slacken a little your prayer. What purpose does it serve as long as I obey you? He sent me in your direction to prove you. Do you want me to tell you by what ordeal? I shall tell you. Who could resist you, O my master?"

"Quiet," Father Donissan replied, equally calm. "The ordeal comes from God. I shall await it without wanting to learn anything about it, especially from such a mouth. It is from God that I receive in this hour the strength you cannot shatter."

At this very moment, that which lay before him faded away, or rather its lines and contours were lost in a mysterious vibration, like the spokes of a wheel turning at full speed. Then slowly these lineaments took on shape.

And suddenly the curate of Campagne saw before him his double, so perfect, so subtle a likeness that it was comparable less to the image reflected in a mirror than to the soul, the unique and profound thought which each man cherishes of himself.

What was he to say? Here was his pale face, his cassock stained with mud, the instinctive gesture of his hand toward his heart; there was the look in his eyes, and in this look he read fear. Yet never would his own conscience, trained though it was in self-examination, have achieved by its own efforts this fantastic doublet. The shrewdest observation directed upon the inner universe can only grasp one of its aspects at a time. And what at that moment the future saint of Lumbres discerned was the general whole as well as its details, his thoughts with their roots, their extensions, the infinite network which linked them together, the tiniest twitchings of his will, just as a body with the skin laid back would show in the design of its arteries and its veins the throb of life. This insight, at once single and multiple, like that of a man who at a glance perceives an object in its three dimensions, was so perfect that the poor priest recognized himself not only in the present, but in the past, the future, that he recognized the whole of his life.... What! O Lord, are we thus transparent to the enemy who watches us? Are we given so defenseless to his pensive hate?

For an instant they stood there, face to face. The illusion was too subtle for Father Donissan to have any real feeling of terror. Try as he might, it was not entirely possible for him to distinguish himself from his double, and yet he half retained a sense of his own unity. No: Here was no trace of terror, but an anguish so sharply pointed that to undertake to threaten this semblance, as though it were an enemy clothed in his own flesh, seemed almost mad. And yet he dared do it.

"Behind me, Satan!" said he, his teeth clenched.

But the words were strangled in his throat and his hand still trembled when he raised it against himself. Yet he grasped that shoulder and he felt its thickness without dying of fright, he tightened his grip to crush it, he kneaded it between his fingers in sudden fury. His face confronted him, his glance confronted him, his breath upon his cheek, his warmth under his hand.... Then it all disappeared.

The voice of the pitiful carrion still stretched out in the mud again made itself heard. "You are breaking me, you are grinding me, you are devouring me," it whined. "What manner of man are you, then, to annihilate so precious a vision before you have even beheld it?"

"*That* is not what I need," continued Father Donissan. "What does it serve me to know myself? The private examination of one's conscience, without other enlightenment, is enough for a poor sinner."

Thus he spoke, despite the fact that regret for the lost vision hurt every fiber in his body. The dizziness of a supernatural curiosity, thenceforward fruitless, forever, left him breathless, empty. But he thought he was close to the goal.

"You're at the end of your tricks," said he to the shivering object which his foot was pushing off the roadway. "Who knows how much time remains to me? Let us hasten! Let us hasten!"

He leaned very low, less to hear clearly than through an instinctive gesture prompted by the zeal which devoured him: "Answer me!" He made the sign of the cross, not over the object, but on his own breast. "Has God given you my life? Am I to die here and now?"

"No," said the voice in the same shrill tone. "We cannot do with you as we will."

"In that case, whether I am to live for a day or for twenty years, I must wrest your secret from you. I shall wrest it from you even if I have to follow you amongst your minions. I do not fear you! I am not afraid! True enough, you once again seem shadowy to me, but a moment since I saw you, O tormented one. Have you not lost enough souls? Must you have yet further prey? You are in my hands. I shall try what God will inspire me to try. I shall say words which are a horror to you. I shall nail you to the center of my prayer as though you were an owl. Or else you will forswear your attempts against the souls entrusted to my care."

To his great surprise, and at the very moment when he thought he was bringing all his strength to bear, irresistibly, he saw the corpse tremble, fill out, resume human form, and it was the gay companion of the first hour who answered him.

"I fear you less, you and your prayers, than Him...." Begun with a sneer, his sentence ended with, an intonation of terror. "He is not far.... For the last few moments I've noticed his scent.... Oh! Oh! How hard a master He is!"

He trembled from tip to toe. Then his head leaned over on one shoulder and his features relaxed once more, as though he heard the enemy's footsteps receding. He went on: "You pressed me close, but I am escaping you. Stop me in my attempts! Fool that you are! I'm not through gorging myself on Christian blood! Today a grace has been given you. You have paid dearly for it. You will pay for it more dearly!"

"What grace?" exclaimed Father Donissan.

He had wanted not to utter these words, and the other immediately seized upon them. The foul mouth trembled with joy.

"Just as you saw yourself a little while ago (for the first and the last time), thus shall you see...shall you see... Ha! Ha! ..."

"What do you mean by that, liar?" cried the curate of Campagne.

As though the cry of curiosity, despite the insult, had altogether restored his equilibrium, brought him back to himself, the strange being gradually straightened up, planted himself on the ground with mincing calm, and sedately buttoned up his leather jacket. The Picardy horse trader was planted on the same spot, as though he had never left it. The future saint of Lumbres's hand fell to his side. What a business! Having borne so many strange and grim visions, he now barely dared raise his eyes to this innocuous sight, this cheery fellow so wonderfully like a host of others. And the contrast between this mouth—the hearty sounds it uttered, the coarse twist of its lips—and the monstrous words it spoke was such as to defy description.

"Don't slink off so quickly. Don't be too greedy for our secrets. Something soon to happen will prove whether or not I lied. What's more, had you only a moment ago taken the trouble to see what I placed before your eyes, you could do without insulting me." That was not the word he used. "In such fashion as you saw yourself, I tell you, you will see certain others.... What a shame that a like gift should be given to such a booby as you!"

He blew into his cupped hands, making his lips vibrate, as does a man in the grasp of bitter cold. His eyes laughed in his ruddy face, and their darting to and fro behind the half-closed lids might just as well have expressed joy as scorn. Joy won out.

"Ha! Ha! Ha! How embarrassed he is! How quiet!" he stuttered.... "You were a trifle friskier a while ago, terror of demons, exorcist, wonder-worker, saint of my heart!"

At each burst of laughter, Father Donissan shivered, then at once stiffened into stupidity; his benumbed brain no longer gave shape to any thought.

The other rubbed his hands together vigorously.

"What grace?... What grace?..." he kept repeating in comic mimicry of his victim. "In the battle you're fighting against us, it's easy to make a slip. Your curiosity puts you at my mercy for the while."

He drew near, confidential: "You know nothing about us, you godlets full of self-sufficiency. Our rage is so patient! Our firmness so clear-headed. It is true that *He* has made us serve His purposes, for His word cannot be withstood. It is true—why should I deny it?—that our attempt of this night seems to turn out to my discomfiture.... (Ah! When I held you close a little while ago, His thought focused upon you, and your angel himself trembled in the gyration of the lightning!) Yet your eyes of mud saw nothing."

He snorted in a whinnying laugh: "Hee! Hee! Hee! Of all those I have seen signed with the same sign as you, you are the thickest, the dullest, the densest!... You plow your furrow like a bullock, you buck your enemy like a he-goat.... From top to bottom, a good target!"

And all the while, Father Donissan, shaken by sudden chills, followed him with his eyes, dumbly fearful. Nevertheless something resembling a prayer—but hesitant, confused, shapeless—wandered through his memory, without his consciousness being as yet able to grasp it. And it seemed that his shriveled heart was becoming a little warmer under his ribs.

"We shall belabor you shrewdly," continued the other one. "Be careful not to annoy us. We'll put the screws on you in our turn. There is no lout whom we cannot make serve our purpose. We'll take the fat off you. We'll put you through the smelter."

He thrust forward his bullet head, aflame with eagerness. "I have held you against my bosom; I have cradled you in my arms. How many more times will you fondle me, thinking that you press the *other* against your heart! For such is your mark. Such is the seal of my hatred upon you."

He placed his two hands upon his shoulders, forced him to bend his knees, made him kneel upon the earth.... But suddenly, giving a single shove, the curate of Campagne hurled himself against him. And he encountered only emptiness and shadow.

Once again the night had gathered round him, within him. He felt incapable of movement. He lived only in his sense of hearing. For he heard words uttered near him, but without coherence, as though hanging in the air, in the unreality of a dream. Then, through a great effort, he succeeded in relating them to beings that lived and moved, close at hand. One of these persons—imaginary or real—drew away. He heard his voice grow fainter, fainter also the grinding of his soles through the sand. At last he felt himself upraised, supported by a bent arm the firm grasp of which pained his shoulder. Something was still bruising his lips and his teeth. A jet of flame pierced his throat and his chest. The blackness which stood a barrier to his vision opened a crack. A thin twilight slowly came to birth in his eyes, slowly took shape. And he recognized, standing on the ground a short distance away, one of those powerful lanterns, such as fishermen carry on very windy nights. An unknown man was supporting him with one hand and making him drink from the neck of a soldier's canteen.

"Father," said he, "at last..."

"What do you want of me?" stammered Father Donissan.

He spoke as deliberately as he could and as quietly. But the vision was still in his eyes, and the man started with an astonishment or fright which seemed beyond the poor, overwhelmed priest's comprehension.

"I am Jean-Marie Boulainville, quarryman at Saint-Pré, brother to Germaine Duflos, of Campagne. I know you well. Are you better?" He averted his glance, with an air of embarrassment, but one full of pity.

"I found you along the road, in a faint. A fine fellow from Marelles, who deals in horseflesh, on his way back from the Etaples fair, had found you before me. The two of us together carried you here."

"You saw him?" Father Donissan cried out. "He's here!"

He jumped to his feet so abruptly that Jean-Marie Boulainville, severely jostled, almost lost his balance. But, interpreting so strange an eagerness after his own fashion, this simple man inquired: "Is there something you want to ask him? Do you want me to hail him? He certainly can't be far."

"No, my friend," said the curate of Campagne. "Don't call him back. Besides, I'm feeling better. Just let me take a few steps."

He moved shakily away. Then little by little his legs grew steadier. When he came close once more, he was calm. "Do you know him?" he asked.

"Whom do you mean?" answered the other, taken unawares. And, at once realizing to whom the priest referred: "The chap from Marelles!" he gaily exclaimed. "Do I know him! Last month at the Fruges fair he sold me two fillies. So! But if you take my advice, Father, we'll walk along a bit together. Walking will do you more good than harm. I'm going directly to the Ailly quarries, where I work. From here to there you can sound out your strength. If you feel any worse, you can get a carriage from Sansonnet at the Flying Magpie Tavern."

"Let's be on our way," replied the future saint of Lumbres. "I've got my strength back. Everything's fine, my friend."

They walked together a little while. And then it was that Father Donissan knew the real meaning of words he had heard: "The near future will prove whether or not I lied."

They traveled, at first slowly, then with more speed, along a rather rough road, so full of ruts from early autumn on that vehicles used it in winter only when the ground was frozen hard. Under such conditions, it soon became impossible for them to walk abreast. The quarryman took the lead. The curate of Campagne followed him, studying his footing, on the watch for obstructions, cautiously maneuvering his heavy shoes, wholly bent on not delaying his companion's progress. His body was still trembling with cold, weariness, and fever, so that his tragic simple-heartedness already more than half forgot the black wonders of this extraordinary night. This was certainly not superficiality or the dullness of extreme exhaustion. Deliberately, though without great effort, he pushed aside any thought of these matters. He innocently postponed examining them to a more favorable occasion, such as, for example, his next confession. How many another would have been torn in double anguish between two thoughts: that he had been the plaything of his madness, and that he had been terribly singled out for great and supernatural ordeals! He, his initial terror once overcome, submissively awaited a new attempt on the part of evil and God's necessary grace. Possessed or mad, taken in by his dreams or by demons—what did it matter, as long as that grace was owing, and would surely be given?… He awaited the consoler's visit with the ingenuous security of a child who, at meal time, raises his eyes to his father, and whose tiny heart, even in the midst of utter poverty, has no doubts of his daily bread.

Within an hour they had traveled together more than three-quarters of the distance to the Ailly quarries. The road was unknown to him and he took great pains not to stray from it, either to right or to left. At times his foot slipped: the slimy mire splashed up into his face and blinded him. So unceasing a tension of the spirit, linked to a kind of inner resistance, the instinctive warning apparatus of an imagination already overstrained, kept his thoughts away from a certain indefinable new sensation, which he would have been hard put to analyze, even had he been inclined to. Little by little this sensation became so lively—or, to be more accurate (since it entreated him with an especial sweetness), so persistent, so incessant, that at last it disconcerted him. Did it come from without, or from himself? There it was, deep in his breast, a warmness seemingly immaterial, a swelling of his heart. And it was also something more, so close in its reality, so pressing, that for a moment he thought the day had come, or else the light of the moon. Yet why did he not dare raise his eyes?

Indeed, he continued ever walking with his glance fixed upon the ground, his eyelids almost shut, perceiving no gleam of light, no reflection except the meaningless glimmer of the muddy water. And yet he would have sworn that he was gradually passing through a soft and friendly light, a golden dust. Without admitting it to himself, or even, perhaps, believing it, he feared that if he raised his head, he would see melt away both his illusion and his joy. He was not afraid of this joy; he felt that he could not have fled it before having made its acquaintance, as he had fled so many others. He was entreated, not compelled, called. He defended himself apathetically, without remorse, sure of yielding sooner or later to the imperious but kindly force. "I'll take ten steps more," he said to himself. "I'll take yet another ten with my eyes lowered. And then again ten..." The quarryman's heels rang out joyfully on firmer, dried-out ground. He heard them with deep and growing tenderness. Little by little he took it into his head that this man was certainly a friend, that a binding friendship, a heavenly friendship, celestially limpid, linked them together, had surely always linked them. Tears came to his eyes. Thus did two of the elect, born for one another, meet one clear morning in the gardens of Paradise.

They had reached the crossing of two roads; one, sloping gently, stretched to the village; the other, worn down by cart wheels, dipped toward the quarries. Far away were to be heard the crowing of a cock and the voices of men: other quarrymen, of course, hastening to their work before daybreak.... It was at this instant that Father Donissan raised his eyes.

Was this his companion in front of him? At first he did not believe it. What he had before his eyes, what his glance grasped—and with the certainty of lightning—was this a man of flesh and blood? Barely would the night allow you to make out the motionless silhouette in the shadows, and yet he had ever the impression of that light, soft, even, living, reflected in his thought, truly sovereign. This was the first time the future saint of Lumbres witnessed this silent marvel which was later to become so, familiar to him, and it was as though his senses did not accept it without a struggle. Thus does a man born blind, when light first enters his eyes, stretch his trembling fingers toward some unknown thing, and is astounded not to be able to lay hold upon its shape and thickness. How should the young priest have been introduced without a struggle to this new way of knowing, inaccessible to other men? He saw his companion before him, he saw him beyond a shadow of doubt, although he could not make out his features, although he sought in vain his face or his hands.... And nonetheless, without fearing anything, he looked upon the extraordinary brightness with a serene confidence, a calm stability, not in order to penetrate it, but sure of being penetrated by it. There was a long lapse of time, as it seemed to him. In reality, no more than it takes for a flash of lightning. And of a sudden he understood.

"In such fashion as you just now saw yourself," the dreadful witness had said. This was in such fashion. He saw. He saw with his fleshly eyes that which remains hidden to the most penetrating—to the most subtle intuition—to the soundest training: a human conscience. Of course, our own nature is partially given us; we know ourselves indeed a little more clearly than we know another, but each man must *go down* within himself, and the deeper he goes, the thicker the shadows, down to dark bedrock, the deep I, where the ancestral shades bestir themselves, where instinct roars, like a subterranean watercourse. And now...and now this wretched priest found himself abruptly transported into the most intimate recesses of another being, surely to the very point reached by the eyes of the Judge. He was aware of the marvel, and was enraptured that this marvel should be so simple and its disclosure so sweet. This burglary of the soul, which someone other than he could never have conceived without thunder and lightning, now that it had been consummated, no longer frightened him. Perhaps he was astonished that its disclosure had come so tardily. Without being able to put it into words (for he never was able to frame words for it), he felt that this knowledge was in accordance with his nature, that the intelligence and the faculties on which men pride themselves played therein but a small part, that it was only and simply the bubbling over, the expansion, the swelling up of charity. Already, unable in the sincerity of his humble thought to consider himself worthy of any singular, exceptional grace, he was close to accusing himself of having through his own fault delayed this initiation, of not yet having loved souls enough, since he had misunderstood them! Yet the enterprise was so simple, the goal, once perceived, so near. A blind man, when he has taken possession of the new sense which is bestowed upon him, is not more greatly astounded at touching with his glance the far horizon, which formerly he reached only at such great labor, through the bogs and brambles.

The quarryman kept moving ahead of him, at his quiet pace. For a moment, Father Donissan was unexpectedly tempted to overtake him, to cry out to him. But only for a moment. This soul suddenly laid bare filled him with respect and love. It was a simple soul, one without a history, heedful, day-to-day, busied with paltry cares. But a sovereign humility, like some heavenly light, bathed it with its glow. What a lesson for this poor, tormented priest, obsessed by fear, was the discovery of this just man, unknown to all and to himself, obedient to his fate, to his duties, to his life's humble loves, under the eyes of God! And spontaneously a thought came to him, adding to the respect and to the love a kind of fear: *Was it not before this man, and this man alone, that the other had fled?*

He would have liked to stop, without taking the risk of shattering the delicate and magnificent vision. Vainly he sought the word which should be spoken. But it seemed to him that any word was unworthy. This majesty of a pure heart cut the words short on his lips. Was it possible, was it possible that in the midst of the human swarm, mingling with the coarsest, witness of so many vices which his simple-heartedness did not in the least judge; was it possible that this friend of God, this poor man among the poor, had clung to righteousness and to childhood, that he breathed life into the image of another artisan, no less obscure, no less unknown, the village carpenter, guardian of the queen of angels, the just man who saw the Redeemer face to face, and whose hand did not tremble upon the scraper or the jointing-plane, full of care to satisfy his clients and honestly earn his wage?

Alas! in one sense, this lesson was to be in vain. The peace which he would never know, this priest was appointed to dispense to others. His mission was for sinners alone. The saint of Lumbres followed his path through troubles and through tears.

They had reached the crossroads before Father Donissan found a word to utter. He relished this sweetness; he drained it dry in the foreboding that it would be one of the rare resting places of his wretched life. And yet he was already prepared to leave it as he had received it, to part with it in silence.

The quarryman came to a stop and said, smoothing his cap with his hand, "We've arrived, Father. Your road is straight ahead, not quite four miles. Are you now in good enough shape? If not, I'll go with you to Sansonnet's."

"That's unnecessary, my friend," answered the curate of Campagne. "Indeed, the walk has done me good. So I am going to bid you good-bye."

For an instant he wondered about seeing him again, but it immediately seemed preferable to leave any fresh meeting in the hands of the same will as had arranged the first. He had likewise wished to give him his blessing. Then he dared not do it.

He looked upon him for a last time. In this glance he implanted all the love which he was to dispense to so many others. And this glance the humble companion did not even see. They shook hands, gropingly.

Once more the road stretched out ahead of him. He recognized it. He swung along fast, very fast. First of all he thanked God, but not in words, for what he had been allowed to see. He walked along as though yet encompassed by the light he had known. This was not its presence, and it was something more than its remembrance. As though you left behind you a melody which long pursued you as you went.

Alas! Here was indeed the ever weakening echo of a mysterious harmony, which never again would he hear, never! The continuance of his joy was short-lived. Every step seemed to draw him further from it, yet when, in his artlessness, he stopped still, its flight appeared even speedier for his having stopped. He bent his back and moved on.

Little by little the countryside, still blurred in the every earliest moments of dawn, became more familiar to him. He recaptured it with sadness. Each object recognized, accustomed things recovered one by one, rendered more indistinct and more vague the night's great adventure. Far quicker than he would have thought, it lost detail and outline, shrank into dream. Thus he passed through the village of Pomponne, left behind him the hamlet of Breme, climbed the last rise. At last he made out below him, in the hollow of the hill, the railway signal suddenly so close at hand, the light of the little Campagne station.

He came to a halt, out of breath, bareheaded, shivering in his mud-stiffened cassock, suddenly not knowing whether it was from cold or from shame, and his ears were filled with confused sound.

At this instant the routine of daily life caught hold of him again with such power and so roughly that in a minute there remained nothing, absolutely nothing, in his mind of a past which was nevertheless so near. And its harsh erasure he felt above all as a painful lessening of his being.

"Did I then dream?" he said to himself. Or rather, he strove to pronounce the syllables, to make them vocal in the silence. And it was to impose silence on another voice which, far more articulately, with dreadful slowness, deep within him asked, "'Am I mad?"

Oh! a man who feels eluding him, as though through a sieve, his will, his attention, then his consciousness, while his dark inside, like the turned leather of a glove, suddenly appears without, suffers a most bitter agony within a space of time no pendulum can measure. But this man—poor priest!—did he doubt, doubted not only himself, but also his sole hope. Losing himself, he lost a more precious good, a divine good, God Himself. In his reason's last flash, he measured the night into which went his great love and vanished.

He was not to forget the site of the new combat. Having reached the last crest, the road turns abruptly and brings to view a narrow strip of land where stands erect an aged elm. The village lies below and to the right, in the last fold of the hill. Answering the station lights, red and green, was the dull glow in the sky from the oven of Joshua Thirion, the baker. The pale daylight still languished in the low places, indiscernible.

On Father Donissan's left, also, was the beginning of a dirt road, which led at a steep slope to the outbuildings of the Chateau of Cadignan. It plunged down immediately through sparse thickets and thus resembled, rather, a ravine or watercourse. It was a spot of shadow in the shadow. Involuntarily, the curate of Campagne glanced down it. The wind among the brambles made a sound like crumpled silk, mingled with abrupt silences. From the sodden ground an occasional stone slipped free and rolled away. And suddenly, among these murmurings...a noise, distinguishable from all others on this lonely morning, the rustle of a living body, which stood up and came close.

"Hey there!" said a woman's voice, very youthful, but muffled, slightly tremulous. "No nonsense! I've been listening to you a good minute. *So you have returned, at last?*"

"And who are you?" Father Donissan quietly asked.

Upright along the edge of the bank, his tall outline scarcely visible against the paler and moving background of the sky, he followed with sad and seemingly inward eyes the little shadow below him, between the ramparts of clay. About this mysterious shadow, some paces away and constantly drawing closer, he knew nothing, although he was already aware with a calm and absolute certainty, a certainty full of silence, that *that* which climbed and gently splashed in the mud was the ultimate and supreme actor of this unforgettable night....

"Oh! It's only you!" said Miss Malorthy, with something like a grimace of pain.

In order to see him, she had raised herself on tiptoe, to his shoulder's height. The tiny, contracted face reflected only dreadful disappointment. In a flash, anger, defiance, a cynical despair in turn flickered across it, so sharply etched and with such a deepening of the features that this child's face no longer had any specific age. Then it was that her eyes met the strange look focused upon her. They could barely support it. And they still retained their flame when the limp bow of the mouth no longer expressed anything more than an anxiety filled with rage.

For that look had not faltered for an instant. Always prudent, even in the aberrations of madness, she scrutinized its expression with her usual distrust. Up till that moment, the young priest who, as Dr. Gallet put it, "turned Campagne's weak heads," had been the least of her worries. Meeting him in such a place at such an hour, she was deeply amazed. For *other reasons* her disappointment was no less acute. A moment earlier, however, she would have felt certain of frightening him, at least of arousing his wrath. And now she read in his look a vast pity.

Not that pity which is no more than the mask of scorn, but a burning, grievous pity, however calm and alert. Nothing betrayed fright or even surprise or the slightest astonishment in the countenance tilted toward her, a little bent over the shoulder, for she could watch only the face. The eyes half escaped her under the eyelids, and when she tried to meet their glance, she became aware that they had little by little lowered themselves to her breast, as though the man of God, disdaining the idle glow of the human pupil, had watched hearts beat.

She was only half wrong. Once again he had heard the sweet, strong summons. Then, like the radiance of a secret glow, like the flow through him of an inexhaustible stream of brightness, an unknown feeling, infinitely subtle and pure, without the least admixture, reached little by little the very principle of life, transformed him in his very flesh. Just like a man dying of thirst who lays open the whole of himself to the water's keen freshness, he did not know whether that which had seemingly pierced him through and through were pleasure or pain.

Was he at that instant aware of the price of the gift that had been made him, or even aware of the gift itself? He who, throughout his life, in the midst of so many tragic trials when at times his will seemed to give way, preserved this power of a sovereign clearsightedness, was probably never fully conscious of it. For nothing could have been less like the slow investigation of human experience, as it moves from observed fact to observed fact, endlessly hesitant and almost always stopped short along the road, when not deceived by its own cleverness. Father Donissan's inner vision preceded all hypotheses, carried with it its own conviction; yet, if this sudden clarification had indeed overwhelmed the mind, the intelligence already in thrall discovered only slowly, and in roundabout fashion, the reason for its certainty. Thus a man who awakens to confront an unknown countryside, suddenly revealed in the bright light of midday, even though his eyes have taken in the whole skyline, only by degrees rises from the depths of his dream.

"What do you want of me?" churlishly asked Miss Malorthy; "is this an hour to stop people along the road?"

She laughed mischievously, but this laughter lied, and he knew it. Or perhaps, rather, he did not even hear it. For louder than any human voice, there cried out to him that sorrow without hope with which she was consumed.

"I was coming along the Sennecourt road," she continued garrulously, "but I turned off toward Corzargues. That astonishes you; it's quite natural—I can't sleep at night.... That's my only reason. But you," she resumed with sudden wrath, "a holy man of God, you don't go lying in wait along the hedgerows to take girls by surprise.... Unless..."

She sought upon the placid countenance the least trace of irritation or embarrassment which could again have set her laughing, but the laughter died away in her throat, for she saw nothing there, absolutely nothing which would allow her even to believe that she had been heard. Thus it was that when she spoke again, her eyes already gave the lie to her voice, which was still mocking: "I see that joking doesn't suit you," she said. "I can't help it, I like to laugh.... Is that against the law? I've laughed so much in my life!"

She sighed, and then continued in another tone: "That's that. We haven't much else to say to each other, I hope?"

In order to get down a dip in the road, she moved ahead of him and, slipping on the incline, regained her balance by laying her five little claws on the black sleeve.

Why did she stop once more? What misgiving kept her motionless for another moment? Above all, why did she add to what she had said words which within herself she repudiated upon the instant?

"So? You think, she has just left her lover; she's on her way home before dawn? You're not altogether mistaken."

Stealthily her eyes circled the horizon. To the right the great Norway pines with their black foliage made a dark, rumbling mass against the eastern sky, already pale with light. It was not the first time she listened to their harsh voice.

Father Donissan gently put his hand on her shoulder and said, simply, "Would you like it if we walked a short distance together?"

He climbed down the bank and, without hesitating, continued in the direction of the hamlet of Tiers, leaving behind him the Chateau of Cadignan and even the village itself. As little by little the path narrowed, it was impossible for them to walk side by side.

Never did Mouchette's little heart pound harder in her chest than at the moment when, still without power to resist or even to use deceit, she heard behind her the tramp of the iron-shod shoes. They went on thus a few paces in silence. At each of his broad strides, the curate of Campagne, literally treading on her heels, forced her to hasten. After a moment or two, this pressure seemed so unbearable to Mouchette that the kind of fear which made her powerless melted away. Lightly jumping onto the road bank, she signaled him to pass.

"You have nothing to fear," said Father Donissan, "and I shall not constrain you. I am not urged by any curiosity. I am merely happy to have met you today after so many days lost. But it is not too late."

"It is even a little too early," replied Miss Malorthy, pretending to smother a shrill laugh.

"I didn't seek you," continued the curate of Campagne; "quite the contrary. In order to meet you, I went a long way round, a very long way, a very strange way. Why should you refuse me what I ask: a brief conversation which will surely be full of consolations both for me and for you?"

She shrugged her shoulders and made no move to follow him.

Yet she was loath to reach a decision, held on the spot by an anxiety which she did not yet know was a secret hope.

The afternoon before she had left her Remangey cousins. The coach had brought her as far as Faulx, where she had asked to be let off, toward seven in the evening. She was to take dinner with her friend, Suzanne Rabourdin, at the Young France Tavern and, she said, would walk after supper the two or three miles between there and Campagne. Ever since her last illness, although her confinement had been kept secret, a few of her relatives were not unaware that she had been seriously ill of a "black sickness." To these good folk, the "black sickness" is incurable, and those who have suffered from it are classified once and for all in the category of poor devils who, as the bitter yet touching phrase goes, "are not all there." Hence for some months it had been rare for anyone to gainsay her fancies. So she had left the Young France Tavern, having refused the company of the Rabourdin boy. Even though she had started off late, she could easily have reached Campagne before ten in the evening, but, crossing the main highway to Etaples, she had, in accordance with a habit already very old, made a slight detour to skirt the Cadignan pleasure-grounds. How many times, without the least fear, but merely ruminating her memories, leaning against the hedge with her two fists under her chin and her feet in the mud, had she weighed the for and against, as she ever did, of a cold brain and a burning heart? Beaten, cast out of her dream, regarded forever as a poor girl beset by idle specters—condemned to perpetual pity—stripped of everything, even of her crime.... And the sole consolation of her sullen little heart was once more to see, at the same unforgettable hour, that roadway along which she had wandered during the course of a unique night, the gate now closed, the mysterious bend in the avenue, and there, furthest of all, the great walls filled with silence, where useless death kept watch, her mute witness.

For over a minute the curate of Campagne awaited her reply, without betraying impatience, but without seeming to doubt either that he would be obeyed. By contrast, his voice made itself more and more humble and soft, almost timid, whereas his attitude expressed a growing authority. And abruptly, without changing his tone, he added these unexpected words which Miss Malorthy felt like an explosion in her heart: "All I wanted was to draw you away first of all, for you know very well that the dead man you await there *is here no longer.*"

Mouchette's helpless amazement showed only in a violent shudder, which she instantly repressed. And it was not fear which made tremble upon her lips the first words she uttered, almost at random: "A dead man? What dead man?"

He answered, in the same calm voice, taking the lead so as to go his own way, while she trotted obediently behind him, "We are bad judges in our own cause, and we often maintain the illusion of certain faults the better to hide from our own eyes that in us which is wholly rotten and must be cast aside under pain of death."

"What death?" continued Mouchette. "What death are you talking about?"

And she mechanically clung to the loose part of his cassock, even though each of his steps pushed her aside, out of breath and stuttering, against the edge of the bank. The ridiculousness of this pursuit, the humiliation of asking questions in her turn, almost of imploring, were bitter to her pride. Yet she also felt something like an obscure joy. She was still speaking when they quit the path and came out upon the plain. She at once recognized the spot.

It was the little crossroads, hemmed in by quickset hedges, planted with scraggy lime trees in the old-time fashion, a couple of hundred yards from the first houses of Trilly. On the first Sunday in August—when the patronal feast was celebrated—itinerant merchants set up there their sorry shops on wheels, and sometimes those who liked such amusements danced with the girls.

Once again they confronted each other, face to face, as they had at the moment of their meeting. The sad dawn wandered across the sky and the tall silhouette of the curate seemed to Miss Malorthy taller still when, with a sovereign gesture, ineffably powerful and gentle, he moved toward her, holding his black sleeve above her head: "Do not be astonished at what I am going to say: above all don't see anything in it able to arouse the astonishment or curiosity of anyone. I am myself only a poor man. But when the spirit of rebellion was in you, I saw the name of God written in your heart."

And, lowering his arm, he traced a double cross with his thumb on Mouchette's bosom.

She bounded backward lightly, without finding a word to say, in stupid astonishment. And when she no longer heard within herself the echo of that voice of which the sweetness had pierced her through and through, his fatherly eyes completed her confusion.

So fatherly!... (For he had himself tasted the poison and taken delight in its long bitterness.)

The human tongue cannot be sufficiently constrained to express in abstract terms the certainty of a real presence, for all our certainties are deduced, and to the greater part of men experience is only, at the evening of a long life, the end of a long journey around their own nothingness. No clarity save logic springs from the reason, no other universe is given save that of species and genera. No fire save the divine which can bend and melt the ice of concepts. And yet that which revealed itself in this hour to Father Donissan's eyes was not at all a symbol or a figure; it was a living soul, a heart sealed to all others! No more than at the moment of their extraordinary meeting would he have been able to justify in words this external vision of ever equal brilliance, which melted and blended into the interior light wherewith he himself was saturated. In like fashion a child's first vision is so full and so pure that the universe of which he has just possessed himself cannot at first be severed from the quivering of his own joy. All its colors and all its shapes flower at once in his triumphal laughter.

When later on he was questioned about this gift of reading within souls, he first denied, and almost always stubbornly. At times, also, fearing that he might be, he gave a clearer account of it, but with so many scruples and so innocent an attempt at precision that his words were often a fresh disappointment to the curious. After such a fashion might some pious villager interpret the ecstasy and union in God of Saint Teresa or of Saint John of the Cross. This is because life is no more than confusion and disorder to anyone who meditates it from without. Thus supernatural man is at his ease as high as love bears him, and his spiritual life involves no dizziness the moment he has received the magnificent gifts, without his stopping to define them and even without his seeking to name them.

What do you see? people would ask the holy man. When do you see? What warning? What sign? And he would repeat, in the voice of a studious child who cannot think of the answer to an elementary question: "I have pity.... I only have pity!..." When he had met Miss Malorthy along the roadside, seeing in front of him merely an almost indiscernible shadow, a violent pity was already in his heart. Is it not thus that a mother wakes with a start, knowing with full certainty that her child is in peril? The charity of great souls, their supernatural compassion, seems to carry them at once to the most intimate inwardness of beings. Charity, like reason, is one of the elements of our consciousness. Yet if it has its laws, its deductions are as quick as the thunderbolt, and the mind which seeks to follow them sees only the flash of their lightning.

The look which the man of God kept lowered upon Mouchette would, perhaps, have made any other person fall to his knees. And the truth is that for a moment she felt herself hesitant and in a sense softened. But then help came to her—a help never awaited in vain—from a master daily more attentive and more severe; a dream once scarcely distinct from other dreams, a desire hardly keener, a voice among a thousand other voices, at present real and living; companion and torturer, by turns complaining, pining, source of tears, then importunate, rough, eager to impose restraints, then again instantly decisive, cruel, fierce, the whole of him dwelling in a sorrowful, bitter laugh, formerly servant and now master.

This all at once gushed forth from within her. A blind anger, a frenzy to set this look at defiance, to close her soul to it, to humble the pity which she felt hanging over her, to mark it with infamy, to defile it. Her outburst hurled her, her whole body quivering, not at the judge's feet but in his face, the judge in his sovereign silence.

At first she could not find a word to say; was there any to express this savage rage? She merely reviewed in her mind, but with a superhuman speed and sharpness, the major disappointments of her short life, as though the pity of this priest were their terminus and their crowning....

At last she was able, in an almost unintelligible voice, to shape these syllables: "I hate you!"

"Do not be ashamed," said he.

"Mind your own business," cried Mouchette. (Yet he had so accurately hit the mark that it was as though her wrath was baffled by it.) "I don't even know what you're talking about!"

"Undoubtedly other ordeals await you," he continued, "and harder ones.... How old are you?" he asked after a brief silence.

For a moment, Mouchette's eyes had betrayed a certain surprise, already come to nought. At these last words she made a violent effort and smiled. "You should know, you who know so much...."

"Up to this day you have lived as a child. Who has not pity for a little child? And such are the fathers of this world! Oh! you see, God helps us even in our madnesses. And when man arises to curse Him, it is He alone Who supports that feeble hand!"

"A child," said she, "a child! You won't find many little choir-singers like me in your vestries; they'd have no use for your holy water. The roads I have traveled—you'd better wish never to know them!"

She uttered these last words with a slightly comic emphasis. He calmly replied: "What then have you found in sin which might be worth so much grief and turmoil? If the quest for evil and its possession involve some hideous joy, you can be sure that another trampled out its juices for himself alone and drank them to the dregs."

Father Donissan again took a step toward her. Nothing in his demeanor expressed any inordinate emotion or the desire to astound. Nevertheless the words he spoke riveted her to the spot and reverberated in her heart.

"Give up such thoughts," said he. "You are not guilty before God of this murder. Any more than your will was free a moment ago. You are like a plaything, like a child's toy ball, in the hands of Satan."

He did not give her time to answer, and besides, she was speechless. Even now, while he talked, he was sweeping her along the Desvres road, taking broad strides amidst the empty fields. She followed him. She must follow him. He spoke as he had never spoken, as he never again would speak, even at Lumbres and in the fullness of his gifts, for she was his first prey. What she heard was not the judge's sentence, nor anything that might surpass the understanding of this lowly and sullen little animal, but—with a terrible gentleness—her own story, the story of Mouchette, not dramatized by a stage manager, adorned with rare and exotic detail, but indeed summarized, reduced to nothing, seen from within. How little substance does the sin which devours us leave to life! What she saw burning to ashes in the fire of words was herself, withholding nothing from the straight, sharp flame, backed to the last turning, to the last fiber of flesh. In proportion to the rise and fall of the dreadful voice, its impact reaching her very bowels, she felt her life's warmth wax and wane, that voice at first a separate entity, with its everyday words, which her terror welcomed as a friendly face in a frightful dream, then more and more mingled with the inner testimony, the harrowing murmur of her conscience, churned to its deep source—so much so that the two voices now made but one lament, like a single ruby jet of blood.

Yet when he grew silent, she felt she was still alive.

This silence was long drawn out, or at least lasted an interval beyond measurement, indiscernible. Then the voice—but come from so far!—reached her ears anew.

"Pull yourself together," it said. "Don't overtax yourself. You've said enough about it."

"Said enough? What have I said? I haven't said a thing."

"We have talked," resumed the voice. "Indeed we have had a long talk. See how the sky is growing light; the night is almost over.

"Did I say anything?" she repeated in a tone of supplication.

And, abruptly (as, at the instant of awakening, the accomplished act looms up in the memory, with brutal clarity): "I've spoken!" she cried. "I've spoken!"

In the gray of dawn she recognized the curate of Campagne's face. It expressed an infinite weariness. And his eyes, in which the flame for the moment was erased, seemed as though surfeited with the mysterious vision.

And she felt so weak, so defenseless, that she could not then have taken a step, she thought, either to approach him or to avoid him. She faltered.

"Is it possible?" she went on. "By what right?..."

"I have no rights over you," he gently replied. "If God..."

"God!" she began... But she could not finish. The spirit of revolt within her was apparently benumbed.

"How you struggle in His hand," said he sadly. "Shall you again escape Him? I hardly know...."

In a most humble voice, after a fresh silence, he added: "SPARE ME, MY DAUGHTER!"

His pallor was frightening. The hand he raised toward her fell back awkwardly; he averted his eyes.

And already she was impatiently clenching her little fists.

He saw her, as he had glimpsed her in the shadows an hour earlier, with that face of a child grown old, shrunken, beyond recognition. The uselessness of his great effort, the scattering to the winds of the divine graces which had just been so lavishly poured forth, there, on that spot—the inexorable foreboding rent his heart.

"God!" she exclaimed with a harsh laugh.

The pale dawn gradually spread about them, and all they saw of it was its pathetic reflection upon their own faces. To their right the hamlet, scarcely free of the fog, in the hollows of the little hills, made a scene of desolation. In the vast plain, infinite, alone, there lived a thin twist of smoke, above an invisible roof.

Then Mouchette's laughter became silent. The flickering flame in her eyes died away. And of a sudden, pitiable, at the end of her strength, stubborn, she begged once more: "I didn't want to offend you.... Didn't you lie to me just now? I didn't say anything. What would I have said to you? It seems to me I was asleep. Have I been asleep?"

He appeared not to hear her. She redoubled her efforts: "Don't refuse me.... You can't refuse to answer.... If only you'll tell me, I'll do anything you say."

Never had this strange girl's voice made itself so humble, so beseeching.

Still he did not answer.

She stepped back a few paces, stared him a long while in the face, ardently, her eyebrows puckered, her forehead lowered, and then she abruptly said: "I confessed everything. You know all!"

But, immediately recovering herself: "Well, suppose you do? I'm not afraid of anything. What is it to me?... But tell me...Oh! tell me, what did you do? Did I really talk in my sleep?"

In her utter exhaustion, her unconquerable curiosity was already propelling her toward a new adventure. The blood was mounting to her cheeks. Her eyes were recapturing their dark flame. And as for him, he contemplated her with pity, or perhaps with scorn.

For, to his great surprise, the vision had been obliterated, had disappeared into the void. His remembrance of it was too keen, too precise for him to have any doubts. The interchange of words still rang in his ears. But the shadows again had fallen. Why then did he not obey the inner impulse which commanded him to depart without delay? Here before him stood a poor creature merely hastily reweaving the briefly torn web of her lies.... Yet had he not been for a moment—for an eternity!—through an effort almost divine, set free from his own nature? Was it despair for this power lost? Or frenzy to reconquer it? Or anger at finding a rebel once more in the wretched child just since at his mercy? He moved his shoulders in a gesture of enormous brutality.

"I have seen you!" For the first time he used the familiar form of the pronoun, and she shuddered with anger. "I have seen you as perhaps no other creature like you has ever been seen in this world! I have seen you in such fashion that you cannot escape me, with all your wiles. Do you think that your sin horrifies me? You have scarcely offended God more than do the animals. You have carried about within you only counterfeit crimes, just as you bore within you only a fetus. Look inside yourself! Stir up the slime within you: the vice on which you pride yourself has long since rotted there; at every hour of the day your heart bursts with loathing. From out of yourself you have extracted nothing but vain dreams, always disappointed. You think you have killed a man.... Poor girl! You liberated him from you. You have with your own hands destroyed the sole possible instrument of your own detestable liberation. And a few weeks later you were groveling at the feet of another not as good as he. And that other one made you eat dirt. You despise him and he fears you. But you cannot escape him."

"I cannot...escape...him," stammered Mouchette. Her terror and her frenzy were such that upon her excessively mobile, now hardened face there manifested itself an ill-omened serenity. "I know that I can," she finally said. "When I want to. People thought I was crazy; what have I done to set them all straight? I was waiting until I'd be ready, that's all."

He pressed his hand so violently on her shoulder that she staggered, "You will never be ready. You pilfer from God only the worst—the mud of which you are made, Satan! Do you think yourself free? You would only have been so in God. Your life..."

He breathed deeply, like a wrestler about to make his supreme effort. And already there was rising into his eyes the same glow of superhuman clarity, but stripped, this time, of all pity. So he had once more conquered the perilous gift, conquered it by force, through a desperate yearning capable of doing violence, even to heaven itself. God's grace had made itself visible to his mortal eyes: they now beheld only the enemy, reveling in his prey. And already Mouchette's pale face, as though shrunk by anguish, was foundering into the same dream, whereof the hideous reflection was exchanged between their two pairs of eyes.

"Your life repeats other lives, all alike, lived listlessly, just at the level of the troughs where your cattle eat their grain. Yes, each of your actions is the token of one performed by those from whom you spring, base misers, lustful wretches, and liars. I see them. God grants me to see them. True, I have seen you in them, and them in you. Oh! How dangerous and tiny is our place here below! How strait is our path!"

And he began to say things even more singular, his voice, however, lowered, and speaking with great simplicity.

How can any account be given of them here? This was again the story of Mouchette, marvelously blended with other old stories forgotten long since, if, indeed, they were ever known. Before she understood its meaning, Mouchette felt her heart contract, as though she were unexpectedly falling, and likewise that surprise which makes the most scatterbrained hesitate at the threshold of a deep and secret dwelling. Then there were names—heard, familiar, or merely brimming with vague recollection, more and more numerous, one casting light upon the other, until the very web of the narrative could be made out, underlying all. Humble facts of daily life, without any luster whatever, embedded in the most commonplace spite—like pebbles in their sheath of mud-dull secrets, dull lies, dull drivelings of vice, dull adventures which a name suddenly uttered lit up like a beacon, only to fall back into the shadows, where the mind would even then not have distinguished anything, but which a kind of holy disgust arraigned for what it was: a crawling mass of dingy lives. Although Mouchette once again felt herself swept away, despite her will and her reason, it was this very disgust which lived and thought on her behalf. For at the frontier of the invisible world, anguish is a sixth sense, and pain and perception are but one. Those names which the again sovereign voice uttered one after the other she recognized in their passage—but not all of them. They were those of the Malorthys, the Brissauts, the Paunys, the Pichons, ancestors and ancestresses, traders beyond reproach, careful housekeepers, loving their own goods, never deceased intestate, the glory of chambers of commerce and attorneys' offices. (Your Aunt Susan, your Uncle Henry, your Grandmothers Adela and Malvina or Cecelia...) But what the voice told, entirely in monotone, few ears had ever heard—the story grasped from within—the most hidden story, the best-guarded; not cut-and-dried, not locked in the interplay of effects and causes, of acts and intentions, but brought into relation with certain major facts, with the basic failings. And assuredly Mouchette's intelligence, left to itself, would have gathered but little from such an account, the terrible gaps in which would have led more clear-headed persons astray. Where the voice found its echo—was it not in her very flesh, which each of these faults had marked with its mark, had weakened at the very instant when she was conceived? At seeing these dead men and women little by little emerge stripped naked from their shrouds, she did not even feel anything you might call surprise. She listened to this superhuman revelation with a heart swallowed by anguish, though without genuine curiosity or amazement. It seemed as though she had already heard it, *or something better yet*. Slanderous lies, hatreds long cherished, shameful loves, calculated crimes of avarice and hate—the whole business gradually took shape within her, just as, when you are awakening, takes shape some cruel image of your dream. Never, never were the dead so brutally torn from their dust, cast abroad, opened. At a word, at a name unexpectedly spoken, as though over the surface of a bubble of mud, something clambered from the past into the present—act, desire, or, sometimes, deeper and more intimate, a single thought (for it was not dead with the dead), yet so intimate, so deep, so fiercely torn free that Mouchette greeted it with a groan of shame. No longer did she distinguish between the pitiless voice and her own inner revelation, a thousand times richer and fuller. Moreover, quicker than any human speech, those numberless phantoms springing up on all sides could not even have been given names; yet, as through a tempest of sounds the dominant rises irresistible, so a clear and active will was completing the organization of this chaos. In vain did Mouchette, in an artless gesture of defense, raise her little hands against the enemy. Whereas another dream, the moment it is examined with composure, steals away and is scattered, this one drew closer and closer toward her, like soldiery gathering for the charge. The crowd, so swarming a moment earlier, in which she had recognized all her own people, gradually shrank. Faces superposed themselves, one upon the other, now forming but a single face, which was the very countenance of a vice. Confused gestures froze into one single attitude, which was the gesture of crime. Even more: at times evil left of its prey only a shapeless mass, fullblown with rot, swollen with its own venom, digested. The misers made up a mass of living gold, the lustful a pile of entrails. Everywhere sin was bursting its shell, was laying bare the mystery of its procreation: scores of men and women bound together in the fibers of the same cancer, the frightful bonds meanwhile retracting, like the severed limbs of an octopus, into the very core of the horrible creature, into the initial failing, known to no one, in a child's heart.... And abruptly Mouchette saw herself as she had never seen herself, not even at that moment when she had felt her pride shattered: something gave way within her, with a giving way more irremediable, and then plunged in hidden flight. The voice, ever low, but with a living, burning touch, had, as it were, laid her bare, fiber by fiber. She doubted whether she existed, whether she had existed. In her mind every abstraction took on a shape and could be pressed to her bosom or rejected. And what is to be said of this buckling of her consciousness itself! She had recognized herself in her own and, in the paroxysm of her frenzy, no longer distinguished between herself and that herd. What! not one of her life's acts which had not elsewhere its double? Not a thought which was her very own, not a motion which had not long since been made? Not alike, but the same. Not repeated, but one. Without her being able to state in intelligible words any one of the clarities which were completing her destruction, she felt in her wretched little life the huge deceit, the huge laughter of the deceiver. Each of those mocking forebears, monotonous in his baseness, having recognized and nosed out in her his or her property, came to take it; she was relinquishing her all. She yielded everything, and it was as though the herd had come to devour her own life cupped in her own hands. What to contest with them? What to take back? They possessed even her rebellion itself.

Now she started up, beating the air with her hands, her head thrown back, then tumbling from one shoulder to the other, exactly like a drowned man sinking. Sweat poured over her face, as though a torrent of tears, while her eyes, devoured by the inward vision, presented to the curate of Campagne only a metal grown hard and cold. No cry issued from her lips, though one seemed to flutter in her silent throat. This cry, which was not heard, nonetheless impressed its shape upon the shriveled mouth, the bent neck, the thin shoulders, the hollowed loins, upon the whole body, which seemed stretched upward for an appeal of despair.... At last she fled.

As far as the first turn in the road, she believed she did not hurry, whereas she was even then almost running. At the foot of the slope, when the thin hedges and the crowded trunks of the apple trees afforded her cover, she took flight with all the speed her legs could muster. Upon approaching Campagne, however, she left the main road and instinctively took the path—deserted at that hour—which allowed her to reach her garden without being seen. Obviously she had no thought, no desire, other than to find herself alone, behind a tight-shut door, sheltered, alone. The outside world, the familiar horizon, even the sky belonged to her enemy. Her dread, or, to be more exact, her derangement, was so acute that, had only the opportunity arisen, she would have cried for help to absolutely anyone, even her father.

But the opportunity did not arise. The kitchen was empty. She dashed upstairs, shot the bolt on her door, threw herself across her bed, then at once jumped up again as though something had bitten her, hurled herself toward the window, pulled back the curtains, and, seeing her own eyes in the mirror, sprang back like a startled animal.

"Is that you, Germaine?" asked Madame Malorthy through the partition.

Only the mirror beheld the new thing in Mouchette's eyes, the frenzied grimace of her lips. She answered in a low, calm voice: "It's I, Mother."

And before the old woman had been able to slip in a word, without faltering, without even thinking about it, she found the only lie not wholly lacking in verisimilitude. "Cousin George drove me back in his wagon as far as the hamlet of Viel. He was going to the Viel-Aubin market."

"At this hour in the morning?"

"He left very early because he had a load of pigs. I had to take the opportunity or walk home."

"You haven't eaten," answered her mother. "I'll make you a little coffee."

"The truth is I've had no sleep and so I'm going to bed," said Mouchette. "Leave me alone."

"Do open your door," Madame Malorthy began again.

"No," Mouchette wildly cried. Recovering herself at once, she added in her small voice, dry and hard, which made her mother tremble: "All I need is sleep. Good night."

And when she heard the sound of the wooden clogs grow fainter at the turn in the staircase, her knees bent under her; she slumped in the shadowy corner without a word, without a glance.

Present peril begets only fear, which dulls a coward's responses. It benumbs before it kills. Terror awakens later, when the blunted consciousness little by little takes cognizance and possession of its ill-omened guest. Sentence strikes the condemned man like the stone from a sling, and the turnkey who takes him back to his cell dumps upon the pallet there something like a corpse. But when he opens his eyes in the deep and gentle night, the poor wretch is suddenly aware that he is a stranger among men.

Rarely did Mouchette take the time to study herself with any care; in such employment she found no pleasure whatever. Her lack of experience in these matters was profound; it resembled innocence. However far back she went in the past, of scruples and remorse she had only known that vague discomfort—the fear of peril or its defiance, the vague awareness of being for a moment outside the law, the totally wakeful instinct of an animal far from its lair, on an unfamiliar path. Even at that very instant nothing troubled her except the mysterious danger glimpsed a little while earlier, the will which had broken hers, the ridiculous priest known to everyone, greeted along the street, commonplace, who saw her bend her knees.

This recollection was still so strong that it pushed aside all the others: she had run into something that blocked her way, and the obstacle was that priest. Formerly such a circumstance would have aroused her wrath and set taut the thousand strands of her guile. What this time held her in utter abasement was the surprise of feeling only a bitter disgust in the bottom of her humiliated heart.

For a moment—for one single moment—the idea occurred to her (but so disconcerted, even at seeing itself take shape): to shatter the obstacle, to repeat the murderous deed. At once she pushed it aside; it seemed to her pointless and grotesque, like something undertaken in a dream. You don't kill for the sake of a few obscure words. Such was the reason she alleged to herself; but it was truer that by striking home to her pride, her harsh adversary had broken her life's one source of energy.

Danger would, rather, have excited her; the hateful would not have stopped her. She feared only something which might have been ridicule or pity. As sometimes happens, the words which suddenly sprang to her lips without her seeking them expressed her deep fear: "They'll think I'm altogether crazy," she muttered.

Crazy!… Here for a long minute she halted her thoughts. Until then, even at the Campagne asylum, she had not doubted her sanity. From the instant when she regained consciousness, she had listened to the discussion of her case with ironical curiosity. What had they known—those fine gentlemen—about her terrible adventure? Almost nothing; the essential portion of it remained her secret. Surrounded by this new audience, she was what she had wanted to be, still resembling her favorite imaginary character, a girl of danger and mystery, with a unique destiny, a heroine among the cowardly and the dim-witted…. And yet, today, this very moment…

What justified her terror? At the bend in the deserted road she had left behind her only the young priest, whom she had encountered many times before, harmless in appearance and even a bit benighted. Of course he had talked. But what had he said that was so serious? At this point the effort she was making to recover herself, to get control of herself, stopped short. As the minutes passed, it seemed clearer to her, however, that in some fashion or other she had been tricked. She had taken alarm over a certain number of vague phrases, of allusions seemingly underhanded— perhaps innocent, clumsily interpreted. And what were they? A word said at random about the crime already so long past, almost forgotten, a word intended rather to reassure her. "You are not guilty before God of this murder…" (in vain did she repeat the very words; she did not recapture the humiliated rage which then so powerfully agitated her heart). What more? Reproaches, exhortations to change her ways… (she could not frankly remember any) and finally… (here her memory stopped short) a certain extraordinary revelation which had upset her to such an extent that, the anguish it had caused being all that remained of it, she was unable to say why she had crouched down in the corner of her room, her face on her knees, prickly from shivering, her teeth chattering. There! *There is the secret.* It was only then that she had fled. It was then that this dreadful emptiness was hollowed out within her. Was it possible? Was it really possible that she should have fled—and with such a despairing flight—from vague tales about her and hers surely winnowed from village gossip? It was true that she had believed them, and she still knew enough about them to be certain that at a given moment she could not have not believed them. No doubt the same presence and the same words would have convinced her afresh. But what of it? Had she ever been fearful of the hatred of fools? But what on earth could he have told that was new, this priest? The terror which, as it were, had torn her asunder in order to hurl her here trembling did not spring from him. She had been deceived by nothing more than a dream...and this dream which she carried away benumbed can suddenly revive... Oh! oh! see how already her heart was beating and throbbing, while the sweat streamed down between her shoulders. The surge of anguish shook her, the frightful icy caress firmly grasped her throat. The shriek to which she gave vent could be heard in every corner of the room, and even the wall trembled from it.

Once again she found herself lying flat on her belly over the foot of her bed. The eider quilt had slipped beneath her and she had sunk her fangs into it, so that her mouth was full of down. The silence was now unbroken, and abruptly she realized that she had cried out only in a dream. And at the moment, with all the strength that remained to her, she was holding back, she was stifling another scream. For in a flash she saw herself brought back to the asylum, the door locked tight behind her, this time crazy for good and all—crazy in her own eyes—even by her own admission.... At first she groaned under her breath and then became silent.

At times, when the soul itself cowers within its jacket of flesh, the most abject creature longs for a miracle and, if he knows not how to pray, at least instinctively, like a mouth spread wide to catch a breath, opens himself to God. But fruitlessly would the wretched girl resort to what life was left her, in order to solve the puzzle she had set herself. How would she raise herself by her own powers to the height where the man of God had suddenly carried her, and from which she was now fallen low? Of the light which had pierced her through and through—poor lonely little beast—there remained but her unknown pain, of which she was dying and which she did not understand. She writhed, the dazzling weapon plunged deep into her heart, and the hand which had driven it home did not know its own cruelty. As for divine mercy, she knew it not and was even incapable of imagining it.... How many others struggle thus, bootlessly clasped against the breast of the angel whose face they have glimpsed and then forgotten! Curiously men watch the antics of some individual among these, sealed with this seal, and are astonished to see him by turns frantically seeking pleasure, despairing in its possession, surveying all things with eyes thirsting and hard, from which even the reflection of what he desired has been erased!

For two long hours, now coiled against herself, motionless, now twisting on the floor in a dumb, convulsive frenzy, and now bludgeoned by a horrible sleepiness, she believed she really was losing her reason, believed she was one by one going down the black steps. Her career was redrawn before her, line by line; she glanced at its various stages. It was like a series of paintings, each appearing with lightning speed. She took account of each of the characters there depicted, scrutinized their faces, listened to their voices. At every image sought for, brought to life, willfully sucked dry, she literally felt her sense and her reason quiver, like a frail ship in the wind; always her transparent anguish once more got the upper hand. She had reached the point of deliberately provoking within her the powers of disorder, summoning madness as others summon death. Yet by a deep instinct, barely conscious, she forbade herself the only outward expression which would have hazarded the breaking of her strength: she uttered no cry, she smothered even her groans: one single witness of her delirium would have been enough to put her out of her depth. That she knew; she did not call, To the extent that, despite herself, her inner resistance grew firmer, her motions became an artificial tossing about; her frenzy was wearing itself out through its very violence. She was gradually becoming the spectator of her own madness. When she saw herself once more breathing vigorously, as in the waning of a great dream—a dreadful calm re-established in her soul—her disappointment was total, absolute. It was like the wind suddenly ceasing over a raging sea on a black night.

The same unknown thing was still lacking to her, was lacking to her life. But what? But what was it? Fruitlessly she wiped her cheeks, torn raw by her fingernails, her bitten lips; fruitlessly she watched the light of dawn through the windowpanes; fruitlessly she repeated in her sad, lackluster voice: "It's finished… it's finished!…" The truth appeared to her; what was clear to see crushed her heart; even insanity refused her its darkling asylum. No, she was not crazy, would never be so. That thing was lacking to her which she had held in her arms—but where? but when? how? And now it was a certainty that for some moments she had been playing the role of madness to hide, to forget—whatever the price—her real, incurable, unknown ill.

(Oh! Sometimes God calls us in a voice so urgent and so gentle! Yet when He unexpectedly withdraws, the howling which bursts forth from the disappointed flesh must astonish hell!)

Then it was she called—from her deepest, her most secret reaches—with a summons that was like the gift of herself—then it was she called to Satan.

After all, whether or not she uttered his name, he was not to come except in his own time and by a roundabout road. That pale star, even when entreated, rises infrequently from the abyss. What is more, she could not have said, in her half-consciousness, what offering she was making of herself and to whom. It had come unexpectedly, rose less from her mind than from her poor sullied flesh. The compunction which the man of God had for a moment brought to life within her was no longer but a suffering among her sufferings. The instant confronting her was wholly anguish. The past a black hole. The future another black hole. The road others travel step by step she had already traversed; however trifling her career by comparison with so many fabulous sinners, her hidden spite had drained all the evil of which she was capable—except for one offense: the last. Since childhood her quest had been directed toward him, every disillusionment having been only an excuse for a new challenge. For she loved him.

Where hell finds its best windfalls is not among the crowd of turbulent spirits who amaze the world with resounding crimes. The greatest of saints are not always wonder-workers, for the contemplative most often lives and dies unknown. Now hell likewise has its cloisters.

So here we behold her, this wide-eyed mystic, little servant of Satan, Saint Brigit of the void. Except for one murder, no spoor of her will remain upon the earth. Her life is a secret between herself and her master, or rather the secret of her master alone. He did not seek her out among the powerful; their nuptials were consummated in silence. She went forward to the goal, not step by step, but by leaps and bounds, and touched it when she thought she was not yet so near. She would receive her guerdon. Alas! there lives not the man who, having made up his mind and having discounted remorse, has not, for an instant at least, hurled himself upon evil with manifest covetousness, as though to choke off its curse, cruel dream which makes lovers moan, maddens the murderer, lights a final glow in the eyes of the wretch determined to die when, the rope already tight around his neck, he shoves the chair away with a wild kick.... So it was, but several times as intensely, that Mouchette desired in her soul, without naming him, the presence of the cruel Lord.

He came at once, abruptly, with no fluttering of wings, dreadfully peaceful and sure. However far he strains his likeness to God, no joy can proceed from him; yet, far superior to the pleasures which move only the entrails, his masterwork is a dumb peace, lonely, icy, comparable to the delight of nothingness. When this gift is offered and received, the angel who watches us, astounded, turns away his face.

He came, and the moment he was there, Mouchette's turmoil miraculously ceased, her heart beat slowly, gradually warmth returned, her body and her soul were but the firm, calculated expectation—free of useless impatience-of an event thenceforward certain. Almost at the same moment, her brain imagined it, clothed it in the fullness of reality. And she understood that the hour had struck for killing herself; above all, without delay, *at that very instant.*

Before her limbs had made a movement, her spirit already fled along the road of release. And she dashed hard on its heels. Strange thing: her eyes alone remained disquieted and wavering. All her sentient life lay at the tips of her fingers, in the palms of her nimble hands. She opened the door without letting it creak, pushed wide that leading to her father's room (at that hour always empty), took the razor from its accustomed place, and fully bared its blade. In no time she was back in her own room, facing the mirror, tiptoe on her tiny feet, her chin thrown back, her throat stretched tight, proffered.... Whatever her inclination may have been, she did not hack at it with the steel, but savagely, consciously, she pressed home the cutting edge and heard it slice her flesh. Her last recollection was the spurt of lukewarm blood upon her hand, fanning out as far as the fold of her arm.

4.

AT THE CHURCH, in the sacristy, the key of which he had always in his pocket, Father Donissan awaited the hour set for his Mass, which he celebrated as usual. For some days Father Menou-Segrais had kept to his room, suffering from a rather more violent attack of asthma. About half past ten, looldng out at the road, he saw his curate and was astonished. Within the instant, however, the heavy shoes echoed on the flagstones in the vestibule, and then on the stairway. Finally, behind the closed door, his voice, ever firm and calm, inquired: "May I come in, Dean?"

"Gladly," cried the pastor of Campagne, his curiosity aroused. "Come right in."

He stiffly turned his head, which was sunk between two huge pillows propped against the back of the big easy chair. The young priest's face seemed indistinct to him in the dimness of the room (the curtains were still half drawn). What he saw of it was quite enough to give the lie to the voice's feigned calm. Yet the older man expressed his astonishment only by a fluttering of the eyelashes over a sharp glance.

"What a surprise!" he very gently began. "How is it you are already back?"

He took good care not to motion him to any chair, knowing from experience that when the poor fellow stood before him, arms dangling, his awkwardness doubled his natural timidity, kept him the better at his elder's mercy.

"I made an ass of myself, as always," replied Father Donissan. "In short, I got lost. . . ."

"So you arrived at Etaples too late and confessions were over?"

"I haven't told you the worst," the curate woefully admitted.

'Well, well!" exclaimed Father Menou-Segrais, violently striking the arm of his chair with a liveliness very different from his usual manner. "And I ask you, what are those gentlemen going to say? To get there late is one thing. But not to arrive at all!"

However little he ordinarily cared about the opinion of others, he feared ridicule with a nervous apprehension which was, if you like, the feminine element in a nature nonetheless quite adequately male. And of what derision would he not be the butt, indirectly, through the person of his curate, already quite enough an object of fun! However, catching sight of Father Donissan's eyes and their magnificent loyalty, he blushed at his weakness and continued placidly: "What's done is done. I'll drop the canon a line tonight, asking him to forgive *us*. Now tell me..."

Taking pity, he waved to a chair with his outstretched hand. To his great surprise, his curate remained standing.

"Tell me," he repeated, in a very different tone of authority and concern, "how did you get lost in a country which after all is not a wilderness?"

Father Donissan kept his head bent to one side, and his bearing expressed humble respect. Yet his answer was surprising: "Should I tell you what I believe to be the truth?"

"You should," replied Father Menou-Segrais.

"Then I shall," said the curate of Campagne.

His blanched face, still furrowed by the terrors and fatigues of the night before, displayed a resolution already formed and inevitably to be accomplished. The only indication he gave of his shame was to turn aside his head. He spoke, with lowered eyes and perhaps a little hastily....

What was more, the plainness of certain things he said, their boldness, the clear solicitude not to withhold anything, would have betrayed, even to a less shrewd observer, the likely secret hope for some interruption, for some vehement disagreement which would have come to the poor priest's aid without having him break his promise. He was listened to, however, in deep silence.

"I did not go astray," he began. "At the worst, I might have got lost halfway, in the midst of the plain. That is why I took the main road; I left it only for a moment. All I had to do was walk straight ahead of me. Even in the middle of the night (for I must admit the night was dark) it was impossible to miss my goal. If I did not reach it, others than I will be to blame."

He stopped to regain breath: "However strange, however idiotic this may seem to you," he continued, "there is something stranger, something madder. Something worse. Another ordeal had been prepared for me."

At this point his voice became unsteady and his hand made the involuntary gesture of a man surprised in the midst of a narrative by some major objection. His eyes fixed themselves, humbly this time, upon the dean's countenance.

"I should like to ask you…is it wholly blameless to recount an adventure like this one—even an absurd adventure—to interpret it as seems proper to me"—again he hesitated—"…by attributing to myself, involuntarily, a certain role…and insights?…"

"Continue! Continue!" Father Menou-Segrais cut him short.

He obeyed, for, after a silence during which he seemed rather to be striving to avoid all useless circumlocutions, all temptation to retain the good opinion of him to whom he spoke, he went on: "God has twice allowed me, and without the least possible doubt, to see a soul, with my own eyes, through the fleshly impediment. And this not by ordinary means, by study and reflection, but by a special, marvelous grace, whereof I owe you my avowal, whatever it may cost me.…"

"Which you consider a miracle?" asked Father Menou-Segrais in his most ordinary tone of voice.

"I believe it to be such," said he.

"You will make a report of it to your bishop," was the dean of Campagne's simple reply.

Moreover, there was not the least surprise in the glance with which he enfolded—literally—the strange form of his curate; no surprise, but a quiet attentiveness, unconcerned with personalities, barely curious about the facts, possessing a hint of lofty pity. The curate blushed to the roots of his hair.

"What on earth did you meet, out in the open country in the middle of the night?"

"First of all a man, whose name I do not know."

"Oh!" was Father Menou-Segrais's only comment.

"Understand," added Father Donissan with a woeful trembling of his lips. "He began the conversation.... I had no thought of anything of the kind.... I did not even see his face.... I did not recognize his voice. We walked along together a little while. We talked of trifling things...the weather...the night...what have you?..."

He stopped, seized with remorse at hiding a part of the truth from his judge. And then, abruptly, to get it over with: "This was the moment when I received that grace, that illumination to which I have referred. As for the other meeting..."

"I know enough about the case...at least for the moment," interrupted the dean. "The details matter little."

He leaned his head on the pillow and, painfully twisting his features, pulled his tobacco pouch from the depths of his pocket; he snuffed his pinch and, indolently raising his hands, as though courteously to excuse himself for interrupting an ordinary conversation: "Would you ring for Madame Estelle? It's time for me to take my dose of salicylate, and I don't know where she's put the bottle."

The bottle was duly discovered in its usual place. He drank slowly, wiping his lips with great care, and then dismissed the housekeeper with an affectionate glance. When the door was closed behind her, he said, "You are going to be taken for a madman, my boy."

He was addressing, however (and well he knew it), one of those men whose experience is wholly internal, as though shaped inwardly, and whose equilibrium is not easily upset. Barely did a slight contraction of the face betray rather more surprise than fear. He quietly replied: "I owed you this confession. God is my witness that I want all this to be forgotten, that I want silence."

"Count on me," resumed the dean of Campagne, "to hide everything which can be hidden without lies. For, of course, I am your immediate superior, my friend, but I have my superiors as well!"

After an interval: "I am going to write...no! I'll go instead, I'll go see Canon Couvremont, the former spiritual director of the Major Seminary. There's a colleague who's very trustworthy, most staunch. He'll consider the matter. What's more, I'm pretty sure that he and

I shall quickly see things in the same light. I can readily surmise his decision."

Perhaps he expected a question, but he did not even get a look.

"We shall request on your behalf a long retreat at Tortefontaine, or with the Chevetogne Benedictines. I must be frank with you, Father. I have believed you, I still believe you, to be marked with a mark, chosen. Enough on that score. This is no longer the age of miracles. Miracles, rather, would arouse alarm, my friend. Such things concern the police. The authorities are only awaiting an excuse to pounce upon us. Then too, the neurological—as they call them—sciences are all the rage. A simple little priest who reads souls as one reads a book.... They'd take care of you, my boy. For my part, what you have said is all I need; I ask no more; indeed, I'd just as soon not hear any more."

He thrust out his two hands as though to ward off this dangerous secret, then let his head sink back into the hollow of the cushion. But at the curate's first movement of withdrawal, he exclaimed: "Mark, my word! I formally forbid you even to open your lips on such a subject without my previous authorization, and before anyone, no matter whom. No matter whom; do you understand?"

"Even my usual confessor?" Father Donissan timidly asked.

"Him above all," quietly replied the other.

Then silence, a heavier silence. Once, twice the curate's heavy body twisted from right to left and back, his eyes turned toward the door. With his right hand he nervously fingered the buttons of his cassock. And suddenly he heard, to his great astonishment, his own voice saying: "I have not told all."

There was no reply.

"What remains for me to tell concerns (how greatly, God knows!) the salvation of a poor soul for whom we shall be answerable, you and I. Providence seems to have entrusted that soul to me particularly, expressly, certainly, for this person belongs to your parochial family, Dean."

"I am listening," replied Father Menou-Segrais, slowly raising his eyes.

Not for a second, during the course of the long narrative which followed, did the clear and powerful eyes turn from the curate's harrowed face. A kind of sorrowful heedfulness could be read therein, and you could watch the manifest resolve little by little take shape. Not a word issued from the tight-closed mouth, not a tremor disturbed the long pallid hands resting on the arms of the easy chair, and the head, a trifle bent to one side, the chin high, was resplendent with intelligence and will.

When the curate had finished, the dean of Campagne unaffectedly turned toward the Florentine Christ hanging over the head of his bed and said, in a voice at once strong and tender: "God be praised, my son, for your having spoken so freely and so humbly. For such simplicity of heart disarms even the spirit of evil."

Beckoning the young priest to draw near, he lifted himself up slightly toward him, looked deep into his eyes, and, face to face, he said: "I believe you, I believe you without reserve. But I need a moment to think over what I am going to say about it.... Would you get from my table, to the right... there... yes; it's the *Imitation of Christ*. Open it, please, to Book III, Chapter LVI, and read, from the bottom of your heart, especially verses 5 and 6. Go on.... Pay no attention to me."

The aged priest, magnificently gifted, whom ignorance, injustice, and envy had in former years made ineffectual, felt at this unique moment that he was fulfilling his destiny. Comparisons are of small worth when we have to borrow them from ordinary affairs to convey some idea of happenings in the inner life and of their majesty. The time had come when this unusual man, at once subtle and passionate, as bold as any other, yet capable of bringing to bear on all things the sharp edge of the mind, was to show his full stature.

"'The shame of having fled glory...'" he murmured, quoting from memory the last words of the chapter. "Now, my friend, listen to me."

Obediently the curate of Campagne left the *prie-dieu* and remained standing at a few paces' distance.

"What you are going to hear," said Father Menou-Segrais, "will doubtless pain you. God knows that up until now I've been too sparing of you! And yet I should not like to upset you. Whatever I say, be not troubled. For you have committed no fault other than a fault arising from inexperience and zeal. Do you understand me?"

The priest nodded.

"You have acted like a child," continued the old priest after an interval of silence. "The trials which await you here are not of the sort one can face with presumption; more than ever—cost you what it may—you must turn your back on them, flee them, without so much as a glance behind you. Each of us is tempted only according to his strength. Our illicit desires are born, grow up, evolve with us. They are, like certain chronic maladies, a sort of compromise between sickness and health. In such case, patience is enough. But it can happen that the disease suddenly grows worse, that a new element..."

He interrupted himself, not without a certain embarrassment quickly overcome.

"First of all, mark this well: in the eyes of all the world you are henceforth (and until when?) merely a silly little priest, full of imagination and self-conceit, half dreamer, half liar, or else madman. So suffer the penance which will surely be imposed upon you, the silence and the temporary oblivion of the cloister, not as an unjust punishment, but as something needful and justified.... Again, have you understood me?"

The same glance and the same acknowledgment.

"Know this, my child. For months I have been watching you, probably with too much prudence, too much hesitancy. Yet from the very first day I saw clearly. Certain graces are showered upon you, as it were, beyond reason, without measure; obviously this is because you are extraordinarily tempted. The Holy Spirit is bountiful, but His generosities are never vain; He proportions them to our needs.

To my mind, this sign cannot mislead: the devil has come into your life."

Father Donissan still remained silent.

"Ah, my poor, dear child! Simpletons close their eyes to such things. Priests there are who dare not even utter the devil's name. What do they make of the inner life? The instincts' doleful battle-ground. Of morality? A hygiene for the senses. Grace is nothing more than a sound line of reasoning which entreats the intelligence, temptation a fleshly appetite which sets traps to corrupt it. Thus are they barely aware of the most commonplace incidents in the great conflict waged within us. Man is deemed to seek only the agreeable and the useful, conscience guiding his choice. Well-suited to the abstract man in books is this average man, encountered nowhere! Such childishnesses explain nothing. In such a universe of feeling and reasoning animals, there is nothing left for the saint, or else he must be convicted of madness. Good care is taken of that, needless to say. But the problem is not so cheaply solved. Each of us—Oh! if only you will remember these words of an old friend!—is by turns, in some fashion, a criminal or a saint— now inclined toward the good, not by a judicious appraisal of its advantages, but plainly and strangely by a thrust of the whole being, a spilling over of love, which makes of suffering and renunciation the very object of desire—now plagued by the mysterious taste for degradation, by delight in the savor of ashes, intoxication with animality, his homesickness beyond comprehension. Oh, well! What matters the experience of the moral life accumulated over the centuries. What matters the example of so many wretched sinners and their anguish! Yes, my son, remember. Evil, like good, is loved for itself, and served."

The dean of Campagne's naturally weak voice had little by little grown muffled, so that it had seemed, for the last few moments, intended for his own ear alone. This, however, was not at all the case. His eyes, under their half-lowered lids, continued fixed on Father Donissan's face. Up till then, that face had remained in appearance impassive. At these last words this impassivity abruptly melted away, and it was as though a mask had fallen.

"Must we believe it!" he cried out. "Are we truly so wretched!"

He did not finish what he had begun saying, and he seconded it with no gesture; an endless distress, doubtless far beyond any speech, so sorrowfully expressed itself in these stammered words of protest—the despairing resignation in his eyes filled with shadow —that Father Menou-Segrais almost involuntarily opened wide to him his arms. He threw himself within their embrace.

Now he was kneeling against the high, padded armchair, his rough head with its close-cropped hair innocently cast against his friend's breast.... But by common consent, their embrace was brief. The curate merely fell back into the attitude of a penitent at his confessor's feet. The dean's emotion expressed itself only in the slight trembling of the right hand with which he blessed him.

"These words scandalize you, my son. May they also fortify you! It is all too sure: your vocation is not that of the cloister."

A sad smile, quickly repressed, crossed his lips.

"The retreat which will soon be required of you will without any doubt be a time of trial and of very bitter abandonment. It will last longer than you think, be sure of that."

With a paternal look, not without its touch of very tender irony, he pondered at length the stooped face.

"You were not born to please, for you know what the world hates best, with a shrewd, knowing hate: the feeling and the taste for strength. They won't let you off easily."

"...The labor which God works in us," he resumed after a brief silence, "is rarely what we expect. Almost always the Holy Spirit seems to us to act against the grain, to lose time. If the block of iron could conceive the file which slowly rasps it away, what rage and what vexation! Yet it is thus God uses us. Certain saints' lives seem frighteningly monotonous, a true wilderness."

Gently he lowered his head, and for the first time Father Donissan saw his eyes cloud over and two tears from the depths well out of them. Then at once, shaking his head, he said: "Enough of this. We must hasten! For before long the hour will sound when, according to the world, I shall no longer be able to do anything on your behalf. Now let us speak plainly, as clearly as possible. Nothing is better than to express the supernatural in commonplace, popular language, in the vocabulary of day-to-day life. No illusion can stand up against that. I pass over your first adventure: whether you did or did not see face to face him whom we daily meet—not at all, alas! at a bend in the road, but within ourselves—how should I know? Did you see him really, or in a dream—what matters it to me? That which can seem to the generality of men the major happening, for the humble servant of God is more frequently only an accessory. There's no way to judge your clear-sightedness and your sincerity except by your works: your works will bear testimony for you. Let's say no more about that."

He hoisted his pillows, caught breath, and continued with the same strange, sly gentleness: "Now I come to your second adventure, with which I cannot say I am unconcerned—far from it. For an error in your judgment may here have been noxious to one of those souls who, as you said, are entrusted to us. I do not know Monsieur Malorthy's daughter. I know nothing about the crime of which you believe her guilty. In our view, the problem must be otherwise stated. Criminal or not, has this young girl been the object of a special grace? Have you been the instrument of that grace? Understand me.... Understand me! At any moment, we can be inspired with the necessary word, the sure and certain mediation—just that—not some other. Then it is that we behold true resurrections of conscience. An utterance, a glance, a pressure of the hand, and some will, until then past bending, abruptly crumbles. Poor fools we, who suppose that spiritual guidance obeys the ordinary laws of human intimacies, even those that are sincere! Endlessly are our projects turned upside down, our finest reasonings reduced to nought, our weak means turned against us. Between the priest and the penitent there stands ever a third invisible actor who now is silent, now murmurs, and now abruptly speaks as master. Our part is often so passive! No vanity, no conceit, no worldly wisdom withstands that! How then conceive, without a certain heaviness of heart, that this same witness, capable of making use of us without the least accounting to us, links us more straitly to His unspeakable activity? If this has been your case, it is because He is proving you, and that ordeal will be hard, so hard that it can shatter your life."

"I know it," stammered the poor priest. "Oh! How your words hurt me!"

"You know it?" asked Father Menou-Segrais. "In what manner?"

Father Donissan hid his face in his hands; then, as though ashamed of an impulsive movement, he continued, his head held straight, his eyes staring at the pale daylight without: "God has inspired me with this thought, that He thus pointed out my vocation, that I was to pursue Satan in souls, and that I should thereby inevitably compromise my peace, my priestly honor, and even my salvation."

"Don't believe any part of it," the pastor of Campagne sharply rejoined. "One compromises one's salvation only by useless activities outside one's proper path. In the place where God follows us, peace can be taken from us, not grace."

"You are greatly deluded," calmly replied Father Donissan, without seeming aware of how remote were such words from his accustomed tone of respect and humility. "I can have no doubts of the will which presses me or of the fate which awaits me."

Father Menou-Segrais's eyes held the joy of the searcher who suddenly glimpses the solution long sought. "What fate does await you, my son?"

The curate shrugged his shoulders slightly.

"I shall not require your secret of you. There was a time when I should have had the right to. But now we are parting company, you and I, and already you no longer belong to me."

"Don't say such things," murmured Father Donissan, his eyes darkened and staring. 'Wherever I may go, however deeply I may plunge—yes—into the very arms of Satan, I shall remember your charity."

Then, as though the image which took possession of his spirit too sorrowfully stirred him, and he wanted to flee it (or perhaps confront it), he hastily stood up.

"Is that your secret?" cried Father Menou-Segrais. "Is that what you claim to hold from God? Have I understood aright that you blaspheme within yourself the divine mercy? Such are no lessons learnt from me! Listen to me, you wretched man! You are (and how long have you been?) the gull, the plaything, the laughable tool of him whom you fear the most."

Both hands raised and then lowered, he made a gesture of horror and discouragement which belied the spontaneous brightness in his eyes.

"I have not blasphemed," replied Father Donissan. "I have not despaired of God's justice. I shall believe until the last minute of my miserable life that the sole merits of our Lord alone are fully great enough to absolve me, me and all others with me. Nonetheless, it was not idly that there was one day revealed to me, in so effective a way, the dreadful horror of sin, the wretched state of sinners, and the devil's power."

"When was this?..." began Father Menou-Segrais.

But, without letting him finish, or rather as though he were not concerned with listening to him, the future saint of Lumbres went on: "Of this, a foreboding was long ago given me. Before knowing the truth, I bore its sorrow. Each human being receives his share of fight; some, more zealous, more learned than I, have doubtless a very lively feeling for the divine order of things. As for me, from childhood I have dwelt less in the hope of the glory we shall someday possess than in regret for that which we have lost." As he continued, his face hardened; a fold of anger furrowed his brow. "Oh! Father, Father! I have longed to thrust this cross aside! Is it possible! Always I have assumed it anew. Without it, life has no meaning; the best becomes one of those lukewarm ones whom the Lord spews forth. In our dreadful wretchedness, humiliated, crushed, trampled by the most vile, what would we be did we not at least feel the outrage! He is not wholly master of the world, so long as the sacred wrath swells within our hearts, so long as one human life, in its turn, casts the *Non Serviam* in his teeth."

Words crowded in his mouth, disproportionate to the inward images which gave them rise. And this flood of speech in a man naturally silent betrayed something close to frenzy.

"I stop you short," Father Menou-Segrais coldly interjected. "I order you to listen to me. The only reason you're talking so much is to deceive yourself and to deceive me along with you. Enough of that. But I know that you are not a man to content yourself with words. Such violence presupposes some resolve, some scheme, perhaps some act, and I want to know what it is."

This blow struck so close to home that Father Donissan looked at his dean in dismay. Yet the old man, subtle and strong, was already forging ahead: "In what fashion have you realized in your life feelings of which the least that one can say is that they are confused and perilous?"

The young priest answered nothing.

"Well, then, I'll tell you," resumed Father Menou-Segrais. "You began with excessive mortifications. Then you hurled yourself into the ministry with an equal violence. The results you won rejoiced your heart. They should have brought you peace. Nevertheless you have it not, even now! Never does God refuse it to a good servant who has strained his strength to the utmost. Is it possible, by any chance, that you have deliberately rejected it?"

"I did not reject it," answered Father Donissan with an effort. "Rather is it that I am more disposed by nature to sorrow than to joy...."

He seemed to reflect for a moment, to seek for his thought a moderate, conciliatory expression. Then, suddenly making up his mind, in a voice which passion actually subdued, comparable to a dark flame, he exclaimed, "Oh! rather despair and all its torments than a cowardly complacence for the works of Satan!"

To his great surprise, for he had allowed this wish to escape like a cry, and had himself heard it with a sort of terror, the dean of Campagne took both his hands between his own and gently said: "Enough; I read clearly within you: I was not mistaken. Not only have you not besought consolation, but you have maintained your spirit with everything capable of pushing you to despair. You have maintained the despair within you."

"Not the despair," he cried out, "but fear!"

"The despair," evenly repeated Father Menou-Segrais, "and it would have led you from blind hatred of the sin to scorn and hatred for the sinner "

"Hatred of the sinner!" cried he, hoarsely (the pity in his look included a certain sullenness). "Hatred of the sinner!"

The violence and disarray of his feelings cut short the words on his lips, and it was only after a long silence that he added, his eyes closed upon a mysterious vision: "I have cast aside a good much more precious than life...."

Then the dean of Campagne's voice resounded in the new silence, firm, clear, impossible to escape: "I have never doubted that there was a secret in your inner life, better kept by your ignorance and your good faith than by any possible duplicity. You have committed some imprudence. I should not be surprised had you conceived some dangerous vow...."

"I couldn't have conceived any vow whatever without my confessor's permission," stammered the poor priest.

"If it is not a vow, it is something very like it," replied Father Menou-Segrais.

Then, painfully straightening himself and pulling away from the pillows, his hands upon his knees, he said; without raising his voice: "I enjoin you to disclose it, my child."

To the dean's great astonishment, his curate hesitated a long while, his eyes hard. Then, with a painful shudder: "It's true, I assure you. I've made no vow, no promise, barely a wish...perhaps...surely ill-justified, at least according to human prudence..."

"It is poisoning your heart," replied Father MenouSegrais.

Then, shaking his head and making the best of it: "This is perhaps what deserves your censure. The possession of so many souls by sin... has often afforded me transports of hate for the enemy. For their salvation I offered everything I had or ever would have...my life, first of all—that is so small a thing!—the consolations of the Holy Spirit..."

Again he hesitated: "My salvation, if God wishes it!" said he, under his breath.

The avowal was received in a deep silence. The extraordinary words seemed to create that silence, of themselves to lose themselves. Then Father Menou-Segrais spoke anew: "Before continuing," he said with his usual directness, "forswear that thought forever and pray God to pardon you for it. What is more, I forbid you to speak of these things to anyone other than myself."

Then, as the priest opened his mouth to answer, that masterly clinician of souls, ever steadfast in his prudence and his sovereign good sense, said: "No arguments. Keep still. The only thing now is to forget. I know all about it. The undertaking was conceived in a fashion beyond reproach and carried out point by point. Not otherwise does the devil beguile those in your likeness. Did he not know how to abuse the gifts of God, he would be nothing more than a cry of hatred in the abyss to which no echo would respond...."

Although his voice revealed no excessive emotion, great depth of feeling was nonetheless made evident by this symptom: Father Menou-Segrais drew his cane from beneath his armchair, got up, and took a few steps around the room. His curate remained standing where he was.

"My dear young boy," said the old priest, "what perils await you! The Lord summons you to perfection, not to peace. Of all men, you will have the least assurance in your life, clear-sighted only for others, passing from light into shadow, fickle. In some fashion your rash offer has been heard. Hope is almost dead within you, forever. Of it there remains only that last glimmer without which every task would become impossible and every merit vain. This extreme poverty in hope—here is what matters. The rest is nothing. Along the road you have chosen—no! into which you have hurled yourself!—you will be alone, definitively alone, you will walk alone. Whoever would follow you upon it, would lose himself without helping you."

"I did not ask for that," cried out the future saint of Lumbres with sudden violence. (In truly pathetic contrast, his voice remained gloomy and willful.) "I did not request these special graces. I want no part of them! I wish for no miracles! I never asked for any! Let me be left to live and die in the skin of a poor man who does not know *A* from *B*. No! No! What has been begun this night will not be brought to completion! I dreamed. I was mad."

Father Menou-Segrais went back to his easy chair, stretched out on it, and replied without raising his voice: "Who knows? Which one of those whom we honor as our fathers in the faith was not accused of being a visionary? What visionary has not had his disciples? At the point you have reached, your works alone will speak for you, or against you."

A moment later he added, with a gentler intonation: "Am I not also to be pitied, my child? My experience with souls and reflection over a period of several months dead me to believe that God has chosen you. Unbelieving simpletons do not grant the existence of saints. Pious simpletons believe that they grow all by themselves, like the grasses of the field. Few know that the rarer a tree's species, the more fragile it is. Your destiny, to which so many other destinies are surely bound, is at the mercy of a trifling mistake, of an abuse of grace even though involuntary, of a hasty decision, of an uncertainty, of a misunderstanding. And you are entrusted to me! You belong to me! With what trembling hands do I offer you to God! No error is allowed me.

How cruelly it afflicts me to be unable to fall on my knees at your side and give thanks with you! From day to day I awaited a supernatural confirmation of God's designs upon your soul. I awaited this confirmation of your zeal, of your growing influence, of the conversion of my little flock. And in your so unsettled, so stormy life, the sign has exploded like a bolt of thunder. It leaves me more puzzled than before. For it is henceforth certain that this sign is equivocal, that even the miracle is not pure!"

He reflected an instant, then, raising his shoulders and with a gesture of helplessness: "God knows there is little chance I should yield to fear! God knows that I am all too tempted to brave the judgment of others! I am frequently accused of independence and even of insubordination. Yet there are some rules which cannot be infringed. Were you to tear yourself to pieces with a penitential scourge, I could put that to rights. Were you to dream the devil, or meet him at every crossroads, that is my business. But this no less improbable tale of the little Malorthy girl enlightens me. I cannot leave you free to speak and to act in this parish as you see fit.... I can't leave it up to you. I must...it behooves me...it is necessary that I unbosom myself of this to our superiors. My support will be of small avail to you! On the other hand, you must hide nothing. From then on—oh, from then on!—who knows when you will at last overcome the distrust of some, the pity of others, the opposition of all! Shall you ever overcome it? May I have been mistaken in you? Have I perhaps expected too much? An old man can no longer botch his life. But I shall have botched my death."

Father Donissan at last broke his silence. Far from abashing him, this last expressed doubt visibly restored his courage. He objected timidly: "I desire nothing so much as to be forgotten, obliterated, to lead an ordinary life and fulfill the duties of my station. Were you willing, what would prevent me from becoming again what I was before? Who would be concerned about me? I attract the attention of no one. I have the reputation I deserve of a very simple, very limited priest. Oh! If you allow it, I think I could succeed in passing unnoticed, even by the Lord and His angels!"

"Unnoticed!" gently exclaimed Father Menou-Segrais (he smiled, but his eyes filled with tears). Yet he immediately stopped short. The staircase resounded from the unusually rapid steps of the housekeeper. The door opened almost at once, and, ashy pale, with that haste old women show in announcing bad news, she said, "Miss Malorthy has just done away with herself."

Then, already satisfied with the effect she had produced, she added, "She has slit her throat with a razor...."

The reader may peruse below a letter from the bishop to Canon Gerbier:

> *My Dear Canon:*
>
> *I owe you my thanks for the composure, the intelligence, and the discreet zeal of which you have given proof during the course of certain events very painful to my paternal heart. The unfortunate Father Donissan this week left the nursing home at Vaubrecourt, where he has been under the most devoted care of Dr. Jolibois. This practitioner, a pupil of Dr. Bernheim in Nancy, yesterday discussed with me the present state of health of our dear young man. He gave evidence of that breadth of outlook and of that tender solicitude which I already have had frequent occasion to admire among men of science whose studies have unfortunately turned them from the faith. He attributes this temporary disorder to a serious intoxication of the nervous cells, probably of intestinal origin.*
>
> *Without lacking in charity, which must be our constant principle, I deplore with you the negligence, to call it by no worse a name, of the dean of Campagne. By acting decisively and vigorously, he would certainly have prevented our appearing to be momentarily in conflict with the civil authorities. Nonetheless, thanks to your judicious intervention, and after a first*

misunderstanding quickly cleared up, Dr. Gallet displayed toward us the highest courtesy by helping us to keep the scandal within bounds. What is more, his diagnosis has been confirmed by his eminent colleague at Vaubrecourt. These two characteristic facts do as much honor to his character as to his professional attainments.

Miss Malorthy's evidence, the secrets she revealed when fully delirious, or during the hours before her death agony, would certainly not have been enough to compromise, in Father Donissan's person, the dignity of our ministry. But his presence at the dying girl's bedside, despite Monsieur Malorthy's formal protest, should in no case have been tolerated by the dean of Campagne. I grant that what followed could not have been foreseen by a reasonable man. The desire of this young person, publicly expressed, to be borne to the church porch in order to die there should have been given no consideration. Apart from the fact that her father and the doctor in charge of the case were opposed to such an imprudence, what was known about Miss Malorthy's past and her religious indifference permitted the belief that, having already at an earlier date been under care for mental disorders, the approach of death had upset her feeble reasoning powers. What are we to say about the altercation which ensued! Of the queer words uttered by the unhappy curate! Above all what are we to say about the veritable abduction committed by him when, tearing the sick woman from her father's hands, he carried her, all bloody and dying, to the church, which fortunately was near at hand! Such excesses are of another age and are beyond words.

Heaven be thanked, the scandal has happily come to an end. Good souls, more zealous than wise, were already heralding this conversion in articulo mortis, whose lack of verisimilitude would have covered us with ridicule. I've cleaned up the whole mess. Our solution has satisfied everyone. Excepting, of course, the dean of Campagne, who, by withdrawing into a disdainful silence and refusing us his testimony, showed himself, at the very least, peculiar.

Under my instructions, Father Donissan has gone to stay with the Trappists at Tortefontaine. There he will remain until there is confirmation of his cure. I grant that his perfect submissiveness pleads in his behalf, and that there is ground for hoping that someday we may be able—these regrettable events having been forgotten—to find for him in the diocese some lesser employment proportionate to his capacities.

Five years later, indeed, the former curate of Campagne was named pastor officiating over a small parish in the hamlet of Lumbres. His works there are known to all. Glory, beside which all human glory pales, sought out in this desert place the new curé d'Ars. The second part of this book, based on authentic documents and testimony which no one would dare challenge, reports the last episode of his extraordinary life.

The Second Part

THE SAINT OF LUMBRES

1.

HE OPENED THE window; he still awaited—who knows what? Across the gulf of shadow streaming with rain, the church feebly glimmered, the only living thing.... "Here I am," said he, as though in a dream....

Downstairs old Martha was drawing the bolts. Far away tinkled the blacksmith's anvil. Yet already he was no longer listening; it was the hour of the night when this fearless man, buttress of so many souls, staggered under the weight of his wondrous burden. "Poor pastor of Lumbres!" said he, smiling, "he's good for nothing...now he isn't even able to sleep!" He also said, "Can you believe it? I'm afraid of the dark!..."

The sanctuary lamp little by little outlined in the night the pointed arches of the three-mullioned windows. The ancient tower, built between the choir and the main nave, from just above them thrust up its timbered spire and its heavy belfry. All this he no longer saw. He was standing, face to the gloom, alone, and as though upon a ship's prow. Around him the great dark swell rolled, with superhuman sound. From the four corners of the compass there rushed toward him the fields and the invisible woods...and behind the fields and the woods, other villages and other towns, all alike, bursting with abundance, enemies of the poor, packed with cowering misers, cold as winding sheets.... And further still, the cities, which never sleep.

"Dear God! Dear God!..." he kept repeating, unable to weep or to pray.... As happens at the bedside of one dying, each minute dropped into the darkness, beyond recall. However short the nights, day comes too late: the flirtatious young widow already has put on her war paint, the drunkard has slept off his wine. The witch, back from her sabbath, still glowing with warmth, has slipped between her white sheets.... Day comes too late.... But justice, justice alone, from pole to pole, will astound the world.

Finally he slipped to his knees, slumping where he stood. That justice, which a generous-hearted people expects from the Minister of Finance, he sought at not so great a distance—but rather over there, just above the horizon, close at hand, full-fledged with the coming dawn, irresistible, in the shattered night. The open hand will not draw shut...speech will wither upon the lips...monstrous Evolution, becalmed forever, will suddenly cease to writhe and squirm.... The fearful dawn, which swells up within men, will give the most secret thought its shape and its eternal volume, and the furtive and double heart will no longer even be able to forswear itself.... *It is consummated*, meaning that all is defined for always.

Monsieur Loyolet, inspector of secondary schools (complete with permission to teach as professor of literature), wanted to see the saint of Lumbres, about whom everyone was talking. He paid him a visit, secretly, with his daughter and his lady. He was a little upset. "I had pictured to myself an imposing man," said he, "with some bearing and good manners. But this priestling has no dignity; he'll munch a crust right out in the street, like a beggar." "What a pity," he also remarked, "that such a man should believe in the devil!"

The pastor of Lumbres believed in him, and that very night he feared him. "For weeks," he later confessed, "I had been tried by an anguish novel to me: I had spent my life in the confessional and I was suddenly overwhelmed by the feeling of my impotence; I felt less pity than disgust. You need only be a poor priest to know what is the frightening monotony of sin!... I found nothing to say.... I could only give absolution and weep...."

Above him the cloud tore itself into tatters. One, ten, a hundred stars came back to life, each by each at the summit of the night. A fine rain, a dust of water, fell from a cloud rent by the wind. He breathed the air, freshened and eased by the shower....

This evening he would defend himself no longer; no longer had he anything to defend; he had given all; he was empty.... This human heart—how well he knew it... (he had entered within it, he and his poor cassock and his heavy shoes). This heart!

This aged heart, where dwells the incomprehensible enemy of souls, the enemy powerful and vile, magnificent and vile. The morning star forsworn: Lucifer, or the false Dawn...

He knows so many things, poor pastor of Lumbres! which the Sorbonne knows not. So many things which are not written, which scarcely are said, of which the avowal is torn from within you, as from a wound healed and ripped open—so many things! And he knew likewise what is man: a great child full of vice and boredom.

What is he to learn that is new, this old priest? He has lived a thousand lives, all alike. No more will he be astonished; he can die. Brand new moralities there are, but never will you put a fresh face on sin.

For the first time he doubted, not God, but man. A thousand recollections surged upon him: he heard the bemused wails, the ashamed stammerings, the pained cry of passion which steals away and which a word rivets to the spot, which words of simple clarity bring back and flay alive.... Once more he saw the poor, distraught faces, the eyes which would and would not, the conquered lips as they fell limp, and the bitter mouth uttering its *no*.... So many sham rebels, eloquent indeed before the world, whom he had seen at his feet, laughable!

So many proud hearts wherein a secret rotted! So many old men like unto dreadful children! And towering over all, coldly staring at the world, the youthful misers, who never forgive.

Today like yesterday, like the first day of his priestly life, the same.... He had reached the last stage of his endeavor, and suddenly that with which he had striven was lacking. Those whom he had wanted to set free, they themselves had rejected liberty as a burden, and the enemy whom he had pursued to high heaven laughed down below, ungraspable, invulnerable. All men had made a fool of him. "We seek peace," said they. Not peace, but a brief respite, a halt in the darkness. They came all in a lather to the feet of the lonely one; and then they returned to their sad pleasures, to their joyless lives. (And he likened himself also to those ancient, affronted walls, whereon a passer-by inscribes a filthy verse, and which slowly crumble, full of mocking secrets.)

Those he had so often consoled would no longer have known him. At this instant, one of the most tragic in his life, he felt himself beleaguered from all sides; all things once more were open to question. Certain more treacherous thoughts, long since thrust aside, abruptly reappeared, and no longer did he recognize them. In all things he found a new meaning and, as it were, a new savor.... For the first time he contemplated without love, but with pity, the sorry human flock, born to graze and die. He tasted the bitter feeling of his defeat and of its vastness. In the uttermost anguish, the fearless will refused to admit that it was beaten; whatever the cost, it wanted to regain its balance....

Now he was standing; his eyes unbendingly stared before him.... How many nights like to this night, until the last night! Yet ever, among the multitude, divine grace will shoot its bolt; ever will it brand some one of these men, toward whom justice rises, across time, like a heavenly body. The obedient star hastens to their call.

No longer was he looking at the little church; he looked above it. He was wholly vibrant in joyless exaltation. Now he hardly suffered, he was becalmed forever. He desired nothing; he was conquered. Through the open breach, waves of pride flooded into his heart....

"I was damning myself unawares," he would say, later on; "I felt myself growing hard as a stone."

The plan he had so often made of going to hide and die in some retreat on the world's edge, some Charterhouse or Trappist monastery, came back fresh to his mind, but as a new image, but with a shriveling of the heart, sharp and sweet, a mysterious swooning. At such moments, formerly, the shepherd did not abandon his flock; he dreamed of carrying it with him, even unto his place of penance, still to live and win it merit. But now even this memory was fading away, the last to go. The tireless friend of souls sought only rest, and something, also, the secret thought of which eased every fiber within him, the need to die, like the desire for tears.... And tears they were indeed which bathed his eyes, yet without unburdening his heart, and in his innocence the old man no longer recognised them, was astonished, and could give no name to this sensual intoxication. He was on his way—and without having opened his eyes—toward yielding to that utmost temptation wherein had sunk before him so many of those ardent souls who traverse pleasure at a bound and find nothingness, to clasp it in an ultimate embrace. At the limit of his vast endeavor, weariness, so often conquered, pushed aside, spurted from him like the shedding of his own blood. No remorse. The enemy, full of guile, wound him in this hopeless lassitude as in a shroud, with infinite skill, the dreadful mockery of a mother's ministry.... Vainly did the crushed old man cast, through the whitening night, a glance in which there stirred a last gleaming, and which was not to reflect the rising day. Within him he saw nothing, no image on which to affix temptation, no sign of the toil which slowly destroyed him, under the eyes of an impassive master. No longer was it the cloister he desired, but something more secret than solitude, the swooning of an eternal descent, into the enfolding darkness. To him who had so long held his flesh in bondage, sensuality in the end discovered her true countenance, covered with a graven smile. And it was not this image, either, or any other, which was to disquiet the senses of the lonely old man, but in his innocent and obstinate heart came awake that other lust, that frenzy for knowledge which undid the mother of mankind, erect and musing, at the threshold of Good and of Evil. To know in order to destroy, and to renew in destruction one's knowledge and one's desire—O clime of Satan!—desire for nothingness sought for its own sake, loathsome outpouring of the heart. The saint of Lumbres has strength only to summon this dreadful repose; divine grace places a veil before these eyes only just now still full of the divine mystery.... That glance so limpid now is hesitant, knows not on what to settle.... A strange youthfulness, a naïve eagerness, like to the first wounding of the senses, warms the aged blood, pounds in the shrunken chest. Gropingly he seeks, he strokes death, through so many veils, with a hand that falters.

Up to this solemn moment, had his life had a meaning? He knew it not. He saw behind him only a desert land, and those multitudes through which he had passed, blessing them. And what now! The flock still trots at his heels, pursues him, presses in upon him, gives him no rest—insatiable, with that vast anxious hubbub, and that trampling of stricken animals.... No! He will not turn his head, he does not want to. They have pushed him this far, to the edge, and beyond... O miracle! there is silence, true silence, his repose.

"To die," said he in a low voice, "to die." He spelt out the word, to impenetrate himself with it, to digest it in his heart.... Truly did he now feel it in the depths of him, in his veins, that word, subtle poison.... He persisted, redoubled his efforts, and with growing feverishness; he would have liked to drain it as a draught, hasten his end. In his impatience there was that need of the sinner to burrow into his crime, always deeper, in order to hide himself there from his judge; he had reached the instant when Satan brings all his weight to bear, when all the nether powers press in unison upon one single point.

And nonetheless it was upward that he lifted his eyes, toward the square of grayish sky, where the night was scattering in mists. Never had he prayed with that hard will, in such a tone. Never had his voice seemed sturdier between his lips, murmuring without, but within resounding, like a roar, prisoner in a block of bronze.... Never did the humble wonder-worker, of whom so many things are told, feel closer to miracle, face to face. It seemed that for the first time his will slackened, beyond resisting, and that a single word, spoken in the silence, would destroy him forever.... Yes, nothing separated him from repose save a last impulse of his sovereign will.... No longer did he dare look at the church, or, in the dawn's haze, at the dwellings of his little flock; some shame held him back, which he longed to brush away through an irreparable act.... What served it to clutter himself with other needless cares? He lowered his eyes toward the earth, his refuge.

2.

THEN IT WAS that the low door which faces on the Chavranches road rattled twice. In the small yard, the whole chicken coop was a beating of wings. The dog Jacquot shook his chain, and all these sounds made but a single pure note in the pure morning.

Old Martha's clogs were already clattering on the steps—click, clack—and, more muffled, in the damp grass—fluck, fluck. The lock grated.

At that moment the saint of Lumbres awoke. There is no absolute silence save on life's other side; through the tiniest chink the real slips in and gushes up, finds its level. A sign calls us back, a word murmured low revives an abolished world, and a given perfume, inhaled long ago, clings harder than death.... The old fellow's eyes instinctively turned toward the sorry turnip watch of silver, a memento of the Major Seminary, affixed to the wall. "At such an hour in the morning," said he to himself, "it's certainly a sick call." Someone sick, one of his children! At a glance—so brief, so sharp—he saw again the scattered village and the smoke plumes among the trees. The whole of the little parish, and so many souls across the world whose strength and joy he was, who summoned him, called him by name.... He listens; he has already answered; he is ready.

What awaited him at the foot of the staircase—his roost, as he liked to call it? What words? What countenance? And, within the hour also, what fresh combat? For he bore within him that thing to which he could not give a name, crouching in his heart so broad and heavy, his anguish, Satan. He had not regained peace, he knew. With him breathed another being. Because temptation is like the birth of another man within a man, and his dreadful enlargement. He drags this burden about within him; he dare not cast it aside; where would he cast it? Into another heart.

But the saint is always alone, at the foot of the cross. No other friend.

"Father," old Martha called, "Father!"

He had come down the steps without thinking what he was doing, and he followed his dream across the kitchen, toward the garden, eyes half closed.... The good woman took him by the sleeve. "In the parlor, Father, in the parlor..."

And she raised her shoulders a trifle, with a smile of pity.

This parlor is a handsome room, a very handsome room, well waxed. Six rush-bottomed chairs are there to be seen, two stuffed snipes on the gray marble mantle, alongside a large sea shell and a monumental statue of Our Lady of Lourdes in white plaster, dreadful bluish white (Sister Saint Mémorin had brought it back from Conflans-sur-Somme last Easter holiday). There was also an Entombment—in an oak frame—all spotted with mildew, and furthermore, against the faded, flower-pattern wallpaper (an inn-keeper's delight of a paper), a great bare cross of black wood without a Christ.

(And this it was which the pastor saw, first of all, and at once turned away his eyes....)

"Father," said Martha, "here is the Squire of le Plouy, about his sick son...."

The Squire of le Plouy had arisen, had had a coughing fit, and had spat into the ashes of the hearth. The empty coffee cup in front of him was still steaming.

"Which one?" the old priest asked without thinking.

...And at once he stopped short, blushed at the look Martha shot him, and stammered, "Everyone knows, good heavens! that the Squire of le Plouy has only one boy!"

But the traveler showed no surprise and quietly specified: "It's our youngster Tiennot. It came over him after he got back from Vespers, an indigestion you might say. After that a splitting headache. Then, in the small hours, here he was telling his mother, 'Say, I can't move any more.' It was true. Not his arms or his legs or anything. Paralyzed. And his eyes all askew. Monsieur Gambillet said to me, 'My poor Arsene! he's done for.' Meningitis, is what he said. Then his mother heard him; you know how it is? You can't make her listen to reason. 'Go get the pastor of Lumbres,' was what she yelled at me.... So I harnessed the horse and here I am."

He fixed his honest eyes on the saint of Lumbres, eyes in which there twinkled even so, through the tears, a bit of irony—man to man, we know what a woman is like, with her ideas. (What was more, this saint about whom so many tales were told, and who does not even know the le Plouy lad, this saint who has to be reminded of things!)

"My friend...my dear friend," sputtered the priest. "I'd like to... that is...I'd like truly, I fear... Come, come! Luzarnes is not my parish, and the pastor of Luzarnes... I'm very touched at Mrs. Havret's remembering me—poor woman!—but I must...I should..."

Above all he was fearful of mortifying a sensitive colleague. And then, truly, he felt so low today!

But the Squire of le Plouy was a man of few words. He had

already wound his muffler about his neck and buttoned up his serge greatcoat. And Martha placed between her master's hands, placed with authority, a hat grown green with age.... He had to go.... He had gone.

3.

THE PASTOR OF Luzarnes was a simple man. He lived on little, on a small number of simple feelings to which his prudence gave no expression. Though past fifty, he was still young, and he always would be; he was ageless. His conscience was clear as the leaf in an account book, without erasures and without blots. His past was not empty; in it he recalled a few joys, he numbered them, he was astonished that they were so thoroughly dead, in such fine order, each in its place, lined up like figures in a sum. Were they truly joys? Had they ever breathed? Had they ever throbbed?... He was a good priest, devoted and punctual, who did not like to have his life disturbed, loyal to his class, to his day, and to the ideas of his day, taking this up, leaving that aside, extracting from all things some small profit, a born bureaucrat and moralist, and a man who predicted the snuffing-out of pauperism—as they called it—through the disappearance of alcohol and the venereal diseases; in short, the advent of a healthy and athletic youth, decked out in wool jerseys, to the conquest of the kingdom of God.

"Our saint of Lumbres," said he occasionally with a thin smile. But in the heat of discussion, he also would say, "Your saint!" in an altogether different tone. For, if he willingly reproached the diocesan administration because of its formalism and its scruples, he did not the less deplore the disorder brought to pass in a peaceable jurisdiction by one of those miracle men who upset all calculations. "In such a connection, His Excellency will never display too much prudence and discretion," he would conclude, cautious as a canon and already bristling with texts.... Good Lord! A saint cannot pass by without upsetting many an apple basket, but better a few spilled apples than to do without the greater good.

Each turn of the wheels brought the pastor of Lumbres nearer this pitiless censor. Through the mist he already saw the gray eyes, so lively, mocking, restless, where danced a little and a very slender flame. Four miles away from his own poor parish, at the deathbed of a wealthy child, summoned there as a wonder-worker—what a ridiculous business! What a scandal! He felt the full impact in advance of the words of welcome, so sly and arch.... What did they want of him? Did they hope for a miracle from this withered old hand which shook at every jolt as it lay on the serge of his cassock, gray now, from long wear?

He looked at that hand, the hand of a peasant, never clean, with a schoolboy's dismay. Oh! What was he, in the midst of them all, but a poor, stubborn peasant, faithful to his daily toil, step by step, in the great empty field? Each day showed him a new task, like a patch of earth to be spaded, in which to sink his coarse shoes. He kept going and going, without a glance to the side, casting right and left some artless word, and blessing with the sign of the cross, tireless. (Thus, in the autumn mists, the forefathers broadcast barley and wheat.) Why came they from so far, men and women, who knew only his name, and fabulous tales? To him rather than to others, so polished in their speech, pastors of towns or large villages, and men of the world? Many a time at the close of day, burdened with weariness, he had ruminated this idea in his head to the point of obsession. And then, letting his eyelids fall, he had finally gone to sleep with the thought of how God's gifts are beyond understanding and His ways strange.... But today! Whence came it that his feeling of powerlessness to do good humiliated him without giving him peace? Was the word of loyal renunciation so harsh, then, to his lips? O strange windings of the heart! A little while before he dreamed of escaping men, the world, universal sin; recollection of his useless great exertion, of his life's majesty, of his extraordinary loneliness were to cast over his death a final joy filled with bitterness—and here he was now, doubtful even of that exertion, here was Satan drawing him further down.... He, the man of sacrifice? The marked and chosen victim?... Not in the least! Rather an ignorant madman, overexcited by fasting and prayer, a village saint, shaped for the wonderment of the idle and the dullards.... "That's it, that's it!" he murmured between his lips at each jolt, his eyes hazy.... Meanwhile the hedgerows sped by on right and left; the trap flashed on like a dream, yet the dreadful anguish ran ahead and awaited him at every milestone.

For this strange man, on whom so many others laid themselves like burdens, possessed the genius of consolation and was never consoled. We know that at times he unbosomed himself regarding this, during those rare moments when he sought relief from his suffering and wept in Father Battelier's arms, calling upon divine pity with artless lamentations and in a child's speech. Deep within the poor Lumbres confessional, which smelt of darkness and of mildew, his sons on their knees heard only the sovereign voice, higher than eloquence, which laid open the hardest hearts, imperious, suppliant, and, in its very gentleness, unbendable. From the holy shadow where stirred the invisible lips, the words of peace billowed to high heaven and drew the sinner outside himself, unshackled, free. Simple words, taken to heart, limpid, terse, telegraphic in essential things, then pressing, overwhelming, shaped to express the whole meaning of a superhuman commandment, words wherein those who loved him better more than once recognized the tone and, as it were, the echo of the most violent of souls. Alas! While he thus lavished himself externally, the bestower of peace found within himself only disarray, tumult, a helter-skelter of distraught images, a witches' sabbath packed with grimaces and cries...followed by a terrible silence.

Many never understood by what miracle it was that the same man whom millions of others chose as arbiter for the most redoubtable conflicts in duty always betrayed himself, in his own strife, vacillating, almost timid. "I am made sport of," said he, "I am used as a plaything." Thus was it that he gave full measure of that peace whereof he was empty.

4.

"HERE WE ARE," said the Squire of le Plouy, pointing his whip toward some smoke arising in the midst of trees.

A little old fellow in horizon-blue breeches pushed upon the gate and took the reins. Monsieur Havret alighted at the courtyard entrance; his companion followed him as far as the house. On the threshold a tall black figure, the pastor of Luzarnes, greeted them. "My dear colleague," said he, "you are awaited here as a great noble of olden days, deep in adversity, would have awaited Saint Vincent de Paul...."

He continued to smile merrily, but with a kind of professional discretion, within a step or two as he was of the lad who was dying. At the same time he compensated for his mocking tone by a hearty shake of the hand, country fashion.

Already, however, the pastor of Lumbres was drawing him away from the house a few yards, into the midst of a flock of frightened hens. "I am ashamed, my friend, truly ashamed," said he in his gentlest tones, "I beg you to forgive...this poor lady's ignorance.... I likewise beg you...to forgive me.... We'll talk about that later," he concluded in a different tone of voice, "and you will see that I am...the more blamable of the two...."

The pastor of Luzarnes felt on his arm the grasp of the vigorous fingers, which trembled slightly. Even in this supernatural man's deliberate self-abasement, the gift he had received gushed forth and he still was masterful in action.

"My good colleague," replied the former professor of chemistry, already less jovial, "no self-reproaches in my presence.... Rightly or wrongly, I've the reputation of being strong-minded, and even, according to some, wrong-headed.... My scientific education, you know, that's the whole reason...shades of meaning, a slightly different vocabulary.... But all the same...I have the greatest regard for your character...."

His eyes lowered, he spoke with growing embarrassment. He felt himself laughable, perhaps hateful. At last he fell silent. But before raising his head, he saw, as though within himself, as though in the deepest mirror, the glance implanted upon his own, and despite himself he had to seek it out, he had to surrender, wholly.... For a second he felt himself naked, before his judge who was full of forgiveness.

He saw only the look in the trembling, slack, ashy-pale face. This look which summoned him from so far, begging, desperate. Stronger than two arms outstretched, more pitiful than a cry, dumb, black, irresistible... "What does he want of me?" the good fellow asked himself with a sort of holy horror. "I thought I saw him in the pool of fire!" he later explained. A pity beyond explaining tore him within his heart.

For an instant he felt the aged hand tremble harder on his arm. "Pray for me..." the saint of Lumbres whispered in his ear.

Yet, tightening his grasp, then abruptly drawing himself away, he added in a changed tone, the harsh tone of a man defending his life: "Do not tempt me!..."

And side by side, without further words, they entered the house.

"Do not tempt me!"

He had flung out this cry alone.... He had wanted to explain... to ask pardon...already blushing with shame at the thought that he was entering this house as giver of life's precious things, bereft of all hope that he could extricate himself without serious wrongdoing and without giving scandal.... And then, suddenly, in a flash of lightning, the powers which had assailed him throughout the dolorous night bestirred themselves anew, and the words he was going to utter, his own and inmost thought, were together dispelled in the sole reality of anguish. However low the wily enemy had dragged him before, every bond had not been broken, every echo from without smothered.... But this time the strong hand had torn him up alive, had uprooted him.... "Save yourself yourself, the hour has struck!..." said also the voice never heard, thundering. "Finish the empty struggle and the wearisome victory. Forty years of labor and of little profit, forty years of tedious strife, forty years in the cattle-shed, flat among the human beasts, level with their rotten hearts, forty years scaled and conquered!... Hasten!... Here is your first step, your one and only step out of the world!..."

And this voice said a thousand other things, and said only one, a thousand things in one alone, and this sole word brief as a glance, infinite.... The past tore itself away from him, fell into tatters. Through the ever-changing anguish there brusquely passed, like lightning, the dazzlement of a terrible joy, a burst of inner laughter to shatter any coat of mail.... He saw himself a fledgling priest in the seminary courtyard on a rainy day.... In the lofty hall, with its hangings of cherry damask, before His Lordship in cape and rochet.... The first days at Lumbres, the priest's house ruinous, the bare wall, the winter wind in the little garden.... And then... And then... the vast labor, and now this pitiless crowd, night and day packed tight around the confessional of the man of God as though he were another curé d'Ars; the deliberate severance from all human help; yes, the man of God wrangled over like some bit of prey. No rest, no peace except that purchased by fasting and the rod, in a body felled at last; recurring scruples, the anguish at ceaselessly touching the most obscene wounds of the human heart, the despair at so many damned souls, the powerlessness to succor them and clasp them through the abyss of flesh; the obsession that it was all time wasted, the vastness of the toil.... How often, including that very night, had he borne the assault of such images!... But this time an expectation, a great and marvelous expectation, illuminated him within, finally consumed the inward man. Already he is the man of the new day, the guest at the new banquet.... How far already is this world behind him! Far behind his restive flock! No longer does he find, never again will he find within him this so lively feeling of universal sin. He is now aware only of the enormous hoax of vice, of its gross and childish falsehood. Poor human heart, barely rough-hewn! Poor arid brain! People of here below, who squirm in your mud, unfinished!... No longer does he belong to that people, no longer does he know that people, he is ready to renounce without hatred. He surges back toward the day like a diver, his whole weight thrust toward the outstretched arms, who, in the dark and vibrant water, already opens his eyes to the light above.

"You have set yourself free," said the other one (another one so like unto himself). "Your past life, your useless yet touching toil, your fasting, your scourging, your slightly naive and vulgar loyalty, humiliation within and without, the enthusiasm of some, the unjust mistrust of others, and certain utterances packed with poison. Oh! all is but a dream, and the shadow of a dream! All was but a dream apart from your gradual ascent toward the real world, your birth, your release. Clamber up to my mouth, harken to the word where abides all knowledge."

And he listened, he waited. He was at the very point whither the ancient enemy wished to lead him, the enemy with but a single wile. Degraded, trampled, spilt upon the ground like dregs, crushed under an immense weight, burned by all the invisible fires, spitted again on the sword's point, pierced anew, hacked to pieces, his last gnashing drowned in the terrible outcry of the angels, this ancient rebel, to whom God has left for his defense only a single and wearisome lie.... Alas! the same lie lodges at the corners of a miser's mouth, or in the eager and dying throat where rattles untamed pleasure, the same: "You will know.... You are going to know.... Here is the mysterious word's first letter.... Enter here.... Enter within me...plunge your hand into the living wound...eat and drink...take your fill!"

For, after so many centuries, it is still you whom he awaited, a thousand times refurbished and grown young again, dripping paint and unguents, shining with oil, laughing with all his new teeth, offering your inhuman curiosity his body drained dry, the whole of his falsehood, where your parched mouth will suck not one drop of blood!

"I saw him, or rather we saw him," the pastor of Luzarnes, former professor at the Cambrai Minor Seminary, long afterward wrote to Canon Cibot.

"I saw him standing in the midst of us, his eyes half closed, and for several minutes we looked at him without wishing to break the silence. The natural expression of his face was one of goodness filled with unction, to which several prudent persons already attributed the character of a certain simplicity. But his bony features seemed to us all, at that moment, as though petrified by a feeling of extreme violence; he looked like a man bending every effort to surmount a difficult obstacle. I noticed that his posture had grown unbelievably erect and that this, in his old age, produced the impression of a vigor out of the ordinary, even an impression of brutality. Although my mind, shaped of old to the severe method of the exact sciences, is ordinarily little affected by the impulses of the imagination, I was so much struck at the sight of this great body, motionless and as though struck by lightning, in the quiet surroundings of a country parlor, that for a moment I doubted the evidence of my senses, and when I saw my respected friend stir and speak once more, it surprised me like some unexpected happening. Moreover, he seemed to be emerging from a dream. I have informed you above, my most honored colleague, that I had gone out to greet our dear pastor of Lumbres, and that I had met him along the roadside, at some distance from the house. Certain things he said, the precise meaning of which perhaps escaped me, had added to my anxiety. I was trying to reply as a prudent friendship dictated when, grasping my arm with violence and staring me in the eyes, he said, 'Tempt me no longer!' Our first conversation stopped there, our feet having already conveyed us to the threshold of the Havret dwelling. I had at that moment a foreboding of calamity.... It was all too justified. The child, whose condition, after all, was desperate, had passed away during my brief absence. The midwife, Madame Lambelin, had scientifically verified the demise, Beyond any possible error. 'He is dead,' this person had told us in a low tone of voice. (But I do not know whether the pastor of Lumbres heard her.) He had passed the threshold and taken a few steps inside when, in a very moving display, and one the sincere piety of which every enlightened person can honor, while yet deploring in it a certain exaggeration due above all to ignorance, the sorrowing mother literally cast herself at my venerable colleague's feet and, in the transports of her despair, kissed his aged cassock, striking her forehead upon the ground with a sound that reverberated through my heart. At the poor woman's touch, and without lowering his eyes to see her, the pastor of Lumbres stopped short. Then it was that we saw him for several long minutes, motionless, in the middle of the room, like a statue, and indeed exactly as I have just described him to you.

"Then, making the sign of the cross over Mrs. Havret's head and lifting his eyes toward me, he said, 'Let us go outside!' Alas, dear and honored colleague, such is the weakness of our minds when enthralled by too vivid an impression that nothing, at that moment, it seems to me, would have kept me from following him, and that, in the violence of her affliction, the unfortunate mother let us go without a word said. Of all of us, only Madame Lambelin had perhaps kept her self-possession. There is much to reprove in that person's conduct and religious views, but through her God was teaching us a lesson in common sense and rationality. Most assuredly during that whole dreadful morning I was like a toy in the hands of an unfortunate man whom sound advice, based on experience and knowledge, might have spared a frightful mishap.... God alone could say whether I was the instrument of His wrath or of His mercy. But the sad events which followed weigh the scales in favor of the former hypothesis.

"The distinguished canon stipendiary, since dead, seems to live again in every line of this truly unique letter, couched in its judicial and cautious phrases, strung like horse chestnuts on a thread, where the foolish will find nothing that is not trite and shallow, but which is enshrouded in the magic of a dream. The only dream of an impoverished life which never knew any case of conscience save this, and shattered itself upon it, sole doubt and sole enchantment! Not many months before his death, this innocent victim wrote one of his old friends:

> "*Obliged to interrupt a task which was my sole distraction, I cannot rid my mind of certain recollections, and among them one of the most painful, the pastor of Lumbres's woeful and inexplicable end. I constantly revert to it. I see in it one of those events, so rare in this world, which exceed the bounds of ordinary reason. My poor health suffers from the results of this obsession, and I see in it the principal reason for my progressive weakening and for the almost total loss of appetite.*"

These last lines will rejoice any one of those pilferers of human documents whom we today allow to splash about and rummage in stagnant waters. But to read them without vulgar curiosity, letting resound in oneself the echo of this artless lament, one will better understand what sincere distress lies in this admission of impotence, written in language not unlofty. The ultimate effort of certain simple men, who are born to toil in peace, and whom some wondrous encounter has hurled into the heart of things, in a single flash of lightning quickly quenched—when we see them striving to the last moment of their unintelligible lives to recall and recapture that which never recurs and which took them by surprise-such is a spectacle of so much tragedy and of so deep and inward a bitterness that we can compare it to nothing save the death of a little child. Vainly do they trace back, step by step, from memory to memory, vainly do they spell out their lives, letter by letter. The reckoning is there and yet the story makes no sense. They have, as it were, become strangers to their own adventure; in it they no longer recognize themselves. Tragedy has pierced them through and through, only to kill another standing beside them. How would they remain callous to this injustice of fate, to the wrongdoing and the obtuseness of chance? Their most strenuous effort will get them no further than the shuddering of some innocent and defenseless beast; in dying they suffer a destiny to which they are not equal. For however far a commonplace mind may be able to reach, and even though you might conceive that through the mist of symbols and appearances it has sometimes touched the real, necessity requires that it may not pre-empt the role of the strong—a role which is less the knowledge of the real than a feeling of our impotence to seize it and retain it whole, the savage irony of truth.

What man better than this so distinguished priest would have been able to delineate for us the last chapter of such a life, consumed in solitude and silence, sealed tight forever? Unfortunately, the former pastor of Luzarnes left only a few unfinished letters, the essential passages in which we have quoted. The rest was meticulously destroyed after the adjournment of the inquiry ordered by episcopal authority, the findings of which were in the interim kept secret.

5.

"LET US GO outside," had said the pastor of Lumbres.

The other priest had followed him, not spellbound as he in good faith came to believe, but simply through curiosity, to see what would happen. The former professor knew little in detail about the old man who had suddenly become guardian of a vast flock, ever on the increase. By what marvel had this old chap with his muddy shoes, always walking the roads alone and at a fast clip, his smile sorrowful, gathered around his confessional what amounted to a people, his people? His reverence the pastor of Luzarnes, a newcomer in the diocese, shared "up to a certain point" the distrust of some of his colleagues. "I withhold judgment," said he ingenuously. And here, today, by chance (one of the words to which he was partial), without further ado, he was being admitted into the confidence of this strange spirit.

They went out into the little walled garden behind the house. The clear sun filtered down upon the lettuces. Bees in the west wind darted like arrows. For a breeze had sprung up with the coming of day.

Abruptly the pastor of Lumbres stopped short and took a step toward his companion. His aged face was disclosed in the full light, branded with the stigma of sleeplessness, as easily recognized as the countenance of a man in his death throes. For a moment the poor mouth relaxed, trembled; then, to the curious eyes which watched him, the other eyes, vanquished, yielded their secret, surrendered.... The old fellow was weeping.

At once the future canon was moved to compassion; he held his slender white hand upraised. "Truly, my dear colleague..." He said a great many things hastily, at random, as is fitting in so grave a case, gradually renewing his courage by the sound of his own voice. As he talked, and in order to be the more certain of convincing him, he kept his eyes fixed upon the priest, shuddering from head to foot, whom his infallible eloquence would soon set to rights. "This fit of exaltation, my devout friend, is but a passing trial, and a warning from Providence, which perhaps does not always approve the excesses of your zeal, the harshness of your penances, your fasts, your vigils...."

He went on and on, eager to reach a conclusion, giving with all his heart his salves and unguents, when a voice—of so singular a tone, ah! indeed a voice so singular, so little expected, the voice of a man who had not listened, who would no longer, listen, the lamentation of which alone vomited into nothingness the disappointed eloquence. "My friend, my friend, I'm worn out. I can't go on." Other words trembled on his lips, but he did not utter them. His watchful colleague, only for a moment out of countenance, began, "This despair..."

Already the pastor of Lumbres was placing his own imperious, feverish hand upon his friend's. "Let us draw away a little further, I beg of you," said he, "just over there."

They stopped at the base of a wall that was crumbling apart. What joyous life hummed all around them! "I can't go on," resumed that pitiable voice. "Oh! for compassion's sake, my friend, now my sole friend, let not your charity lead you astray. Be hard with me! I am merely an unworthy priest, a poor priest, a barren soul, a blind man, a wretched blind man...."

"Surely not...surely not..." the future canon politely corrected him, "surely not you, but perhaps some foolhardy minds who take advantage of your ere...of your candor.... It's so easy to believe in all the good things said about us!"

He smiled, brushing away with his hand a troublesome wasp (the wasp and this bemused mouth, full of talk, two buzzing animals).... Then he said, in a tone precluding debate, "I am listening to you."

The pastor of Lumbres fell on his knees, at his feet. "God puts me in your hands," he declared, "gives me to you!"

"What childishness!" exclaimed the future canon. "Get up, my friend. Your imagination is magnifying beyond measure what is no more than the impress of fatigue, of overwork. Oh! I am only an ordinary man, yet a certain amount of experience...." he concluded with a smile.

The pastor of Lumbres responded to this smile by another, a wounded smile. What did it matter! All he wanted to see in this man was a friend, before the final turning, not one he had chosen, but one received, obviously received from God, his last friend. Ah, assuredly he no longer hoped to turn backward, find peace again, live once more! Already he had gone too far along the accursed road. He would go further, further, till his breath failed, with this his only companion.

"Alas!" he cried, "such was I at the Major Seminary, such have I remained, a stubborn head, an arid heart, utterly unspirited, in a word—a worthless man whom Providence has used. All the talk there has been about me, people's willfulness in seeking me out, the friendship of so many sinners, so many signs and ordeals of which I understood neither the meaning nor the purpose. A saint ripens in silence, and silence has been refused to me. Just now, even, I ought to have kept still.... If I had, I should not now have to confess something to you.... (Yes...my heart bled at leaving—and in such an hour—that poor woman on her knees—so hard—yes, so hard hit....) It was not without a reason...not without a reason.... Because... My friend, just as I was crossing the threshold...a thought...such a thought came to me..."

"What was it?" asked the pastor of Luzarnes. Involuntarily he had leaned over toward the old priest, bringing his ear close to the mouth whence there now issued only a confused murmur.... Then he drew up, overwhelmed. "Oh! my friend..." he cried out, "oh, my friend!"

He raised his arms to heaven and then crossed them on his breast, letting his broad shoulders slump back in dejection. The pastor of Lumbres was still kneeling, his head lowered. Only the grayed nape of his neck could be seen, bent in shame.

"And so," the pastor of Luzarnes spoke very slowly, "this thought came to you, suddenly, for the first time?"

"For the first time."

"And never before?..."

"Lord!" exclaimed the aged man, "never before! I am only a poor wretch. For years I have not known the meaning of an hour of peace. How can you believe.... What! I, trampled under the very feet of Satan! A miracle, I!... Truly, my friend, perhaps throughout my life I have not made one single act of divine love, even imperfect, even incomplete.... No! it took the dreadful toil of this last night.... Literally, I am no longer master of myself.... I was in the contortions of despair.... And it was then...then, as though in mockery...that this thought came to me..."

"It was your duty to thrust it aside," said the other.

"Understand me," humbly continued the old fellow. "I said, 'this thought came to me.' That was a misstatement. Not a thought at all, but a certainty.... Oh! Words are my undoing, they have always been my undoing," he exclaimed with naive impatience. "I must go on to the bitter end, my dearly beloved brother, to this last admission.... Even on my knees before you, plunged in sorrow, doubtful even of my own salvation...I believe...I have to believe...invincibly...that this certainty came from God."

"Have you had—how shall I say?—a material sign..."

"What sort of sign?" guilelessly asked the pastor of Lumbres.

"How should I know?... Have you seen or heard?..."

"Nothing.... Only that inner voice. Had an order been given me, with equal preciseness, I should instantly have obeyed. But it was less an order than the simple assurance, the certainty that this would be...if I wanted it. God is my witness that the avowal I am making you tears out my heart, I should die of shame for it.... I knew...I know...always...I am sure...that a word from me would have...Lord, Lord!...would have brought back...yes, would bring back to life this dead child!"

"Look at me," said the pastor of Luzarnes, after a long silence and with authority.

With both hands he was lifting him off the ground. When he saw him standing close to him, knees caked with mud, head held low, he loved him....

"Look at me," he repeated. "Answer me frankly. Who held you back from putting to the test...from putting to the test your power, that very instant?"

"I do not know," said the old priest. "It was a terrible thing.... When the instrument is too lowly, God casts it aside, after He has made His use of it."

"Yet your...conviction remains unimpaired?"

"Yes," repeated the pastor of Lumbres.

"And now, here and now, what is your decision?"

"To obey," replied this strange man.

The future canon briskly pulled out his spectacles and brandished them.

"My advice will be only of the simplest," said he. "First, you will come in behind me, you will excuse yourself as best you can. (So abrupt a departure on your part must have seemed most extraordinary, inconsiderate.) While I complete this duty of politeness, you will go—listen to me carefully—you will go perform your devotions in the room where the body lies—the best you can—as you please.... I should not want to leave the least doubt in your mind, upset as it already is.... I'll be responsible for everything," he concluded after the most trifling of hesitations, but with a sharp gesture of decision.

(Thus did he hide from his own eyes the weakness of an impulse of curiosity whereof he was barely aware, and which he did not admit to himself. For at times the most humdrum man, wandering through a gaming room, is caught up in the rhythm of all those fleet hearts, throws a gold coin on the baize, and lays bare a little portion of himself.)

Then, raising his spectacles to the level of his eyes: "After which, my friend, you will prudently go take a little rest."

"I shall try to," said the old priest humbly.

"You can if you try. The act of resting, say the specialists, is an act of the will. Among many sick persons, even insomnia is one of the thousand forms of abulia. Have faith in one who is well-versed in these matters. Such a moral crisis as this is certainly no more than the natural reaction of an overworked organism. Let us speak frankly between ourselves, my dear colleague. Nine times out of ten the peace you go so far to seek is within your grasp. Proper rules of health will restore it to you. Of course in a priest's mouth, these truths are at times dangerous, or need to be handled delicately. But from a superior intelligence, such as is yours, I need have no fear of one of those exaggerated interpretations…which certain scrupulous souls…"

"You believe me insane," said the pastor of Lumbres, with gentle sweetness.

He lifted his eyes toward the younger man, his eyes which had been lowered and were full of a mysterious tenderness. Then he went on: "Alas! Not long ago I should still have wished it. There are times when seeing is in itself so hard an ordeal that you would like God to break the mirror. You would break it, my friend…for it is hard to remain standing at the foot of the cross, but even harder fixedly to look at it. What a sight it is, my friend, to see innocence in its death throes! Yet, all in all, that death is nothing…you could, perhaps, finish it off at a single blow, bring it to an end, stuff with dirt the ineffable mouth, smother its cry.… No! The hand which presses Him is more knowing and stronger; the look which gluts itself with Him comes not from human eyes. To the appalling hatred which broods over the dying Just Man, all is given, all is yielded. Not only is the divine flesh torn, it is violated, profaned by an absolute sacrilege, even in the majesty of its last breath.… The mockery of Satan, my friend! The laughter, the incomprehensible joy of Satan!…"

"For such a sight," said he after a brief silence, "our filthy clay is still too pure.…"

"The tragedy of Calvary," began the future canon…

He did not finish. From that moment on, this sacerdotal follower of Descartes ceased to see clearly within himself. Had even Descartes, whose discourses long ago revealed to so many lovely bluestockings another sensible universe, and who by an expert compounding of mathematics and wit made out of the problem of being a pastime for gentlefolk—had he one day heard one of his strange animals, concocted out of springs, levers, and cogwheels, speak—even he would not have been more overwhelmed than the unhappy priest, until that moment so level-headed, who, suddenly turned inside out, no longer recognized himself.

The pastor of Lumbres placed one sharp finger against the future canon's forehead. "Wretched are we," he said in a voice slow and harsh, "wretched are we who have here only a bit of brain and the pride of Satan! What have I to do with your prudence? Now my fate is settled. What peace did I seek, what silence? There is no peace here below, I tell you, no peace whatever, and in a single instant of true silence, this rotten world would melt away like a wisp of smoke, like a smell. I prayed Our Lord to open my eyes; I wanted to see His Cross; I saw it; you don't know what it is.... The tragedy of Calvary, say you.... Why, it stares you in the face, there is nothing else.... Look! I who speak to you, Sabiroux, I have heard—yes—even in the cathedral pulpit...things...beyond my telling.... They speak of God's death as they would of an old legend.... They embellish it...they add to it. Where do they find all that stuff? The tragedy of Calvary! Mind you remember, Sabiroux..."

"My dear friend...my dear friend," stammered the other, at the end of his rope, "such overexcitement...such violence...so far removed from your nature..."

And indeed the words themselves frightened him less than that voice, become so hard. But what was worst of all was his own name, the three syllables pilloried, snapped out like a command: "Sabiroux.... Sabiroux...."

"Mind you remember, Sabiroux, that the world is not a cleverly built machine. Between Satan and Himself, God hurls us, as His last rampart. It is through us that for centuries and centuries, the same hatred seeks to reach Him; it is in the same poor human flesh that the ineffable murder is brought to completion. Ah! Ah! however high, however far prayer and love may bear us, we carry him along with us, affixed to our flanks, the frightful companion, bursting with boundless laughter! Let us pray together, Sabiroux, that the ordeal may be short, and that the wretched human multitude may be spared.... Wretched multitude!..."

His voice broke in his throat, and he covered his eyes with his trembling hands. All around the limpid little garden whistled and sang. But they no longer heard it.

"Wretched multitude!" he repeated under his breath. At the memory of those he had so greatly loved, his mouth shook, a kind of smile slowly came to his face and spread over it with so gentle a majesty that Sabiroux was afraid he would see him fall there, in front of him, dead. He called out to him twice, timidly. Then, like a man awakening from sleep:

"I had to speak thus. I feel better. I believe it was allowable for me, Sabiroux, to rectify your judgment of me a little. It would distress me to let you believe that I have ever been favored with...with visions...apparitions...in a word with uncommon temptations. Such things were not made for me. No! What I have seen, my friend, I have seen in my little sacristy, seated on my rush-bottom chair, as clearly as I see you. You see, we don't know what a sinner is. What is a voice in the darkness of the confessional, which purrs along, hurriedly, hurriedly, coming to rest only on the first syllables of the *Mea culpa*? Here's a good thing for the children, poor little ones! But you must see, you must see the faces where all things are limned, and the eyes. Men's eyes, Sabiroux! One can never exhaust that subject. Indeed! I have been at many a deathbed; that is nothing; the dying are no longer frightening. God veils them. But the wretches I have seen before me—and who argue, smile, writhe, lie, lie, lie—up to the very moment when an ultimate anguish casts them at our feet like empty bags! This one still cuts a figure in the world, I assure you! That one still prances before the girls. The other blasphemes pleasantly.... Oh, for a long while I didn't understand! I saw only stray sheep whom God gathers up as He goes by. But there is something between God and man, and not at all a personage of secondary importance.... There is...there is that obscure thing, crafty and stubborn beyond compare, to whom nothing can be likened save, perhaps, that atrocious irony, cruel laughter. To him God yielded Himself for a time. In us is He clutched, devoured. From us is He wrested. For centuries the human race has been placed in the press, our blood squeezed out in torrents in order that the tiniest particle of the divine flesh might afford satiation and hilarious laughter to the dreadful torturer.... Oh, our ignorance is deep! To a learned, well-mannered, prudent priest, what is the devil, I ask you? Hardly do they dare utter his name without a smile. They whistle to him like a dog. What then? Do they think they have tamed him? I tell you! I tell you! It's because they've read too many books and haven't heard enough confessions. All they want is to please. They please only fools, whom they reassure. Our vocation is not to induce sleep, Sabiroux. We are in the vanguard of a struggle to the death, and our little ones behind us. Priests! But then they don't hear that cry, the cry of universal wretchedness! Then the only confessions they hear are their sacristans! Then never have they held before them, face to face, a countenance wholly distracted? Then never have they seen dart forth one of those unforgettable glances, already filled with hatred for God, to which there remains nothing we can give, nothing! The miser gnawed by his cancer, the lustful man like a corpse, the ambitious absorbed in a single dream, the envious who ever keeps watch. Come now! What priest has never wept in impotence before the mystery of human suffering, of a God outraged in man, His refuge!... They do not want to see! They do not want to see!"

The louder the harsh voice became in the wind and the sun, the more the sturdy little garden challenged it with all its stalwart life. The May breeze, driving its gray clouds across the sky, betimes jammed the vast herd of them below the horizon. Then it was that a ray of dazzling light, like the flash of a sword, skimming the whole darkened plain, came to burst in the resplendent hedgerow.

"I felt," later wrote Father Sabiroux, "as though I were upon an isolated summit, exposed defenseless to the blows of an invisible enemy.... And he, once more grown silent, stared at the same point in space. He seemed to await a sign, which did not come."

6.

WE MUST FALL back upon the words of that witness from whom we draw the cream of this narrative, and who was chosen by One more skilled and more powerful to stand beside the old man of Lumbres during his last struggle. Like what has been previously quoted, the following sentences have been extracted from the voluminous report addressed to his superiors by the scrupulous canon. Granted, you will see fear and self-esteem expressed here, sometimes with an innocent cunning. But there is nothing wholly worthless in the pleadings of an unfortunate man who defends his prejudices, his ease, his vanity, his reasons for living.

"Indeed, it is most difficult to picture to oneself with sufficient vividness an event already long past, yet a conversation like that which I am trying to recount here is, as it were, elusive to the grasp, and the most faithful memory could not, at such a distance, recreate the attitude, the tone, the thousand little facts which proportionately modify the meanings of the words and dispose us to hear only those which agree with our own hidden feelings. The respect which I owe the formal orders of my superiors and my desire to enlighten them must triumph over my reluctance and my scruples. Hence I shall try, less to report the exact words, than to reproduce their general meaning, and the extraordinary impression they made upon me.

"'Remember, Sabiroux!' my unhappy colleague had suddenly cried out, in a voice which riveted me to the spot. His eyes shot out flames. Once or twice I tried to make myself heard, without his deigning even to lower his glance. Must I admit it once more? I was under his charm, if you can describe as charm a dreadful tautening of the nerves, a consuming curiosity. As long as he continued speaking, I no longer doubted that I was in the presence of a man truly supernatural, in the very midst of ecstasy. A thousand things of which I had never thought, and which today seem to me full of contradictions and obscurities, or even of childish imaginings, then enlightened at once my heart and my reason. I believed that I was penetrating into a new world. How to reproduce in cold blood those singular utterances in which, by turns entreating and threatening, now pale with rage, now streaming tears, in a heart-rending tone, he despaired of the salvation of souls, recounted their useless martyrdom, raged against evil and death as though he held Satan by the throat. Satan! That name ceaselessly returned to his lips, and he pronounced it with an overwhelming intonation which pierced your heart. Were it permitted to human eyes to glimpse the rebel angel, to whom the holy innocence of our forefathers attributed so many marvels today better understood, such words would have evoked him, for already his shadow lay between us two humble priests in the little garden. No! Gentlemen, such discourse cannot be repeated in cold blood! You would have to have heard this venerable man, transfixed with horror and, as it were, carried away with hatred, summoning the most secret recollections of his sacred ministry, dreadful avowals, the work of sin in souls, and even the countenances of those unfortunate ones who had become the devil's prey, whereon his visionary eyes saw retraced, line by line, the death agony of Our Lord upon the Cross. I was in the transports of a sort of enthusiasm. No longer was I one of those ministers of Christian morality, but a man inspired, one of those legendary exorcists, standing ready to tear away from the powers of evil the lambs of their flocks. Miracle of eloquence! I spoke incoherently, I should have liked to hurl myself into combat, defy dangers, perhaps martyrdom. For the first time it seemed to me that I glimpsed the true purpose of my life and the majesty of the priesthood. I cast myself, yes, I cast myself at the knees of the pastor of Lumbres. Far more! I clutched between my hands the folds of his poor cassock, I pressed my lips against it, I watered it with my tears, and crying out, alas! in the overabundance of my joy, rather than saying them, I hurled forth these words: 'You are a saint!... You are a saint!...'"

Not once but twenty times did the canon, stooping on the ground, repeat this exclamation, and he stammered it in his intoxication. The soil scorched his heavy shoes, the horizon revolved like a wheel. He felt himself lighter than a man of cork, marvelously free and light, in the elastic air. "I believed myself severed from mortal bonds," he observes.

What utterance was then strong enough to lift so high this heavy weight, or what even more miraculous silence? What did he whisper in his ear, this tragic old man, whom temptation was then stirring to his depths, and who, spurned by all and even by God, compelled, spent, turned in his dying toward a friendly eye? But that, we shall not know....

"Oh! Satan holds us under his feet," said he at last, in a voice gentle and defenseless.

The pastor of Luzarnes, stuttering with astonishment: "My friend, my brother, I misjudged you.... I did not know you.... God has made you to be the honor of the diocese, of the Church, of the rostrum of Truth.... And, possessed of such wonderful gifts, here! You are still sighing, you consider yourself vanquished! You! Let me at least express to you my gratitude, my feeling, for the good you have done me, for the enthusiasm..."

"You have not understood me," the pastor of Lumbres only said.

He knew he should remain silent; nevertheless he was going to speak. Weakness has its logic and its propensity, as has heroism. All the same, the old man hesitated before dealing his final blows.

"I am not a saint," he continued. "Come, let me speak. I am, perhaps, one of the damned.... Yes! Look at me.... My past life becomes plain to me, and I see it like a landscape, just as from above Chennevières you see the town of Pin, beneath your feet. I labored to sever myself from the world; I wanted that, but the other is stronger and more wily; he helped me to wear out the hope within me. How I have suffered, Sabiroux! How often have I not said what I was tempted to say! I harbored in myself this loathsome thing; it was as though I had clasped to my heart the devil, like a child. I was at the end of my tether, and now this crisis has finally shattered everything. Fool that I was! God dwells not there, Sabiroux!"

Again he hesitated, before the innocent victim: this flushed priest with his candid eyes. Then, madly, he struck and struck again: "A saint! The word is on the tips of all your tongues. Saints! Do you know what they are? And yourself, Sabiroux, keep this in mind! Rarely does sin enter within us by violence, but rather by cunning. It seeps in like the air. It has neither form nor color nor taste proper to itself; it assumes all forms, all colors, all tastes. It wears us away inwardly. For the few wretches whom it devours alive and whose cries appall us, how many others are already cold, and are not even dead bodies any longer, but empty sepulchers. Our Lord has said it, Sabiroux! The Enemy of mankind pilfers everything, even death, and then flies off laughing."

(The same flame once more passed over his staring eyes, like a reflection on a wall.)

"His laughter! That is the weapon of the prince of this world. He hides himself away just as he lies; he assumes all countenances, even our own. He never waits; nowhere does he take a stand. He is in the glance that defies him; he is in the mouth that denies him. He is in mystical anguish; he is in the self-assurance and calmness of the fool. Prince of this world! Prince of this world!"

Why this wrath? Against whom? the pastor of Luzarnes asked himself in all sincerity. "Oh!" he exclaimed. "Men like you…"

But the saint of Lumbres did not let him finish; he moved closer to him, to put his arm around his shoulder. "Men like me! Holy writ tells you, Sabiroux; they faint away in their wisdom."

Then suddenly he asked, his voice cutting, "Prince of this world… what do you yourself think of that world?"

"Dear me, of course…" whispered the poor fellow between his teeth.

"Prince of this world; here is the ultimate answer. He is prince *of this world*, he holds it in his hands, he is its king."

"...We are trampled under Satan's feet," he resumed after a silence. "You, I more than you, with a desperate certainty. We are inundated, drowned, covered over. He does not even take the trouble to thrust us aside, puny as we are; he makes us into his instruments; he puts us to his own uses, Sabiroux. At this instant, what am I myself? A scandal to you, a thorn which he thrusts into your heart. Forgive me in the name of divine pity! I have borne this thought, ripened every day, in silence all my life. No longer do I contain it; it has devoured me. It is I who am in it, my hell! I have known too many souls, Sabiroux, I have too often listened to human speech, when it no longer serves to hide shame but to express it; taken at its source, spurting like the blood from a wound. I, too, I thought I could fight, if not conquer. At the outset of our priestly lives, we fashion for ourselves so strange, so generous an idea of the sinner. Rebellion, blasphemy, sacrilege—all that has its wild grandeur; here is a beast we shall tame.... Tame the sinner! Oh, what a laughable thought! Tame weakness and slothfulness themselves! Who would not grow weary of raising up an inert mass? All alike! In the outpouring of their avowals, in the release of forgiveness, liars still, always! They play the part of the strong and skittish man who has taken the bit in his mouth despite convention, morality, and all the rest; they beg for a firm hand to hold them in. Oh, wretched they! They are foundered! I have seen some, mark my word, I have seen some whom the name of a woman cast into convulsions of frenzy and who, torn by fear, remorse, and desire, groveled at my feet like animals.... I have seen. No! No! This vast fraud, this cruel laugh, this way of profaning what he lolls, such is Satan victorious! Have you understood me, Sabiroux?"

The professor's azure eyes met the old man's glance with a candid curiosity, an infinite, everlasting good will. Ah, let it at last be shattered, that blue enamel! And the aged athlete, confronting the great, wide-eyed child, by turns flushed and grew pale. His heart pounded regularly in his chest where the powerful will, never wholly subdued, already was growing taut, bursting its bonds. He shoved Sabiroux against the wall, he cried into his ear, and in an unforgettable tone: "We are conquered, I tell you! Conquered! Conquered!"

For a minute, a long minute, he listened to his own blasphemy, like the last shovelful of earth tossed into a grave. He who thrice denied his master one look alone could absolve, but what hope for the man who has denied himself?

"My friend! My friend!" cried out the pastor of Luzarnes.

But the saint of Lumbres gently pushed away his hands. "Leave me," said he, "leave me…listen to me no longer."

"Leave you!" retorted the other, his voice piercing. "Leave you! I have never encountered anything like you. Forgive me rather for having had my doubts about you. I am ready to serve you as the witness you had proposed.… Nothing is impossible or incredible in a man such as you are.… Go ahead! Go ahead! I follow you; it was God Who inspired you not long ago. Come! Let us return to the house together. Go restore to the mother her dead child."

The pastor of Lumbres looked at him in amazement, passed his hand over his forehead, sought to understand.… Even for a moral philosopher, what a tragic, astounding forgetfulness! What! He no longer remembered?…

"Come, my friend, my venerable friend," he repeated, "is it up to me to remind you what, a while ago, in this very place?…"

He remembered. Mercy's last appeal, the dazzling promise which would have saved him and which he heard only with mistrust, rather than obeying it like a child whose little hands do great things unawares—was it possible? Another had to remind him. The obsession to which for two days and two nights the wretched man had lashed his thought—madness!—perhaps at the moment of his deliverance, and at what hands! had got hold of him, entire. At the decisive moment, at the unique moment in his extraordinary life—sovereign, absolute mockery—he was no longer anything but a human animal, with power only to suffer and cry out.

Ah, the shipwrecked mariner who in the morning mist is not able, any more, to descry the rosy sail; the artist who, having exhausted his vein, dies while yet alive; the mother who beholds in the eyes of her dying son the look of recognition slip away—none of these cast to heaven a harsher outcry.

Nonetheless, even under this blow, the heroic old man did not bend his knees. He no longer prayed. He coldly measured the depth of his fall; for the last time he reviewed the superior tactics of the enemy who had overcome him—"I have hated sin," said he to himself, "then life itself, and whatever unutterable thing it was I felt during the delights of prayer was perhaps this despair which was melting me away at the heart."

Images one by one wear out their patterns upon us; then, with the consciousness in full disarray, reason comes and finishes us off. As much as the instincts themselves, this high faculty on which we pride ourselves has its panic. The pastor of Lumbres felt it. He completed the thought which was killing him. "What, at the very moment when I believed myself...what, in the deepest intoxication of divine love!..."

"Has God made game of me?" he cried.

In the scattering of a dream which has ever seemed to us reality itself, and to which our destiny has become linked, when the disaster is complete—has reached its point of perfection—what other force still entreats us, be it not the bitter desire to provoke misfortune, to hasten it, to know it at last?

"Let us go," said the pastor of Lumbres.

7.

HE STRODE ACROSS the garden, which a cloud had thrown into shadow. He reappeared at the threshold.

"Here he is!" exclaimed she who awaited him, heart pounding.

She moved forward toward him and stopped, stricken unto her very hope at the sight of this altered countenance, where she read only grim determination, countenance of a hero, not of a saint. But he, not lowering his glance toward her, went straight toward the closed door, behind the large oak table and, his hand on the knob, with a gesture stopped short his overawed colleague. The door opened on the dark and silent room, with its closed shutters. For an instant the candle at its far end flickered. He entered and closeted himself with the dead.

The room, its walls whitewashed, was narrow and deep; it lay directly behind the kitchen, and the doctor had wished the sick boy moved there because it was more spacious and had two windows facing the east—the garden, the Sennecourt woods, the Beauregard hills, filled with hedgerows in flower. A worn carpet had been thrown over the red tile floor. The single taper barely illuminated the naked walls. And what daylight crept in—you could not tell how—through invisible chinks, gathered and floated about the white sheets, unwrinkled, stiff, and falling away most evenly to the floor on each side of the little boy, now wonderfully well-behaved and quiet. A busybody fly buzzed.

The pastor of Lumbres remained standing at the foot of the bed and watched without praying the crucifix on the clean linen. He did not hope he would again hear the mysterious command. But the promise had been given, the command heard; that was enough. Here was the unfaithful servant, at the very spot where his master had in vain awaited him, and now he listened, impassive, for the judgment he had deserved.

He listened. Outside, behind the closed shutters, the garden blazed and hissed under the sun, like a stick of green wood in a fire. Inside the air was heavy with the perfume of lilacs, of hot wax, and of another solemn odor. The silence, which was no longer the silence of earth, and which the exterior noises pierced but did not break, mounted around them, from the deep soil. It mounted, like an invisible vapor, and now animate things, seen through it, were loosened and set free; now sounds slackened within it, now a thousand unknown things sought each other there, and there were joined. Like the gliding motion, one upon the other, of two fluids of unequal density, two realities were superposed, without blending, in a mysterious equilibrium.

This was the moment when the saint of Lumbres's glance met that of the dead boy and remained fixed upon it.

The glance of only one of those dead eyes, the other being closed. Probably the eyelids had been drawn shut too soon, and by a tremulous hand, and so muscular retraction had lifted one of them a little, and you could see under the stiff lash the blue pupil, already tarnished, but strangely dark, almost black. Of the wan face in the hollow of the pillow, you saw only that, in the midst of a black ring, widened as though by a cavern of shadow. The little body in its shroud strewn with lilacs already had that stiffness and angularity of a corpse around which our atmosphere, so in love with living shapes, seems solidified like a block of ice. The iron bedstead, with its tiny cold burden, seemed like a ship of wonder which has cast anchor forevermore. There was only that backward glance—the long look of one exiled—as clear as a motion of the hand.

Assuredly the pastor of Lumbres did not fear that look; but he sought from it an answer. He tried to hear it. Just before, in a sort of defiance, he had crossed the doorsill ready to play within these four white walls a desperate game. He had strode toward the dead boy without being moved to compassion, without pity, as though toward an obstacle to be cleared, something to be pushed over, too heavy.... And behold, he who was dead had outstripped him: *it was he who awaited him*, like a determined foe, on his guard.

He stared at this half-open eye with curious attentiveness, from which pity gradually disappeared, and then with a kind of cruel impatience. Most certainly he had looked upon death as often as the oldest soldier; such a sight was commonplace to him. To take a step, stretch out his hand, with his finger close the eyelid, cover the pupil which watched him, which was now utterly defenseless—what could have been easier? No terror held him back today, no disgust. Rather the desire, the unavowed expectation of an impossible thing, which was going to come to pass outside of him, without him. His mind hesitated, drew back, again moved forward. He tempted this dead boy as, shortly, without knowing it, he would tempt God.

Once again he tried to pray, moved his lips, relaxed his tight throat. No! One more minute, one short minute more... The mad, absurd fear that an uncautious word would drive away forever a presence invisible, divined, wanted, feared, nailed him dumb to the spot. The hand, which was sketching in the air the sign of the cross, fell back. In its passage, the broad sleeve bent the flame of the taper and put it out. Too late! Twice had he seen the eyes open and close in a silent appeal. He smothered a cry. The dark room was already more peaceful than before. The outside light slipped through the shutters, floated about, outlined each object against an ashen background, and the bed in the midst of a bluish halo. In the kitchen the clock struck ten.... A girl's laughter rose in the clear morning and long continued to pulse.... "Come! Come!..." said the saint of Lumbres, his voice ill-assured.

With comic haste he fumbled through his pockets looking for the touchwood lighter which had been given him by the Count of Salpene (but which he always left behind on his table), found a match, vainly tried to ignite it, repeated, "Come...come," his teeth clenched. In emptying his pockets, he had scattered over the floor his horn-handled knife, some letters, his cotton handkerchief—its color such a lovely red!—and in vain did he feel here and there over the tiles, trying to recover them. The bed, close at hand, cast a denser shadow. But higher up, in contrast, the luminous vapor around the closed blinds broadened and spread out. Now the dead boy's face appeared...by degrees...re-ascended...slowly...to the surface of the darkness. The old fellow leaned over to touch it, looked.... The two eyes, now wide open, looked upon him also.

For another moment he met their gaze with a wild hope. But no crease budged the retracted eyelids. The pupils, dull black, no longer held any human thought.... And yet... Perhaps some other thought?... Irony quickly recognized, in a flash.... The challenge of the master of death, of the thief of men.... It was he.

"It's you. I recognize you," exclaimed the woeful old priest in a low, strained tone. At the same time it seemed to him that all the blood in his veins fell back upon his heart in an icy rain. A lightning-like pain, unutterable, pierced him from one shoulder to the other and at once spread throughout his left arm, even as far as the numb fingers. An anguish such as he had never felt, wholly physical, emptied his chest as though a monstrous suction were at work just above the stomach. He stiffened to avoid crying, calling.

All certainty of living had disappeared: death was close, sure, imminent. The dauntless man struggled against it with a desperate energy. He stumbled, stepped forward to regain his balance, grabbed the bed, sought not to fall. In this simple misstep, forty years of a generous will, at its highest tension, were spent in a second for one last superhuman effort, sufficient for one moment to stop fate short.

So it is true that, until the night conceals him, covers him over in his turn, the obstinate torturer, who diverts himself with man as though he were a prey, surrounds him with his illusions, summons him, leads him astray, bestows commands or caresses, withdraws or renews hope, assumes all voices, of angel or of demon, is countless, effectual, powerful as a God. As a God! Oh! What matter hell and its flames, provided that once, only once, the monstrous mischief be crushed! Is it possible, does God wish, that the servant who has followed Him shall find in His place the laughable king of the flies, the beast seven times crowned? To the mouth which seeks the cross, to the arms which press it close, shall only this be given? This lie? Is it possible, repeats the saint of Lumbres under his breath, is it possible? And then, at once: "You have deceived me!" he cried out.

(The sharp pain which girded him with its terrible shoulder strap a little loosened its clasp, but his breathing became more labored. His heart beat slowly, as though drowned. "I have only a moment more," the wretched man said to himself, lifting from the floor, one after the other, his leaden feet.)

But nothing stopped him; his jaws clamped tight, mustering his whole self in one sole thought, he advanced upon the conquering enemy and measured his blow. The saint of Lumbres slipped his hands under the stiff little arms, drew the light corpse half out of its coverings. The head fell over and rolled from one shoulder to the other, then slipped backward and came to rest. It seemed to say, "No! No!" with the pretty, lazy gesture of spoiled children. But what mattered it to the rough peasant, assaulted to the very depths of his supreme hope and kept on his feet by a superhuman wrath, one of those elementary feelings, frenzy of a child or of a demigod?

He elevated the little boy like a host. He looked wildly heavenward. How can we hope to reproduce the cry of distress, the curse of the hero who asked neither pity nor forgiveness, but justice! No, no! He did not implore this miracle, he demanded it. God owed him. God would give him, else all was but a dream. As between him and You, say who is master! Oh, the mad, mad words, but made to resound even unto heaven, and shatter the silence! Mad words, loving blasphemy!...

Upon him who brought death into the human family the power is perhaps bestowed to destroy life itself, to restore it to the void from whence it is drawn. Granted that he had suffered in vain! But he had believed. "Show Yourself," he cried out in that inward voice in which is made manifest to the invisible world the incomprehensible power of man, "show Yourself before abandoning me forever!"... Oh, the wretched old priest, who cast what he had to the winds in order to obtain a sign in the heavens! And this sign would not be refused him, for the faith which moves mountains can surely bring a dead boy back to life.... But God yields Himself only to love.

8.

The saint of Lumbres himself has left us only a very brief account, or rather notes hastily written, and in a confusion of spirit bordering on delirium. Its wording is clumsy, so artless that it is impossible to transcribe the lines without toning them down. Nothing here recalls the extraordinary man upon whom were tried all the seductions of despair; quite on the contrary, here you rediscover the former pastor of Lumbres, with his open humility, his respect for his superiors and even a rather low deference, a cringing fear lest he set tongues wagging, a perfect distrust of self, joined to a profound despondency, beyond remedy and all too indicative of his end.

Nevertheless, a few of these lines deserve to be rescued from oblivion. They are those in which, anxious only to record very precisely the succession of events of which he was the sole witness, he transcribed, as it were, word for word, the final moments of his wonderful story. Here they are, exactly as written:

"For a minute or two I held the little body in my arms," he wrote, "then I strove to raise it up toward the crucifix. Light as it was, it was most painful for me to support it, so weak and aching was my left arm. However, I succeeded. Then, focusing my eyes upon our Lord and forcefully recalling to my mind the penance and the fatigues of my poor life, the good I occasionally could do, the consolations I have received, I gave all, without reserve, in order that the enemy who had relentlessly pursued me, and who at that very moment was robbing me even of the hope of salvation, should finally be humiliated in my presence by One more powerful than he.... O Father, to this I should have sacrificed even eternal life!...

"Father, it is all too true; the devil, who had taken possession of me, is strong enough and cunning enough to deceive my senses, lead my judgment astray, mingle true with false.... I accept, I receive in advance your sovereign decision. But the marvel still dwells in the eyes which saw it, in the hands which touched it.... Yes! For an interval of time about which I cannot be precise, the corpse seemed alive again. I felt it warm under my fingers, throbbing. The little head, tumbled backward, turned toward me.... I saw the eyelids flutter and the features take on life.... I saw it. During that moment an inner voice repeated these words to me: *Numquid cognoscentur in tenebris mirabilia tua, et justitia tua in terra oblivionis?* I was opening my mouth to utter them, when that same sharp pain, beyond description, which I can compare to nothing else, once again overwhelmed me. For another second I tried to hold up the little body which was slipping from my grasp. I saw it tumble back on the bed. Then it was that behind me there resounded a dreadful cry."

He had indeed heard it, this dreadful cry followed by more awful laughter. Then he had fled the room, like a thief, straight toward the open door and the garden full of sunlight, without turning his head, without seeing anything save the shadows, which he pushed aside without recognizing, waving both his outstretched arms.... Behind him the voices were extinguished one by one, finally to blend into a single vague murmur, soon hushed.... He took a few more steps, caught his breath, opened his eyes. He was sitting on the bank of the Lumbres road, his hat fallen near him on the ground, his eyes still vague. A trap rolled by at a fast trot, in the golden dust, and in passing the driver even smiled broadly and raised his whip.... "Have I been dreaming, then?" the miserable priest said to himself, his heart throbbing.... The pastor of Luzarnes stood before him.

A pastor of Luzarnes pale, out of breath, stammering, but little by little regaining his impressiveness and his self-assurance at seeing the wretched fellow who was scrambling to his feet with great difficulty, forcing himself to stand upright, bareheaded, his gray hair in disarray like an ancient schoolboy's.

"Unfortunate man!" exclaimed the future canon as soon as he was sure of speaking with suitable firmness. "Unfortunate man! Your situation could well arouse pity; I am sorry for you. But I am also sorry for myself, in that I yielded to your folly and have drawn upon this poor house another frightful harm and compromised the dignity of all of us—yes!—of all of us by a ridiculous display.... And this flight! Oh! dear colleague, this lack of courage astounds me in you.... And now," he resumed after a silence, during which he seemed still attracted by the sound of his own voice and kept his eyes shut, "and now, what shall you do?"

"What would you have me do?" replied the saint of Lumbres. "I have committed a fault the gravity of which I scarcely can estimate. God knows it. I fully deserve your scorn."

He added a few confused words in an inaudible tone, hesitated a long while, then, humbly, his head inclined toward the ground, he said in a voice almost unintelligible: "And now...and now... if you will tell me...the dead child, whom I held in my arms?..."

"Don't speak of him!" replied the pastor of Luzarnes with deliberate asperity.

At this blow the old man shuddered without answering, yet cast a strange glance at his judge.

"The almost sacrilegious comedy you performed (with no bad intention, my friend!) has produced a catastrophe of which you seem unaware.... But seriously, it's not possible that you neither saw nor heard..."

"Heard..." replied the saint of Lumbres, "heard... What did I hear?..."

"'*What did I hear*'!" exclaimed the former professor. "Explain yourself! After all, you are quite capable of having listened only to imaginary voices. I'm unwilling to believe that a man like you, a minister of peace, should remorselessly have left behind him a woman, a mother, whom your hateful play acting almost killed* and who is, at this very moment, wholly out of her mind?"

Since the old priest, however, gazed at him in what was obviously genuine stupefaction, he lowered his voice when he spoke again, with a fool's eagerness to pour out his sad and tragic tale.

"So you don't know! You are unaware that the unhappy woman had slipped into the room behind your back? What took place? You must know better than I.... We heard a cry, a burst of laughter.... Then you crossed the kitchen like someone bewildered.... She wanted to follow you; it was all we could do to restrain her; what a dreadful spectacle.... Alas! Why should I be astonished that a weak woman in misfortune should have been carried away by your eloquence, the contagion of your gestures, of your exalted imagination, since I myself...a brain like mine...a little while ago... had reached the stage of not knowing what was true and what false.... She kept repeating, 'He lives! He lives! He will live once more!' She wanted us to run, to bring you back.... Mercy on us!"

He stopped a moment, panted, and asked, his arms crossed: "There are the facts.... What do you make of it?"

"I am at a loss," replied the pastor of Lumbres, calmly, drawing himself to his full height.

Then he seemed to search with his eyes in the empty sky for his invisible enemy. "I am at a loss," he resumed. "I was mad...a dangerous madman.... I should take steps against myself—yes—I must myself make myself harmless.... One hope remains to me, and that is that my time is short; very short.... My friend, a little while back I felt the first attack of a disease which I attributed...well, a very strange pain, and one which, I feel certain, will, at one moment or another, redouble its attack, and carry me off...."

"He described to me very precisely," reports the pastor of Luzarnes in the notes already quoted, "a classic attack of angina pectoris. I most plainly told him so. I should have liked to have added some advice (based on experience, alas! my venerable mother having died of this fearful disease). But, after having twice made me repeat the term angina pectoris, which he had never heard, I saw him pick his hat up from the ground, wipe it on his sleeve, and stride off without wanting to listen to me."

9.

HOW LONG IS the road back, the long road! The road of armies beaten, the road of the evening, which leads nowhere in the fruitless dust!... Yet you must go on, you must tramp on, as long as beats this poor old heart—to no purpose, to use up life—for there is no rest so long as the day lasts, so long as the cruel star watches us, with its single eye, above the horizon. So long as beats the poor old heart.

Here was the first house in the village, then the short cut, between two hedges of unequal height, through meadows and apple trees, which led to the cemetery entrance, in the very shadow of the church. Here was the church of Lumbres, like a shadow.

The pastor of Lumbres entered, without anyone's seeing him, through the small door which opened directly into the sacristy itself. He let himself fall into a chair, his eyes fixed upon the brickwork of the floor, kneading his hat with his hands, still unable to focus upon anything his routed memory, merely hearing the regular throb of the blood in the arteries of his neck, with stupefied attentiveness.

There remained nothing indeed of the grand old man in full rebellion, in full defiance! Not for a second, until the end, would he find the strength necessary to gather up his recollections, or to disentangle them. Even the idea of so painful a winnowing was to him hateful, unbearable. Oh, if only he could preserve within himself, rather, this half-sleep! The struggle had been too violent and he had fallen from too great a height; ordinary temptations are no more than children's dreams, a wearisome rumination, a repetitiousness like the wily droning of some judge. But he—he had been put to the question by the torturer.

Unconsciously he held one hand tight against his chest, at the very spot where the pain, quiet now, had its root. More than terror of a fresh spasm, however, fear weighed him down; fear first of all of the judgment of his colleagues, of their gossip, of the archbishop's reprimands and disciplinary measures. The tears were welling to his eyes. He dragged his chair up to a small table and, his head empty, his heart dispirited, his back bent under the impending blows, he forced himself to write very legibly, very neatly, with an eye to a possible inquiry, in a fine schoolboy's hand, the sort of report a few lines of which we have already quoted.

He wrote, corrected, tore up. But the more he recorded its details on paper, the more his miraculous adventure melted away in his mind, was blotted out. He no longer recognized it; he was, as it were, a stranger to it. The very effort he made to recapture it broke within him the last, the fragile thread of memory, and left him with his elbows on the table, his eyes vague, his faculties numb.

How many hours would he remain thus, looking at but not seeing a narrow grilled window, in the stone wall's thickness, outside of which an elder branch moved to and fro, stirred by the wind in the sun, now black, now green? The man who came at noon to ring the Angelus saw through the little panes in the door, in the shadows, his hat fallen upon the floor, and his breviary, its holy pictures and place-markers scattered about. At five o'clock a youngster who was studying the catechism in preparation for his First Communion, Sebastien Mallet, came to look for a book he had forgotten, discovered the door closed, but then, hearing nothing, ran away. "I did not dare knock too loud, or call," said he later, "for the church was already full of people, and I was very fearful they would question me."

This was indeed the hour when the crowd of pilgrims daily brought to Lumbres by the Plessis-Baugrenan bus flocked to the saint's confessional in the Chapel of the Holy Angels, A strange crowd, where one saw so many tragic or comic personages elbowing each other, so many famous puppets which the warmth of a great soul for a moment raised above the level of day-to-day lies, restored to the kingdom of mankind! That particular evening, more numerous than usual, fidgety because they had had to wait, or perhaps stirred by a vague foreboding, in the murmurous ancient church... Each time the main door swung open, distressed faces—those taut faces which those who "constantly saw this pilgrimage will never forget—turned toward the threshold briefly bathed in light, and then in unison fell back into shadow. The cautious whispers, the nervous coughings smothered behind hands, a thousand different little gestures of impatience or of curiosity, ultimately blended into one single strange sound, comparable to the trampling of a herd in the tempest and the rain. Suddenly even this noise ceased; all was silent. The sacristy door grated amidst a solemn soundlessness. The pastor of Lumbres appeared.

"Lord! how pale he is!" said a woman's voice, far back in the nave.

This cry, clearly audible, broke the spell. The herd rediscovered its master and breathed.

Now the old priest was approaching his confessional, slowly, his head a little bent over the right shoulder, his hand still tight against his heart. At the first step he had thought he would fall. But an eddy in the crowd had already borne him to his destination; it closed in around him. Once again, he was their prey.

Never again did he escape them. He remained standing, his tall figure sharply bent over, the nape of his neck against the low oaken ceiling, his breath labored. He abandoned to suffering a body inert and humiliated, his mortal remains. His doltish patience would weary the torturer.

But who could ever weary that invisible one who observed him, and gloated at his agony? It was needful that the wretched old man, for a moment a rebel and almost a conqueror, should feel upon himself until the very end that power he had defied.... Would to God that he might at least recognize his enemy, face to face! But it was not that voice that he would hear, that last challenge.... Then it was that through the keen anguish awareness by degrees returned to him that he was listening.... He listened to a murmur soon more distinct...monotonous...inexorable. He recognized it.... It was they. One by one, men and women, there they all were, whose breath he felt rise up toward him, less hateful than their impure speech, dismal litanies of sin, words sullied for centuries, ignobly tarnished by use, passing from the mouths of the fathers to those of the sons, like the most read pages of an obscene book, and marked by vice with its sign— countersigned-in the filth of thousands of fingers. It arose, this speech; little by little it wholly encompassed the saint of Lumbres as he yet stood there. How they hurried! How fast they went!... But the moment they caught their breaths, you would see them—Oh! you would see them, those dreadful children!—seek, touch with their tongues the hideous udder, which Satan squeezed for them, swollen with the beloved poison!... Until death, raise the hand, forgive, absolve, man of the cross, vanquished beforehand!

He listened, he answered as in a dream, but with utter clarity. Never was his brain more free, his judgment swifter, keener; whereas his flesh was heedful only of the growing pain, of the fixed point from which the sharp pangs radiated, thrust in all directions its wonderful branches, or ran beneath the web of nerves like a darting shuttle. It had penetrated so deep that it seemed to have reached the division between the body and the spirit, made two parts out of the one man.... The saint of Lumbres in his death throes had concourse only with souls. He saw them with those eyes over which the lids already had dropped—they alone.... Wedged against the resounding partition, the small of his back painfully pressed against the bench where he did not dare sit, his mouth open to breathe the heavy air, streaming with sweat, he heard only that murmur, barely distinct, the voices of his sons at his knees, filled with shame. Ah! whether they spoke or remained silent, the great impatient soul had already forestalled their avowals, commanded, threatened, entreated. The man of the cross was not there in order to conquer, but to give witness until death of the savage guile, of the unjust and abject power, of the iniquitous decision which he was appealing to God. Look upon these children, Lord, in their weakness, their vanity, as light and as swift as a bee, their curiosity without constancy, their short-range, elementary reasoning, their sensuality full of sadness...listen to their language, at once rough and treacherous, which seizes only the shapes of things, rich only in equivocation, firm enough when it denies, always cowardly in affirmation, the language of a slave or a freed-man, made for insolence and to caress, pliant, insinuating, dishonest. *Pater, dimitte illis, non enim sciunt quod facient!*

10.

"ALAS," EXPLAINED THE pastor of Luzarnes, "I have paid a rather high price for what I have gone through! My unfortunate colleague very nearly died in my presence of an acute attack of angina pectoris, and you yourself will very shortly agree..."

As he uttered these words, he was tramping along the road to Lumbres, followed by the young Chavranches doctor, who had to trot to keep up with him. This still beardless practitioner, who had had his shingle out only a few months, enjoyed a professional reputation merely a little beyond his deserts. The self-possession of his small talk, his medical student's impudences, and, above all, his scorn for his patients had won him all hearts. Not a lady of substance in the neighborhood who did not dream, on her daughter's behalf, of a proposal from this insolent mouth, and of the assistance of his two skilled hands, as well suited as the legendary blade to heal the wounds they inflicted. Not a dying soul who did not aspire to hear, beside his deathbed, a few of those consoling, spicy words, uttered in a soothing tone, and with the facetiousness of a cannibal. For this fop no longer bothered to number those who, under his ministrations—and to borrow his own expression—passed away with a good laugh.

"Heavens! That's altogether likely, Father," he replied in a conciliatory tone.

He had been summoned in great haste and on the advice of the pastor of Luzarnes, and he had found the Squire of le Plouy's lady in a violent attack of delirium which exhaustion alone brought to an end. But, toward evening and once the sick woman had fallen asleep, the priest had exclaimed, "My dear doctor, I have a personal favor to ask of you. Your automobile, you said, is to come here for you at about seven? It is barely five now. Stroll over to Lumbres with me. What stands in the way of your telephoning your chauffeur at Chavranches to come get you there? In the meanwhile, you will have had time to give my poor colleague a thorough examination, and I shall have your opinion on him."

"You have long known what I think!" said the young medical man, not uncheerfully. "Food that gives little nourishment, no exercise, quarters in a dilapidated rectory, the damp church, the confessional without light or air, thirteenth-century health rules—upon my word! Quite apart from a weak heart, all that is enough to finish off an organism already overtaxed!... But what would you have me do about it?"

"I have my ministry and you have yours," replied the pastor of Luzarnes, with nobility. "'The reason for our existence is pity for the weak, mankind. What matters it to you whether my poor associate be this or that? And even though what you say is true, it would still be only one of those cases of exaggerated professional zeal, which deserve the concern of an observer and the care of a medical man...."

"All right! I'll go..." he yielded. "After all, it's a pleasure to discuss things with a priest like you," the Chavranches doctor added.

Thus did they decide to make the pilgrimage to Lumbres together—and with feelings much alike. As they entered the village, it began to rain lightly; the white roadway under their feet took on an ochre tint; a mist tasting of ivy hung in the air. They visibly hastened their pace. The grass in the cemetery was soaking wet; the iron gate, endlessly opened and closed, grated its lament, and the high gray stone portal, whipped by the tempest, seemed in the dying shadow to stretch and shiver like a sail. Then, side by side, they entered the now almost empty church.

Once inside, the pastor of Luzarnes, placing his hand in fatherly fashion on his companion's shoulder, said in a low voice: "Dr. Gambillet, I should gladly have spared you this visit to a church, which you might find embarrassing, but won't you find it more cheerful to wait here than in a rectory parlor, as cold and bare as the reception room of a nunnery? Moreover, the greater part of the crowd has happily scattered. I see no one waiting at the confessional, and if my venerable colleague is taking a brief rest in the sacristy, he'll raise no objections, I trust, to coming with us at once to his house!"

Having said this, he disappeared. The young man from Chavranches, continuing to stand quietly near the holy-water stoup, in a moment heard only the echo of his distant voice, the creaking of a door, the tread of heavy shoes on the flagstones. Before run one by one, the lingering devout women, taking quick, short steps, their hands furtive on the brim of the marble basin, passed within touching distance, glancing at him with their grave eyes. Then the peasant sacristan blew out the last lamps. At last the pastor of Luzarnes reappeared.

"Here's a strange business!" said he. "My colleague must have left the church; we can't find him anywhere. What is more, confessions, they tell me, stopped at least forty minutes ago.... We have to yield to the facts, Dr. Gambillet.... Surely he must have gone back to his residence by the cemetery door.... Bear with me a little longer," he added in that tone of intimacy which never meets with refusal.

"What does it matter to me?" obligingly replied the Chavranches doctor. "My car is to pick me up here at about seven o'clock; I have time. But for a dying man, Father, your friend is pretty nimble...."

He rounded off his thought by whistling heedlessly. For, awaiting without impatience, with manly firmness, the moment when it would be his turn to take charge, he would have thought it unworthy to betray any surprise. Yet vainly did they question old Martha in the parlor with its pair of stuffed snipe; she had not seen her master and did not expect him soon.

"Poor dear man, he eats at impossible hours, and more than once has spent the livelong night kneeling on the pavement of the Chapel of the Holy Angels!

"That's where he still is, gentlemen, sure as you're standing there! You'll find him in the little recess in the wall, behind the cruet table—a place he likes—as much alone as though he were in the middle of the Bargemont woods.

"Ladislas!" said she to the sacristan, who had just appeared in the doorway with a pile of linen on his arm, "did you see him, while you made your rounds?"

But the old fellow shook his head.

"We close the church doors," she explained, "at six, and Ladislas will not open them again until nine, for evening prayers and benediction. This is the time our pastor sets aside to put things a little to rights, down there, you see, and straighten them up to his taste.... Just think! He has secured the bishop's permission to have the Blessed Sacrament exposed all night long! Will you give these gentlemen the keys?" she asked Ladislas, a trifle embarrassed.

"I'd rather go with them myself," the sacristan crustily replied. "After all, I have my orders, too! Time to eat a bite and drink a glass of wine."

Behind his back, the old woman wagged her head. "I was very much afraid it would be that way, gentlemen," she said. "But it won't take him long to eat supper, for he hardly touches a thing. He has a rough way of talking, you see, but is no more ill-natured than a child."

"Well then, we'll wait for him," stiffly said the pastor of Luzarnes, questioning his companion with a glance.

"And...and I have still another proposal to make you," began the aged Martha, after coughing to clear her throat. "In the room next door (the one our good saint of the Lord calls his oratory, on account of his hearing confessions there also) there is a grand gentleman come from far away on purpose to see our pastor, an old man with the Legion of Honor, very much the gentleman, I assure you, very pleasant, and who must find the time heavy on his hands."

The Chavranches doctor made a gesture with both hands, consigning to the devil the old man as well as his cross of the Legion.

"Some retired general?..." suggested the former professor of chemistry with a smile of sympathy for the doctor.

"His card is on the table—yes, there in front of you, gentlemen," said she, disheartened. "But he has such soft, gentle eyes. No! He just can't be a military man!"

The square of stiff paper was already under Gambillet's nose, who blushed like a child. "Oh! Oh! This is another story!" said he with the tone of a connoisseur....

He held the card out to the pastor of Luzarnes, who was staggered. "Antoine Saint-Marin..." stammered the future canon, his lips moist.

"Of the French Academy," replied the other, like an echo. The young medical man took a stance, and for a moment seemed to be seeking something.... "Introduce us!" he said, at last.

11.

FOR HALF A century, this celebrated old man had reigned supreme over the kingdom of irony. His genius, which prided itself on respecting nothing, was of all geniuses the most docile and the most commonplace. If he feigned modesty or wrath, teased or threatened, it was the better to please his masters and, like an obedient slave, by turns bite or fondle. In his artful mouth, the safest words were deceitful, truth itself was servile. A curiosity, of which age had not yet blunted the edge, and which was what you might call the strong point of this ancient juggler, drew him constantly to renew himself, to work upon himself before a mirror. Each of his books was a milestone where he awaited the passer-by. Fully as well as a girl educated and polished by the bleak experience of vice, he knew that the way of giving is worth more than what one gives and, in his frenzy to contradict himself and forswear himself, he succeeded each time in presenting the reader with a man wholly new.

The young word-weavers who made up his retinue praised to the skies his expert simplicity, his sentences as crafty as a theater *ingénue*, the twistings in his dialectics, the vastness of his knowledge. The spineless race, chill to the marrow, recognized in him its sovereign. They rejoiced, as though at a victory won over mankind, in the spectacle of impotence which at least makes mock of that which it cannot embrace, and demanded their share of the barren caress. No thinking being had debauched more ideas, despoiled more venerable words, offered a richer prey to the most contemptible of his fellows. From page to page, the truth which he first proclaims with a rake's abandoned, foolish, gibing pout, turns up again in the last line, after the ultimate somersault, stripped naked, sitting on the knees of the triumphant, conniving manservant of an old farce.... And at once the little troop, enlarged by a public both anxious and devout, salutes with a discreet laugh the latest trick of the urchin approaching the century mark.

"I am the last of the Greeks," he said of himself, with a strange grin.

At once twenty simpletons, hasty experts on Homer by virtue of the marginal notes concerning him which they have been able to read in a history of literature, cry out in praise of this new miracle of Mediterranean civilization and rush off to awaken with their sharp clangor the dismayed Muses. For it is the ghastly old fellow's coquetry, and the most cynical of his graces, that he pretends to await glory upon the lap of the lofty goddess, cradled against the chaste girdle, over which he lets wanton his ancient hands.... Singular, dreadful nursling!

Long since he had decided to visit Lumbres, and his disciples kept it no secret from the profane that he would carry with him to that place the idea of a new book. "The chances of life," he confided to his flock, in that tone of intimate sauciness with which he aspired to dispense the treasures of a fashionable skepticism, baptized in his view as antique wisdom, "the chances of life have allowed me to draw near to more than one saint, assuming you wish to apply this word to those men of simple manners and ingenuous minds, whose kingdom is not of this world, and who nourish themselves, as do we all, on the bread of illusion, but with exceptional appetites. Yet such people live and die, recognized by very few, and without having spread very far the contagion of their folly. Forgive me for having reverted so late in life to a child's dreams: I should like, with my own eyes, to see a different saint, a true saint, a miracle saint and—in a word—a popular saint. Who knows? Perhaps I shall go to Lumbres to finish my job of dying in this good old man's hands?"

These words, and others too, were long regarded as an amiable fantasy, even though they may have expressed, with a sort of comic modesty, a sincere feeling, low but human, a sordid fear of death. The famous writer, unfortunately for him, was merely debased, not mediocre. His strong personality, painfully held in check in his books, had abandoned itself to vice. Vainly did he struggle to conceal from all, by heaping on skepticism and irony, the dreadful secret which sometimes oozed out between the words. The older he became, the more the wretched man saw himself tracked down, assaulted in his lie, day by day less able to beguile his growing ravenousness with snacks and tidbits. Powerless to control himself, aware of the disgust he inspired, finding only through cunning and toil a few rare occasions to sate himself, he hurled himself like a glutton on what passed within reach of his gums and, once the dish was emptied, wept with shame. The idea of an obstacle to be hurdled, and of the delays required by the comedy of seduction, even when held to its briefest, the fear of ever-possible physical impotence, the capriciousness of his fits of hunger, discouraged him in advance from chance encounters. The housekeepers whom in former times he had maintained with a certain show were now succeeded by rustic wenches and servant girls who were his domestic tyrants. As best he could, he found excuses for their familiarities of speech, affected a distressing equanimity, distracted attention by a laugh which rang false, while his eyes secretly followed the short petticoat on which he would, in a little while, go roll his hoary head.

But alas! this dismal debauchery wore him out without satisfying him; he could imagine nothing lower; he was touching bottom in his grotesque hell. After desire, never keener and more urgent, there followed a pleasure too brief, stealthy, fickle. The hour had come when the need outlived the appetite, ultimate riddle of the fleshly sphinx.... Then was it that between this old, inert body and the vainly importuned delight, death raised itself, like a third comrade.

She whom he had so often fondled in his books, and whose sweetness he thought he had sucked dry, Death—visible, what was more, everywhere through his cold irony, like a face seen lying under deep, clear water—dreamed a hundred times, savored, he did not recognize. From thenceforward he saw her too close, mouth to mouth. He had chosen the image of a slow old age, sloping gently through a flowered land, and which falls asleep content, after the last step. But he did not at all expect this surprise in full daylight, this housebreaking.... What? Already?

He strove to drive away the thought, to disguise it at least; he spent infinite resources in this wretched game. Scarcely dared he confide to his most intimate friends a little something of his anguish, and they only half understood him; no one wished to see in the great man's eyes the tragic look in which was expressed a child's terror. Help! said those eyes. And the audience cried out: What a wonderful conversationalist!

12.

Dr. Gambillet advanced toward the famous author of *The Paschal Candle* and introduced himself, not without brilliance, for he was not wholly lacking either in roguishness or in a feeling for the appropriate. Then, turning toward his companion and yielding him the floor, he said: "The pastor of Luzarnes is better fitted than I to wish you welcome in this miraculous land of Lumbres, but a step or two from the little church you have come to visit."

Antoine Saint-Marin turned his long pale face toward Father Sabiroux, examining him from tip to toe, bored.

"Cherished and renowned master," said the priest in measured tones, "never did I expect to see you so close at hand. The ministry I perform in the depths of this countryside condemns us all to isolation until death, and it is a great mischief that France's clergy should thus be held apart from the country's intellectual cream. At least may one of its most humble representatives be allowed…"

"The country's intellectual cream, reverend Father, is a very noisy and a very disagreeable society which I should advise you, rather, to keep far removed from your rectories. And as for isolation," he added with a little laugh, "would that I might have been condemned to it like you!"

The former chemistry professor, for a moment abashed, chose to smile likewise. But the young Chavranches doctor, already free of any ceremoniousness, interjected: "Come, come, Father! Here you are acting like a lord mayor upon the king's entrance into his good town. The renowned master has not journeyed a hundred leagues to hear his own praises. Must I admit it, sir," he continued, bowing toward Saint-Marin, "I am myself ready to commit a more heinous offense against you."

"Don't stand on ceremony," blandly replied the novelist.

"Allow me merely to ask you for what reason..."

"Not another word, if you value my good opinion!" exclaimed the author of *The Paschal Candle*. "I presume that you wish to know the reason which led me to undertake this brief journey? Yet, thank God, I know no more about it than you do. The toil of writing, young man, is of all work the most vexatious and the most thankless; it's quite enough to compose my books; I do not compose my life. This page is a blank page."

"I hope you will write it, nonetheless," sighed the pastor of Luzarnes, "and I have the boldness to say that you owe it to us."

The renowned master's glance, always slightly vague, fell from aloft upon his sanctimonious suppliant and flicked over him without coming to rest. Then he inquired, his eyes half closed: "So we are all three awaiting the whim of a saint?"

"The keys to the temple, first of all," remarked the Puck of Chavranches, "and the whim of the sacristan Ladislas."

"How so?" asked Saint-Marin, without deigning to notice the pastor of Luzarnes's gesture, requesting a chance to speak.

Gambillet, however—the quicker of the two—after his own fashion recounted the day's events, a score of times corrected by his frowning companion, whom a slight movement of impatience on the renowned master's part each time cast back into nothingness. When he had heard the whole story, the novelist said: "Upon my faith, sir, I did not expect so much from a day badly begun. Oh! the refreshing surprise of a bit of the supernatural and the miraculous!"

"Supernatural and miraculous?" the pastor of Luzarnes protested, his voice grave.

"Why not?" sharply asked Saint-Marin, turning the whole of his body about to confront his innocuous enemy.

(However low the great man had fallen, naked stupidity made him ashamed. But above all he was fearful of encountering his own image in the folly or the baseness of others, as in some tragic mirror.)

"Why not?" he repeated, hissing each word rather than pronouncing it between his long, clenched teeth. "We all hope for a miracle, sir, and the sad universe invokes it as we do. Today or in a thousand centuries—what matters it to me, if some liberating event is someday to breach the walls of universal mechanism? I'd just as soon expect it tomorrow and go to sleep happy. By what right would the brutish technicians awaken me from my dream? Supernatural and miraculous are adjectives full of meaning, sir, and words which a cultivated man utters only with longing. . . ."

Never had the pastor of Luzarnes felt himself more unjustly put to shame than at this avowal. "Monsieur Saint-Marin," he remarked to his friend Gambillet, "seems to me more a poet than a philosopher, and capable of interpreting the words of others according to his own fancy. But why lose one's temper?"

The author of *The Paschal Candle* would himself have been hard put to it to reply, for by instinct he hated that which resembled him and relished without admitting it the bitter intoxication of despising himself in others. Better than anyone else he knew by how light and fragile a shade of difference the man whose only profession is his wit is removed from the fool, and in certain well-spoken simpletons the old cynic was enraged to catch the whiff of a puppy from the same litter.

"If you have not seen the hermit," resumed the Chavranches doctor in order to break the silence, "are you at least acquainted with the hermitage? What a curious house! How lonely it is!"

"A little while ago I was under its spell," said Saint-Marin. "In life the only truly precious thing is the rare and the singular, the moment of waiting and of foreboding. Here I have known it."

Dr. Gambillet nodded, giving his approval with a cautious smile. The tall old man, however, moving close to the window, began to draw his long fingers over the panes. The lamplight made his shadow dance upon the wall, now shortening, now lengthening it. Outdoors, one's eyes could distinguish nothing save the wan streak of the road.

And in the deep silence, the Chavranches medical man heard the slight grating of the fingernails on the polished glass. Suddenly Saint-Marin's voice startled him: "That devilish sacristan," said he, "wants to slay us with melancholy. I'm a dreadful fool to wait and yawn here when I have a whole day ahead of me. For I shall not leave Lumbres until tomorrow. Upon my word, what's more, I am extraordinarily weary."

"Then too," observed Dr. Gambillet, "if the imaginings of Father Sabiroux bear any relation to the truth, his unfortunate colleague will be in no condition to converse with you tonight."

"For this occasion, moreover," replied the celebrated master, "it is sufficient to have made the acquaintance of this country presbytery; a unique spot."

(He indicated the room and its four bare walls with a caressing gesture, as though it were some rarest trinket to tempt a collector.)

To the self-esteem of the pastor of Luzarnes, this simple sentence was like a healing balm. "I must point out to you," said he, "that this room is improperly termed an oratory; my venerable colleague rarely makes use of it. To tell the truth, he hardly ever leaves his own bedchamber."

"Well, now?" said Saint-Marin, his interest aroused.

"I should be delighted to take you there," eagerly added the canon-to-be. "The reverend pastor of Lumbres, I am sure, would gladly show you this mark of esteem, and I should be doing no more than giving effect to his own thought."

He took the lamp, lifted it above his head, and then, dramatically waiting a moment with his hand on the doorknob: "If you gentlemen will be good enough to follow me?"

At the top of the first flight of stairs, the pastor of Luzarnes pointed to a half-open door at the end of a long corridor and said, "Allow me to show you the way."

They entered after him. The lamp, held at arm's length, illumined a long room with a sloping ceiling, whitewashed, and at first appearing to be absolutely empty. The deal floor, freshly scrubbed, emitted a clinging odor. A few bits of furniture, artlessly ranged against the wall, grew visible, betrayed by their own shadows; two cane-seated chairs, a *prie-dieu*, a scanty table laden with books.

"This is like any poor student's garret," said Saint-Marin disappointed.

But the future canon, indefatigable, drew them further, bending his smoky and faltering light toward the floor. "Here is his bed," said that amazing man with a land of pride.

Chavranches's little terror and the literary man, though they were both of them without shame, changed an embarrassed smile over the broad back. The straw mattress, ridiculously narrow and meager, covered with a pile of wearing apparel, by itself alone afforded a spectacle of sufficiently pitiful sadness. Saint-Marin, however, scarcely saw it; he was looking at two great gaping shoes, greenish with age, one of them upright, in an odd position, the other on its side, showing its rusted nails, its warped leather, the turned edges of its sole; two poor old shoes, filled with an infinite weariness, more wretched than men.

"What a picture!" he said in a low tone; "what a laughable and wonderful picture!"

He thought of the circular flight of all human life, of the road vainly traveled, of the ultimate misstep. What had he gone to seek so far away, this great-hearted vagabond? The same thing as he himself awaited, in the midst of familiar objects, his beloved prints, his books, his mistresses and his courtesans, in the town house on the rue de Verneuil, where Madame de Janze died. Never had the patriarch of the void, at his best moments, lifted himself higher than a lyric disgust with living, a caressing nihilism. Nonetheless his throat tightened, his heart beat faster.

And then the words came, in a flood. "We are here," said he, "in a consecrated place, as venerable as a shrine. If the broad world is a tilting yard, it is worth marking the spot where the great endeavor was made, where the most foolish of hopes was essayed. The men of antique days would probably have viewed our saint of Lumbres with contempt; but a long experience of misfortune has made us less harsh with this kind of wisdom, wisdom a trifle barbarous, which finds in the very glow of action its reason for being and its reward. The difference is less great than you imagined between him who wishes to embrace everything and him who thrusts all aside. There exists a wild grandeur of which antique wisdom was unaware...."

The lovely, ponderous voice of the renowned writer remained as though perched upon the last syllable, whereas his glance was fixed upon the corner of the room that the assiduous Sabiroux was at that moment illuminating with the light of his lamp. In a sort of hollow, formed by the exterior angle of the roof, a bit of plank, crudely nailed to the wall, supported a metal crucifix. Below it, tossed upon the floor, in the darkest corner, a lash lay in folds, one of those the cattle drovers call a "cutlass," sharp at its point, three fingers wide at its base, like a flat black snake. But neither the crucifix nor the whip held the master's attention. It was, rather, at a man's height, a strange spattering, covering almost a whole section of the wall, made up of a thousand tiny specks, so close together toward the center that they there constituted a uniform mass of pale reddish brown, a few fresher, still vivid pink, others scarcely visible in the lime's thickness, as though blotted up, dried out, in color indescribable. The cross, the leather thong, the reddened wall... That wild grandeur of which antique wisdom... The distinguished musician had not the courage to thump out his last chord, and abruptly cut short his melody.

Stock-still, Dr. Gambillet several times muttered, into his mustache the words "mystical folly," covertly watching the silent Saint-Marin. The irresistible intimate of Chavranches society, so quick to strip the sheet from woeful nakednesses, and who often boasted of seeing everything and hearing everything with a brow of bronze, felt, as he later admitted, shivers down his spine. The most thick-skinned of men does not behold untroubled the violation before his very eyes of a great love's humble secret, the poor man's private portion, his sole treasure, and that which he takes with him beyond the grave.

The reverend pastor of Luzarnes, turning away the lamp, said at once, utterly unperturbed: "My venerable friend, gentlemen, deals harshly with himself and seriously compromises his health! God preserve me from finding fault with his zeal! But I must say that these violences against his own person, not forbidden, only tolerated, were nevertheless regarded by many as a dangerous means of sanctification, too often a scandal for the weak or a laughing-stock for the ungodly."

The former professor emphasized this last word with a familiar gesture, his thumb and index finger joined, the little finger extended upward, in the manner of a man who states precisely a point under contest. The doctor's embarrassment, the other's silence, seemed to him a rather flattering proof of their benevolent attention. He bestowed a smile upon the matter, then moved on satisfied, for the mediocre priest is, above all other men, impervious.

"How nervous indeed is this great man!" Gambillet said to himself, following close on Saint-Marin's heels, and curiously watching the long ivory hand fidget with the cane and occasionally tap the floor with it. For several minutes the author of *The Paschal Candle* had truly been making an almost heroic effort to hide his distress and control himself. Most likely he had not remained unconscious of the lugubrious poetic quality of the poor man's dwelling, but many long years had gone by since the novelist had been tricked by any stirring in his aged heart! Any emotion barely taking shape and, as it were, in the state of coming to birth was at once pigeonholed, put to use; here was the raw material which his busy genius fashioned to the customers' tastes.

The old comedian could be reached only through the senses; the reddish spot upon the wall in the lamp's halo had stripped him to his quivering nerves.

We are all aware of—even know by heart—a score of his impudent pages, in which, with all the resources of his art, the wretched man exerted himself to lay his unruly ghost. No one has spoken more freely of death, more heedlessly and with more loving scorn. No writer in our tongue seems to have observed it with so candid an eye, made game of it with a pout so mocking and so tender. By what mysterious compensation, his pen once laid aside, did he fear it like a beast, like a wild animal?

At the thought of the inevitable ending, it was not his reason which grew dizzy, it was his will which gave way and threatened to break. This sophisticate knew with despair the upheaval of the instinct, the hateful panic, the recoil and stiffening of the animal in the slaughterhouse which has just caught the smell of the butcher's club. Thus years ago, if we are to believe Goncourt, Zola, the father of naturalism and the Rougon-Macquarts, awakened in the middle of the night by the same terrors, flung himself out of bed and afforded his dismayed wife the spectacle of a prosecuting attorney in his night shirt and trembling with fear.

Upright upon the first step, his face turned toward the shadowy stair well, his brow knotted, his throat dry, he breathed heavily, the only remedy for such attacks. Behind him Gambillet, unable to move on, was astonished and anxiously listened to the master's heavy, irregular respiration. He lightly rested his hand on the old man's shoulder: "Are you feeling unwell?" he asked.

Saint-Marin turned about with some difficulty and replied in a forced voice: "Not at all! Not at all…just a little discomfort…a slight suffocation.… It's better…wholly passed by…"

But he still felt so weak and so low in his mind that the Chavranches doctor's commonplace sympathy was unbelievably sweet to his heart. In the sense of well-being which accompanied the relaxation of his nerves he had thus often been tempted to speak, to yield his secret, to beg of him nearest at hand advice and succor. By good fortune, his benumbed pride always awakened him in good time from his had dream.

"Doctor," said he with a fatherly smile, "experience will make you realize that traveling is no longer capable of educating old age, but only of hastening its end. Which still has its advantages! For at the last turning, when a poor old fellow wishes and fears the little misstep which will hurl him into nothingness, just the hint of a shove is sometimes needful."

"Nothingness!" politely protested the pastor of Luzarnes, "surely that is a very strong word?"

(For a second Saint-Marin studied his insufferable fawner over the medical man's shoulder.)

"What matter the word?" said he. "Have we any choice?"

"There are words so full of despair...so anguished..." exclaimed the poor priest, already going pale.

"Come! Come!" continued the author of *The Paschal Candle*. "I have no hope that a syllable more or less will bestow immortality upon me!"

"I don't make myself clear," parried the canon-to-be, passionately eager to be conciliatory. "Very likely a mentality like yours conceives...the future life...in another likeness...probably...than the generality of our faithful...but I cannot believe that...your lofty intelligence...accepts without being revolted...the notion of a total forfeiture, beyond remedy, of a disappearance into the void?"

The last words were strangled in his throat, and meanwhile, with a moving self-abasement, his glance implored the indulgence, the pity of the great man.

The savageness of the scorn which Saint-Marin betrayed before fools was especially astonishing because on other occasions he freely affected a complaisant skepticism. Thus it was, however, that he was able outwardly to make manifest, at very slight risk, his natural hatred for the lame and the weak.

"You have my thanks," said he to the pastor of Luzarnes, "for reserving to me a Paradise different from your curate's and choirboys'. Yet may the gods spare me from going up there to find another Academy when the one we have here in France bores me to tears!"

"If I properly understand your jest," replied the future canon, "you accuse me..."

"I accuse you of nothing," abruptly exclaimed Saint-Marin with extraordinary violence. "But please understand that I should fear nothingness less than your silly Elysian fields!"

"Elysian fields...Elysian fields," mumbled the poor dumbfounded fellow. "Far be it from me to distort doctrine.... I only wanted to bring within your grasp...speaking your language..."

"My grasp...my language!" repeated the author of *The Paschal Candle*, with an envenomed smile.

He stopped for a moment to catch his breath. The lamp, which shook in the pastor of Luzarnes's hands, fully illuminated his pale countenance. The old man's flabby mouth took the shape of one about to vomit, to spew forth even his heart. And it was his heart indeed, his true heart, that the old comedian would hurl, would spit out, once for all, at the feet of this stupid priest.

"I know what the most enlightened of your species offer me, Father: the wise man's immortality, perched between Mentor and Telemachus, at the feet of a good Lord talking dialectics. I find Berenger's just as attractive, with us all dolled up as national guardsmen! Mr. Kenan's classical antiquity, the prayer on the Acropolis, high-school Greece—all tommyrot! I was born in Paris, Father, in the back room of a Marais shop, to a father from the Beauce and a mother from Touraine. I was an altar boy along with the rest of them. Had I to get down on my knees, I should still go straight to my old parish of Saint-Sulpice; no one would see me making faces at the feet of Pallas Athene, like a drunken professor! My books! To hell with my books! I, a dilettante! A fine talker? I've taken from life everything I've been able to, mind you, in great gulps, by throatfuls! I've drunk it down in a steady stream, straight from the bottle, come what might! One must make the best of it, Father. When you enjoy life, you fear death. It's just as well to try to look it in the face as to seek distraction in the philosophers' scribblings, just as someone in a dentist's waiting room leafs through the illustrated magazines. A sage crowned with roses—I! A classical old fogy! Oh!... There are moments when the worship of dolts makes you long for the pillory. The public never lets go of us, always wants us to make the same faces at it, applauds only these, and tomorrow will look on us as liars and mountebanks. Ho! Ho! If only the bigots knew how to paint! At bottom we are dupes, Father, we lose our hand, doubled and redoubled! A plasterer's helper, who thinks only of filling his belly, displays more wit than I; up to the last moment he may hope to eat and drink his fill. But we!... You leave school with the illusions of a poet. You see nothing more desirable in the world than a handsome flank of living marble. You fling yourself headlong at the women. At forty you sleep with duchesses; at sixty you must already be content to go on a spree with the girls. And later... Later... Ha! Ha! Later... you are envious of men like your saint of Lumbres, men who at least know how to grow old!... Do you really want to know what I think? What the famous master thinks, my thought in the raw? When a man is no longer able..."

He finished his sentence, and raw it was indeed, in a very explosion of disgust. His features—so fine-drawn—had then that expression of stupidity, the sly smirk, the fearsome immobility of vice on an old man's face. Gambillet was quietly watching him with a cruel smile. The pastor of Luzarnes had stepped back a pace or two. His distress at that instant would have melted the heart of immortal Villiers's Baron Saturne.

"Come...come...master," he stammered. "The religion of which I am a minister...has treasures of indulgence...of charity.... Scruples regarding dogma...can...in some measure should...harmonize with a fatherly solicitude...even a special kindliness...for certain exceptional souls.... I did not think that a sincere attempt at conciliation... at synthesis...a certain broadness of view.... The future life...according to the teachings of the Church."

Arguments thronged in his poor, confused brain; he would have liked to have produced them all at once, his thought jumping from one to the other, like the jittery needle of a mariner's compass....

Then the hearty old man marched over toward him, blotting him out with his broad shoulders: "The future life? The teaching of the Church?" he cried out, defying the priest with his pale eyes; "do you believe in them? Flatly...do you believe in them without cavil? Without any quibbles? Yes or no?"

(And indeed there was in the voice of the author of *The Paschal Candle* perhaps something other than a tone of insulting challenge....) But who could hope to hold fast the pastor of Luzarnes within the twin jaws of the pincers? He had never seriously doubted the truths he taught because he had never had any doubts of himself, his infallible criterion. Yet he hesitated. He hastily groped for a happy formula, one of those adroit phrases.... Alas, his formidable opponent was certainly pressing him too hard.... The clergyman raised toward him a hand requesting his forbearance.

"Please understand me..." he began in a dwindling voice.

Saint-Marin cast at him a glance truly flaming with hate. Then he turned his back. The poor wretch struggled in vain; the sentence he had begun was choked off in his throat; meanwhile there rose to his eyes real tears, tears of shame.

Dr. Gambillet never understood by what miracle a conversation, at first friendly, gradually becoming higher tempered, was able to conclude in such a squabble that all three of them for a second glowered at each other, face to face under the lamplight, as though they were irreconcilable enemies. It was because they were living through one of those peculiar moments when speech and attitude had each its different meaning, when witnesses question each other without any common understanding, pursuing each his inner monologue, and each thinking that he grew indignant against the others whereas they were merely becoming angry with themselves, with their own remorsefulnesses, just as cats, mysterious, play with their own shadows.

In the silence which followed, pregnant with a fresh storm, the outside door abruptly opened, and the steps of the stairway creaked one by one under a heavy tread. Their overexcitement was so great that they looked at each, other with a kind of sacred terror. But, upon recognizing Martha's serene countenance, Father Sabiroux first among them breathed easy.

"A fine business!" muttered the old woman, out of breath. Then, on the last step, gently patting her apron to smooth out its wrinkles, she took in the three men with a quick glance. "Ladislas is waiting for you, gentlemen."

They followed her to the garden gate, obediently, without speaking. The sky was full of stars.

"Ladislas will have gone ahead," resumed the servant, pointing with her finger at a lantern swinging in the gloom, the other side of the cemetery. "I can hear his step. You will find the church open."

For an instant she held back the pastor of Luzarnes, grasping his sleeve, and, tiptoe in her clogs, she whispered these words into his ear: "At least make him listen to reason. Since yesterday evening, he's not had a bite to eat! If it's in any way possible!"

She disappeared without awaiting any answer. The canon-to-be caught up with his two companions at the church's portal. Above them the lofty building towered in the night, alive and sharply defined beyond compare. Within, the sacristan's iron-shod shoes could be heard dragging over the flagstones.

"So we shall continue to pursue our adventure in company," Saint-Marin amiably remarked to the former professor, whom the great man's smile brought back to life. "I'd have no heart for my dinner before you have ferreted out your elusive saint; and, after all, it would require nothing less than this intervention from above to bring a close this evening to our little quarrels."

The freshness of the air after the shower had blown away his bad temper. Apart from the poor room of the pastor of Lumbres and the magic circle of the lamp on the wall, his fit of fury was now scarcely more than a bad dream.

"Let's go in, then..." was all that Sabiroux said (but with what a look of gratitude!).

As soon as he saw them, Ladislas hastened in their direction. The future canon greeted him cheerily: "Well, now, Ladislas," said he, "what's new?"

(The old fellow's face expressed profound amazement.)

"Our pastor is not there," said he.

"How extraordinary!" exclaimed Sabiroux, in a voice which long echoed under the vaulting. He crossed his arms, deeply upset. "But seriously," he continued, "are you so sure that...?"

"I've looked everywhere, in every corner," Ladislas replied. "I certainly thought I'd find him in the Chapel of the Holy Angels; he goes there each day, after supper, in a little nook you have to know how to find.... But neither there nor anywhere else...I've even poked about in the pulpit, so..."

"But what do you suppose?" interjected Gambillet. "What the devil! A man doesn't lose himself!"

The future canon nodded his agreement.

"My thought," said Ladislas, "is that his reverence may have gone out by the sacristy and taken the Verneuil road, as far as the Roû crucifix. It's a walk he likes to take at nightfall, while saying his rosary."

"Oh! Oh!" loudly sighed the Chavranches doctor.

"Let me finish," added the sacristan. "At this hour—twenty minutes before the Benediction of the Blessed Sacrament, he would be back, he would have been back long ago.... I've given that careful consideration.... He was so weak this evening, so pale.... Fasting since last night... What I think is that he may have fallen from weakness...."

"I begin to fear so," said Sabiroux.

He reflected for a moment, his arms still crossed, more self-possessed than ever, blowing out his cheeks. Suddenly he reached a decision: "I am overwhelmed, dear master...to be...indirectly...the cause of an inconvenience..."

"None...no inconvenience at all," protested the dear master, now wholly relenting. "All in all, I should almost say that the episode amuses me, did I not have to share your anxiety.... However, I shall not suggest my going any further, on these old legs of mine.... I prefer to await you here...."

"It won't take us very long, I hope," concluded the former professor. "It's a certainty we shall find him over there.... Dr. Gambillet will be kind enough to keep me company; I am more in need of his help than ever. Come with us," said he to the sacristan, "and get the blacksmith's son as we go by. If our unfortunate friend has to be carried..."

The voice little by little grew dimmer as it moved away. The door closed behind it. The celebrated author of *The Paschal Candle* found himself alone and smiled.

13.

MAGIC SMILE! THE old church, slightly warmed by the day, breathed about him with a slow respiration; a smell of ancient stone and of worm-eaten wood, as secret as that of the deep forest, glided along the thickset columns, wandered mistily over the ill-fitted flagging, or piled up in the dark corners, like stagnant water. A hollow in the floor, an angle in the wall, an empty niche gathered it as though in a granite trough. And the red light of the sanctuary lamp, far off, toward the altar, resembled a lantern over a lonely lake.

Saint-Marin delightedly sniffed this country night, between sixteenth-century walls, filled with the perfume of so many seasons. He had made his way to the right side of the nave and was huddled against the end of an oak pew, hard and invigorating; a copper lamp at the end of a bit of wire swung above him, creaking slightly.

At intervals a door slammed. And, when all was perhaps about to be still, there were the dusty panes shivering in their leaden cames, jarred by a horse trotting along the road.

"And now," said he to himself, "the Chavranches medico and his unbearable friend are trotting I know not where, withdrawing themselves just far enough to allow me to enjoy in peace a perfect hour!..." (For he gladly believed in these civilities of chance, in mysterious concurrences.) This church, this silence, the play of the shadows... Come now! All was his...all awaited him. At least, may they not come back too soon, was what he wished.

They would not come back too soon.

(The dying know well what they want, but they keep still about everything, used to say Mécislas Golberg, that ancient Jew.)

The eminent master's anguish had little by little been dispelled in the great inner silence he had so rarely known. A thousand recollections caught fire from it, like the pricks of light in a city after dark. His memory passed them in review and rejoiced at their confusion, at their intoxicating disarray. Across the bounds laid down by our calendars, how the days, the years, the hours summon each other and answer!... A bright summer morning, with the fine ring of copper resounding from the preserve kettle...an evening with a clear and ice-cold brook flowing beneath motionless leaves...the surprised glance of a blue-eyed cousin across the family table and her little, panting chest...and then, abruptly—a half-century cleared at a bound—the first gnawings of old age, a broken tryst...the great love, dearly cherished, defended step by step, contested, even to the ultimate moment, when the lips of the aged lover pressed upon an unsettled and stealthy mouth, tomorrow turned cruel.... There was his life—all that time spared of it—what of his past still retained shape and features; the rest was nothing: his work or even the renown. Fifty years of struggle, his distinguished career, thirty famous books.... What then! Did all that come to so little?... How many dolts go about exclaiming that art... What art? The wondrous minstrel had known only its serfdom. He had borne it like a burden. The melodious chatterbox who had talked of nothing else had not once expressed himself. The whole wide world, which thought it loved him, knew only the mask which hid his face. He was exiled from his books and, before the event, dispossessed.... So many readers, not a single friend!

What was more, this caused him no regret. The certainty that he thus slipped through men's fingers forever, that there would remain of him only an image, made his mischievous eyes glitter. The best of his work deserved no other consequence than this jest at the hour of death. He wished for no disciple. Those around him were enemies. Powerless to create anew a spell, a gracefulness of which their master held the secret, they satisfied themselves with adroitly mimicking his style. Their boldest strokes were on the level of syntax. "They take my paradoxes apart," said he, "but they know not how to put them together again." That younger generation—its ranks so desperately reduced—which had seen Péguy lying in the stubble, in the face of God, drew away with disgust from the divan whereon the hypercritic polished his fingernails. It left to Narcissus the labor of refining even more upon his delicate impotence. But it even then had come to hate, with all the strength of its genius, the sturdiest and the most successful of the flock, who aspired to be the heirs of the unworthy master, who leeringly distilled their complicated little books, scolded and gnashed their teeth at the greatest, and had no better hope in this world than to strew their stale and fastidious dung around the edges of all the spiritual springs where poor wretches went to drink.

Yet what did the author of *The Paschal Candle* care about the nibbling of so many busy little teeth within his shadow? He had gnawed more from necessity than relish, wearily. Make way for the young rats, with sharper fangs! This evening he could muse upon them without wrath. He dreamed, shivering with pleasure, of the great distant city, of its bubbling multitude, under the vast dark sky. Would ever he see it again? Did it even still exist, somewhere, over there, in the so tender night?

Almost directly above his head the clock ticked softly, like a heart beating. Briefly he closed his eyes the better to hear it, live and breathe with it, this ancient, ageless forebear, which for centuries had reluctantly dispensed the pitiless future. This sound to which he listened, barely audible in the resonant framework of the church, this monotonous purring, interrupted only by the solemn voice of the hours, would outlast him, would journey on through years and yet more years, through fresh stretches of silence, until that day.... What day? What day would have singled out, for the last time, at the stroke of midnight, the two rusty hands, the two old gossips, before they came to a stop forever?

He opened his eyes. In front of him a tablet of grayish marble, affixed to the wall, bore an inscription, the broad letters of which, free of their pristine gilt, he slowly deciphered.

> *To the memory...of...Jean-Baptiste Heame, royal notary 1690–1741...and of Mélanie-Hortense Le Peon, his wife...of Pierre Antoine Dominique...of Jean-Jacques Heame, Lord of Hemecourt...of Paul-Louis-Francois...*

...and so to the bottom of the list, to the last name:

> *Jean-César Heame d'Heme-court, cavalry captain, former warden of the parish, deceased at Cannes...in 1889...benefactor of this church...*
>
> *Pray for this Family entirely extinct.*

the old stone still pleaded, humbly, as though to excuse itself for being there.

"What a terrible loss!..." murmured the author of *The Paschal Candle* between his teeth. But he smiled a hearty smile of protective sympathy. The generous piece of marble, conscientiously carved, embellished with fine gold, as solidly substantial as any other bit of bourgeois furniture! Nothing is sadder than a burial plot with a white stone marker, its boundaries set off by chains, whipped by the rain on a winter's day. But sheltered against the cold and the heat, facing the official pew, where the deceased church warden took his bit of blessed bread,* this stone, as smooth and polished as on its first day, waxed each week by a painstaking sacristan—what a consoling picture of death. The writer's sensibility was touched by this posthumous comfort. He spelled out all those names, as though they were the names of friends, whose nearness reassured him. Together with this dynasty of the Heames, how many others also were there, under the floor slabs with the letters worn smooth, here and there, right up to the foot of the altar, good folk who wanted to sleep under a roof, to last as long as the solid stone footings! You could dream of sleeping there, in their company.... Never had the famous novelist felt himself so resigned, so docile. An exquisite weariness relaxed him to his least fiber, made float before his eyes the image of the dark church fast asleep, henceforward without a secret, friendly, intimate. He savored a peace he had never felt, an extreme well-being, almost religious.... He took his ease, he stretched; he stilled a yawn which was like a prayer.

Outdoors the sky darkened; a final transept window blacked out altogether. From then on the door opened and closed upon a background of black velvet, where the exterior world revealed itself only through its perfume. Scattered shadows came close, gathered together. A discreet whispering echoed through the trusses, from oaken pew to oaken pew; brief, impatient footsteps gained the threshold; little by little the church emptied itself of its invisible commonalty. The hour of daily Benediction was long since passed, the sacristy remained closed, out of twelve lights only three illumined the ark. What was going on? Why wait any longer?... They sought each other out, groping, they called to each other from afar, with a little lingering cough, they talked it over as between those who belonged. For with the last Vaucours bus, the male and female curious had disappeared; at that late hour, Lumbres retained only its old friends. And meanwhile the last of these moved off. Saint-Marin was to remain alone.

14.

For him alone this great plaything, a trifle funereal, but charming all the same—for the author of *The Paschal Candle* alone—for him alone! Lovingly he traced with his eyes the ribbing of the vault, gathering together in rosettes, and falling back three by three on the pilasters of the lateral walls, with so supple a movement, so living, almost animal, a grace. The master-mason who in olden times had shaped their aerial course—had he not, unawares, labored to rejoice the vision of the aging genius? What more did they expect, the devout men and women and even this peasant priest, when they lifted their noses toward their empty sky, than a loosening of their bonds, a brief peace, the temporary acceptance of fate? What they artlessly called God's grace, the gift of the Spirit, the efficacy of the Sacrament, was the same respite which he relished in this solitary place. Poor people, whose ingenuousness ladened itself with so much useless talk! Worthy country saint, who believed that each morning he consumed Eternal Life, yet whose senses were aware only of a rather crude illusion, scarcely comparable to the lucid dream, to the willed illusion of the wonderful writer. "Why did I not come earlier," said he to himself, "to breathe the air of a rustic church!... Our 1830 grandmothers knew secrets which we have lost!" He regretted his visit to the rectory, which very nearly had led him astray, the idiotic pilgrimage to the saint's room (that section of wall the sight of which had for a moment made his reason totter), a spectacle, in short, slightly barbarous and made for a less fastidious public.... "Saintliness," he asserted to himself, "like everything in this world, is beautiful only when you see it in its theater; behind the scenes it's stinking and ugly." His buzzing brain hummed with a thousand new, bold thoughts; a young hope, still confused, stirred even his muscles; for many a day he had not felt so lithe, so vigorous.

"There is a joy in growing old," he exclaimed to himself, almost aloud, "which has been revealed to me today. Love itself—yes, love itself!—can be left behind without a violent break. I have sought death in books, or in base city burial grounds, now inordinate, like a vision shaped in dreams, now cut down to the measure of a man with a cap on his head who, they say, keeps in good repair the fences around the plots, makes entries in a book, directs matters. No! It is here, or in other like abodes, that one must greet it with good grace, just like the cold and the heat, the night and the day, the imperceptible progression of the stars, the seasons' return, taking example from the wise men and the beasts. How many precious things beyond compare can the philosopher learn from the mere instinct of some old priest like this one, very close to nature, heir to those inspired solitaries from whom our fathers long ago created the divinities of the fields. Oh, unconscious poet who, seeking the kingdom of heaven, finds at least repose, a humble submission to the elementary forces, peace profound..."

By stretching out his arm, the illustrious master could have touched with his finger the confessional where the saint of Lumbres dispensed to his people the treasures of his empiric wisdom. There it was, between two columns, daubed a dreadful chestnut-brown, vulgar, almost sordid, closed in by two green curtains. The author of *The Paschal Candle* deplored so much useless ugliness and that a village prophet should utter his oracles in the depths of a deal box; all the same he curiously examined the wooden grill-work behind which he imagined the old priest's calm face, smiling, attentive, eyes closed, the hand lifted in benediction. How much better he liked him thus than all gory with blood, up yonder, confronting the bare wall, whip in hand, in his cruel frenzy! "The most kindly dreamers," thought he, "probably need these rather sharp stimuli which bring back to life in their minds images that are fading. What others ask of morphine or of opium, this man obtains from the bite of a lash on his back and his sides."

At the tip of its wire, the copper lamp swung gently to and fro. Each time it returned, its shadow spread out as far as the vaulting, then, driven back again, lay in wait in the darkness of the columns, and there turned back on itself to deploy once more. "Thus do we shift from cold to hot," Saint-Marin mused, "now boiling with ardor, bubbling over, now cold and weary, according to unknown and presumably unknowable laws. Once upon a time our skepticism was still a challenge. The very indifference in which we later believed we should gain all is soon no more than a pose rather tedious to maintain. What twisting pain, O Lord! behind the epicurean smile. But our great-nephews will succeed no better than we. The human mind endlessly varies the shape and the curvature of its wings, beats against the air at every angle, from negative to positive, and never flies. What is now more disparaged than the name of dilettante, which a while back was borne with honor? The new generation was clearly signed with another sign; we have known what it was, since: it was that of its own sacrifice, honorable fate, coveted by the military. I have seen young Lagrange, trembling all over with a holy impatience, like a living premonition.... Before me, he is savoring the repose he detested. Believers or freethinkers, by whatever name we are named, it is not enough that our search should be in vain; every effort hastens our end. The very air we breathe burns within, consumes us. To doubt is no more refreshing than to deny. But to be a professor of doubt—what a Chinese torture! Then again, at the height of one's strength, seeking after women, the obsession of sex commonly congests minds, repels thought. We dwell in a half-delirium of gloomy enjoyment, broken by crises of lucid despair. But as the years go by, images lose their strength, our arteries circulate a thinner blood, our motor idles. We ruminate college abstractions in our old age, which acquired all their virtue from the eagerness of our desires; we repeat words no less threadbare than ourselves; we watch in the eyes of young people for secrets which we have lost. Oh! The hardest ordeal is endlessly to compare one's own failings to the ardor and activity of others, as though we felt uselessly slipping over us the powerful groundswell which will lift us up no longer.... What good is it to attempt what can only once be attempted? This poor old priest has acted less foolishly by withdrawing himself from life before life itself withdrew. His old age is without bitterness. From what we regret losing he wishes to be freed as quickly as possible; when we bewail that we no longer feel any urge to desire, he deludes himself that he is less tempted. I should swear that at thirty he had made for himself the happinesses of an old man, upon which age could not fasten its teeth. Is it too late to imitate him? A peasant mystic, brought up on old books and lessons from commonplace masters, in the dust of the seminaries, can by degrees raise himself to the serenity of a sage, but his experience is limited, his method artless and sometimes far-fetched, complicated with useless superstitions. The means at the disposal of a renowned master, at the end of his career, but in the full potency of his genius, are of a different efficacy. To borrow from sanctity the likable in it; to recapture without stiffness the peace of childhood; to become accustomed to the silence and the solitude of the countryside; to bend one's mind less to regret nothing than to remember nothing; to observe within reason, within measure, the ancient precepts of abstinence and chastity, assuredly precious things; to rejoice in old age as one does in autumn or in twilight; little by little to become intimate with death—is not all this a difficult pastime, but nothing more than a pastime, for the writer of many books, for the bestower of illusion? This will be my last work," concluded the celebrated master, "and I shall write it for myself alone, by turns actor and public...."

But that last book is precisely the one a man does not write, barely glimpsed in his reveries. Meditating it alone is a fatal sign. Thus do old cats about to die still caress with their claws the carpet's wool, and languish upon fine colors a glance full of obscure tenderness.

It was this same glance which the author of *The Paschal Candle* fixed on the thin wooden trellis behind which he envisioned his mealy-mouthed hero, a patriarch with an indulgent laugh, his speech full of vigor and relish, rich in his experience of souls. He loved him already for all the good he might expect of him. Even though you may be a saint, you are nonetheless appreciative of a certain rare form of courtesy, that attentive, penetrating sympathy which is the ultimate politeness of a great lord of the intellect. He who is disgusted at flattery relishes better the higher forms of praise. Ha! Ha! Others besides the illustrious Saint-Marin have knelt here, have listened to the good old man, and have departed less heavy of heart. Why not? In confession is the experience of sin ever complete? Is there not, in the shame of the avowal—even though incomplete, insincere—a sharp and strong feeling which is like unto remorse, a slightly crude and queer remedy for the growing insipidity of vice? And then, too, were not the frenzied freethinkers silly indeed to hold the Church in contempt for a method of psychotherapy which they considered excellent and novel in a fashionable neurologist? This distinguished medical man, in his clinic—was he doing anything other than a simple priest in the confessional: provoking confidence, setting it in motion, in order later to influence by suggestion, when he saw fit, a sick man lulled and relaxed? How many are the things rotting in the heart from which merely this rupture sets you free! The famous man, who lived in his own shadow, saw himself in all eyes, heard himself on all lips, recognized himself even in the hatred and the envy which swarmed around him, might well have been tempted to escape from his own obsession, to break the enchanted circle. He never opened himself to an inferior, he always lied to his equals. Were he to leave behind him truthful memoirs, his natural double-dealing would be redoubled by one of those fearful outbursts of posthumous vanity with which the public is thoroughly familiar. Nothing is of less account than what is said from beyond the grave. Well, then...well, then, it was fitting that once, by chance, this precious gift of himself, which he had always withheld, should be bestowed at a venture, as a man might throw a fistful of gold at a beggar.

Not for an instant, did the man—even though he had keenness and, lacking true taste, at least felt the vulgarity of others as a physical constraint upon him—escape the snare of his own baseness. He concocted these ideas helter-skelter, with a naïve assurance, deluded himself that he had only to make his choice among so many well-founded motives. Finally he looked at the wooden steps, worn down by the knees of penitents, with as much curiosity as desire.... Once there, the rest would be automatic. Who would hold him back? What in the same spot was so often given to illiterate old maids would surely not be refused to this most shrewd observer, and one who has his self-composure better in hand, delicious banterer! It required but a tiny effort, after having sucked dry so many rare and difficult sensations, spoken so many tongues, grinned so often and so knowingly, to end up in the guise of a country philosopher, disillusioned, become peaceable, opportunely pious. Since the emperor who planted turnips, we have seen more than one great personage of the world insure himself a bucolic death. In theater talk, this is called living your part so fully that you confuse yourself with the character you are playing. And thus, at the end of long and dedicated study, some actor—well fattened, pink with pleasure—swallows his beer, closes the book and cries out: "I've got my Polyeucte letter-perfect!"

15.

"I HAVE MY saint letter-perfect!" the famous master could have remarked at that moment, had he felt inclined to banter. And indeed he did have him, or would have him, quite literally. He reflected, ingenuously, that having tried with a disdainful tooth the most precious fruits gathered in the garden of kings, he could still chew with appetite a bit of coarse bread torn from a poor man's mouth, for such is the curiosity of genius, ever new.

It's a fine thing to taste so late the joys of initiation! From Paris to Lumbres, true enough, the road is long; but from the presbytery so close at hand to the peaceful church—what another distance had he covered! Only a little while back troubled, anxious, without any hope other than promptly to return with lowered head to the small house on the rue de Verneuil, there one day to die, useless and forgotten, in the arms of some servant girl who would murmur to someone off-stage that "the poor gentleman takes his dying very hard"—now set free, liberated, with a project in mind... O joy!...his skin tingling... In six weeks all could be settled, arranged. He would find somewhere, at the edge of a wood, one of those half-peasant, half-middle-class houses, between two moist green lawns. Saint-Mann's conversion, his withdrawal to Lumbres...the cries of triumph of the pious...the first interview...a subtle restatement of position...which would be something like the great man's testament: an ultimate caress for youth, for beauty, for pleasure, all lost, not in the least forsworn; then the silence, the great silence, wherein the public would piously enshroud, side by side in their solitude at Lumbres, the philosopher and the saint.

The obsession became so strong that he thought he was dreaming, was for a moment bemused, shivered, and once again realized that he was alone. This too abrupt awakening upset his equilibrium, left him upset and nervous. Suspiciously he eyed the empty confessional, so near by. The closed door with its green curtain invited him.... Come now! What better opportunity to see something else besides the poor old fellow's dwelling, his pallet, his disciplinary scourge: the very place where he made himself manifest to souls? The author of *The Paschal Candle* was alone, and in any case it disturbed him little to be seen. At seventy, his first impulse was always clear-cut, direct, irresistible-the dangerous privilege of writers with imagination.... His hand groped, found a knob, abruptly opened.

Hesitation followed his movement rather than coming before

it; reflection came too late. An indefinable remorse, regret at having acted so hastily and by hazard; the fear or the shame of surprising some ill-defended secret made him lower his eyes a second. But the reflection of the lamp on the flagging had as soon discovered the yawning open space, slid over to it, risen slowly up its height.... His eyes rose with it....

...Stopped... To what purpose? Never can that be concealed which the light has once discovered, forever.

...Two rough shoes, like those discovered over there; the fold of a cassock in a queer tuck...a long thin leg in a woolen stocking, starkly stiff, a heel square upon the threshold—here was what first he saw. Then...little by little...in the heavier shadow...a vague whiteness, and suddenly the terrible, thunderstruck face.

Antoine Saint-Marin was capable of showing, under extreme circumstances, a cold and calculated gallantry. Besides, dead or alive, this unexpected old fellow was at least as irritating as he was frightening. In brief, the writer had been brutally interrupted at an auspicious moment in the midst of his reverie; the last word remained with this strange witness dead in his somber box, with this upright corpse. A professor of irony had found his master, and aroused himself abashed from a slightly silly, heart-warming dream.

He opened wide the door, stepped back a pace, measured his odd companion with his eyes, and confronted him without yet daring to challenge him.

"A fine miracle," he hissed between his teeth, a little peevish. "The good priest has died here, without a sound, of a heart attack. While those idiots roam the roads looking for him, here he is, quiet indeed, like some sentinel, killed by a bullet in his sentry-box, point-blank!..."

Erect against the partition, the small of his back held up by the narrow seat onto which he had tumbled at the last moment, buttressed by his legs stiff against the thin bit of wood which trimmed the threshold, the saint of Lumbres's forlorn body in its grotesque immobility retained the attitude of a man whom surprise has brought to his feet.

Others may be laid out to rest by a friendly hand, beneath a fresh white sheet; this man ever rears up in his black night, hears the cry of his children.... He still has something to say.... No! His last word is not uttered.... The aged athlete, pierced by a thousand blows, bears witness for weaker ones, names the traitor and the betrayal.... Oh! the devil, the other one, is surely a skillful fellow, a wonderful liar, this wayward rebel in his lost glory, full of scorn for the heavy and moody human cattle which the thousand resources of his guile arouse or subdue, according to his wish, but his humble enemy faces up to him, and beneath the forbidding hue and cry shakes his stubborn head. With what a tempest of laughter and shouting does joyous hell acclaim the artless speech, barely intelligible, the confused and maladroit defense! What matter! still another hears it, whom the heavens will not forever hide!

Lord, it is not true that we have cursed you; may he perish, rather, that liar, that false witness, your mocking rival! He took everything from us, left us wholly naked, and placed in our mouth an impious word. But suffering remains to us, which is our part in common with you, the mark of our election, inherited from our fathers, more active than the chaste, incorruptible fire.... Our intelligence is heavy and commonplace, our credulity endless, and the suborner subtle, with his gilded tongue.... Upon his lips familiar words take the meaning that suits him, and the loveliest of them lead us astray the better. If we are silent, he speaks in our stead, and when we seek to justify ourselves, what we say condemns us. The peerless pleader, scorning to rebut, amuses himself by prying their own death sentences from his victims. Perish with him the treacherous words! Through its cry of pain does the human race express itself, the lamentation wrested from its flanks by an inordinate endeavor. You have cast us like a leaven into the lump. The universe, of which sin has stripped us, we shall recover, inch by inch, we shall hand it back to you just as we received it, in its order and in its holiness, on the first morning of the days. Reckon not the time for us, Lord!

Our needfulness falters, our mind so quickly turns aside. Constantly the eyes espy, both right and left, no possible way out; constantly one of your workmen casts aside his tool and goes away. But your pity, no, your pity grows not weary, and everywhere you hold out to us the tip of the blade; the runaway will resume his task, or he will perish in the wilderness.... Ah, the enemy who knows so many things will not know that! The vilest of men carries away with him his secret, the secret of effective, cleansing pain.... For your anguish is sterile, Satan!... And as for me, here I am where you have led me, ready to receive your final blow.... I am only a poor priest, rather simple-minded, of whom your slyness for a moment made sport, and whom you will roll like a stone.... Who can struggle against you with his cunning? When did you first take on my Master's features and His voice? On what day did I yield for the first time? On what day did I accept, with mad complacence, the only gift you give, the deceiving image of the saints' utter forsakenness, your despair, unutterable to a man's heart? You suffered, you prayed with me, O fearful thought! Even that miracle... No matter! No matter! Strip me! Leave me nothing! After me another, and then yet another, raising the same cry, holding embraced the cross.... We are not at all those rosy saints with blond beards which good folk see in paintings and whose eloquence and sound health the philosophers themselves would envy. Our portion is not at all what the world conceives. Compared to it, even the compulsion of genius is a frivolous game. Every beautiful life, Lord, testifies for you, but the saint's testimony is as though torn out by iron.

Such was probably, here below, the ultimate lament of the pastor of Lumbres, raised toward the Judge—and his loving reproach. But to the famous man who had come so far to seek him, he had something else to say. And, if the black mouth in the shadow, which resembled a wound opened by the explosion of a last cry, no longer proffered any sound, the body altogether mimed a fearful challenge:

"You wanted my peace," cried out the saint, "come take it!"

CLUNY MEDIA

Designed by Fiona Cecile Clarke, the CLUNY MEDIA *logo depicts a monk at work in the scriptorium, with a cat sitting at his feet.*

The monk represents our mission to emulate the invaluable contributions of the monks of Cluny in preserving the libraries of the West, our strivings to know and love the truth.

The cat at the monk's feet is Pangur Bán, from the eponymous Irish poem of the 9th century. The anonymous poet compares his scholarly pursuit of truth with the cat's happy hunting of mice. The depiction of Pangur Bán is an homage to the work of the monks of Irish monasteries and a sign of the joy we at Cluny take in our trade.

"Messe ocus Pangur Bán,
cechtar nathar fria saindan:
bíth a menmasam fri seilgg,
mu memna céin im saincheirdd."

www.ingramcontent.com/pod-product-compliance
Lightning Source LLC
Chambersburg PA
CBHW020930310726
48980CB00007B/706/J

* 9 7 8 1 9 4 4 4 1 8 9 3 9 *